Briksanna's Sacrifice

A Novel of the Four Realms: Book One

Sabrina Rawson

Copyright © 2014 Sabrina Rawson
Graphic Artist: Victoria F. Alday
Cover Design: Whit&Ware Design
Editor: Rayna Penning
Associate Editor: Franklin Campbell-Jones
Interior Format: KDP & CreateSpace
ISBN-13: 9780996013901
ISBN-10: 0996013903

Dedication

This book is dedicated to two women who encouraged me to put
pen to paper two years ago. Kim Lupsha and Jessica Knight two
wonderful women who will never be forgotten for their witty ideas and
laughing comments which helped drive my life when I thought this
project would go no further than my personal computer.
To all the women and men suffering from cancer throughout
the world; dreams can come true no matter what because cancer
cannot discourage hope.

Many people will walk in and out of your life, but only true
friends will leave
Footprints in your heart.

Eleanor Roosevelt

Table of Contents

Prologue

Somewhere lost in the Four Realms

"Y ou will never have him!" she screamed; spitting out what little was left in her mouth. She could barely lick her cracked lips let alone wet her tongue. When was the last time she tasted water? Cracking her eyes, dark all around, she could barely see her surroundings. This must be the thousandth time she had said those very words. How many times had she denied him her fealty? "You can't make me do this. This thing you speak of is an abomination to all that I believe and hold true."

Exhausted, she closed her eyes and waited for peace to fall upon her. Speaking frailly, "I know the truth as so do you. The Prophesy does not tell of my commitment to your Master only to bear the love of Lord Drakkoon. There is nothing that you can say or do to me that will convince me that this monster you serve could be the person I would freely give my love to."

Raising her head ever so slightly, she could sense his presence in the room. Eyes closed she searched for the voice of her tormentor, always near, but outside of her range of vision. She could hear the constant drip of water from the corner of her cell, but knowing she was shackled to the opposite wall, when he was not in the room torturing her, she had long ago learned not to consider the idea of using the water as an answer for her thirst. There was a drain somewhere in the middle of the room, she could hear the water running down it now, as she hung suspended from her chains. The damp smell of the room had her gagging, but she choked down the bile and forced herself to pay attention to the man in the room intent on causing her harm.

After all this time he never let her see him, always staying close enough for her to sense his presence never revealing who he really was. He smelled like rotten, dried earth. Something that once was beautiful turned for the worse with a deep suffocating stench. The foulness would remain with her.

Steeling herself for another verbal battle with her tormentor, she pressed on with her argument. "I am not to be forced, for to do so would forfeit all, and death will be your Master's ruler, as the Great Seer Vakgdona spoke not long ago". Raising her head higher, eyes still closed, she shook her head lightly trying to shake the hair out of her face. Her hands were bound, suspended above her. Her ankles were shackled to the floor with feet dangling allowing enough room for the tips of her toes to touch ground leaving little room to support her full weight.

Gods she was tired. For weeks she has been enslaved to this room, bound like an animal, left alone with the exception of the visits from her tormentor, or so she began calling him. He never gave her his name, whenever she asked he evaded by issuing his own demands. She learned early on, the less she asked of him, the sooner he would get tired of hearing his own voice or beating her, whichever came first, then he would leave her alone for the guards to release her, only to shackle her opposite a wall of dripping water with only enough energy to lay on the floor mat, waiting for the next round of interrogation to begin again.

What else was there, but to call this man an idiot; a man who asked the same question over and over again, day after day, so much that she knew the full moon had risen three times since she'd first awoken in here. Her energy was strongest during the cycle of the full moon as was known to all royal families. To not have been able to hold her head up during those times was a testament of her weakened physical state. Escape seemed possible with despair beginning to cloak her being. He was insistent.

"Pledge yourself to my Master, heart and soul; body and spirit, giving him that which he desires the most, a son? Something so profound, that in all the four realms, only you, princess can give him. By him you can have your son, the prophesied instrument of peace. By saying yes, to my Master, the campaign against the Four Realms will cease allowing peace in the land. For you, he will do this. He will give you what you need to fulfill The Prophesy; a son, and in return you shall give my Master yourself, willingly. Have you forgotten princess, you and my Master are destined for one another? Agree to this now, and stop this madness. Agree to give yourself to him, and I will take you from here this very moment. A bath and full meal await you, succulent of the finest foods, prepared only for you. Give me your word and I will cut you down myself."

Soft movement on the ground to her left, led her to believe for the first time, he was very close to her. She was tempted to open her eyes, but knew this would alert him she was paying attention, and the more she stayed active in the conversation, the more he was inclined to stay. Not, saying nothing would make him angry and the sooner he got angry, the sooner he would leave her alone. Peace is what she craved, no longer caring if she was to see daylight again. All she wanted was to be left alone.

She knew who she was and where she came from hating him with every ounce of her being, she thought, *I am Princess Briksanna of the High Royal Realm, First Princess to the House of Akmond, loving daughter of the High King and Queen, devoted sister and completely loyal to the Realm of Skaldanna. You have not only broken many laws by kidnapping me, but the act of torture you have inflicted will never be forgiven by me or the Realms of Skaldanna. The crimes you have committed will be met with utter retaliation. There will be no place you can hide; no place for you or your master to run to where the warriors of Skaldanna will not be able to find you.*

Instead she said, "You are a dead man." Speaking matter of fact, mentally scolding herself for her outburst. He knew exactly who she was and if he cared at all about her stature, he would never have kept her in such a humiliated existence let alone whipped her repeatedly for simply not conforming to his wishes.

She let her head drop back down, hair falling in front of her face, obscuring any chance of a clear view of her present surroundings. She knew her dismissal would be met with pain.

The Tormentor breathed deeply; again from her left, steps coming closer. Her only chance might be this very moment; knowing this game needed to end now.

How much longer could her she survive? How many more moons will pass before the Master's patience ran out awaiting her compliance? She guessed not much longer if her senses were correct, considering her tormentor's visits had become multiple of late.

She could almost feel him now. "You will bend to my Master, as was also foretold by Vakgdona. Have you so conveniently forgotten the rest of The Prophesy, princess?" He whispered near her left ear.

She hated how close he was to her right now with his foul stench oozing the smell of rotten carcasses. Yet the hands that held the whips, when he beat her, never bore the look of filth or decay. Frowning, at her thoughts, surely she smelt what was rotten within him that carried the putrid scent of a decayed sprit permeating the air each time he entered her cell. She was going to rip that spirit from his very being the moment she had a chance.

All members of the High Royal Family were highly gifted energetically, able to absorb energy from their living surroundings as if it were a breath of fresh air. Only the High Royal House was able to wield the energy they absorbed. In the days, years, before the attack on her home and family, they were the guardians of all the energy on Skaldanna, collecting and distributing, often blending the different realm energetic signatures, creating a stronger source that could be used for growing larger crops or shaping stronger metals. She and her best friend Katerina, had been demonstrating, to the High Royal Court, the use of energy during hand-to- hand combat when their house was attacked by dark magic.

Got him. Focusing on his energy through her mind's eye she could pick up his energy signature, locking on him visually, targeting on the man who made her nightmares come true.

Blocking everything out around her, she delved deep into what little energy she had left within herself and focused, filling herself with as much energy as she could, knowing she had one chance to catch him off guard.

Average height for one of her kind, six feet tall, broad in shoulders yet lean in shape. His hair was tied back, customarily worn in this manner only by nobles of the realms, how strange. He seemed familiar. For a split second, the way he stood, waiting for her reply, seemed like a familiar vision her mind recognized, but as quick as the association came, the thought disappeared. She concentrated on the rest of him, where his hands were. Gods she hated his hands. They always held implements of horror. Each day those implements were getting worse, lasting longer with him striking her harder and deeper than the last. She could barely move her legs from the last beating he gave.

"How much longer do you think you will last in my torture chamber, princess? There are great pleasures awaiting you if you would only yield to my Master's bidding. He has such dreams of a beautiful future for the two of you. Why prolong the inevitable?"

Taking a calm deep breath, centering herself, she remembered all that she lost, the future she once believed in. Her siblings, her parents, all the people that used to look upon her for their children's future, she did this for them. Centering her spirit, she held her courage tight knowing what she had in mind to do. She had not heard of anyone being able to energetically kill a person, but she hoped with all of her anger and fear she could inflict enough damage by draining him, siphoning his life's energy fueling her own.

Remembering her training, as the child of the High King, she stilled her movements, balanced on her toes and forced her movements to be slight of eye as she prepared her next move. Holding tight to the chain binding her hands up above, she focused on the man to the left of her.

"Gods grant me strength for all things done are by your design alone. Fill me with the energy you believe I am destined to wield so I may destroy as prophesied. I ask this of you in my lowest moment, hear my plea. Make me your weapon," she murmured. For the first time in three moons she took a deep breath and felt a familiar rush of warmth fill her. *You can do this. You don't want to die*, she thought.

Striding quickly up to her stopping directly behind, close enough casting his rotten breath onto her neck, he inquired, "What did you say? Say the words again and I will release you."

She whipped her head back head butting him with all that was left in her, not wasting a second longer. A loud crack echoed off the walls of the room where she had been held captive, hitting her target for the first time, dead center on the bridge of his nose, felling him in one hit. Keeping her eyes closed, she could still see him, grasping his nose as he crumpled to the ground, with a loud yelp, blood pouring from his nose and mouth. She smiled knowing her aim held true and power could be gained from his pain. As he had drained her for weeks on end, she will return a hundred fold to her Tormentor, as she believed was her right in being the violated Princess of The Prophesy.

"It worked." Remembering the royal combat trainers' words to aim small but hit big, she closed down her mind of memories that would distract her; instead she focused on the task at hand.

"The Prophesy is not inevitable for me as you would think, but certain death for your Master it speaks of," she screamed at him straining in her bonds. "There is no future for your Master!"

Fueled on tortured adrenaline, she felt her inner energy pulling greedily from the injured man behind her. Focusing on his pain, she pulled harder on his life force, determined to drain her tormentor dry. She screamed from the sheer strength of his life force, pouring into her as if a big wind had pushed her, straight from the sea itself, cleansing the air of the putrid stench within her cell along with it.

Pulling the remaining bits of life force from the dying body behind her; flinging her arms wide, she snapped the bonds above her. Eyes changing; lighting up the entire room with a bright violet glow, she was filled with an unknown power like she had never felt before; reviling in the strength of the power she now carried, assuring her again she had purpose; reminding her she was the First Princess of Prophesy.

Hearing her own voice from afar pouring from her, building within her, she spoke.

"It has begun, The Prophesy has awoken. Nine princesses will bear nine sons born from the blood of the four realms and distant lands; a mixture of this time and that of the great divide. To restore balance within the universe, the First Princess of Peace, she whom the Great Gods have marked with violet green eyes, of the Four Realms, will bear the first son; she shall bear Lord Drakkoon's love, fealty and be the Instrument of Death. Her first son born too shall bear the same color eyes as his mother, marking him as the Instrument of Peace. He will be born of this world and of the one called Earth, who only by his hand will be the instrument of death for Lord Drakkoon thus freeing all the worlds from imminent destruction".

She screamed again, inhaling a great breath, filling her lungs with much needed air. Looking down checking for injuries she saw herself whole, no longer with injury, no longer shackled like an animal. Strength poured through her entire being for the first time in many days.

She closed her eyes arms stretched wide, she vowed. "I will avenge the ones I love, hear me my Gods. I will not rest until I have my vengeance, fulfilling The Prophesy of the First Princess, this I vow. So mote it be."

1

Present Day
Somewhere in the hills of Northern California

She sighed, rubbing her eyes tiredly trying to focus on what it was she was doing. "Not much planning left to do." Looking over the topographical maps surveying the area for their next assignment she felt antsy about her past recently thinking after centuries of living in the Earth Realm she wanted to go home. She noticed she was irritated at herself for staying here. She knew she could not hide much longer. The Prophesy had remained silent in her mind for many years until lately and she did not like how it made her feel.

"I just want to make sure there no obstacle's I may have overlooked," she snapped.

"In all the years I have known you, there hasn't been a mistake Bri. You are thorough, before you bring the plans to the table. It is what makes you a great leader and us your willing followers," said her most trusted companion and leader.

Nathanial Angelo, the captain of her mercenary team Lightning Strike, and like all members, Nate was built better than a Mac truck and even easier on the eyes. All members of her team were a close knit, fun, loving family combined with a healthy dose of demons hiding in their personal closets more than any normal person should have. If not for the assignments she had been given, no one in the world would ever accept let alone succeed in the dangerous missions they took. They were the one team, where secret agencies, the mortal world called upon for aid. They were that good.

At six foot six, Nate was her one weakness; at least she thought he was.

Looking in his direction, she slowly raised her head, dragging her eyes away from the table. Dressed in his usual black military style cargo pants and black t-shirt resting over a firm six-pack abs, *Gods this man makes me feel*, she thought. And all the more knowing at the bottom of that view, most assuredly were a pair of strong thighs and legs, a testament of his strength, without a doubt, encased in a pair of steel toe shit kickers. She could feel her heart pick up and her mouth go dry as she tried to choke down a swallow.

Eyes travelling up his torso hung a pair of arms made for pounding the dirtiest souls into the Under Realm. Resting her gaze on his mouth for a few seconds, she wondered what his mouth would feel like. Would it be soft and full like she had imagined? Feeling irritated at how quick she could be easily distracted by looking at him, she flicked her eyes away from his mouth and decided starring at his deep set dimples framing a full mouth was better. She noticed his mouth was starting to spread into the most erotic grin she had ever seen. It never failed when the dimples appeared she would always stumble in thought. How aggravating.

"Like what you see Princess?" He taunted continuing to smile at her.

Her heartbeat picked up again, if that was even possible. Letting go of what little energy she had left, her gaze continued to the top of his face, settling on deep green eyes, framed by dark black eye lashes, he peered between strands of hair that had fallen over his brow looking as if he had no cares in the world. His expression seemed both challenging and inviting standing across the table from where they had spent the past two hours hashing out their plan of rescue for the latest mission which she had not yet accepted.

"You know we haven't even accepted this mission and you are treating it as if we are leaving within the hour. You need to rest, Bri," he said with a tone of compassion, which he did not usually convey.

Her heated energy surged again, filling her with a rising heat that left her system flooding with warmth and excitement all rolled into one. She did not want to be reminded of what it could be like if she were to feel for a man again. If there was anyone, in both worlds, that could have made her forget who she was or what it was she was fighting for, it would be Nathanial Angelo.

She could not afford to feel, to dream. Could not conjure feelings which could possibly be damaging to her world from so long ago.

"Nathanial, I do not care how you pretty up those words, a thorough soldier is a soldier alive and you had best not forget my telling you. There are too many lives, in this world and throughout the universe, that depend on me to be without mistakes. Tire is not something that I can afford!"

"You can't keep doing this to yourself. The world can't afford for you to fall over in battle because you won't rest," he countered. "Besides, you have been up for the past thirty six hours and counting, since our last mission in Belize. All is safe, Bri. Our team made it back in one piece, we have rested and eaten. What have you done, shower?"

His voice was gained an edge the more he spoke. He was becoming angrier.

Slapping her hand on the table, her voice too gained a sharpness of its own. "Do I look like a child to you?" Her temper began to snap, "I have spanked older mortals both men and Skaldannians bigger than you, who did not have the chance to shoot off at the mouth, as you dare challenge me now."

Even though she was pissed off for being chastised by a mere mortal, Nate was right and she knew it. She knew they both understood what to do next and what to expect; this next mission would be a cakewalk for the both of them. Crazy thing is so did Nate and he was right. They did not need to take this job. They should pass on it and not get involved.

She did not want anyone to know, she no longer found comfort in being alone. She no longer found sustenance in eating food. She was starting to think of giving up her quest for vengeance. What would it be like to be the one who walked away for a change? These new thoughts deeply angered her, even more so frightened her.

How could this man know exactly when and what she needed most in life? Even scarier, she had begun imagining what, it would feel like, to share that much needed rest time with him; the most handsomest man she had ever laid eyes on in almost two millennia. What would it feel like to have him look at her for comfort, nourishment and rest? What would it feel like for him to slate his needs with her? She would have to trust him completely.

Gods he made her feel so vulnerable and vulnerability leads to capture and capture leads to death for all worlds. Feelings were not an option.

Scowling she gathered her energy like a cloak, surrounding her, consoling her scared heart of all the new feelings he stirred within.

Challenging him caused her fear of trust to turn into anger. "How dare you tell me when I think I have done enough, studied long enough or sacrificed enough? How dare you tell me when anything I do is enough, so that I can take a rest, eat some food or..."

Stepping around the table, his face flashed to fury in a matter of seconds. "Or what Bri, you might recharge fully for once, like you should do? Or maybe you could fill the energy stores you are so eager to deplete on all those around you, for the sake of perfection on a mission you aren't even sure you are going to take!"

Without fear, he had stepped right up into her kill zone completely telling her what he thought.

A fool's mistake. Did he not remember whom it was he was speaking to? How tempting it would be to let her energy go just a little, teaching this fool a lesson. Her sea green eyes, which moments before held deep admiration now flashed in anger. She had sunk daggers into the hearts of enemies just for speaking out of turn from afar and he dared to enter her kill zone with a look and tone of complete contempt.

Not an option. The air within the room began to crackle with static electricity signifying her steel cage surrounding her energetic control was cracking. Nate was starting to look purple, indicating her eyes had visibly turned from green to violet, alerting anyone in her presence her heritage did not belong to this world.

She could barely hear him over the hum of static electricity.

"What are you going to do Bri? Zap me with your big bad lightning bolt? Am I being a bad boy who needs a lesson?" Raising his left hand, poking her in the chest, "Go ahead, fry my ass, but in the end you are still going to need to eat and sleep." Crossing his arms along his chest looking smug at the point he thought he made still standing in her kill zone.

All of the sudden he did the unthinkable. Leaning close to her face, knowing he was pushing her temper. "So Princess, you got it right the first time I said it, I absolutely dare you to fry me."

Outside she heard lightning strike in rapid succession, one, two, three strikes.

Again, one, two, three strikes. Lightning flashed through the windows, crashing right outside the compound. Upon the third strike that hit the ground her vision was illuminating his entire face. Nothing mattered to her at this point. Her only focus was on the man in front of her and what he had just said. She was not concerned that their hair was standing on end or that lightning was striking outside, knowing no storm was in sight. Neither was the fact she had not felt this much channeled energy flow thru her in over a two thousand years.

That should have been her first clue something was wrong. A stray thought nagged at her that something was wrong with the situation but her emotions were all over the place and she just wanted to get rid of feeling out of control. She was terrified of feeling anything right now and the man standing in front of her was the cause of it all. Who was he to tell her what to do? It did not matter. She knew once she rid herself of the problem she could push her fear aside and go back to whatever it was she was doing. But something about the way he was looking at her kept nagging at her consciousness.

It was the sweat dripping off the creased brow of the best friend staring back at her that triggered her memories. This was Nate, the man she had grown to care about above all else. This was the man whose wicked grin, from fifty yards off, starring down a scope lens of a target during a night ops mission could make her heart pitter patter, like some child from long ago. That very same man was about to be drained of life and all she would have to do is be the instrument who unleashes her energy in his direction. After all, he was in my kill zone. It would be too bad doing this thing to him, then she could go back to who she used to be; the cold, hard, demanding Briksanna. It would be that easy to go back to the way things were before she started feeling this way.

She felt energy flow through her faster than before, waiting for the moment she could release it.

"Bri, you have to breathe. Take a deep breath and breathe. You are letting go of your control and your energy is building. Breathe Bri, breathe. Calm the storm inside you," Nate yelled.

Noticing, his face seemed worried, no longer frowning in anger. He looked scared, but she was struggling with why she would care about what this mortal thought of her, after all he is just another mortal. Their life spans were insignificant compared to a Skaldannian.

"Briksanna," he yelled louder, this time gripping both of her upper arms, firmly, bringing her closer to him, staring right into her eyes. "You have to control your energy, for all of us or you have already let Lord Drakkoon win."

Lord Drakkoon, what was it about the name that sounded familiar? Drakkoon, Skaldanna, Father and Mother, her Tormentor. Blinking rapidly breathing in and out she uncurled her fists not remembering when she began holding them closed in the first place. Her chest ached to release the energy she had unknowingly gathered, waiting for a single thought to unleash her madness on the man before her. Raising her hands she grasped his arms to keep her upright not wanting to let go. She felt so weak. How did she let herself become so vulnerable?

"Nate?" she whispered looking up at him.

He stilled, staring at her for a few seconds, searching for some sort of recognition within. With a slight nod and sigh, he pulled her close holding her tight.

"Nate, what happened? Oh Gods, what have I done? Is anyone hurt?" She sobbed while gripping his arms tightly for support and strength. She no longer knew what she needed. But, in that moment she wanted him to hold her more than anything else in her life.

"I was going to strike you down," she choked. "You were challenging me and I was going to melt you right where you stood, all because I did not like what you had to say."

He continued holding her, squeezing tighter close enough to feel his breath rustle her hair. Closing her eyes in self-disgust she said to him, "I could have killed you, not feeling a bit of remorse over it." Putting her head down in deep shame. Her eyes closed as she tried to pull away from him but he refused her wish and held her tighter

"Let me go. I need to leave now more than ever. Nate, let me go, please, let me go." Feeling defeated in every way she begged him to understand, "Please Nate, if you have any respect left for the person I used to be, you will let me go from here. I cannot lead Lightning Strike anymore. I have compromised all that I believe in risking those that I call family. I almost took the life of the..."

Tears spilled over when she choked on what she was about to say, finally admitting he held her heart. It was too much for her. She pulled in earnest from him, "How can you stand to touch the one who almost destroyed you, let me go!" She screamed with tears running down her face, "I almost killed you," she added.

Her sobbing must have been his undoing, because he reached for her again, enfolding her within his embrace.

She was not sure how much time had passed or how long they stood encapsulated, while she cried, but it was long enough for him to reach down and pick her up, cradling her head to his shoulder while she wept. With her hand on his heart; he strode out of the planning room down the hall that led into her bedroom. With a full size bed against one wall, a large easy chair in the opposite corner, one upright chest of drawers; the room looked plain. No shoes lying about on the floor. No clothes thrown on the chair or floor. No perfume or jewelry bottles on the dresser waiting to be put on. This was a room with a purpose; a bed to sleep in and a place for her clothes. Nowhere did her room appear lived in. For the past ten years she had spent her alone time doing her damndest to keep her emotions buried. To do that she believed the only way to protect herself and those she loved was to have strict discipline in how she lived. That included her living space. Plainer the better, this way she did not cater to fanciful thoughts or entertained dreams of what she wanted most out of life. Peace, love and happiness for those around her.

He gently laid her on the bed. Taking swift measure to comfort her, he pulled her boots from her feet rubbing them firmly and smoothly. She began to cry much quieter than before at his tenderness knowing that her resolve to remain emotionless. Coldness no longer dwelled within her.

She knew the woman she used to be was gone and a part of her mourned her as well. Suddenly she felt the bed dip as he stretched out beside her. He reached across her waist and turned her on her side to face him. Looking into her eyes, he lifted her chin with his finger. All traces of anger and worry dissipated giving way to warmth and comfort. In his face she beheld absolute adornment and desperation rolled into one.

Her heart caught in her throat as she swallowed more tears and struggled to articulate the words she wanted to say to Nate as he laid so tenderly in the bed next to her.

"Yes, I engaged you, taunted you; daring you to strike me down. You held back, only showing me what you could do, but never really doing anything to me. Don't you believe I see you as a strong woman? Even as weak as you are, you hesitated in striking me; reasoning with what you were about to do with what you know to be true. Don't close your eyes. You know what I'm saying is true, I watched you. I saw every emotion flow across your face through your soul, as if it were my own. I know you're tired, weak and hungry, needing to take the time to care of yourself. Who better than me to be the one you can lean on? Trust me to care for you when you no longer have the will to do it yourself? Let me be the one to feed you when you are hungry, help you undress when you can't lift your arms because your body aches from battle. Let me be the one you can count on to be there for you. I need to do this for you more than I have needed anything in my entire life."

Searching her face he raised a trembling hand, gently wiping away the remaining tears that had fallen down her cheeks while he spoke. "You are everything to me, don't you know that? I don't want to lose you anymore than you want to lose me." Speaking softly almost akin to fear "Please say you'll let me do this for you? Care for your needs, as if they were my own. Let me be the only man who can provide for you. I give you my heart as your warrior, I would never hurt you or betray you. May you strike me down, this I promise you. Please Bri, I need you now. Let me take care of you. You can trust me."

He held his breathe, waiting for her to say something, do anything; yet, her stillness was starting to frighten him. Never had he spoken words like that to anyone. He was putting his heart and life in the hands of the most beautiful woman he had ever known. What would it take for her to believe he would never betray her? Better to die than to violate such trust than hurt the one most dear to his heart. She kept her heart guarded, constantly protected because of a relationship gone badly long ago. More like an ancient memory needing burying. Although years had gone by pictures on her mindscape remained fresh just above the emotions that bore the scares of anguish. He sensed this at times when her mental shields were at their lowest; when she let him slip into her thoughts. He admired her fortitude.

For years she resolved in holding people at a certain distance, never engaging the opposite sex in any way except when on rescue missions they contracted out. And even then, when they were done she looked upset during debriefing, recounting the events surrounding her interactions with the enemy. It was torture for him knowing how he felt about her. He had desired her for a decade, never once acting on his feelings for her. He understood who she was and what she believed in. He understood her love for the children she had brought into their lives over the years. She deserved to have those needs fulfilled. After tonight he knew she needed more than the love of a family. He knew she needed his love and he was no longer going to sit by and let her struggle on her own.

Bri looked deeply in his eyes holding onto his every word. But, her eyes soon turned from his and fixed upon the flame dancing atop the candle on the shelf in the upper corner of the room. She knew what must be done if she were to remove the cage from around her heart allowing her emotions free reign. He could hear every thought she was thinking. Already she began to pull away from him.

2

He tenderly kissed her brow then her cheek slowly, reverently expressing his deep love for her as he moved closer to her mouth. He brushed his left hand down her head knowing he really wanted to reach out and grab her to him, but kept in mind she was not in a place to accept that right now. He moved slowly, kissing her lightly along her jaw as her head stretched of her own accord granting him better access. He didn't want this moment to become too intimate too quickly, he loved her too much to take advantage of her in this vulnerable state. He only wanted to lie next to her on the bed, bring comfort and assure her that he believed in her.

Tonight's display made him think of her would be control and he didn't like it. She deserved more than the bitter resolve of emotional restraint. Bri was the one who was used to being the protector. Her on the bed tonight, she needed shelter. Needed comfort. If only she allowed him to provide that for her.

He pulled away from kissing her and looked directly in her eyes. "Come on beautiful; tell me what you are thinking in that pretty little head of yours?"

"Why me?" she whispered, averting her head from the scrutiny of his gaze.

"Why not you?" he said, slowly smiling. "You deserve more than you give yourself credit for."

Brushing his hands away she strained to get up from where they laid. "You overstep with your words of admission. I am First Daughter of the High King." Sighing, she sat on the edge of the bed and looked into his deep green eyes, "I am two thousand years old. In that time I have never lost control nor have I let my guard down, striking an innocent in a fit of rage until now."

"Until now, Bri, you have been in control, always guarding your heart and your energy, only we, your family, know you possess and for what? To be driven to exhaustion, constant disappointment on your face every time we complete a mission.

He rose from the bed and slowly moved around the edge near her. "What is it you keep searching for or should I say running from?"

His question caught her off guard offering up a surprised look on her face, clear as day, before she hid it behind those beautiful sea green eyes. "You think I don't see your disappointment every time we reunite a lost one with their loved ones, but I do. You want to know why? Because I've always been the one watching out for you."

"You do not know who I am or what I have done, let alone what I have yet to do." He could see her closing up her heart keeping her burdens closed off from the people who cared for her the most. Especially how close they had all become over the past decade. She loved her team. They were her family. He knew this and yet here she believed she thought of them as more than just a team. Is this what she was willing to become? A cold woman willing to close her heart off to anyone who cared.

"Would it matter what I think or believe in? Will it change how you feel about me? Will it change how you feel about me when you let me in that heart of yours? No, I can tell you it won't."—holding his hand up to stop her from speaking—"I, also, can tell you will always be able to count on me in keeping my word of honor when it comes to you. I will never betray your trust."

Tears that previously threatened, now flowed freely down her cheeks. The longing on her face revealed how lonely her existence had been to hear those very words from him. Could she believe in those words, spoken in his promise? He could tell, lately, her heart had been troubled believing in his gut it was more what he initially had thought. A deep fear of commitment. Maybe her fears had more to do with faith in herself than with the people in her life.

In one of the few times she shared a piece of her past with the family, she explained she had been alive longer than she practiced her worship of the Gods she had once held dear and she longed to feel the conviction she once had for them. She missed what she used to practice every day: building her inner strength and faith which built an unbreakable inner strength. He knew the lack of faith in herself bothered her. Ever since this was revealed to him he knew it was the key to what made it emotionally difficult for her to commit to him right now.

The sullen expression on her face helped prepare him for the words that were about to be conveyed, words he knew would be pivotal in their relationship. After all he had said a moment ago, he prayed silently to whomever was out there that she would open her heart putting her trust in him. No more words could be expressed to prove to Bri that he would never betray her trust. She had to believe in his willingness to commit to her unconditionally before she could step forward in any personal relationship. He knew what she needed to do next. She was standing in the precise moment in time where her next choice was going to be a step towards a role in their relationship.

He could see her resolve to stay away from him emotionally falling away. The way she stood there looking back at him as if he was the one man she knew she could no longer hide her feelings from him. He had to mean as much to her as she meant to him.

She was the most beautiful woman he had ever seen. Waist length thick brown locks of hair always filling him with need to run his hands through each strand. She always wore it in a single braid; if it were up to him she would always wear it down, that way he could have constant access. Sea green eyes ringed with violet glittered like emeralds in the light when she was happy. Whenever she lost control of her emotions, especially in anger, which he had seen enough times to count on one hand, the violet rings expanded taking over her entire eye color. When she was royally pissed which he could say he'd seen on one occasion outside of tonight.

A few days ago when they were on mission and encountered that crazy bastard, Jackson, Lord Drakkoon's right hand man, she became enraged when she saw him go after the twins nicking them here and there with his crazy ass sword fighting. Rage overcame her as she tried to cut a path with both swords. Her eyes lit up in frustration knowing she needed to get to the daughters she had raised since babies before they were seriously hurt. He had never seen her so intent or deadly. She was beautiful in that moment of pure rage just as she was a second ago.

His heart beat a pounding rhythm as he mulled over where his thoughts were leading to. Shaking his head he pushed those thoughts of flowers and butterflies aside. There would be time to delve deep into his heart later. First he had to win the woman.

Truly seeing her before him, straight nose and full lips begging him to kiss he watched her cheeks flush on her pale face knowing he was staring right back at her willing her to believe in him. She stood close to six four almost as tall as he was. She was thin but strong. Her arms and legs were defined like a fighter but sensual keeping his line of sight whenever she wore her jeans and tee shirts. Never once did she gain muscle mass from all the physical exertion swinging her mighty sword.

And now, the mighty warrior he loved struggled with a decision that seemed to stall even her, something that he had never witnessed.

She spoke, "There is much you do not know. I will not lie to you, if there is to be anything here, between us"—waving her hands back and forth between them—"then I must be honest with you about why I have sheltered myself over the years. I will not start a relationship, with the man I love, with lies or unspoken truths."

"Nor would I..." She stopped him as he began to speak with the raising of her hand. Wiping away the last of her tears she swung around giving him her back, pacing the large room before stopping in front of her window out looking their compound. Raising her head she looked up into the darkness. He noticed the full moon had risen and was visible through the clouds.

"There is something I have to do first before we speak again, okay?"

Keeping her back to him he held his breath waiting for her next words. Before giving her a chance to say anything else he hurried to reassure her of his intentions, "I'm not going anywhere, Bri. Whatever you need to do, do it."

Raising her arms, bowing her head in front of the moon she began to pray.

"Gods, please remember your daughter, who humbly approaches you tonight. Please grant me the serenity and courage to accept the tasks, in hopes I will accomplish that which you have placed before me. Help me to believe in myself, to be the woman you need me to be, all the parts not the scattered pieces I have broken, left lying on the ground all those years ago. Grant me the strength to fulfill that which you have put in front of me. I now realize I cannot turn away from who you need me to be or what you will me to do." Closing her eyes with deep sincerity in her voice she continued, "Please forgive my disobedience and allow me time to love him, fulfilling part of what was told so long ago. You alone are the only ones who can delay the inevitable by granting me this boon, granting me time to spend with the fruits of this union. I do not doubt his sincerity or conviction he has towards me. I give him my heart, my allegiance and to you, I give my will to do that which was foretold long ago. I will obey your command fulfilling The Prophesy. I trust you, my Gods, as you asked of me so long ago. This I vow to you."

As the last words left her a mouth, a loud crack thundered form the heavens sending a flash of light that assaulted her eyes throwing her to the floor.

"Briksanna!" Nate shouted running towards her only to be thrown back in the opposite direction, as if he ran into an invisible barrier that surrounded her.

"Do not move." Muttered Briksanna seized by the energy coursing through her. "Kneel with your head down. Do not look up no matter what you hear." There was desperation in her voice although strained and stalled.

"Only because I trust you will I do this, Bri. If I hear anything I don't like, I am gunning for you and there will be hell to pay if you are damaged in any way." Rising to a kneeling position he said out loud, "Do you hear me, who or whatever you are, you better not hurt her or you will deal with me." Taking a long look at her, he slowly bowed his head in supplication.

He recognized the tone she used. He'd heard it many times during their most dangerous missions. Something otherworldly was happening here and she was the only person who would know what the hell it meant. She could hear his thoughts running through his head at the same time he complied with her request relaxing his facial expression from rage to caution. So despite his anger and downright fear, he thought it best to listen to her and take heed.

She was proud of him in that moment for his trust in her. He did followed her instructions without pleading. She was astounded he held her in such regard to put their lives in such a vulnerable position.

The room was filled with electric energy that became evermore intense and bright. With a sudden burst, the light collapsed in on itself, settling to one corner of the room releasing her from it grasp. Briksanna knew at once she was in the presence of the Gods. Quickly dropping to her knees she bowed her head.

To have a response to her prayer so quickly after thousands of years never giving a thought to the deities she held so close in her heart at one time filled her with shame. How naïve she had been, to hold pride as the mature one, simply because she was older than everyone around her. In fact it was a mortal who reminded her of her Fathers words long ago, "You cannot be better or more than the people around you let alone your family, Briksanna. You have to treat them as you would desire to be treated, knowing your inner wisdom is filled by the Gods above. You have to believe here," he said pointing to her heart. "And here," he said pointing to her head. "And here," he said pointing to her hands. "Let the Gods guide you in all that you think, say and do. They shall never forsake you in what you endeavor, neither will they misguide you." She remembered her father clearly; vivid was the moment in her mind, as if it just happened yesterday. Her family had so much open love for one another even when they spoke to one another. Trust was never an issue among them, they believed in one another's words without question.

Tears flowed freely from her downcast lashes. So ashamed was she in allowing her vengeance to overshadow her beliefs. She no longer wanted to be a person alone in the world. She used to be more than that on the inside. She had once been a strong warrior, great leader and good mother to her children. But something was missing deep inside of her, something she lost long ago.

Clasping her hands at her knees she waited for what was to come next.

"Wise words spoken from your father, Princess. I have watched you, and have waited, for you to seek that from the Gods which you know to be true."

"I have been childish allowing my quest for vengeance to overshadow my faith. I beg your forgiveness." Bowing lower, almost prostrate to the ground, "How you honor me appearing here, to one who has shown such blatant disregard and arrogance for so long." she responded humbly.

Gentle hands touched her shoulder, "Rise Princess." Commanded the voice of a woman. She was so startled at the contact she yelped jumping back from where she had been kneeling. Her actions must have alerted Nate, because she quickly glanced his way, seeing his body visibly stiffen, hands clenched in tight fists on the floor. He was visibly battling his instinct to protect her.

She stared at the woman before. She was slight in build wrapped in a white robe that had been worn by ancient civilizations long ago. Long black wavy hair hung below her waist, gold jewelry adorned her body; earrings, necklace and rings. As she turned towards Nate she noticed her feet were bare shimmering anklets adorned her ankles. She was moved by her visual beauty so much so that she quickly forgot her shame. For the first time in eons, she felt peace within herself. Maybe it would be enough to participate in The Prophesy, become the courageous woman she needed to be in order to accomplish all that would be demanded of her. For the first time, she felt she could be that woman.

"There is no need warrior", said the Goddess before her. "No harm will ever befall her, for she had been chosen long ago." Moving away from her striding closer to Nate, she kneeled directly in front of him, touching his shoulder. "Rise, Nathanial Angelo, for you, warrior, are to play a part in Briksanna's fate as your voice is tied to her ear as is your heart tied to hers. You have a great role and responsibility and that is why I have chosen to speak to you both."

Looking directly into her eyes Nathanial asked without hesitation, "Who are you?" He did not fully understand the woman before him.

"Nate!" she interrupted.

Turning to the two people in front of her, she spoke directly to both of them knowing she had to settle any fears by her presence. Hoping to ease their discomfort she replied honestly. "No, Briksanna, he is not from our realm, therefore he does not disrespect me with his question, but asks with the sole desire of understanding." Smiling she looked over at Nate, "Maybe a bit overly protective towards you, as well."

Turning back to her charge, she stepped closer, gesturing for Nate to follow doing her best in assuring them she was not here to cause doubt. "I will speak to you as one, so you may hear what I have to say, not only with your ears but with your hearts, for it is with both you will need to believe that which is expected of you."

Looking vulnerable, Briksanna reached for Nate's hand and held it tightly.

In all the years Merridian had watched over Briksanna, she had never seen such an outward display of fear or trepidation in what was to come next in life. If the grip on Nathanial's hand was any indication, she knew Briksanna was scared. Squeezing her hand back, afraid to take his eyes off her Nathanial held her hand tracing his thumb back and forth reassuring her of his presence. He believed with his whole heart he was her champion. He was absolute in his conviction he would die for the woman standing beside him before any harm could touch her. His display of protective affection moved her more than she had felt in centuries.

Hearing Briksanna say her prayer confirmed her own personal thoughts. Briksanna was ready to step into her role within The Prophesy and she had chosen in her mind Nate would be the man to help her fulfill her role. She chose to do what was right by helping the both of them on their path, despite what her heart wished for. She would do everything possible to be the guardian they both deserved.

The tenderness, sincerity, not to mention the reverence Briksanna had displayed, with her prayer made him want to wrap her up in his strong arms, beating back anyone who dared to hurt her again. She looked magnificent, under the moonlight, invoking her Gods, beseeching their forgiveness for sins, he hadn't know she committed nor did he care, because she was and would always be the one woman he would pledge his life for.

Merridian knew the role Nate would play beside Briksanna. He felt the same admiration toward Briksanna as she felt herself. She was completely moved by her words acknowledging the time had come for her to reveal herself not only to the Gods but to her family and to Skaldanna. Not everything was known to her with regards to what was to become of them, but she knew the time had come for the beginning of the end in the way universe had been drifting along over the centuries. She had to help Briksanna on her path in order for her to become the strong woman she would need to be. There were great sacrifices to be made and great rewards to be gained not only for them, but for the entire universe if they would only believe in themselves. She had to convince them to remain steadfast in their love for one another and that faith will conquer any obstacle in their path.

Focus Merridian, you cannot be what Briksanna needs you to be if you are busy contemplating the unknown.

"Do you mean what you say mortal?" Starring at Nate intently waiting for a reply she did not have to wait long for his response.

"I didn't say anything."

"I can hear your thoughts, as if you spoke them aloud. I have been listening for a long time and am very pleased with what I see, with my own eyes, to be true. I ask again, do you mean, that, which you thought?"

"Who are you? You answer my question and I will answer yours." Crossing his arms on his chest, he starred back at her, clearly challenging her authority.

"You are very brave or, how do they say it in your realm, very stupid; however in this I will grant you. I am known as the Messenger of the Gods; daughter to the First God. Keeper of Light and Energy, Guardian of The Prophesy.

She could tell he was frowning when he turned his head away from her gaze, he wondered how could she do that psychic stuff. She could hear his thoughts, opening up her mind to them, he was thinking back on all he knew and had experienced with Briksanna. What was a little mind reading in the grand scheme of things, right?

She almost burst out laughing hearing his thoughts. She could see herself getting to know this mortal and his way of thinking. She looked away to keep from ruining the moment with laughter.

Turning back to him she noticed he had raised one eyebrow acknowledging her humor in reading his thoughts and he did not look impressed.

Straightening his stance, holding Briksanna's hand tight, as if it was possible to lose her, he said the one word. A word he believed would change his life.

Looking at her directly in the eye he answered her question without hesitation, "Yes."

With a slight nod of her head she acknowledged him. "I have been tasked, by the First God, to send you both on a mission of great importance." Looking at Nate directly, "Are you familiar with The Prophesy involving Briksanna?"

Shaking his head, "No."

"I shall say this once, commanding you to remember it well, for in your moment of doubt, you are both to believe, I as your guardian, will never let you down."

3

*I*nsecurities were put to rest immediately, like a balm of the coolest water. Dare she believe there was hope in coming out of this nightmare with her heart and soul intact? After all these years in doubt, could she trust the words of a Goddess? Yes, she believed for the first time she could be the person she was supposed to be. Scared as she prayed in her heart the sacrifice, in The Prophesy, would not be more that what she could endure. Every choice she would make, from this moment forward, had the potential of becoming a sacrifice.

"The Prophesy demanded there to be a sacrifice, balancing, that which we all call life. This much I have surmised over the years. Is this true?" Feeling her heart pound in her chest she wanted to have answers to her long awaited questions surrounding her role with The Prophesy.

"Just tell us what you need for us to do. Can't you see she's scared not wanting to offend you, not to mention she is exhausted?"

Moving faster than she could track the Goddess touched her forehead commanding her in a loud voice, "Speak, The Prophesy of the First Princess, Lady Briksanna."

A loud clap of thunder rolled off nearby. She saw Nate try and raise his hand in order to block the Goddess from reaching her, but his arms and legs wouldn't move. He was stuck in a state of horror parallelized within his own body unable to protect her.

"Don't hurt her, you promised!" He yelled the moment she realized he was stuck in some sort of stasis.

Her heartbeat sped up as she began to speak in a mechanical voice, completely outside her own control.

"Nine princesses will bear nine sons born from the blood of the four realms and distant lands; a mixture of this time and that of the great divide. To restore balance within the universe, the First Princess of Peace, she whom the Great Gods have marked with violet green eyes, of the Four Realms, will bear the first son; she shall bear Lord Drakkoon's love, fealty and be the Instrument of Death. Her first son born too shall bear the same color eyes as his mother, marking him as the Instrument of Peace. He will be born of this world and of the one called Earth, who only by his hand, will be the instrument of death for Lord Drakkoon thus freeing all the worlds from imminent destruction."

The thunder stopped rumbling at the same time Nate was released from his hold immediately pulling her into a bear hug.

"Nate, you are squeezing me," speaking with a muffled voice, her face plastered to his chest.

"I was scared for you. Lady, I swear, I tell you I love you, and then you pull the sacrificial lamb shit on me. I lost a few years of my life trapped not able to move or protect you. I was left to watch you praying the entire time nothing bad would happen to you."

"Still squeezing," she squeaked.

"Oh, sorry," he said, letting her go reluctantly, but not completely. Looking into her eyes he asked, "Are you ok?"

"I have been better," she said slowly raising her eyes to meet his. "Did you mean what you just said?"

"Hell yes, I was scared."

"Do you love me?" She asked bluntly not wanting to mince words with him. This was important to her.

Pulling her closer again, remembering not to squeeze the life out of her. "I will love you until the day I die, this I promise you. Even then, I can't guarantee my love for you will end."

She saw the relief in his eyes when her whole face lit up from his response. His worry over how she would react to his declaration fled the moment she believed in him. She felt beautiful smiling with her whole being. It had been a long time since anyone had seen her smile like this. A very long time.

Then something happened, she thought another lifetime would pass before she could experience it. She reached up, put her arms around his neck and pulled his head down, inches from her face. She trusted Nate with her heart enough to share her first kiss with him. Looking directly into his eyes, she believed this was the man for heart and soul. The one person she had waited her entire life for.

"You are my warrior, the most honorable man I have ever known. I pledge my life and my love to you, for all eternity. My promise to you before the Gods I shall never break." Pulling him closer she whispered, before allowing their lips to touch, "This I vow to you."

She was kissing him. Not some, seal the bargain kind of kiss or a chaste kind of kiss, to appease a lover, but a promise of passion yet to be explored. Before it could get any better, she remembered they were not alone, tamping down her rising emotions, she broke off the kiss. Years of training to stay in control overwhelmed her body. If there was ever a time to throw all of her psychic awareness out the window now would be a perfect time.

From afar the Goddess cleared her throat, "There is more for you to hear warriors."

Reluctantly parting both of them turned to face the Goddess, her hand still caught in Nate's tight grasp.

"My name is Merridian. If ever, you need me, reach down within your heart and whisper my name. I will hear you, no matter where you are. I am your Guardian, and as such I will be with you every step of the way, along your journey, fulfilling the words spoken by the Great Seer Vakgdona, long ago. The Prophesy speaks of an Instrument of Peace and of the Instrument of Death. Allow me to explain. You, Princess Briksanna, are the Instrument of Peace but in order to do so, you will have to be the Instrument of Death."

"What do you mean, like a knife or something?" Nate asked sounding confused running his hand through his hair. He clearly was becoming agitated. "Let me finish warrior, then you may ask your questions." Chastising him with a pointed look, Merridian waited for him to settle down before speaking again.

Nate sighed loudly; alerting Briksanna he was losing his patience. She rushed to speak first before he vented without thinking. "We apologize, Goddess, please forgive our interruption, right Nate?"

"Right." Dragging his hand down his face in resignation, "I apologize for the interruption."

"In answer to your question, yes the Instrument of Death is a sword and a life; in order to seal the death of Lord Drakkoon, forever, you will have to sacrifice a life. This is the way the Gods believed balance in the universe could be restored. It is the will of the Gods, and Lord Drakkoon is the son of a God."

Hearing a loud gasp come from her mouth, Nate whipped his head around in her direction. "What's wrong? I don't understand what you're telling us." Looking back and forth between her and Merridian, "What does this mean?"

She ignored Nate's questions her mind raced in different directions. If Lord Drakkoon was a son of a God, singular not plural, oh no, could this be what she was thinking it could be? Pulling her hand out of his hand waving him off, "Give me a second to process this," she said speaking to the both of them.

Could Lord Drakkoon be Merridian's brother? That would make him the son of the First God. Surly that cannot be. No father would condemn his son to a lifetime of misery, as the Lord of the Under Realm.

"But the Under Realm is keeper of all that have been punished by the Gods, to wait the time when they are given permission to ascend to the Four Realms, how can this be? Why would a father punish his own son this way?" Briksanna asked with such compassion clearly trying to understand what had happened to them. If she believed what she was being told to be true then their father, the First God, had abandoned his child to a horrible fate. No one deserved that.

"What has he done to deserve this?" Afraid of the answer she was going to receive she stopped pacing and looked directly at Merridian expecting the truth about the man who had hunted her for two millennia.

Tears glistened in her eyes when the Goddess returned her gaze, looked as real and vulnerable mirroring what she felt inside. "Nothing. He has done nothing to deserve any of it. Drakkoon is, and will always be, a great man who has sacrificed the good in his own self for the balance required in both the universe and Skaldanna. His pain and suffering is part of that sacrifice. His obsession is a side effect, one that I cannot intervene with nor can I persuade him from changing his ways. He has been too long in the Under Realm, suffering the effects of being their Over Lord." Merridian chocked on her next words, "That is the way of the Universe, balance, light and dark, love and hate, life and death; this is what the universe requires of all of us. I do not know how else to explain it to you other than the First God knew he would have to sacrifice for the sake of balance in the universe. He has not just sacrificed one son for the sake of balance, but a daughter as well."

At that moment Briksanna knew, the other part of the sacrifice would need to be her and Nate. Eyes wide with fear, "No, I can't. I just found him, please Goddess; I beg you do not ask this of me." Her own eyes welling up with tears, panicking she pleaded with Merridian putting her hands together as if she were praying. "I beg you Merridian; do not ask this of me. I have not the strength or the courage to walk this path you have lain before me."

"Bri, what is going on?" Nate asked clearly getting agitated over her despair, "What does all of this sacrifice mean? Will someone explain what the hell is going on?"

Looking directly at her ignoring Nate, Merridian responded tearfully. "You have always been his greatest obsession. You can, also, be his salvation. Please Briksanna, hear me out before you pass judgment, you are our only hope. Please, both of you, can you listen for a while longer?"

"He is your brother, isn't he?" she stated flatly no longer willing to wait around for confirmation while she resumed pacing.

"Twin brother, to be exact, the only thing you can tell we are related is our green eyes. In all other ways we are very different." Looking away with haunted eyes, turning back around speaking to the both of them, "The First God tasked Drakkoon, four millennia ago, to keep order and maintain harmony within the Under Realm. Doing so would continue the prospect of all inhabitants within both the Upper and Under Realms maintaining balance for the universe, until the time of The Awakening."

Looking at Nate directly she said more for his benefit, "The Awakening is when all the people within the Under Realm are to be judged, hoping to gain permission, ascending to the Upper Realm, thus gaining a second chance at life. Now understand, Nathanial, these people are being punished for the crimes committed against human kind, all they know, have been wiped from their memories when they were first sent to the Under Realm. Those granted permission to ascend have a true fresh start in a new beginning of life."

"Goddess, I mean Merridian, how often does the Awakening occur? I mean how long are those people punished for their crimes, awaiting judgment?" Nate asked openly trying hard to hide his agitation over her distress in what the Goddess was revealing.

"Every hundred years."

"Obviously something went wrong or none of this would be happening. Help me understand, how we are to be the Instrument of Peace and Death?" This whole thing was starting to really make her head hurt. She looked over at Nate and saw his face pale over what Merridian had just told him. His face started to change before her eyes, going from shock to anger.

"Merridian, my first concern is to Bri, then the rest of the world, so spill whatever it is you came to say, because I don't think the Princess here is going to be able to handle much more and frankly neither am I."

"You are brave to speak to me thus," green eyes glowing. "You over step with your words, warrior. I believe the words spoken to you, recently were; I have spanked older men than you for daring to speak to me in this manner." Static electricity began to build around them within the room.

"This can't be good," she groaned. First me, now a Goddess, does he not know when to keep his mouth closed?

Dropping to her knees, grabbing Nate by his hand dragging him with her she bowed. "Merridian, please forgive his words. He does not mean to speak to you without the respect you deserve. I beg your pardon for his offense to you."

Hands and hair still rising the Goddess spoke, "And you warrior, do you share this belief? Do you beg my pardon?"

Raising his head speaking from his heart, she trusted him to find the right words to say not wanting to piss off a Goddess who supposedly was their guardian.

"Forgive me for offending you. I should not take my frustrations out on you. More than anything, I don't want to embarrass this woman next to me. She has suffered enough and I only want to protect her, give her a better life. Don't you see, I just want to give her peace?"

The glow within her eyes dimmed, she sighed, taking the charge in the air within her, visibly calming the storm of emotions she had felt circling the room moments ago.

Looking directly at Nate, Merridian spoke with tears in her eyes, "Peace is what I am trying to do for my brother and everyone in all worlds. It is exactly as you spoke, I wish for my brother to return. He has suffered for too long. By doing so, he has become blinded, corrupted in despair he now believes those corrupted thoughts, emotions and desires from those first sent to the Under Realm. The ones where the taint of their sins fill the land with a stench reminding everyone within of the reason they are there." Tears flowing freely down her face reflecting her broken heart over her brother. "He is my womb mate, the other half of me and for thousands of years, I have felt this burden he bears weigh him down to the husk of a man he is today. Strong he may appear, but I know his heart has been broken. Only the actions of the First Princess can right the wrong that has been left unchecked. Please, do not turn away from destiny. His, yours and all of those involved." Choking the last few words she broke down and cried.

"May I stand?" Nate asked.

Wiping her eyes, clearly embarrassed, in displaying such un-Guardian like behavior, Merridian nodded her head. She could completely relate to feeling like that, vulnerable. It was not long ago when she was bearing her worries and fears to Nate in tears. It was unsettling and invigorating, at the same time, to be able to release all of that emotion when years had been spent bottling them up inside of her afraid anyone would know the love she kept for another could be used against her at any time. It was a horrible way to live and she knew it. She had lived this way for thousands of years hiding her emotions from both the people of Skaldanna and Earth.

Nate didn't wait long for her reply, he stood and approached Merridian, by the time she had given her consent. "I don't know what is done where you come from when a woman is in pain; but my brother raised me well. To me you are a woman who needs some love from a man whom you have just humbled with truthful words."

Without hesitation he took the remaining steps and pulled her into his embrace. This strong man hugged a Goddess like a cherished sibling.

Speaking into her hair he said, "I am very sorry for your loss in a brother, the disappointment in your father and for the pain you have had to endure for so long, while you watched all that you love drift further away. I can only imagine how hard it has been for you. Knowing my lifespan of thirty six years, I would be an emotional wreck if I had to witness my brother going through what your brother has had to endure for thousands of years. That doesn't mean I condone the actions he has done against Bri. It just means I understand now what has lead him to where he is today and I understand what brought you to us."

Pulling back arm's length from Merridian, holding onto her shoulders, he looked in her eyes searching for her approval, "What can we do to help save your brother and fulfill this Prophesy?"

Searching Nate's gaze for any sign of half-truths she appeared astonished. "Remarkable, in my entire existence, no one has dared touch me with affection as you have." In clear amazement, of the contact she had just received, she blinked a couple of times, making sure this moment was real. "It has been so long since someone beside my companion, Ellena, has shown compassion for me, especially over my brother."

Pulling away from him she smiled to the both of them. Nate returned to her side holding her hand again. How easy it felt to have him by her side when earlier today she would never have dreamed to publicly display her true feelings for the man beside her. Looking up at him she was proud he selflessly comforted a stranger, albeit a Goddess, but a stranger no less. His empathy and immediate action would make him a great king.

"I am most touched by your earnest sincerity to my pain. That action and your compassion will not be forgotten. Thank you for your humble apology and sincere show of concern." Smiling now, stepping back, no sign of tears left in her eyes, "We have much work to do, but the greatest sacrifice will be from the both of you. If you do this neither one of you will die, but by following through The Prophesy to the end you will have eternal happiness within each other's arms, this I promise you. You will never again have to sacrifice one or the other, for anyone in anything. You must listen to me with an open mind and heart."

Taking a deep breath she began to tell them the mission set before them. All details they would need to know about the sacrifice, most importantly who would need to be saved first. This would be great if she could remember anything Merridian said before a loud clap of thunder sounded in the room, right as she was speaking the details of their most important mission.

Could they survive everything she was saying and stay safe while saving the universe at the same time were her last thoughts right before darkness hit.

4

Somewhere lost in the Four Realms

Crouching down, hands reaching deep into the dirt surrounding his body, she grabbed a fistful of the rich soil in her right hand and released what was left in the other as she stood. "To remind me the pain this place has brought me. I take this dirt as a reminder never to forget what you have done to me."

Stepping closer to the shriveled body lying on the ground she gathered enough courage to see the face of what was left of the man she had labeled her Tormentor.

Gasping falling to her knees she almost dropped the clump of dirt she she clutched in her palm. "No, it is a trick, it cannot be him. Oh Gods no, please not him."

Closing her eyes, a deep soul searing pain of betrayal lanced through her as she lifted her head screaming into the now empty room. "Why Lysinous? Why"?

Tears fell freely she lowered her head and remembered the pain he dealt her over the past several months. She had been shredded body and soul by the very man she had mourned during her captivity. She could feel her heart break physically and emotionally from this knowledge than he could have ever done to her chained against that wall. She never wanted to be the naïve woman she had been before he laid his hands on her. Dreams she once cherished now lay empty as the shell of a man lying before her.

Gathering the surrounding energy in the room she channeled her fury over the injustice of her imprisonment, her broken dreams and battered body, into a force of energy wrapping it around her like well-worn blanket. The fiery hot band of energy grew as she remembered the pain she felt the moment her parents had died. Months of not knowing what had happened to everyone tortured her as much as his beatings. What had happened to her sister or her best friend? Did they escape? And what of her people? She had spent many days and nights alone with nothing but her own thoughts give voice to her despair. Had anyone been spared when their castle had been conquered by his troops?

The more she thought the more her fury mounted believing their sacrifices had been made so a man promised to cherish her could destroy everything she held dear in life.

She spoke out loud to no one, yet the words were forcefully ripped from her chest. Her pain was inconsolable. "They died defending the lives of me and my family despite the threat of dark magic; even in their anger, their protection and caring of us children, was to ensure we could survive. They had died trying to protect the lives of their faithful subjects, taking the death magic and turning it upon themselves so as not to harm even the guards at their sides; that is the kind of rulers they were. My parents died trying to defend the future of all who lived within the Four Realms; this was their unwavering faith."

Leaning over, she gripped the tunic on his body tearing a large enough piece for her to settle the dirt she held in her hand. Leaning over desperate to complete her task she was unable to stop the flow of tears raining down her face mixing with the dirt she was placing in the fabric. Folding the fabric carefully knotting the top so the soil would be protected, she placed the newly made totem in the pocket of her gown.

Swallowing her pain she shoved aside her need to grieve. She knew she had to escape this place of torture. Gripping her fists tightly feeling the bulge in her pocket brush against her leg reminding her she would never feel vulnerable by a friendly face again. "So I never forget what betrayal feels like nor what death looks like by my hand, this I vow to the Gods above." Looking around she wiped the tears from her eyes. *"No crying. Cry later. Pull it together Briksanna, you have to get out of here first."*

Bowing her head, she closed her eyes, praying from deep within her soul. She released her plea in the form of energy up into the great realm of the Gods raising her arms above her pleading her case into the unknown. "I beg you for your guidance. I know not where I am or where I am to go. Please do not forsake your faithful daughter. I feel abandoned and afraid. Please, Great Gods above, give me the strength and courage to face what lies before me. Grant me your protection from any more harm. Show me a way home."

Opening her eyes, tears flowed freely as a fresh wave of despair threatened to overwhelm her. She reached again into her pocket and touching the talisman, not wanting to forget what she had recently endured in the hands of her once betrothed.

Staring off into the distance she allowed her mind to wander. Thinking back it all made sense why she never saw him. He made her feel only pain and humiliation day after day after day. How could she have been so blind to who he really was? She had grieved daily for him even more so during her torture believing her body would never be perfect like she had once believed because of the many scars she would have due to the constant beatings she had been given.. She grieved for the future she had lost, holding tight to a little girl's long list of what could have been. She had loved Lysinous with a young girl's heart. Her family, along with her father's kingdom had prepared for the announcement of their marriage at the time the castle had come under attack. Lysinous was the great noble son of the Second Realm from the House of Kastekanos. A realm rich in farming. Crops flourished with the most beautiful gardens under the watchful eye of the Kastekanos family. The Second Realm had been the first realm stricken by Lord Drakkoon's malevolent hand. Devastated where its people for many had died and only a scat few families remained. Some fled to the Fourth Realm warning the High King, her father, what had happened seeking shelter and protection. Princess Katerina, Lysinous's younger sister and her best friend, was with her when Lord Drakkoon sent his armies into the Second Realm seeking to extend his rule over the Upper Realm. He had dared the impossible and done the incredible. From the many stories she overheard brought to the High Council, her father being a member, the coat of arms worn by the armies where that of a large bird clutching a spear and a scroll in its claws. No realm bore this symbol as a representation of their kingdoms and no one in the High Council had ever heard of it before assuming it was that belonging to Lord Drakoon.

Lysinous was known, throughout all the lands, as a fair man in heart to be generous in nature and the man who had swept her off her feet with just a smile. She had believed he would protect her, honor her filling her heart and home with love and children. She believed she was the woman he would cherish for all time. Remembering the countless hours sobbing first from the relentless pain he had inflicted only to move onto more lonely hours left in solitude.

"I thought you dead!" She screamed spitting on his face as an ache deep within her heart ripped further in pain.

She looked down at the shriveled up shell of a body no longer seeing the man whose eyes would twinkle with mischief when she and his sister would relentlessly tease him. The body lying on the ground belonged to a man who had caused her untold amounts of pain both to her body and to her heart. He once was her knight in shining armor now he lay dead by her hand a coward who did not have the courage to show his face when he beat her.

Searching his face she noticed his body was bathed in violet light. Taking in the appearance of the rest of his body she forced her eyes to take everything in. The man he used to be to and the person he swore he would be for her to the beast he had become that loved to torment her.

Fury like nothing she had ever felt before mounted with each sweeping glance. How he looked in death. The smell of his burnt body and the way his clothes were half burnt, yet remained half clean still maintaining the formal appearance worn by high ranking noblemen in all realms. Her mind seemed to operate of its own accord for all she could concentrate on was what he had last said and done to her. The blows he dealt to her body, never by his hands always with the rod or whip and sometimes with both. There was no place on her entire body except her face and the tops of her hands that had been spared from the wrath of his beatings.

Gathering her strength raising herself upright she reached into her pocket wanting to look at her talisman one more time as if the bundle of dirt and tears held all her answers. Gripping it tight in her right hand she spoke softly to the empty room.

"Why."

Serenity flowed around her in the form of a gentle breeze gracefully filling her mind, heart and soul with a cleansing sweep giving credence to the presence now belonging to her Gods. They had not left her behind.

"You did not forsake me. I am not alone," she sobbed bringing both hands to wipe her eyes hoping to regain her composure. She wanted to honor them as a strong woman all the while giving thanks there were some things she could still count on to remain steady and honest in her life when there were no arms to physically hold her. She knew she could always trust in her faith to hold her up when the actions of people beat her down.

"To shape you we had to forge you, in the fire of despair. Your destiny required it, daughter ours." Spoken by a male disembodied voice not from any particular place within the room but from all around. Shaking her head at the thoughts of who was speaking, she stilled as she let the words the God had said sink in. Snapping her eyes open fisting her hands at her sides she felt her anger spike to volcanic proportions.

"To shape me as I hung chained to a wall tormented by my betrothed. For months you left me grieving for all that was good in my life had become lost to me, you wanted to shape me?"—she screamed as the words of the God shredded her very soul with the worst betrayal of all—"We of the four realms have given you our fealty and prayers unconditionally, which I believed was due to you from the first moment I can remember and you say my destiny required it? My heart is hardening as I speak from your lack of integrity for your faithful subjects." She spat out feeling her very soul begin to burn with a searing pain. Her anger fanned its' flame.

"Careful daughter ours you let your grief and anger rule you. Control that which festers within. Give us your pain and we will replace it with strength, courage and guidance; that which you prayed for just moments ago."

Flashing with spurts of molten fury she gave him the only answer she had left in her. "I will give you nothing from this day forward. I will shape my own destiny. I spit on your prophesy and I will not be the vessel in which my son will beholden to such treacherous Gods. Gods who allow their children to fall upon misery and suffering for their amusement." Throwing her hands up into the chamber head raised high she closed her eyes drawing the fire pressing within her demanding its release, a mixture of her rage and her energy bubbling to the surface. Never had she felt her own energy core burn so fierce nor feel as powerful as it had in that moment. She no longer cared what happened to her. The only thing she cared about was destroying anything in her path.

"I will no longer serve you the Great Gods of the universe!" Unleashing her wrath on the ceiling above her straight from the depth of her soul right out of her fingertips. Levitating up from the force of the energy she was pulling from the center of whatever realm she was in she floated through the chamber dodging debris. Nothing touched her and she did not care if it did. She remembered the people who had suffered coming before the High Council. They were the very ones along with her father's people she heard screaming every time she closed her eyes. After each torture session she would pray for their souls. May they be in peace cherishing their loved ones in the afterlife. The same Gods she had been taught to have faith in had allowed her to be tortured by the very hands of her betrothed so she could be forged in the pits of despair.

"You could have stopped all of this. You could have saved everyone from such destruction and mayhem." Screaming at the top of her lungs she blasted lightning bolt after lightning bolt all around her while simultaneously floating out of her prison.

She was going to blast her prison down to the depths of the Under Realm where all souls good and bad are to be judged fit to move onto the next life. Lord Drakkoon is ruler of the Under Realm until the Day of Judgment.

Wanting him to hear her fury for it was him her Tormentor spoke of her giving fealty to. "I shall never give over my son to you so you can use him as your instrument of destruction. I will never follow you again, do you hear me, never."

Lightning and thunder rolled striking all around her as she unleashed months of physical torture and emotional pain determined to reduce the mountain of rock into rumble openly defying the Master's command. She screamed and screamed and kept on screaming until sound no longer had a voice just like her heart no longer retained faith. Her trust had been broken for the last time.

5

She felt like she had been weighted down franticly struggling to break the surface of the dream threatening to drown her. Despite her efforts she could not free herself. She did not want to open her eyes and face reality, she was so angry at herself for remembering that weak moment in her life when she had first looked betrayal before her in the flesh and blood only to discover betrayal came in different forms. Trust could be broken in the physical sense like what had happened when Lysinous had tortured her, but it could also come in the form of faith like when the Gods had abandoned her. They had watched her as she was stripped of her dignity fooled by the naïve notions of a little girls dream that they would always be the ones to help pick her up if and when she fell down. She put all of her faith in them, the invisible ones, and the very same entity who told her she needed the experience in order for her to be forged within a pit of despair. She had become that woman without their help. She was a strong, intelligent woman who still retained the capacity to love and empathize with the people around her. That was the very nature of her mercenary team. She wanted to, no needed to bury the past once and for all. She was no longer that person and no matter how much she hated it, her experience made her the woman she was today.

Part of her knew where she was and part of her was still rationalizing what she had dreamed about. She felt trapped and was beginning to panic. Kicking her legs and arms, wiggling her entire body in earnest, she struggled to rise up from where she was being held down. She squeezed her eyes tightly deeply afraid her fears would surface once she fully awakened.

"Bri, wake up for me baby. Come on you can do it. That's it, open your eyes," Nate coaxed. "I'm not going to let anyone hurt you. You're safe in our bed in our time."

Time, oh Gods, I must have spoken out loud. Scrambling out of bed, running towards the bathroom; it wasn't until she reached for the bathroom door did she realize she was fully clothed. "Huh?" This makes no sense. Why was she dressed in yesterday's clothes? Running her hand through her hair still confused from the remnants of the dream she turned around eyes landing on the man sitting on her bed staring at her intently, patiently waiting for her to do what she did not know.

"Why are you here?"

"You were having a nightmare, Bri. You were thrashing in the bad and I was afraid you were going to hurt yourself." Easing himself to the back of the bed he leaned back against the headboard stretching his legs out resting his hands on his lap.

"You did not answer my question. Why are..."

It all came back to her, the meeting they had trying to gauge the value of taking on another mission piggybacking the confrontation with Lord Drakkoon's lackey, Jackson. Their argument, her almost killing him, his confession, her admission and then to her utter horror wrapping up one of the worst nights in several millennia, she shared her nightmare projecting her life's horrors while lying in her own bed with the man she loved. He was the man she had wanted to lie beside for the past decade. She wanted to be awake when they were lying together. At least that was how she had dreamed it would be for their first time.

Walking back to the bed flopping down on the edge contemplating her thoughts, it dawned on her she might have spoken out loud. "Oh, Gods what have I said?" Feeling the heat of embarrassment climb her neck, she covered her face with her hands. "Did I speak out loud by any chance? Did I say anything?"

"Everything. You said everything, Bri." He said quietly reaching out to run his hands down the length of her hair. "It's ok, you are safe with me always."

"No, I did not. How would you know what I said, I was dreaming you couldn't possibly know what I dreamed."

Pulling her arms down looking up at him, her breath caught in her throat. His eyes had turned a molten green as he leaned to whisper beside her ear. "I was there beside you in your dream. Don't you remember what the Goddess Merridian said to us?"

Goddess Merridian? Who was that? she thought.

Oh, this is just freaking fantastic. We get the pleasure of meeting a Goddess... who charges us with the quest of a freaking lifetime, but hey who's counting, right? I must seriously be losing my mind to be this sarcastic.

"You could say that again." Snorting responding nonchalantly.

"I must seriously...hey wait a minute. You can hear my thoughts just like I can hear your thoughts. This is not cool, Bri." Pulling away from her frowning he did not appear as if turnabout was fair play. This could be interesting she thought to herself. They had always been able to speak telepathically but never their personal thoughts. They all had mental walls perfected over time to keep stray thoughts from being picked up on. Speaking of thoughts what was that he was thinking of doing with, oh my God. He could not possibly be able to do all that and the other person would like it. Could they, hmmm.

"I could get used to it if what you are thinking of doing with your hands are going to happen anytime soon."

Breaking into a full grin having been caught in the middle of his thoughts. "What I can do with my hands has been outlawed in many time zones."

Suddenly frowning, feeling horribly out of place. She got up from the bed deciding she might be able to wash away the pain in her chest over what he just said. "Oh, I didn't know that."

"Bri, I was kidding." Jumping up he rushed around the bed to soothe her. "I'm trying to sound sexy towards you and it back fired. What upset you, my comment about my hands?"

"Yes, it implied you are an experienced man. One who has been with many women, is this true?" Hoping she did not sound desperate when all she wanted to believe was he would never betray her trust by comparing her to other women or seeing anyone else for that matter. She wanted to be the only one he sought out, the center of his universe. That was the person she wanted to be to him.

Grabbing her shoulders staring her straight in the eye, "No, there has only been one person I have slept with and that didn't go too well. I didn't want to share the deep dark Nate secrets before the pillow talk."

"Pillow talk, what is that?" Feeling completely out of depth with relationships, she averted her gaze turning her head slightly hoping he did not guess her lack of knowledge. He might decide she was too much work between their argument and the Goddess declaration she had enough baggage she was bringing into the relationship she should leave him be. Cut off her emotions and sever his along the way.

Lifting her chin turning her face back towards him, he reassured her. "You know the intimate conversation post sexual experience?" Blushing he hurried to explain, "I pictured our first pillow talk conversation to be sharing secrets of one another's most embarrassing humorous moments or something like that. Mostly I just wanted you to fall in love with me more just by getting to know the stuff I have never shared with anyone else."

Raising her hand to his cheek wanting tell him the truth. "I am already in love with you and for my people once it happens it happens deeply and forever. We do not try out partners as the people of your world do. We mate for life and I give my heart to you freely. I love you, Nathanial Angelo. You are the mate I have chosen for life."

Touching his head to hers pleading for her understanding. "Don't leave me Briksanna. Promise me you will stay with me tonight? Stay with me as a husband and wife do in my world. I don't know what it means in your world but in mine, I also pledge my heart to you freely and forever. We may not have said it in front of a priest but I know we said the words in front of a Goddess." Holding his breath waiting for her to respond he felt her mind shifting, sorting pictures of recent experiences like a person would flip through a picture book. "Bri, you remember don't you?"

"I don't know. There are bits and pieces like a movie screen flickering; Nate what happened can't you..." Screaming she put her hands to the sides of her head bending over.

"Bri, what is it? What's wrong, baby, tell me where it hurts. I'm going to get help," he started to turn and go, when the candles in the room he lit earlier seemed to jump all at once, shinning taller, brighter than before scaring the crap out of him causing him to jump. Turning around not wanting to abandon her while she was in pain not knowing what was wrong. He wanted to be there for her.

"Nate, I remember everything that happened tonight." Briksanna said softly. "Do not get anyone just yet. We have to talk before we will tell the others." Raising herself up from her crouched position she laid her hand on his check. It was the same place she had held him just moments ago. She kept the pain hidden knowing her yelping had probably upset him. From what he could surmise she was already healing internally. Her head didn't appear to still hurt and from his mental scan she was not particularly worried about any lasting effects. He overheard her thinking what had happened was normal for her kind when information was transferred or when an event prevents a person to immediately remember what happened they regain their memories and the painful assault on her brain was the result. He brushed it off as long as she did. It was good enough for him. "We will call a meeting with the team in the morning to strategize and organize for our quest."

"You'll decline the special ops mission you were grueling over earlier?" Crossing his arms over his chest doing his best to intimidate her with his frequent stare down look.

"You can wipe that look off your face. I have every intention of putting The Prophesy and Skaldanna before I ever accept another mission on this realm. You have my word." Reassuring him with her crocked grin. It wasn't a full smile but it was enough to get his blood pumping nonetheless.

"Humph, well if you say so, I'll bite. If I see you're not taking care of yourself or making good choices for this family because you've pushed yourself too hard we're going to have this talk again."

Feeling her temper want to snip at him she immediately opened her mouth then closed it before she could challenge him. He remembered the scene earlier where she was going to blast him to kingdom come just for pointing out the fact she had not taken proper care of herself. She had become a threat to herself and to the people she called family for what? Pride?

How embarrassing for the leader of the team, not to mention a much older woman, make such an immature mistake. Could a hole open up and swallow her now?

Reading her thoughts he put his finger on her mouth effectively silencing her. "No talking until you're taken care of." Trying to keep a serious look on his face knowing he could read her thoughts and if she found out she would be pissed.

Groaning mentally she must of heard his thoughts. No longer able to resist he looked up at her narrow her eyes mirroring her facial expressions of wanting to yell at him but was holding back out of courtesy, plain and simple. That and she did not want him to know he was right.

"I mean it, Bri, I'm going to take care of you first then you and I can talk, deal? That is the best I can offer after all we have been through tonight." Sounding very serious he was putting all his mental effort to block her from his thoughts so she was unable to ascertain if he was lying or not. He wanted her to trust him.

Looking at her mate her grin managed to reach her eyes for the first time in many years, "Deal Mate." *Two can play at that game.*

He stilled his body, eyes turning a molten green, like an animal ready to pounce before shaking it off knowing he needed to put her needs before his allowing the cool Nate to come to the forefront. Smiling he picked her up, "Mrs. Angelo, you have made me a very proud man. I swear I will do all that I can to keep my promise to both you and the Goddess. Now let's get you showered, some food in you and a clean change of clothes. With the way I am feeling right now not necessarily in that order."

"Warm or hot?" he asked walking into the large bathroom.

"What?" Licking her lips he wondered what it would feel like to have his arms wrapped around her all night long. She seemed distracted by his touch before, but now she couldn't keep her thoughts in the present tense. She kept projecting her own fantasies of them together under the running water, he was afraid he would lose his cool and jump her. If she didn't get her head out of the gutter soon he was going to combust from his own desires boiling inside of him.

He smiled at her knowing she was distracted with her own private thoughts and this touched his heart knowing he excited her with just a thought. They were the same reasons he was struggling with by putting her basic needs first. He did not need her attacking him like an animal clearly as her mind was demanding her to do because if she did he wouldn't last a second.

"Water, warm or hot?" He repeated poised by the head of the shower stall.

"Warm, please." Shaking her head slightly trying to clear her thoughts he figured she should try deep breathing if focusing on the present moment continued to fail her. Goodness sakes, she was acting like a crazed teenager around him and he liked it.

Suddenly feeling doubtful of her worth to him sobered up her libido real quick. She stole a quick glance at him hoping to reassure herself of his commitment towards her but he saw her looking at him from the corner of his eyes anyway.

I have got to let go of this self-doubt. Those thoughts have no place between us in this moment. If I say that enough times maybe I will believe it?

Setting her down carefully on the bathroom counter, holding her around the waist with one arm he leaned into the shower stall to turn on the water. She was too quiet for his liking, because after turning the water on he turned back and stared at her. After a couple of debatable seconds he went with his gut pulling her into a hug wrapping his massive arms around her filling his senses with her scent. She had endured so much. He wanted to give her so much and not frighten her with his presence in her life in the process. He knew he was the man for her and she was the woman for him but she still had a hard time with trusting despite what her heart and mind were saying. There was still a piece of her she kept hidden. Some things were just hard for her to let go of. That he could defiantly understand.

Will she ever trust him enough so they could endure The Prophesy and defeat Lord Drakkoon? More importantly could he trust her to endure the upcoming battle for the sake for the universe? What a complete mess this was. When he dreamed of confronting Bri with the truth of his feelings for her he didn't count on all of this drama to go with it.

Frowning he thought about where his thoughts were heading. He would lay down his life for her no matter what, so what the hell was he worried about? For him there was no one else in the world he would rather spend his days with. She was the one for him and there was nothing anyone could do or say that would cause him to betray her trust.

He let go of her, turned around and adjusted the water temperature. She heard a stray thought from him float by her like a breeze in the bathroom.

I don't know if I can trust her not to forget me. She has been alive longer than I can imagine. I don't even know if there is someone else on Skaldanna waiting for her to come back to. She could have someone who's been waiting for her all this time and I show up. She deserves someone who has more knowledge in all of this prophesy stuff than me. What can I bring to the table that I have gained in my whopping thirty six years of life?

He was frightened he would not measure up to the man she needed him to be in order for her to succeed with her role in The Prophesy. She understood, in that moment, he had always been in the present tense with her. What was going on in that very moment, between the both of them, was the most important thing in his world and he knew it. He had not been keeping the truth of his commitment to her hidden, she had chosen not to look into his heart seeing what was right in front of her. This man was her chosen mate and she believed she had chosen well. Her father would be proud of her choice.

"You are my purpose now, Nathanial." she said quietly from behind, placing her hand on the small of his back to reassure him of her presence. "I will do the will of the Gods for the sake of the universe but never lose sight that I do this for the sake of the life of our future son."

Turning around slowly, Nate looked at her for just a few moments, and then gave a clipped nod. "Let me help you get out of these clothes." Keeping his eyes trained on her beautiful lips he pulled her t-shirt over her head. He looked like a man who was staring at the world's greatest problem and she was the answer.

He reached around her and unclasped her bra careful not to frighten her with his actions. "You are beautiful to me." Pulling the bra away slowly gazing at her making her feel like the most beautiful woman he had ever laid eyes on. "You are so beautiful to me." Bringing his eyes up to her face she recognized the aroused expression on his face mirrored hers.

"Baby, I want you more than I want to breathe, right now, but what kind of husband would I be to you if I start this relationship off being selfish?" His voice sounded deeper, gravely like he was straining to get the words out. His voice sent chills up her spine despite her warmth and she was getting hotter by the second.

Knowing how exhausted she was, he bent on one knee to unlace her boots. Lifting her right leg he pulled off one boot repeating the action with her other foot. Still in a kneeling he reached up to unbutton her pants and pulled the zipper down holding his breath until the zipper went as far as it could go. Chancing a look at her face before he continued with pulling her pants down, he wanted to make sure she was ok with him helping her undress. She stopped him mid motion with a slight touch of her hands.

"I can hear your thoughts as if they are my own. I want you to know before we go any further, I have never laid with a man." Not waiting for his response, she straightened her shoulders hoping down from the counter pulling her pants down in front of him while he remained kneeling in front of her.

What was he going to say? Here I am old enough to be his grandmother, more than several times removed, and I am just a plain virgin.

Grabbing her hand before she could step into the shower, he said "There is nothing plain about you. I am both humbled and honored that you have chosen me to share your love, no don't look away, that's right, I said love. Bri, I will not turn away from this thing we have to go through. I love you more than I want to breathe. I may have doubts now and then, but in the end I will always do the right thing. Now get in there and wash up. The sooner you do that the sooner we can eat."

Eyes glistening listening to his declaration of love for her, she felt another crack in the armor she had built around her soul. "I love you. I have wanted to say that for a long time. I did not know how or if you felt the same way. I was afraid to tell you before, but am no longer." Sounding more confidant she pleaded with her eyes for him to believe her. "Thank you for being here with me. I do not know what I would have done if you were not here with me. Truly, I do love you."

Not hesitating when he spoke next, "I love you forever"

Appearing as if it was the hardest thing in the world to do, he closed his eyes, kissed her lightly on the forehead then turned around and walked right out the bathroom, closing the door, allowing her the privacy of a warm shower.

Walking back into the bedroom he stopped saying to himself, "Get a grip man, you have got to use the big head not let the little head," adjusting himself breathing deeply counting to ten then back down to one again reigning in his raging hormones.

First things first, striding over to the end table he picked up the phone and dialed the one person he knew he could trust with his worries more than anyone. Briksanna was his life not just his wife, but the other half of his soul. He needed his big brother.

His brother answered on the second ring, "Stark?"

"What's up, bro?" His brother said jokingly, "What's wrong early night? I told you what to do, bro."

Interrupting his brothers speech "Stark, this is serious, I need for you to run interference with the family until tomorrow afternoon. Tell everyone to be prepared meet in the big room tomorrow night for a briefing so Bri and I can have the night alone."

No longer joking around, his brother turned professional in an instant. That was the way it always had been between the two of them and this was why he knew he could trust him with his most precious possession.

"Briksanna with you?"

"Yes," not wanting to say any more than the bare minimum regarding their relationship until he had a chance to sort out the details with Bri first. She would want to talk to the family with him. For some reason that made his heart feel real good thinking of the both of them as a team of their own even with the family. It was Bri and him discussing everything, not just missions or discussions regarding the kids, but everything and anything, from now on, the would share with one another trusting each other's thoughts and ideas to formulate the best possible solution.

"You're calling from her room, so she is safe and by the tone of your voice there is more to say on the matter is my guess. You not going to clue your big brother in are you?"

"No, not yet. Stark if anything that happens to us, I want you to know; don't believe everything you see or hear. There is a lot more at stake than any of us ever dreamed possible and I know this sounds crazy telling you like this but I need you to trust me sight unseen. I respect you and as your brother I would never do anything to betray that trust. I trust you with my life, bro, just as I will trust you with the most precious thing in my life. You have to hear me out and know I can't tell you everything right now. We have been through too much together to start doubting each other. So I need you to go out on a limb here and trust me. You with me, brother?"

"Still here man, but I got to tell you, you're starting to scare me." He sounded like he wanted to ask more questions but he was holding himself in check because he had asked him to.

"I will tell you everything tomorrow night," sighing deeply he sat down on the edge of the bed and looked back at the bathroom door. He made sure he could still hear the water confirming Bri was still showering. "I guess I just needed to hear your voice more than anything."

"Now you're really scaring me. Nate what's up, man? It's not like you to keep me in the dark like the rest of the team," sighing too, he gave in not sounding entirely happy about it. "If what you need is for me to stall everyone until you too have had some time to sort out whatever it is you too have to deal with then you got it little brother. And I got your back too, no matter what, you dig?"

Blowing out a breathe he had been holding waiting for his brothers reply, he was relieved Stark understood he wasn't ready to talk about what he wasn't willing to deal with at the moment but had his back anyway. Stark was the constant in his crazy world. He said that years ago and believed in it today, just like he believed it would be that way between them in the future. Stark taught him long ago, family was a non-negotiable in their relationship. You don't give them up, or throw them away because you are afraid they will sell you out one day. Stark would always have his back and he would forever have his.

He laughed out loud repeating Starks famous words, "You da man, always."

"Don't you ever forget it little brother. Get some sleep. Oh and Nate?"

"Yeah?" Bracing himself for what his brother was going to say next.

Speaking softly whispering into the phone, "Don't forget, I've touched both you and Briksanna, so be easy with her bro. She deserves you, but you deserve her as well." With that statement he hung up before he could even say a word.

Nate thought, wiping a hand down his face, his brother already knew what they were dealing with. The night just kept getting better and better.

6

Stark hung up the phone before he could give his brother a chance to speak. Turning around he looked at the people around him and sighed resigned to the path is brother had accepted in life. "It has already started. That was Nate on the phone and after the electrical shit storm we just experienced I expect him and Briksanna have met the Goddess and have been informed of the quest we were briefed on this evening. I believe it will take all of us to help them with what Merridian has explained needs to happen. They will need our support in sorting out this prophesy and I want all of us to be in on this."

Running his hands through his hair not really knowing where to begin, he needed a minute to get his legs under him before saying another word. Anything to do with his brother tended to get his emotions worked into a lather.

Closing his eyes expecting darkness to fill his mind instead he was met with green eyes staring back at him. The pull of her eyes brought forth the memory of the forest north of their compound, what he considered the most peaceful place on earth. One look in her eyes and his brain went on meltdown. He couldn't think of anything or anyone else but the Goddess that left the room a little while ago. It was embarrassing the way he just stood there staring at her when she first appeared to them. The twins probably noticed the drool he had to slurp up because damn the woman was one fine piece of work. He caught her alarm when she first locked eyes with him, he was sure of it. The way she stopped mid-sentence for ten seconds before a mask of indifference fell over her face shadowing any potential knowledge he could have gleamed from her facial expressions. One minute she was talking about some prophesy and the next she stood there staring at him with the same thunderstruck expression he had on his face except he couldn't keep his mind on task like she did. The whole time she talked his mind kept going back to those green eyes, high cheekbones holding a slightly rounded face with a beautiful cleft in her chin begging to be kissed. Long black tresses brushed her hips adding to the allure of a beautiful body wrapped in some sort of robe held together by some tightly woven rope she kept fidgeting with throughout her entire speech. Seems like the beautiful Goddess was nervous about something or she was scared as hell to be in the room with them. Either way she didn't appear, to his critical eye, what he had pictured an omnipotent being should be. Bringing his head back into the present moment he chastised himself for letting some woman break his concentration especially in front of the kids. "Pull it together Stark, get your head back in the game," he mumbled to no one but himself.

"What did you say?" asked Trinity the Great Healer in the group who loved to tease him any chance she could.

"Still trying to wipe the drool he dripped from our last visitor." said Harmony their team's Land Healer high fiving her identical twin sister Trinity. "Too bad she left in a flash, boss, you could have gave her some of that Angelo charm you've been bragging to Nate about." Giggles erupted around the room.

Slamming his fist down on the table zero to sixty pissed, "Ok, that's the last slanderous comment to be made about the Goddess or myself period, understood?" Glaring at everyone in the room itching for anyone to naysay him on the matter so he could pound some flesh. He didn't care who at this point, everyone in the room was deadly with their hands or a weapon. He just wanted to beat something up and if he could knock the smart look off the faces staring back at him it was an added bonus.

"She risked everything to bring our team in the loop so we could work together not because we are a great team, but because we are family, so back the hell off H and T!"

All laughter ceased. Looking seriously uncomfortable Trinity spoke up first, "Let me be the first to say, you are right"—waving her hand around the room stopping at her twin—"and we are wrong," finished Harmony in the usual twin speak everyone was accustomed to.

"To do this means we've got to have our head in the game, right twin number two?" pleaded Harmony looking at Trinity for support.

"Right twin number one, right. Umm...so boss we're sorry. No more jokes about you and the Goddess." Trinity waited expectantly for him to acknowledge their apology.

Nodding at the twins, "Now that *that* is out of the way, let's talk about what Nate just called me about." Pulling out a chair from the desk he sat down intent on finishing the conversation. He wanted to get out of here so he could examine his mental state with the Goddess, deal with it and move on. He didn't like not having his head in the game. Distraction led to mistakes and mistakes cost lives. "You know the drill, kick your shoes off boys and girls, grab your snacks and get comfortable this should only take a few minutes."

Groans around the room could be heard along with some shuffling. No matter how old they got, to him they will always be his kids, his family. He looked around the room as everyone got settled taking inventory at who was on hand noting everyone was present. This group was not only his team but they were his family.

First there was Striker Wells native to Southern California, surfer born and bred; he stood six foot four; radio man and strategist for the team. He was the eyes and ears on all missions whether in the field or on base of operations he was a master coordinator and everyone trusted him to guide them through any situation. He could coordinate a fly out of a spiders nest from two clicks if he needed to that's how good he was. Briksanna swears she can smell the wheels turning in his head whenever they're briefing for any mission. Blue eyes, blonde hair, he's the pretty boy of the group. Rarely does anyone get a chance to see his deep dimples in a full smile, always for the women and only on covert missions for his targets. Striker never showed interest in anyone for personal pleasure. He swears he'll know her when he sees her and so far that hasn't happened. Out of everyone on the team, Striker was the one who always came out on top in command center training missions. He was the first person everyone argued over when it came to who was going to be guarding their backs during hand to hand combat. He was the wickedest man on earth with a blade next to the twins. He'd never seen him without some type of blades strapped to his body. He wouldn't put it past him if he slept with the damn things.

Sitting together on the loveseat were Harmony and Trinity or H and T; the Rasoul twins, identical except for their hair length you would never know who was whom if Briksanna hadn't raised them with different hair lengths. We all know the difference between the girls but anyone outside of the family, good luck. Harmony and Trinity had been abandoned as infants somewhere in the mid-west. Briksanna raised them took care of them herself after she had found them swaddled in blankets under a willow tree. Story was she rescued them from being eaten by animals in some forest in the outskirts of the middle of nowhere, took them in and it was just the three of them before he and Nate showed up. He knew there was more to the story but he always let it go because of the pain the memories caused her whenever he asked so he stopped asking. It was obvious she loved them with all her heart to have done something like saddle herself with two infants while being a mercenary. They met when they had been contracted to do the same job twelve years ago saving each other and have been together as a family ever since. The twins were nine at the time and seriously adept to the task at hand given the mission back then was to rescue a senator's daughter from some drug lord in the middle of a third world country, but who was he kidding, they were raised by a two thousand year old warrior princess from another realm for crying out loud. Stunning beauties they both stood at six foot two, reddish blond hair, hazel eyes and deadly on the field when needed. Both girls were healers not in the traditional doctor medicine sense, but in the psychic "lay your hands" on a person and viola said person was healed. They called Trinity "T" for short or by her title the "Great Healer" as there hasn't been an injury she hadn't healed; however that didn't mean there wasn't a cost to herself both physically and mentally. At times too great a cost he thought.

They called Harmony "H" for short and she was the Land Healer. She could put her hands to the ground and sing the land new growth literally creating new life within the soil she touched. What was dead would bud again just from her touch and a whisper from her mind. Both girls were fiercely protected by Briksanna not to mention by the team as a whole. On the day to day they appeared to be the average young selfish adult, always complaining of wanting new clothes, nails painted or a eyebrows waxed, but underneath they were fierce warriors taught by the best person in the world.

Their number one complaint was the need for a day at the spa. That's their camouflage, what they want you to see them as spoiled snobs with no care for the world but the next manicure; but they're deeply devoted to Briksanna and as honorable as Briksanna was, the girls would never shame her with pettiness. To them, he and Nate were their father's and big brothers rolled into one. Truth be told they were the daughters they wish they had. That's how much he and Nate loved those brats; hence the last name Rasoul. When they were toddlers Briksanna said she called them her rascals. They couldn't pronounce the word always saying *Rasoul* so she came up with the idea to make that their last name.

That leaves Gabriella and Kenneth Nomane brother and sister rescued by Briksanna as teenagers caught in a Los Angeles gang war. She brought them home one day and had been their mother slash mentor ever since. Those two were their weapons experts. They have been with their family for the past nine years and although he admitted being the negative one on bringing the two teenagers home straight from gangland war into their super-secret life he was more concerned with the two little girls, a few years younger, who would now be looking up to a pair of pistol, K-BAR wearing teens as examples.

For the first six months neither kid spoke to anyone except Briksanna and always privately. Then one day Kenneth looked at him and said, "Does everyone have mothers like Briksanna?" What was he to say to that? He thought for a minute then looked at him and new he was looking at his little brother when he was at that age standing on a precipice of making an important decision. Already weighing against what he felt in his heart to be true observing the boy for several months he figured the kid was about to step on a new path of his choosing just like Nathanial had. He hoped the kid went with the right choice, because any choice was better than sitting on the fence going nowhere.

So he told him what he thought, "Children who do are blessed by God themselves," he said, hoping his words would be enough to push the kid into making the right choice.

"Then that means Gabby and me are safe because not only do we have Briksanna for our mother we have you and Nate, the twins and now Gods." Sounding relieved he walked away with the first mile wide smile he'd seen from the kid.

He must have told his sister what he had said to him because from that day forward he couldn't keep them from learning all there was to learn what they all did especially about weapons, ammunition and the act of guerrilla warfare. The more brutal the more they wanted to master it. He had asked Gabriella one day why she didn't want to spend time with the other girls. "Honey don't you want to go with the twins to the mall and have a spa day too? Even Briksanna is going this time?"

She was quiet for about 20 seconds while she thought about it then she shook her head vigorously as if the thought was taboo. "No, I might forget what we are doing or where I came from if I go and I might want more of it. It's better I don't know what those things are like so I can never want them." She stared right at him resigned not to allow herself happiness.

Putting his hand on her shoulder he told her as delicately as he knew how, given he was a man, "Bri is the oldest and most dangerous out of all of us and she is going. Give yourself a break, Gabby; being all that you can be is exactly what that saying means. Part of that is learning how to become a woman. You my dear have grown up to become a very beautiful young lady and there is nothing wrong with taking a day off to feel beautiful. It is what every species does." She thought about it for several minutes and next thing he knew she was walking outside, head held high back stiff as a board, like he had just sent her off on the deadliest mission with odds of coming back against her. Thinking back on that day always made him want to laugh out loud because out of all the women living in this compound, Gabriella was the most feminine woman in the house.

Both kids were of Hispanic descent with raven black hair. Kenneth wears his a bit too long, always tied at the nape of his neck. Gabriella's hair was the longest in the house next to Briksanna's, flowing in tresses except when on mission then she efficiently braids and hides it under a cap. Kenneth was six feet four inches and Gabriella was a hair shorter than her brother standing at six feet two inches.

Pulling his thoughts back from the past he focused on the family in front of him. "Looking around this room we all have two options," he paused seeing if there were any protests or changes in positions from the people in the room. Everyone stilled whatever they were doing knowing if they moved or deviated from what they were listening to it would clue Stark in to what was going through their heads. Everyone in the room was a master at masking their emotions just like he could. No one doubted the person next to them. They all trusted one another with their lives. He knew sharing with them how he felt about the family being asked to support The Prophesy, according to Merridian, would affect not only Nate and Briksanna but the entire family as well. He wanted to be sure everyone was in agreement with him. At all costs, their family was number one and as such they would do anything to make sure their family was not harmed in the process. They were about to head into uncharted waters and he would be damned if anyone got hurt.

"Option number one; we do exactly as Merridian has laid out for us in this particular quest which was to wait for further instructions from Nate and Briksanna when they join us tomorrow?"—raising his hands in a command for silence from especially H and T—"or we go with Option number two; we do what Merridian says but with a bit of investigating on our own? You all are a part of this and you all herd the Goddess, you will each have a role to play in the upcoming battle, to what depth, I don't know." All eyes were so focused on him no one blinked for the first ten seconds after the last words left his mouth.

"Well, shall we do this the Lightning Strike way or not? I want us to vote on it and if we all don't agree then we do it Merridian's way period, deal?"

"Deal," they said in unison knowing the lives of every family member was at stake.

"Well what is it going to be?" he said looking around the room again.

Again in unison they all spoke "Option number two boss."

"That was a no brainer, twin number two," said Trinity

"Can I say double duh on that, twin number one," said Harmony

"I swear can you guys get brain surgery or something? The twin thing is really getting on my nerves." Gabriella said glaring at the twins.

"Get over it, already all of you!" Stark shouted bringing his fist down on the desk this time splitting the wood in two knowing his super strength was a direct result of his short temper. "I have had enough of the sarcasm here. I don't know about all of you"—he spoke hazel eyes beginning to brighten, a sign of his rising emotions—"there are two people in the other room who are about to go through the most hell I can't imagine a new couple should have to go through and it is up to us not only make sure they succeed in their task but sacrifice everything they have built up within themselves that make them who they are today just to keep our world and all the worlds in the universe safe. Do you read what I am saying to you?"

"Yes sir," the girls said in apologetic voices. "We're sorry."

Harmony got up and walked over to him, "I'm sorry, you know when I think of a mom and dad I think of you and Briksanna. You and Nate that is, I mean as a dad... argghh, this isn't coming out right is it twin?" Eyes tearing she looked at Trinity for confirmation then back at him. "Don't be mad at us girls for letting off some steam. We would never let any of you down, ever."

Crazy thing was Harmony was his favorite out of all of them and if anyone could calm the raging monster straining to break free of him was her. Always her, until Merridian stepped in the picture.

Man what a woman she was, I have to seriously get in the game today dreaming about a Goddess, what is wrong with me?

Shaking his head to clear his vision, he looked at the broken table and the teary eyes of the girls, right then he knew he'd lost his cool. Grabbing Harmony's hand he motioned for the other two to come over with his other hand and just like that they flew across the room into his embrace.

Man this was going to be a long night.

Having the air squished out of him by his lovely ladies, he looked over his head at the two remaining men in the room. They just shook their heads and smiled at him. It was Striker who spoke up first.

"Yo man when you're done with the family moment could Kenneth and I get in on this group hug thing you got going on? It looks re-vit-ali-zing," enunciating each word for added emphasis.

Smiling ear to ear looking over at Kenneth for confirmation he noticed one thing and one thing only; Striker was flashing his megawatt smile, dimples and all, damn he was feeling the love right now with the people in the room.

Flipping him off as he held the women in his arms. Yes indeed, it was going to be a long night.

7

"**D**o you have what I asked for?" He said slowly, looking out of his study balcony, watching his armies train in the bailey below. What he saw outside pleased him more than what he was about to hear, this he already knew. Closing his tired eyes, he could almost imagine her standing beside him. Bright violet green eyes haunting his existence was enough to bring him to his knees with intense longing. Feeling his fury mounting tangled with his frustration at not being able to have what he coveted most made him want to lash out at the world in a destructive rage. It took everything he had in him to keep himself from the instinct to cause damage.

Raising his voice slightly, he growled, "You have not answered me therefore I take it, you do not. It is not that I cannot tolerate mishaps, I can. I consider myself very forgiving. It is that I cannot abide with failure," he continued turning around quickly eyes glowing, a deep forest green, now fixed on the man kneeling front of him. "Where is my Blood Stone?" he yelled unleashing pent up rage, loud enough to reach the army training outside in the courtyard causing their swords to stop mid swing and grunts to grow silent. Although men of great bravery, they knew that when the Master's roar pitched as it did death was sure to follow.

"I do not have what you asked for Master, please forgive my failure," came a shaking voice draped in fear.

Jackson the best slave recruited to his army from the Earth Realm, whose sole purpose for going back to the Earth Realm was for the retrieval of the Blood Stone. Keeping his eyes trained on the plush carpet he stretched out before his master in complete submission knowing it was best not to look upward unless commanded.

"I asked you to do one simple thing, and now you kneel before me asking for forgiveness?" He yelled unleashing a sonic blast sending his minion crashing against the back wall.

He struggled to control his emotions that caused pain to rise in his chest. All he wanted was the woman that haunted his waking dreams. It took everything within to bury deep inside obsessive emotions that made him what he had become. This was how he survived this place, bury, avoid and cover ancient scars only his mind knew how to remember and even then he kept those under lock and key. It is how he waited for her. He shook his head to gain composure and fully assume the resemblance of Lord Drakkoon, a name when mentioned anywhere in the universe struck fear in the hearts of all listeners. Smiling after regaining full form and composure, he looked down at the man who would die for his failure but had come to speak to him in person anyway. Either a brave heart or a stupid fool. Which was it? Maybe there was some hope for the warrior's survival after all. No one else who had been close to Briksanna could tell him of his woman so he knew he had to reign in his temper before he let loose leaving him with no knowledge of her. He quieted himself and decided to hear what the man before him had to say.

"Rise Jackson, you are forgiven, for now. Please sit over here."—pointing to a set of armchairs facing an open fireplace recently lit—"Help me understand what difficulties were encountered while doing my bidding."

Rising Jackson walked cautiously to the chair where directed. Blood streamed down his face from both ears and his vision was blurred. These were obvious effects of the sonic blast unleashed by his fury. Once seated, he continued to stare at the carpet taking care to evade his master's eyes. He sat directly across from and he could sense how deeply his Master wanted any information he knew about his beloved Briksanna. A heavy sighed oozed from this master.

"Start from the beginning," commanded Lord Drakkoon.

"I took the team to the building we had assumed housed the Blood Stone. It was there like you had said but so were the Princess and her team. She must have gotten there minutes before us because we entered the chamber housing the stone at the same time." Jackson paused and began shifting his feet nervously.

"What happened next?"

"I let my arrow fly at the Princess."

"You what!" He shouted knocking him over in his chair with his sonic voice.

It took a few minutes for Jackson to stand and gather himself as best he could. Setting the chair upright, he leaned on it for support. His vision remained blurred as he stumbled around to the front of the chair. His crimson stained cheeks were now accompanied by a deep cough that came with a mixture of spittle and blood out of the corner of his mouth. Managing as any proud warrior, he gathered what was left of himself to face his Master.

"Tell me you did not hurt her in any way. Speak quickly and truthfully because nothing can save you once my mind is made up."

Looking directly at Lord Drakkoon, knowing he risked his wrath, he replied. "I did not hurt the Princess, Master. I turned my bow at the last second and the arrow lodged into the wall directly above her head. That is the truth. I swear it upon my life."

"I noticed you did not walk away unscathed and that you also came back alone. What happened next?"

"All hell broke lose is what happened, pardon my familiarity, Master, he mumbled casting worried glances his way.

"I find myself losing patience quickly, Jackson." Feeling his agitation surfacing within his facial expressions he fought to keep his own fears hidden.

"Distracted by the sudden presence of the princess, Nate Angelo quickly retrieved the stone. We were ill prepared for the theatrics from the Lightning Strike team. The blonde twins were tenacious warriors whirling their knives as if it were a stroll in the park. It took all of my training, Master, to fend off those two, and especially the one they call Harmony. She was vicious in her attack. Honestly, I had to use centuries of training in keeping away from the death strike of her blade. They sure are fierce when it comes to defending the Princess...not that I intentionally harmed the Princess...I mean she wasn't harmed at all Master."

"How is it you come to be here and no one else on your team was fortunate enough to survive?" he questioned.

"They let me go to deliver a message to you, Master," returning his gaze to the carpet with tightly clamped lips.

"Who sent the message and what is it exactly," beginning to lose his patience again setting the surrounding area in a green glow.

Clearing his voice before speaking, Jackson responded, "The Princess, Master. She said to tell you 'The time has come. It is time for the Prophesy to be fulfilled. Tell your Master I am coming for him, it is time for our dance. Prepare yourself for I am coming.' It is as she spoke Master, word for word."

Once finishing, Jackson waited for the peace and silence of death to fall upon him. Minutes ticked by but he remained standing, staring at the carpet in complete submission for what he believed was coming next. However, nothing happened. Instead he allowed his green glow to fade giving way to the sound of laughter that filled the room. Soft giggles came first followed by deep chuckles giving way to outright booming laughter. He began to tremble because he had not heard his Master's voice give sound of cheer in centuries.

"I believe I can offer you leniency for your failure in doing my bidding," he managed between chuckles. "Yes, I will grant you the opportunity to be a part of the next step." Rising from the chair he began to pace back and forth in the middle of the room. "What we need is an instrument, for them to target themselves with. Sort of a focal point you see? Yes, this can work, I will do this. I see it already."

"Master, I am forever in your service" Jackson said flinging himself prostrate onto the carpet. "I give my life to do as you please, Master"

"You are correct, Jackson. You are mine to do with as I please." Quickly striding toward Jackson eyes lit up the room with a bright emerald glow. He reached for Jackson and grabbed him by the back of his neck picking him up to hold him as if he was a puppy in need of a scolding. Jackson paled, turned his eyes to the carpet deathly afraid of what was going to happen next.

"Look into my eyes Jackson," he commanded.

He reach deep within himself drew upon dark energy that swirled deep within him. Forcing energy into a person had never been done before. But, just because it had never been done, did not mean it couldn't happen. It simply meant that no one had ever succeeded, however, was determined to get his hands on that bloodstone and with the right adjustments Jackson could pull it off for him.

"I said look into my eyes!" He sent the command using his sonic voice. Energy surged through him like never before, bursting from his mouth projecting a black stream of energy straight into the mouth of the victim dangling in front of him. Jackson was his most trusted warrior want and now he was in the process of molding him into something more. More fierce, more cunning, more deadly.

Jackson's transformation was immediate. He raised his head looking directly into his master's eyes, screaming horrifically when the energy hit him. The room went super nova, bathing the walls a deep green. Jackson's screams became gargled as he was forced to consume more and more dark energy. After a few minutes he focused the energy surge at Jackson's chest specifically the part of his body that housed the man's heart. He now tapped the last place were humanity dwelled making it empty filling it with thousands of years of resentment for the prison he was forced to oversee. He needed Jackson to be formidable in the eyes of his enemies and depositing years of abscessed emotions where any shred of humanity was removed ensured his goal. His intention was to give his enemies a target to focus on that could withstand their foolish games of resistance. He wanted Briksanna for himself, by any means possible even at the hands of his own creation. As far as he was concerned this act was completely justifiable, in fact it was sheer genius. No longer would Jackson have reason to fail. All of the rage and anger he held in being trapped in the Under Realm flowed through Jackson. The harboring stain of hatred within his heart had kept him going when he felt the walls of servitude to the First God's wishes in overseeing the balance of the

Under Realm threatened to bury him. That was why he was sent to this place by his father only to be abandoned by the same God for four millennia with not a single word from him. His saving grace was and would always be his sister. She had kept him grounded when no one else would dare communicate with him. Four thousand years and the only friend he had been that of his sister. He would have died for her as he would for Lady Briksanna. There is no doubt of his loyalty to those he cherished. Thinking of all of his loneliness he poured his anger over his situation into Jackson not holding anything back.

Jackson no longer screamed as the pain overtook him in totality. But, as quickly as he had attacked him with his Dark Energy it all came to an abrupt end. The screaming, the pain and the light ceased to exist like someone had blown the fire out. The only thing he could figure was they both were still alive. Panting while hanging from his Master's grip he rubbed shaking hands briskly across his chest. He was still there. But, not as the man was before. Something had change or was changing physically about him. He felt different.

Croaking, "My eyes Master, I can't see clearly through my eyes."

"Give it a few seconds Jackson. Soon, you shall see more than you had before. In fact, there are many things you will be able to do that before were impossible for you do previously."

Eyes blinking in confusion while streaming tears fell unchecked down his face, Jackson nodded. He noticed the room was dark recognizing night had fallen in the Under Realm since he first entered the room. As Jacksons eyesight continued to clear, he realized Lord Drakkoon was staring at him. Uneasy with the weight of his stare, he averted his eyes for a moment taking stalk of the room around him. Nothing seemed out of place. The two chairs were sitting in where still facing each other by the fireplace. The desk still had papers and maps scattered all over it, which was not unusual for his Master as he liked to account for all matters of affairs within the Under Realm and more so of the Upper Realm than any one person here should know.

However, something was very different. He reached up and began to carefully feel his face. Cheeks, mouth, nose, chin, and then the forehead all told his fingers that his hunch was correct. He now was aware of the surge of energy emanating off his body. At this, instinct took hold and he stretched out both arms, drew his head back facing the ceiling and roared. Startled, he drove back a deep desire to pounce upon the man in front of him as a huge surge of energy flowed throughout his entire being wanting to answer his deepest desire to destroy Lord Drakkoon. He wanted to howl like a wolf but, he tamped it down someplace deep inside. Solitude, he needed to be alone, away from everyone.

Lowering his new creation to the ground, Lord Drakkoon spoke. "From this day forward you will be forever known as the Realm Keeper; Leader of Shadow Riders." Letting go of his creation he staggered back a couple of steps, losing balance for a moment before composing himself once again shaking off weariness suddenly coursing through his body. Looking at the Realm Keeper, glowing eyes no longer visible nor was there any sign of what he had just done or who he had become in order to commit such an act could be seen. He valued the man Jackson and trusted him to keep his wishes kept. He was the one person he counted upon to help him achieve his greatest desire. He trusted Jackson with the life of Briksanna yet somehow it always ended in danger for her and Jackson disengaging with a failed mission. The reasons he was told made perfect sense, but they happened every time they encountered one another. Why did Jackson always come back with tales of battle that could have ended her life? A sharp pain to his head occurred at the moment of his last thought thrusting him back into the present.

"You look formidable now, Realm Keeper. Lightning Strike will not be so quick to break you. Now you are a force to reckon with."

Gripping the chair back he once occupied, he secretly held on to support himself. The energy transfer had taken much more than he anticipated. He had never felt so week before when transferring light energy. His sudden weakness had to be a result of transferring dark energy. He would think of it later, now he needed to rest and did not want his new creation to see how weak he really was.

Standing on his own breathing deeply Jackson, reveled in the energy coursing through his body for the first time. Eyes closed lifting his arms out wide, making a fist with his hands he spoke excitedly. "Master, I feel stronger, invincible even. Indeed, I am a force to be reckoned with. I could crush the Princess and her little team now."

Laughing out loud at his comment, the Realm Keeper never saw the backhand coming before it struck him across the face and sent him flying thirty feet from where he once stood leaving him sprawled in a heap on the other side of the room.

"You are not to harm a single strand of hair on the head of Princess Briksanna or her family. Am I perfectly clear?" He hovered over his creation, panting, filled with rage over his protégé's arrogant statement. Eyes glowing brightly, briefly thinking it might be best to destroy what was newly created before things got out of control and he harmed Briksanna or her family. That was not what he wanted. He wanted her trust, love and companionship. If that included her family, great, if not, it was of no consequence, he only needed her.

"Forgive me Master if I have offended you. I misspoke about the Princess. I know not to harm her. The power in me is new and strong, I misspoke. I shall obey your commands completely." Cowering on the floor, returning submissively head bowed in front of him.

Straightening himself, Drakkoon informed his warrior, "You are excused for the evening. Report back to my study, promptly, after breaking your fast."

"I am confused, Master. I am dismissed from evening training? Am I free to do as I please?"

"Within reason Realm Keeper. You are now the highest ranking official within my realm and as appointed said official you will receive certain privileges in return, like having your evenings free. You are the highest ranking warrior within my armies and should be rewarded with that status such as evenings free. However, should you go against the few rules I set before you, I will terminate you on site as I see fit. Are we understood?"

"Yes Master," swallowing the bile that had risen in his throat.

"You may go and return on the morrow, but remember my words, Realm Keeper, that which was given can be taken away and this time I do not have to be near you to kill you, so be warned."

Jackson held his breath as he absorbed the warning, nodding, he acknowledged him as he rose from where he was kneeling heading out the way he came and hoped to still be alive when he made it to through the door.

He was lucky enough to close the door and live. It seemed today was his lucky day. First was meeting head on with the Lightning Strike team and then dealing with his Master. Straightening his armor he was noticeably disturbed. His face felt weird, his voice sounded different, and he just didn't feel the same. Striding over to a room in search of a mirror, he opened the door and walked inside careful not to bring attention to himself in case someone was watching. How would that look if his Master's second in command needed a mirror? He would never hear the end of it from within the warrior ranks.

He crept further into the room towards a mirror mounted in the far corner. Just before looking into the glass, he paused. Partly fearing who would stare back at him, yet the need to know overbid the fear. He took a deep breath and stepped in front of the mirror. He attempted to gasp, but instead a low growl came from deep within his lungs. Shocked at what he saw no thought of any kind prepared him for what looked back at him.

A great sadness threatened to overcome him, "No one will be able to find me now. I am forever lost to this nightmare." Lowering his head not wanting to look into the mirror he felt sorry for what he had become in service to Lord Drakkoon. He flashed on broken memories images of a happier time, laughter and the smell of jasmine flowers. The need to be wrapped in the calming blanket the memory represented threatened to overwhelm him.

His self-wallowing loneliness lasted for a moment until another surge of energy shot through his system, reminding him of the being he had become. Snapping his head up he remembered where he was and who it was looking back at him in the mirror. He stared back at the highest ranking official within the entire Under Realm. A formidable opponent for Lightning Strike, Lord Drakkoon had said. That is who he was today and today was all that mattered. The memories of his past always brought pain and desperation. There was no room in his life for the weakness of old memories never to been seen again in his lifetime.

"Best defense is a good offense. Shadow Rider training begins tomorrow." He said smiling at himself for the first time taking one last look at his new reflection.

His next course of action having been decided he turned around and slipped out of the room, closing the door behind him. Striding along the hallway, he never noticed the door closing behind him in the servant's stairwell or the whispers in the hall that followed. Something had awakened in the Master's castle.

— ⁓ —

She and her handmaiden Ellena were on their way to see her brother when they felt their psychic energy ripped from their souls. Ellena barely had time to catch her, before she collapsed a few feet from her brothers study doors. Holding her upright she had ignored the force of whatever was occurring behind his study doors which seem to be the source of what was draining them, physically and mentally. Using all her strength, keeping her upright she could barely retain her consciousness as Ellena dragged them both to the nearest door. Fearing the harm that could befall the both of them in this helpless state she felt terrified for their lives for the first time visiting her brother's home. So great was the pull on their energy, her friend could barely drag the both of them through the door. She could offer no help in assisting her friend; her limbs wouldn't obey her at the moment.

Ellena closed the door to the stairwell with her foot quietly, trying not to alert anyone of their presence. Leaning back against the door, they both slide down the length of the door. Swearing mentally at her father for his lack in protecting her again she knew she would protect her best friend with her very life if it came to that, yet at the same time she pleaded with him to protect them from harm as was habit. She begged him to bless them with courage and wisdom to escape this trouble they were trapped in.

She was eager to test her limbs for range of motion. Never had she felt so violated in all of her life nor had she felt utterly helpless before. Knowing it had happened in her brothers home, more than likely at his hands, left her bereft of emotion. Shoving her grief down she put her energy into moving her limbs wanting more and more to be out of this place. Something horribly had happened and she needed to get her and Ellena out of there fast.

"Mistress we are safe for the moment. I have brought us to the servant's stairwell outside Lord Drakkoon's study." Ellena spoke in a shaking voice clearly not able to hide the horrifying fear of their recent psychic violation.

"What do you make of it? I am so weak." Rubbing her temples with shaking hands she tried to understand what had happened.

"As am I, Mistress. I do not understand what happened other than a great pull on our inner energy. The force of the pull was so great you lost ability to stand and almost collapsed in the hall had I not caught you. I almost screamed for your safety but immediately clamped my mouth closed, remembering where we were. I believe I bit my tongue in the process. Tis not a place I want to be found screaming in."

Casting a nervous look around the stairway they were in she nervously ran a hand through her hair. "Right you are and I am eternally thankful to your quick thinking, Ellena. Please let me rise so I may assist you." Shakily she rose from where she lay in her lap. Reaching down grabbing her arm, she helped her friend stand.

"Mistress I hear some voices coming from your brother's study. What shall we do?" she whispered.

"Step back and let me listen with the door cracked. Maybe we can find out what my brother has done this time." Pushing her hair around her shoulder she moved passed her friend.

Moving as quietly as possible she cracked the stairwell door peaking for any person who may discover their hiding spot she did not realize Ellena was holding her arm tightly ready to yank her back into the stairwell if necessary. She smiled inside knowing her friend was there with her. It was good to know she did not have a ninny for a companion instead she had her very own personal guard. No one would expect her delicate friend to be a fierce warrior in servants clothing. That was what they both had agreed upon long ago when they first came to be friends. She was to be her personal guard, instead becoming her most trusted friend and she would not have had spent their time together any other way.

She was touched her friend thought quickly in moving them to safety while she could barely hang on to consciousness. Suddenly the study doors opened and she saw what looked like the body and hair of Jackson yet it was not the face of Jackson that she saw.

"Oh Drakkoon, what have you done?" She whispered believing this was the reason for the drain on their inner energy. Whatever he had done had to have been dark to cause this kind of physical alteration. Energy was never supposed to be used in this manner. It was a clear violation of the laws of natural order. He knew that and yet the person who walked past them was the very proof of how far brother had lowered himself to.

Jackson walked by and entered a room two doors down across the hall from where they were currently hidden. He was in the room for several minutes, doing Gods knows what, when he left the room whistling as if all was well in the world.

That was defiantly Jackson who left the room. He whistled that tune all the centuries he served her brother. The body was Jackson but the face belonged to another person. He looked scarier, stronger than before. A person who, she would bet, had it in him to inflict death whenever the mood struck. All of a sudden she knew what was bothering her about Jackson. He was not only visibly different, but his energy signature was stronger, darker and much more volatile than before.

Why Drake? Why would you do this? It is unnatural and not a part of this universe, yet you have gone too far, brother. I will no longer be a part of this life you have chosen.

Feeling the last straw of hope for her brother she had been holding onto for several millennia snap, there was nothing left she could say to sway him from the path he had chosen to tread upon. The time had come for her to choose the path she needed to walk in order to do what she believed to be the right choice. Staying there trying to reason with her twin was no longer something she could do. She had to stand with the people she believed were the true champions in this war.

"What shall we do know Mistress? Jackson does not look or act the same. I fear there is something truly dark that has occurred this time with Lord Drakkoon, something that cannot be undone." Shaking her head trying to clear her vision physically as if that would change what they had seen with their own eyes.

Watching Ellena stare back at her while she spoke; more than likely witnessing her facial expressions give way to her desperate attempt at reaching some semblance of understanding over her brothers actions. She knew the choice she had to make and the pain of such understanding stood visible upon her very face. She no longer had it within her to continue pleading with her brother to change his ways. She had to let him go and it was breaking her heart. He was her other half. Her twin. There was nothing in the universe like the connection they both shared.

She knew there was something he had been keeping to himself the past few times they visited. He would not tell her what it was no matter what she did to pry it out of him. The last time they spoke he asked her if she remembered the man he was before being sent to the Under Realm. He said he cannot find that man any longer and the loss of the memory scared him. He shut down refusing to elaborate knowing if she were to press him he would have told her to leave denying he had spoken on the matter. No, she knew there was more going on with her brother than what she had seen or heard. She needed to get the both of them out from the Under Realm fast. She was too tired to think any longer and where they were was not a safe place to be.

Reaching behind her, Ellena closed the door quietly pulling her into a giant hug. "Mistress, I am sorry for my careless words. I know how deep your love and hope is for your brother. Your sadness touches me now. Please forgive me for my rash words. I was not thinking but only speaking, most likely from all this fear running through my veins. Do not worry for I will not abandon you. You are my dearest friend and I remain your friend always."

Touched by such honest words twice within the same evening must surely be a sign from the First God Himself. Looking up at her best friend, wiping away freshly fallen tears she studied her companion closely. Sincerity and strength shone back at her with words spoken straight from her soul. Her friend had spoken words of truth.

Grabbing her by the arms speaking directly at her confident with the choice she made would keep them safe. "Your sincere kindness will not be forgotten. When I was feeling such despair over my brother and his obsession, you held fast and remained by my side. You have been with me for many centuries yet never have you forsaken our friendship for your own needs. You are my trusted companion whom I am most honored to call my dearest friend. One day I shall repay your kindness and compassion this I vow."

With a loud clap and the last of her energy she whisked both of them away from Deepsong, Lord Drakkoon's castle within the Under Realm, racing them back to the Earth Realm. A compound in Northern California was the first place her mind pictured when she thought of their safety.

A gripping pain in her heart almost risked their escape distracting her with grief. She realized her time convincing her brother to change his ways were over. Their long talks, reminiscing of times past, sharing dreams of the future, their hopes and desires turned obsessions were no longer for her to deal with. She was now only the Guardian for the Princesses of The Prophesy. This was her choice and in making it a great burden lifted off her shoulders.

Guilty emotions pressed her psyche. Why did she not do more for her brother? She could have spent more time showing him life in the Under Realm could be beautiful. Why did she not take more interest in his affairs despite his raging mood swings? She could have saved her brother from his horrible choices. His obsession with the Princess was something like she had never seen before. He truly did believe he loved her and would stop at nothing to afford himself the opportunity to prove his love to her mistakenly doing everything possible to gain her attention yet driving her away further with his actions. Lady Briksanna was stuck in the past and he was trying to find it. No matter how she explained this to him he shut down and over the years became more and more withdrawn about all matters concerning the Under Realm and in the Upper Realms with the exception of Lady Briksanna.

She was so afraid. Afraid for all people everywhere, if she could not bring The Prophesy to fruition. Afraid for the people waiting for the next Reckoning; who have been denied all these years because her brother did not want to concern himself with matters in the Under Realm. She feared for fate itself. Hazel eyes belonging to the man called Stark Angelo was what her soul craved. . Her desire to be held in his strong arms brought thoughts of comfort when she was so afraid and in pain from her shattered heart. Racing towards that beacon of saving grace she believed she would find in his embrace fueled her all the more to fight for their safety. She knew everyone in Briksanna's family had a role to play in completing The Prophesy and everything would depend on the choices of the ones that walked that path. Being a goddess did not change the fact that she knew she had a role to play in allowing the freedom of choice to map out the path before her. As frightened as she felt flying through the portal knowing the last of her energy was being used in bringing them to safety, she pressed on fighting the darkness threatening to overwhelm her.

She had not needed anyone since her brother had been sent to the Under Realm as their Guardian and Overseer. Right now more than ever she needed Stark to save her and that scared her to her core. She did not know if she could put her heart or the lives of all worlds in the hands of a mortal because that was what she would be doing if she were to allow her heart any room to feel for him other than a friend. Her head said Amen, but her heart was very quiet. She had better get her heart in sync with her head if she was going to help anyone let alone herself.

8

Nate turned around to hang up and realized he was no longer alone. Briksanna had opened the door to the bathroom sometime in the last couple of minutes and was leaning on the bathroom door studying him.

How much of the phone conversation did she over here? Argghh, I hate it when she just stares at me.

"You feeling better, Bri?"

"Much, you should take one and I will wait here for you. Then we can talk", she said quietly padding to the chair near the bed. "I am so tired of everything, you were right, I need to rest. I really need to just"—waving her hands in the air searching for the right words as she flopped into it.—"loosen up a bit," searching for his approval in her choice of words.

Nodding he told her, "You are the most beautiful woman I have ever laid eyes on. I just want to make sure you understand when I look at you; I only see you, not the clothing, not the hairstyle and definitely not the scars. Have I told you this already, because I might have missed saying it, with all this fate conversation we've been having the past couple of hours? I only see you."

Feeling his desire for her mount to volcanic proportions with his declaration, he walked towards her with purpose in his gait. With each step he took the more tense she appeared to be. She became so still he almost missed it.

The vein in her neck pulsed, revealing her increase in heart rate. Bri wasn't afraid of anything so it couldn't be fear, which left the opposite. His baby was excited. He was the one making her excited and it was the sign he needed. The need to close the gap between them beat at him like a living entity.

Watching her hold her breath turned him on. He put on a burst of speed to reach her barely stirring the air around them. Holding her captive, heart, mind and soul he kept his green eyes trained on her face tracking her tongue lick her bottom lip made him hiss with desire for the woman sitting before him. He knew he was pushing his limit, right now, being this close to her knowing his mind was screaming to throw chivalry to the wind and grab the woman caveman style to an undisclosed location. His selfish sexual side was screaming to take her and ravish her until neither one of them could move. He strained with everything he had not to give in to that half of him knowing he wanted to show her how much he could love her, but it was hard. She was now biting her lip clearly thinking about something. He couldn't concentrate when his libido was beating at him to take what he wanted. Trying to rain in his hormones he thought maybe it was time he took that other half of himself outside and shoot him.

Mesmerized by the depth of her stare he tuned into her sexual emotions and waited for her to reveal, in words, what he knew she felt in her soul hoping it matched what he believed was already in his heart.

"You are most precious to me. To the end of my existence, I will endeavor to be all that you envision me to be, strong, fearless, wise and accepting."— holding up her hand to keep him from saying anything else—"I believe I can be what the Goddess says I am to be for both Lord Drakkoon and for you in order to save the universe, but I want you to always hold fast this one thought. It is you, Nathanial Angelo, whom, I will forever covet with the depth of my soul as my one true mate."

Holding her breath under his watchful eye she waited for his response. He wanted her and she was held captivated by the way he studied her, intently searching her face for any sign of deception. She knew his thoughts as if they were her own. Giving him time to reason her words she had spoken she continued to hold her breath. A lock of hair fell over his eyes when he turned his head studying her as was his habit when in deep thought. She wanted desperately to brush herself against him while she pushed that lock back in place with her own hands. Breaking concentration from his hair, once again briefly looking at his eyes, down his nose past the places where dimples tended to appear when he was smiling finally settling on his mouth. Why her gaze stayed on his lips of all places she did not know, but there they stayed for what seemed like eons. Her heart beat a rhythm sending a trail of heat to pool between her legs indicating her arousal simply by the way he looked at her. She knew he was turning everything she said over in his mind and that was fine with her. She wanted him to be the person he believed he could be, not some silly notion of a man he thought she wanted. His trust in her was just as important as her giving her trust over to him. She did not want to search his mind or heart for the answer. She needed him to prove it to her with more than words and she would do the same, expecting no less from herself than she expected of him.

He continued to study her not saying a word licking his lips like she had done to him a moment ago brought up an image of her mouth following the trail of his tongue. Her mouth watered, she wanted to taste him. She imagined wrapping her hands around his body bringing him close twining her arms around his neck just so she could weave her fingers through his long dark hair. Moisture pooled between her legs, something she had never felt before. She wanted to trace her tongue along his jaw, down his throat, around his chest not stopping until every area had been explored by her mouth. She was close to losing control of her emotions knowing if she did not do something she was going to attack him like an animal in heat.

The need to take care of him overrode the sexual desire coursing through her veins. She did not want his body or his heart to be hurt in any way because of the path she believed she would need to travel in order fulfill her role in The Prophesy. Realizing she wanted to protect him from any emotional damage because of the course her life was about to take reminded her the true depth of the love she had for him. Knowing her trust must not be too far behind she wanted to be careful not to rush their relationship. There was too much at stake and much more to lose than either of their hearts and souls. Allowing full reign on her emotions could be the end for everything if she was not careful.

"That is where you are wrong, Bri, your welfare will always be placed before mine." Dropping his gaze he turned as if he was to walk away, but before he took one step he turned back towards her, smirking flashing his dimples. "Let's eat something before I forget food is what you need and shame myself before the best meal in the world, because lady, you are the tastiest thing I have ever seen."

Bending over he grabbed her hand leading her towards the door. He never glanced back confident she was not was not going to put up a fight when he pulled her behind him. Where this self-assurance came from she did not know nor was she going to question it. She liked it. She was his and that was what she desired most.

Before they left the room she stopped at the dresser by the door opening it retrieve a small item. It looked like a pouch held together by a leather cord. Nothing extraordinary just an old necklace she held in her hand. Closing the drawer she turned around never taking her eyes off what was in her hand. He watched the emotions play across her face anger flashed for a moment as she gripped the leather cord briefly followed by resignation when she sighed bringing her eyes up to him. She looked so hurt by whatever it was she was thinking about. He didn't want to violate her trust by entering her mind taking the information from her so he waited for her to tell him instead.

"I made this the day I broke out of my prison long ago. I wanted to have something to remind me of who I was when I was kidnapped and who I became because of my torture in the Under Realm. After two thousand years of harboring this talisman I realize it has kept me from getting close to anyone a constant reminder to close my heart off the living so I could feel safe by protecting my heart at the same time. I believe I no longer need this, Nathanial. You are my future. Our love for one another is my talisman. I want to give this to you to do with as you please. Every step I take from here on out is towards a future where doubt and betrayal no longer belongs in."

He was both humbled with her words to share her feelings with him and glad she took the steps to trust him with a possession he believed she has used to keep herself separate from the rest of the world for so long. He wanted a future with her where their love was absolute. He knew what he needed to do with her gift.

Taking hold of the item in her outstretched hand he held both her palm and the talisman together not letting go of her hand. She looked surprised when he held her hand not wanting to scare her he kept his voice even knowing this was a pivotal moment for her. He wanted to honor her hoping what he had to say would be exactly what she needed to hear.

"I want you to destroy this, Bri, right here, right now. If I could I would do it for you, but my gut is telling me this is something you need to do with me being witness. This was your promise to yourself made a long time ago and like me I have had my share of demons to deal with growing up, but for me to be the man I am today I had to let go of those demons and move forward in my life for me to truly be free. I am grateful more than you can possibly know that you trust me enough to give this to me, but you have to do this on your own. I'm not going anywhere, baby. I am right here by your side where I will always be for as long as I am alive."

Nodding her head, he let go of her hand holding his breath willing her to understand he wasn't throwing her gift back in her face, but giving her the chance to let go of her past hurts on her own. Her eyes watered but never spilled. He knew she was scared to put her trust out there having been hurt so bad long ago. He didn't know the details of what had happened that drove her to make the thing she held in her hand and he didn't care. Nothing mattered to him more than the woman standing before him because she was his future, the present Briksanna, and that was all he cared about. Casting her eyes down at her palm he saw the determination to end her lifetime of resentment towards what happened to her in the past. The talisman grew bright encased in a purple ball of energy. She brought her other hand over the ball of energy and within seconds the ball glowed so bright he wanted to shield his eyes, but remained still knowing his promise to stand by her side meant watching her do this. The ball of energy left her palm taking the talisman with it.

She lifted her eyes not to look at him but at the ball of purple glowing energy and for a split second he felt her whole being shift as she poured all of her resentments into that ball of energy seconds before the energy folded in on itself becoming nothing more than a speck of light before blinking out of existence.

It was over and the smile lighting up her face was worth every second of worry he held for her while she did what he believed she needed to do for her to be free from of her past.

"That felt good. Better than good. In fact, I feel great." Pushing her hair away from her face she looked around the room nervously keeping her eyes averted.

Grabbing her hand wanting to soothe her anxiety, "You are an amazing woman, Mrs. Angelo. I am proud to stand by your side and will do so forever. Don't worry, Bri, you are the best person for me and I am the best person for you. You have let the past go and I, for one, believe you look a little bit lighter having let go of all that resentment you've carried around. Not that you weren't hot before, you're just as hot looking now; however you have this inner glow thing going on now. It's very sexy and if we don't get out of this room I am going to lock this door and have my way with you. Do you read me Mrs. Angelo?"

Grinning at her wiggling his eyebrows adding emphasis to what he was thinking would to lighten the mood. He knew his head was going down the gutter while she stood there looking nervous, but he didn't see nervous he only saw a sexy woman that belonged to him and he wanted nothing more than to put his hands all over her to sooth her worries from her mind, body and soul.

Nodding her head she didn't move or say anything. His speech left her speechless. Reaching out for her he pulled her in for a brief hug squeezing her while he kissed the top of her head. "I love you."

He said three words he knew she needed to hear not worried if she returned the words to him or not. None of it mattered to him. He just knew she need to hear them and damn if he didn't want to give her anything she needed.

Letting her go, he said huskily wanting to hold onto her longer than he should. "Let's get out of here."

Leaving the room they walked down the hall and looked over his shoulder, "Is there something in particular you want to eat?"

"Not particularly. Is there something you desire to eat Nate?" She did not hide the husky sound from her voice.

Nate spun around and stared into her green eyes for a few seconds before responding. "There is only one thing I desire, Princess, and that is not something meant for public view." Wiggling his eyebrows grinning playfully, "Unless you're no longer hungry and wish to release me from my honorable quest, I can think of a dozen things I'd like to do with you."

Smiling, feeling her heart rate increase in response to their flirtatious banter she felt her body temperature spike. Her attraction towards him was clouding her sense of reasoning.

"You seem quite capable of fulfilling my wants in this moment, but if it is food you speak of, then yes, I am hungry." Stepping closer he hissed at her audacity to seduce him when she knew his control was hanging by a thread.

"This is a dangerous game you play, Bri. I want you so bad I can taste you on my lips without having put them on you that's how bad I want you." Grabbing her head with his right hand he didn't waste time. He pulled her mouth to his before she could say anything contrary.

Explosions went off, behind her eyes, when his lips met hers. She was immediately consumed with his kiss. Where Nate began, she ended. The same must have been for him because his grip tightened on the back of her head moments after bringing them together. Weaving his left hand through her hair he held her securely pressing his tongue into her mouth, exploring, seeking for what she could not tell. She was afraid he was searching for something she was terrified to give. One by one her emotional restraints began to fall enabling her to become a part of the moment. His kiss shattered the last bit of restraint she had been clinging to granting her heart freedom to desire more of what he fed her mouth.

I want all of you. Give me all of you, Bri.

There was no care left in the world when she heard his words whisper in her mind, silky words floated through her conscience like a lover's caress. Only her desire to fulfill the demands of her mate remained fanned by the heat of their kiss. He stroked her tongue creating an elaborate dance between their mouths matching the sexual emotions that had sparked between them for the past decade. The way his hands wrapped around her body felt better than any fantasy she had ever dreamed of. He stripped her of her doubts, laid them to waste and replaced each one with a desperation built not on ownership, but of a love to be shared by one another equally. He was strength, desire and honor matching her most cherished values. His mouth weaved magic while he brought her body to places she had only dreamed of being. This was what women have spoken of all her life. How a man ignited passion within a woman so fast a woman would lose all perspective simply by a kiss. She understood, now, how easy two thousand years of existence went right out of her mind while she gave into the moment loving emotion for this man. The feel of his lips had her whole body lit up with fire.

The kiss deepened, became rougher, their heads slanted allowing better access searching hungrily for more of what she did not know. She reached up and linked her hands around his neck simultaneously molding her body to his while she wrapped her legs around his waist in effort to pull herself closer to him. It seemed they stayed that way in the middle of the hallway not aware of what or who could be around them. All she wanted was more of him, but she knew she had to take care of herself. Whether those were her words or his whispered into her mind she did not know, but it cooled the raging inferno reminding her to slow their actions from where they were leading before it was too late to stop.

Breathing heavily they both broke apart at the same time. Unwrapping her legs from around his waist, he helped to steady her by not letting go. They just stared at one other panting heavily.

After a minute or two her eyes widened and he felt her body go stiff in his arms as static electricity gathered around Bri and latched on her energy with so much force she physically lurched to the side. He helped her right herself but before he could say anything she connected with him and he could sense the tug on her core energy which he could tell, from her thoughts, was not freely given. This was an abomination, an act of the worst kind for the people of her world, this was what she shared mentally because what frightened her the most was she currently was in the Earth Realm and this should not be happening. She felt another pull on her energy, harder and more violent than the first almost ripping a cry from her mouth. Only thing that could do this was if something horrific had happened on Skaldanna and Skaldanna needed an energy infusion from her to sustain the damage that had occurred in her homeland for the realms to repair itself. This is what being High Royalty meant, he understood now. She was the keeper of the realms energy and he knew whatever was happening on Skaldanna had to be pretty bad for her energy to be ripped from her like this.

He tensed when she closed her eyes and he knew by the way his hands had tightened on her arms they might leave a mark, but he didn't care. What was happening to her was not like anything he had ever seen while living with her this past decade and by the look of confusion on her face neither did she. She pulled her arms down from his neck and wrapped them around her waist franticly trying to break the connection with her energy. He stayed mentally connected to her trying to sort out her thoughts, seeing if there was anything he could do to shield her from whatever was happening. Her body would not work when she commanded it to move. The pain had overwhelmed centuries of her mental discipline. She could not form a mental shield to block whatever it was that had attacked her energy. She was too overwhelmed by the intensity of the pain associated with the pull of her energy that it magnified her fear of violated against her will. She couldn't do anything but slide down the wall to the floor and all he could do was follow her down as he watched the woman he loved fall prey to some unknown force.. The pain was so intense for her she didn't make a single sound. He was frantic to take the pain away from her and was sending reassurances via their mental link trying to assess with his eyes what the hell was happening to her. She pried her eyes open wide searching for his face relieved he was still there. Tears welled up in her eyes and her breathing no longer came in short gasps. He was crouched down starring at her intently waiting for her to say something.

He knew he was coiled like a snake ready to kill whoever hurt his woman and there wasn't a doubt in his mind this was a deliberate attack on her. Never had he seen her react to anything either here on Earth or in her realm to put her in such a state of shock. The way she held herself while it happened he was afraid if it went on any longer she could have been died. He was more than pissed, he was volatile and judging by her thoughts she had no idea what had happened. What scared him the most was she had no memories in her two thousand years of existence of this type of event occurring. He was ready to explode.

All the years of working and living alongside him she knew in order for Nate to be this tense there was something wrong. Her mind was still a jumble of residual pain and confusion. In a flash she saw how much he wanted to throw himself in harm's way just to spare her a single drop of pain yet on the other he wanted to tear apart whomever caused her the pain with his bare hands. This wasn't pain caused by their actions, but by something else going on in the world she was certain.

"Bri, what is it?" Looking around for a threat he began testing the kinetic energy surrounding the area they were sitting in, expanding his senses throughout the compound. She was still connected to him mentally choosing to let her senses open fully for him so she could feel the possessiveness of their shared mental bond flow through her, strengthen her with how much he cared. She would do everything in her power to keep him from feeling an ounce of pain.

"Bri, tell me what you know," he whispered into her mind.

"He knows I have the red diamond and has disturbed the Universes balance. How I do not know, but I felt his rage at that knowledge quickly followed by immense pain. My connection to Skaldanna told me there had been a great disturbance within the realms. Something unnatural pulled a great deal of energy from the Upper Realms so much so my connection to Skaldanna had been affected despite my location."

Closing her eyes she concentrated on Skaldanna desperate to form a mental communication link with her most trusted friend in the Fourth Realm. Katerina Kastekanos was still her most trusted confidant after all these years of self-exile. They saw each other twice a year when she traveled to Skaldanna, depositing the much needed energy from the Earth Realm, feeding the core energy on Skaldanna like all of the High Royal predecessors before her. If there was anything going on within the Realm of Skaldanna, she would be the person to talk to.

Centering her thoughts deep within herself, she did what she had never done before. She contacted Katerina from Earth without formal mental preparation or ceremony nor did she wait for Sahmain or Beltane, to try and contact Katerina when it was easier to access Skaldanna because of the thin veils accessing the various realms. There was no time for formalities.

"Kat, are you there? Can you hear me?" Her call was met with silence. Speaking louder mentally pulling years of experience communication with energy threads she tried again. *"Kat, answer me, can you hear me. If I do not hear from you in ten seconds I am coming to get you and that is an order!"*

"Keep you skirt on!" Came a faint reply from a familiar voice.

"What has happened? Enormous amounts of energy was just ripped from my being a few seconds ago. Something is very wrong do you know if anything has happened within the realms?"

"We have felt it here too. I fear something very bad has happened. As we speak I am leaving the dining hall, heading up to the ramparts hoping to get a better view of my kingdom."

Relieved Katerina was okay and taking active measures to seek out the problem she felt a moment of hesitation to send her friend into the unknown fully aware of what it felt like to have her energy violently ripped from her being. *"Be careful whatever it is, I have a very bad feeling and I haven't felt this uneasy since the attack on my home years ago."*

Sounding nervous trying very hard to mask her emotions from her friend she concentrated on securing the mental link she formed with Katerina all the while drawing on Nate's energy to help sustain her knowing he was in her mind as an observer to their conversation. She was not concerned with keeping him out but instead welcomed his comforting presence. Him being here to support made her feel content and reassured her of his strength. If she was not careful she could easily see herself putting all her trust in him.

Where did that thought come from? Careful to keep her personal thoughts out of the conversation away from her mental observer she focused on Katerina's voice.

"I know what you mean. All I can tell you is that the nobles and I were enjoying the evening meal when our energies began to be syphoned from us. It lasted for about a minute stunning everyone into silence. Afterwards most everyone became ill to their stomachs no longer interested

in eating fearing they may have been poisoned. Some ran from the room to the nearest bathroom to be sick, some never made it that far spilling the contents of their stomachs along the way. Some were so ill they fell over passed out cold from whatever evil had attacked us."

"Oh Gods, are you ok. Do you have need of me?" There was no answer just silence as her anxiety for what her friend had faced mounted.

"Katerina, do you have need of me?" Still no answer just silence. She panicked believing this had to do with Lord Drakkoon. After all that had happened, this evening, it could not be anything but a direct attack on Skaldanna. Concentrating harder than she had ever done before she forced more energy into her communication link hoping to press Katerina into a response. "Katerina, answer me. Do you have need of me?"

"I think, Princess, I do," was the quiet response spoken into her mind, so unlike her friend.

"Thank the Gods, I thought I lost you and was prepared to come to you, veil or no veil," she said sounding relieved to hear her voice. She loosened her grip on Nate's arms not realizing how tense she had become waiting for her to respond.

Sounding very confused and scared Katerina stated, "I am standing on the northern ramparts overlooking the northwest section of my kingdom, you know where the pond meets the forest? Well, you would never believe what I am seeing here. I truly am frightened, Briksanna. I was just down to the forest this afternoon with the children of my court picking berries and it did not look like this. I swear all of it did not look like this. Oh Gods, what has happened to my lands." The last part was whispered as she heard Katerina's voice break into tears."

"What...Katerina, tell me what you see. I do not know if I can maintain this connection. You have to tell me what you see." She felt herself start to fade and with it the last of her reserved energy she had clung to in order to maintain the mental connection with Katerina. Suddenly Nate was there feeding her more of his energy soothing her fears while feeding her his strength. His actions told her she was not alone.

"The whole forest has died. A few leaves are trees which this morning were full of growth, no shrubs exist on the ground, just lifeless trunks trapped within a barren wasteland. All of the crops in my fields have withered to dust. A few scattered blades of grass remain. Everything around me looks dead, worse than what is seen during winter months. Briksanna I am as old as you and I have never seen anything like this throughout my years of existence. In the manner of minutes death has become of my realm for as far as the eye can see. I have no idea of the state of my people who reside within those lands outside my castle. Oh Gods, my people could be in *mortal danger or worse already dead? I am not strong enough to fight this malevolence on my own. Briksanna, if ever I needed your help it is now. You must come home."*

Katerina wept softly. She could feel her despair through their connection as if she were standing beside her. She wanted to weep with her. She remembered how beautiful the forests looked bordering her castle admiring them the last time she had visited. How tall the trees stood, how bountiful their branches stretched offering shade to those who ventured to take shelter under their leaves. How vibrant the castle gardens bloomed after she had infused Skaldanna with her energy. She made it a habit to stroll throughout the gardens with Katerina before returning to the Earth Realm during every visit because it was a beautiful reminder of the home worth the sacrifice of self-exile to prevent war with Lord Drakkoon. A place she could count on to help her settle her mind filled with longing before heading back to her home on Earth. It always felt like the land knew, through its majestic beauty, it was giving back a piece of itself by filling her with harmony in return for her devoted service to Skaldanna. Her service as High Royalty was to deliver energy gathered from the Earth Realm and release it to everyone. For centuries, servitude to the High Royal Court she donated her energy towards the sustainability of all realms on Skaldanna. It was her duty, her legacy and she took pride in being the one being to fulfill that role for all the inhabitants on Skaldanna.

The beauty of Katerina's gardens inspired the name she gave one of the twins. The little cherub she had held in her arms always reminded her of those exact moments when she released her stored energy upon Skaldanna. Only a person of High Royal blood could disperse the combined energy necessary to feed the core of Skaldanna. This task had been passed down from father to son, mother to daughter always belonging to the High Royal family. An honor not a responsibility of servitude, something she was grateful to do her entire life. The moment she released her energy on Skaldanna she always had a feeling rightness fill her heart as if this was the way energy transfer had always been meant to be. Two forces sharing equally in the balance of existence.

Kat knew how deeply she felt about the land of Skaldanna. Seeing Kastekanos lands was all that she had time for in the past several millennia. Any communication or Ruling Council governing meetings, if ever needed, were always conducted on the Kastekanos estate or via Katerina. Her lands had been her home for the past several centuries. She felt devastated by the news.

Pushing those thoughts aside quickly thought of what needed to be prioritized as her leadership instinct kicked in. She reached out to her friend once more. *"Calm yourself Kat. First and foremost you are Princess of the Second Realm. Your duty is first to your people. Organizing your castle will fortify your kingdom. You know what you have to do. Keep the people close and inside the castle walls. Account for all that is within and if anyone comes seeking aid, give it; careful to separate the sick from the healthy."*

"Take stock of your resources, which includes your people. Healers to the sick, the elderly and young should be kept separate from the strong this way everyone can focus on the task at hand not be distracted with assisting one another. If need be use the older children residing in your castle for inner guards, that should keep them busy, not to mention bustling full with pride. Everyone should be given a task. Assign them, Kat, letting them know that to fortify your castle right now is to fortify their kingdom. This devastation may not be limited to your lands. Use your advisors for labor, no one healthy, is to be left without a task, do you understand me?"

"Yes." No longer crying she sounded stronger and clearer of mind than she had a minute ago.

"You are to place your realm under high alert. Send your fastest scouts, but only the ones you consider trustworthy as you do not want to scare your people into a panic. Have them alert your tenant farmers that they may seek refuge within the castle walls until more can be determined. It is best for safety, a reason your scouts will understand. They are not to force the people into following their orders, but to suggest it is in their best interest to follow your proclamation of refuge. Have them report to you directly, who knows what they may find. No one is to eat or drink anything until you have your alchemist test all food and water supply for any signs contamination and report their findings only to you. Again not to start a panic if they were to find anything, that could prove disastrous considering what you have told me has happened with the surrounding lands. What you have in your food stores and that of your tenets is all that remains for you until we can get there. Harmony and I should be able to help with the healing the lands once we can better access the situation."

Feeling her energy draining fast, she was quick to ask, *"You are quite sure of what you are seeing and that you yourself are not suffering ill effects of this energy drain?"*

"I am quite certain that I am in control of my mind," she snapped. *"You forget whom it is you are speaking to. I am just as strong and wise as you are. What you have said I would*

have put in place given time, but Briksanna, you are not looking at what I am seeing. Truly you would have been more careful with your question if you could see the impact all this death has had on the land. I am seeing what the lands would look like if they were to die before my own eyes. It would break your heart as mine has already been broken. This will be disastrous to all of Skaldanna not only to my people. Who will feed the other realms? We are the only source for all grains and ninety percent of all remaining crops. My worry is not only for my realm, Briksanna, but for all the people of Skaldanna."

Sighing Briksanna felt at a loss of words hearing her speech. Regaining her composure she sought to console her friend. *"I am sorry to have offended you my friend. I am just as frightened without seeing or experiencing what you have recently endured and I am in another realm no less."*

Feeling mollified by her words, Katerina sighed herself, *"I must leave you to begin all that we have discussed."*

"Kat, you will be careful? That is a request not an order. You are my oldest and dearest friend. I would truly grieve if anything happened to you. Please be careful." Hoping her words expressed sincerity instead of the desperation they sounded like when she spoke mentally with her friend.

"As do you, Princess. Stay safe. Will you be coming, then?"

"Yes, we all will be coming this time Kat. You will finally get your wish to meet the children. I should have brought everyone with me years ago, but I let my fear of the unknown keep me from acting on what I knew to be right. Do not tell Fenrir I said that or I will never live it down." Sighing, sounding wearier by the moment she guessed she had a minute before her energy ran out.

"Bri, break the connection. You are draining yourself dry, baby. Tell her we will be ready to enter the realm in twenty four hours if need be with supplies for her kingdom." Nate commanded into her head.

"Kat, I will organize the family and we will bring as much supplies as the veil will allow. Do not tell anyone of our arrival, so as to not raise any alarms or false hopes. Meet me at the same location we met last Beltane at the edge of the forest by the servants entrance, with only a select few for your protection to keep our initial arrival quiet."

"What time?" Katerina asked, her voice getting fainter by the second almost a whisper in her mind.

"Midnight", Briksanna replied.

"Until then, Briksanna. I shall wait for you where the flowers once grew."

"Until then, Katerina. May the Gods watch over you and your kingdom."

Suddenly snapping her eyes open she stared with eyes glazed, unfocused and squinting. "Nate?" She spoke one word not able to keep the darkness threatening to take her at bay any longer she promptly rolled her eyes allowing darkness to claim her. The last thing she heard was Nate's frantic cry of alarm as she passed out in his arms.

9

Somewhere lost in the Four Realms

*L*ightning struck all around her as she raged over his betrayal. Thunder shook the walls from the force of her wrath. She the First Princess of the Four Realms floated up from the pits of despair where she had been tortured, betrayed and left broken for days upon end by the very Gods she had blindly given her faith to. She awoke this morning form her worst nightmare not knowing if she had the courage to endure another day. After all she had seen and learned she vowed she would never be a woman who trusted easily again. From this moment forward she would do everything possible to empower herself with knowledge, the skills for survival and most of all, she would guard her heart. She would never giver her trust willingly based upon words spoken by any man, woman or God. She would be the controlling factor in her life from this day forward.

Floating upward, she cleared the crumbling castle reaching the top of a cliff landing gently on two feet. She noticed for the first time where she had landed. No longer was she within the realm of Skaldanna. The sun was brighter than she had ever seen and there was only one within the sky not two as she was accustomed too in her home realm.

The second thing she noticed, looking down, was she had subconsciously created a portal and she was looking back to the place she had just destroyed, hence the difference in landscape. Her parents spoke to both her and her sister about their ancestors within the High Royal bloodlines having the ability to create portals and if either her or her sister felt such power within them they were to seek them out for guidance. Her parents did not want their children to test out that particular ability so they could be lost. She did not have any inclination of how to create a portal so she put the conversation completely out of her mind at the time.

She recognized some of the landmarks surrounding her from old stories passed down through generations of stories; often times to keep ornery children from sneaking around at night. She felt a stab of curiosity to spend time exploring the surrounding area. First she had to deal with where she came from and closing the portal. If there was anything she retained from her lessons as daughter of the High King was the lesson of follow through. She meant to finish destroying the place that held so much heartbreak and pain.

Looking down the entire area she saw nothing more than a dark castle surrounded by a moat conveniently shielded by nothing less than a dark forest of unnaturally darkened trees. Nothing surrounding or within the castle held any life that she could see. To the left of the castle was where she had just freed herself from. She smiled a little knowing the place now lay in crumbles with the exception of a towering pillar standing in the middle of the rubble. That must have been where she blasted her way out with her lightning.

While she searched the area for life her focus kept going back to the unusual object sticking of the rubble. The solitary pillar held a coat of arms near the top. A familiar symbol leaving her cold despite the warmth from the sun on her back created a feeling of dread within the pit of her stomach. She stared at the symbol for a long time never taking her eyes off the object absorbing herself in its simple design. Three moons in the downward shape of a half crescent, floated above a phoenix bird. The phoenix held a sword in one claw and within the other it held a scroll.

"Deepsong," she whispered. She did not know if any monsters were about in this new realm. The idea of being tortured by her betrothed was enough for her to bite her tongue until the familiar copper taste filled her mouth. Seeing the bowels of Lord Drakkoon's realm stirred her blood again sending a bright light of rage shooting through her system. She could smell the smoke floating through the portal from the ruins reminding her where she had recently come from. She understood who the Master was. She knew who was responsible for the atrocities that befell her family and their castle the day she was kidnapped. Lord Drakkoon's fortress lay in partial ruins. Her rage threatened to consume her once again. She bit down harder wanting to keep herself from lashing out despite the overwhelming desire to destroy everything in front of her. Her emotions threatened to overshadow every reasonable thought left in her mind.

"Why do you not attack? I am here, take me now you cowered!" she screamed igniting lightening all around her.

Charged with a vengeful rage she still had enough reason in her mind to remain strong. She would never allow herself to be put in a vulnerable situation again. She would prepare herself, mind and body.

Seeing no sign of movement around the castle she was appeased further solidifying her reason to stand firm in what she believed more and more. Courage filled her heart while she stood on the edge of a cliff in a different world breathing different air. Closing her eyes she breathed in the salty air and allowed it to flow through her calming her mind and body. Slowly the fury left her body while her fingers loosened their grip and her mouth no longer tasted like blood from her constant biting. She was still very angry but she wanted to remain alive to exact revenge. She needed gain control of her emotions and learn how to stay alive.

Looking away from the gruesome sight of her past she realized she could never wage a war of vengeance with Lord Drakkoon right now. She was no match for him in her current physical and emotional state. She wanted to be strong of mind and body never feeling powerless again. She needed to access the damage to the Upper Realm, see who had been spared and what condition all the Realms of Skaldanna were in while she had been imprisoned. When enough time had passed, when she had gained all that she sought to empower her she would strike out at him with a force that not even he would be able to recover from.

"I will avenge the Four Realms of Skaldanna, on the boarder of my new world and yours. I First Princess Briksanna, daughter of High King Akmond, violet green eyed princess of peace foretold in The Prophesy, spoken by the Great Seer Vakgdona, shall strike the death blow of the Master within the Under Realm. My life and the lives of all those who have already paid in death demand vengeance and vengeance shall be mine to exact. You will die by my hand, this I vow, sealed in my blood."

She brought down a thin bolt of lightning aiming the hot white light to her outward palm striking clean through ripping a scream of pain from her. Ignoring the new sensation of pain she fought the desire to sit down and cry over all the pain she had recently endured. Kneeling at the edge of the portal she reached the ground with her bloody hand and grabbed a handful of dirt from the ground intent on duplicating the symbol in this realm mixed with her blood so she would never forget what had occurred to bring her to this place. Out of the corner of her eye she saw the coat of arms on the pillar. Three moons in a downward crescent shape above a phoenix holding a scroll in one claw and a sword with the other. To seal the vow she sent a lightning bolt straight towards the symbol scribing a jagged line across the breast of the bird signifying where the Master would die by her hand.

Three moons, three months she had been tortured. This is what she interpreted reading the symbol. She believed it would be three months for her act of vengeance to begin once she decided to act upon The Prophesy. How or when that would occur she had no idea, yet she no longer concerned herself with the details of life. She felt better simply having made the choice to empower herself without the pressure of a timeline to begin her trek towards retribution. She would learn patience in order to become methodical. When she struck the Master she wanted the moment to be downright dead on. She could wait a hundred lifetimes for that particular stealth both in body and of mind.

She was the Phoenix, arisen, yet today she remained a woman kneeling in a strange land no longer the naïve princess. A strong magical being long believed, by all the people within her realm, to be the favored pet of the Gods. She would need to become the Phoenix again to defeat the evil which had torn her kingdom apart.

The sword held in its claw would the instrument of death for the Master, whom she know to be Lord Drakkoon. She would see that he received nothing less than death.

The scroll represented The Prophesy of the Four Realms spoken by the Great Seer Vakgdona. She knew at some time she would have to acknowledge her role in The Prophesy but for now she had more important things to focus on.

The new mark she added was the death mark she, First Princess Briksanna, would bring down on Lord Drakkoon.

"This I vow upon my very soul." Lifting a bloody hand filled with dirt she whispered a promise that blew with the wind a mingling of dirt and blood towards the edge of the portal. When all the dirt left her hand she saw her hand had begun to heal and the pain subsided.

That was different.

Shrugging the thought of what other things she would learn about herself in this new place she stood up and looked one last time at the place she knew would be forever burned into her memories. She closed the portal simply by willing it so and it was done. Alone she took in the forest in front of her and the cliff behind her. Her senses were filled with the sounds of nature clamoring around while she stretched her senses far wary of any unknowns. She did not think she could handle much more that day for her cup had run over many days ago. Not picking up on possible threats she tested her abilities happy she still had retained the command of the elements. Another thing she noted was if she needed to protect herself from harm she would have no problem killing again. Some things just needed to die. That was the lesson she had learned.

Looking one last time over her shoulder towards the cliff she saw the horizon across the great body of water looked beautiful. She could start life here without the threat of pain. She would learn everything to be the best warrior this world had ever seen. She heard a sizzling sound not in accordance with nature. Looking for the source of the sound she realized it was coming from the ground by her feet. That was when she saw the symbol she had drawn on the ground had hardened into the earth forming an image similar to rock. She bent over intent on touching the image to find there was no heat emanating from it despite the sizzling sound she had heard earlier. Running her fingers over the symbol felt like a balm to soul. She was no longer captive within the Under Realm. She was no longer within the safety of her homeland in the Upper Realm. She was in a new place to begin her new life.

Having this symbol embedded on the land of her new home solidified her resolve to be the strongest warrior she could be never to forget where she had come from or what needed to be done in order to defeat Lord Drakkoon.

10

Screaming in his head for help, he picked up his love running towards the infirmary praying to anyone and everything she stayed alive long enough for him to get them some help. *"Stark, can you hear me brother?"* He screamed telepathically to his older brother. *"Stark, the Princess is down. Unknown source. I am headed to the infirmary with her in my arms."*

"Roger that. On my way, what happened? We all felt a psychic pull on our energy for a minute, but before we could track it we lost the link." Stark sounded calm and cool, but he knew his brother was all business as he spoke. Gathering Intel on the run was Stark's cup of tea.

"What's your ETA?" Stark asked, not sounding stressed at all considering how upset he was holding his woman. He was normally the calm person of the team, the one everyone counted on all missions to never panic like he was sounding right now.

"Thirty seconds or less, hoping for the less. Stark we got some major shit going on here and my first instinct is to pick her up and cage her in so I can keep her safe, but I know that wouldn't work. She would kick my ass all kinds of mid evil. Ten seconds, Stark, you almost there?"

"Looks like the whole damn team heard the psychic call. It's like our teams personal alarm system." Muttering mentally to no one in particular but himself. He knew everyone was in tow based on his brother's comment.

"We're right behind him Nate. I am sending a signal to the Infirmary now setting it up." Trinity piped in sounding confident no doubt running right alongside Stark punching a bunch of codes into her new smartphone. She was probably turning everything on since Striker wired her phone up to the system overseeing the compound last week. Knowing Striker, access was restricted to areas only she would need immediate access to thus having the necessary codes to turn everything on remotely. He was glad Trinity had that piece of technology in her hands right now. He still wasn't getting a response to his mental probe from Bri and he was worrying more by the second.

"She's our mom as well as our best friend we won't let you or Momma down." Harmony spoke confidently sounding just a sure as her sister. She probably had her nine millimeter in her hand appearing all business on the outside searching for a possible threats to those she considered family. Man she could never fool anyone when she was seriously pissed on the inside. They could always tell by the vibe she gave off when she was really mad about something. It never failed to irritate her that she couldn't hide that part of herself from the rest of them. The rest of the team would shrug it off both her emotions and her irritation just like everyone had their own issues to deal with, himself included. No blame or accusations there, not from him.

"We would never think any less of you ever; I hope you both know that." Softly spoken from the woman he held in his arms.

"Briksanna!

Mamma!" Speaking as one telepathically while stopping in the hall directly in front of the infirmary doors; he looked down at the woman in his arms and could've wept serious tears.

"Woman, I keep telling you, this shit has got to stop. You took ten years off my life passing out like that." Straining not to sound like a puddle of mud with the anxiety of seeing her pass out not knowing what had happened or what he could do to help her.

With barely enough energy to spare she picked up a trembling hand and looked directly into his eyes, she whispered. "It is not time for me to leave you, my love." Promptly she dropped her hand looking as if that one action was the last bit of energy she had left in her. "I think I am going to take you up on your offer to rest. Can you take me to my own bed and watch over me? With all that has gone on I trust you to take command of the team while you keep watch over me. I am so tired, Nathanial." Yawning into his shoulder she snuggled her head deeper into his chest, closed her eyes promptly falling asleep.

He pulled her closer kissing the top of her head before looking up whispering in her hair, "I promise, I will never fail you. I give you my word, baby, you will be protected with my life."

Looking up he stared into the eyes of his family, "I am taking Bri back to our room, H &T, she will need an IV bag set with all the nourishment you can pump into her while she is sleeping allowing her to heal properly. You can evaluate her when we get to our rooms to make sure, but I gather you two will know what is best for her. I can't even begin to tell you what she needs now other than sleep and nourishment."

He looked over to the rest of the group, "Striker, I need recon of the portal Bri used last for her trip to the Four Realms on Beltane. Any Intel you can gather about her trips, what she takes with her, what she brings back, I want a list. Then I want you to take inventory of what we have on hand that correlates to that list in the way of supplies. Gather them in sixty pound packs, same items for each pack. That means one pack for each of us. Idea is to bring as many supplies as possible when we go on our next mission. Before you ask, since I mentioned a pack for each of us, yes we are all going to Skaldanna, this is our next mission. Don't ask for details, you will all get them at the same time once Bri wakes up. Suffice to say there has been a great travesty done to the Second Realm and in speaking with Katerina it was the entire realm, hell maybe all of Skaldanna. We will need everything that we can bring. So mentally pack up expecting what we bring maybe all that is on hand initially until we have a clearer understanding of what the hell is happening over there."

"Kenneth and Gabriella, I need visual surveillance of the perimeter, inside and out. Once secured, I want you to meet up with Striker and take a look at what he has inventoried. You two are going to look at that list and compare weapons and ammunitions that she had with her at the time of her visit with what we currently have on hand. Same thing as with the packs, I want each member of the team to be outfitted with as many weapons as possible keeping in mind what each person prefers, then load each team member up accordingly."

Looking directly at his brother already dismissing everyone else, "Stark, you and the twins are with me."

Whirling around not waiting for a reply he headed back in the direction he recently came from knowing he'd have full cooperation from the team. Feeling secure he had instructed them well, given the situation at hand, he believed if there were any questions Stark would field them gaining absolute cooperation. Knowing that his brother had his back, he put on a burst of supernatural speed arriving in their room seconds later and closed the door.

Laying Bri down on their bed gently, he brushed her hair away from her face. He gathered up the blankets around her so she would be warm. Sitting beside her on the bed he wondered at all of his thoughts and emotions that came crashing down on him when he looked at the love of his life laying in their bed looking beat up emotionally and physically. He wanted to protect her, laugh with her, see that smile that took up her entire face that left him on cloud nine for days. Just the act of her uninhibited happiness made her the beautiful he had grown to love. She was the most beautiful woman on the face of the universe and he loved her completely.

Her long hair laid spread around her pillow looking brittle and grey accentuating her pale face. Seeing her weak brought up his insecurities of helplessness that still held the power to put him to his knees with worry. It was years ago when he realized his heart was lost to her strange green eyes. He didn't know if he had the courage to let her know of his feelings then and was shaking like a leaf inside when he confided in her earlier. One thing he knew for certain was he would never allow anyone or anything to come between the love he held in his heart for her. He realized tonight, they both could still be harmed or even killed, but nothing could touch his love for her. He believed in the kind of love spoken of in the fairytales they used to take turns reading to the twins when they were little. He'd never seen it in real life, but God as his witness he wasn't going to pass up on his love of a lifetime just because he was scared to be King of her realm.

Wiping his hand over his face he knew he was exhausted, he wanted to curl up right beside her and never let go. So much had happened tonight, how much more could she take? He started to doubt not only his worth but his courage to be the man she would need him to be when they go to her homeland. He knew she was deathly afraid of The Prophesy, so was he, but he also knew there was no way out of the path they were on but to go forward. He had an uneasy feeling there was more to this prophesy than what he knew and he didn't like not having all the facts. If it was only The Prophesy holding her from returning why would the Goddess show herself now? Knowing what Merridian had said earlier made sense, Bri hadn't been ready or willing to take everything on years ago and whatever demons held her back all this time he would get to the bottom of it eventually because like him, she believed the same way as he did. Keeping secrets during missions killed your own team faster than a bullet from your opponents.

Seeing her lying in the bed looking relaxed he realized without a doubt he would to do everything possible to be exactly the man she needed him to be for them to come out of this nightmare in one piece. He hoped he wouldn't mess things up too bad along the way. He wanted to be the man she trusted with not only her whole heart but her life, because this woman held all the power to destroy him just by rejecting him.

"How is it you picked me to be your knight in shining armor? I'm just a human." He said out loud.

He stilled looking at the woman laying before him as a scent of lemon blew through the room filling his nose with what smelled like his favorite merengue pie. No one could make lemon merengue pie like Gabriella. Odd their room was too far away for that smell to be detected in here and Gabriella was doing recon with Striker so that was out of the question. Looking around the room they were in he saw no one and the door to the room was closed so where the hell was the smell coming from. Shaking his head he was just about to chalk it up to craziness not being able to explain this experience let alone anything else that he'd experienced over the past decade he bowed his head shoving the question aside when the smell of lemons hit his nose again. Rubbing the back of his neck in absentminded frustration his thoughts once again returned to what he chalked up as his human inadequacy over the situation he was in. How the hell was he going to be the Prince to his Princess when he was only human?

"And she is just a woman," said a female voice from the other side of the bed.

Startled at the person who appeared out of nowhere, he jumped up throwing knife in hand ready to let loose on this unwanted intruder who breached his personal sanctuary. He saw a woman on the other side of the bed; make that a hologram, at least that's what his brain processed at the time.

"Relax human, I mean neither you nor the Princess any harm. My name is Vakgdona and I am the Great Seer of Skaldanna coming to warn you both."

The beautiful six foot three blonde hair blue eyed beauty watched him from the other side of the bed. Studying her, he itched to grab Bri from the bed. Almost identical to what he saw earlier this evening on the Goddess, she wore a robe like attire but in light blue with a white and gold apron looking thing over it keeping the robe like dress closer to her body revealing a great figure hidden underneath, not like he was ogling the woman, it was plain as day she was a beautiful woman. A silver chain adorned her left side wrapping around her waist holding the whole robe slash apron dress together. Her long wavy blonde hair hung lose around her shoulders flowing past her hips. She wore no make-up that he could see come to think of it Bri preferred not to wear anything too unless she was out on Spa Day with the girls then she caved in and wore it just for them he suspected. That must where the scent of lemons had come from because the smell intensified filling the entire room once she had spoken. Looking closer he noticed she had a circlet on her head. From first glance it looked like it was gold in color sitting on her head wrapped around her temple and forehead tight like it had been pressed onto her head rather than placed.

"That is because it is not sitting on my head, it was forced upon me by the Tormentor long ago. It is what keeps me in a constant state of unconsciousness. This is why no one has seen me in so long. Even though I appear asleep I am aware of all that goes on around me," she said simply as she continued to observe me.

She looked down at Bri, but spoke directly to me. "It is time for the Princess to begin her role in The Prophesy and you must see to it that she follows through with everything no matter what appears too costly to endure. The losses, if failure where to occur, would be so great death would be for everyone. This is what I see when I travel down that paticular vision path. You are the key to her success, Nathanial, that and her trust in herself. She believes it is her fear of trust in others that has kept her away from her destiny, but in truth it was fear within her that has kept her from moving forward in life and in her destiny. You have the power to change that for her as much as you fear she has the power to destroy you."

Looking back at him she cocked her head as if listening to a voice from far away before she straightened herself once again all attention on him. "It is because of Lord Drakkoon's energy transfer that in two thousand years of stasis I can come to you at this time. That and something darker, much darker added to it that has caused all the damage to everyone and everything. Despite my efforts to root out the person behind the curtain of darkness I believe they have connected themselves to The Prophesy. I am forever blind to the malevolence that continues to circle The Prophesy and it has frustrated me for quite some time. This person is more sinister than Lord Drakkoon. Every time I look deeper I am filled with pain beyond my power to stop it and it takes much time for me to recuperate in order to see anything but the darkness I have been encased in. Maybe it is as it should have been, I do not know. I only know that it is time for you both to begin your quest. I tell you this so you may share my thoughts and observations about this hidden villain with everyone so you are aware of the dangers ahead of you. Rest easy warrior, truly, I am no foe for you to worry over."

Taking a chance leaving Bri vulnerable he quickly glanced at the door knowing his brother was going to show up with the twins any minute. "My family is on their way to us right now. I don't know how you feel about company, but I thought you'd like to know."

"Although time has little meaning while in stasis, I do appreciate taking the time to explain things." Blue eyes flashed at him showing the first signs of irritation. Not moving but remaining still, hands at her sides she closed her glowing eyes, visibly trying to calm herself. Taking a deep breath she opened revealing bright blue orbs. She remained quiet while she looked round their room before settling her eyes on him once again. Still she did not speak. What seemed like minutes had only been moments before she spoke again, but it was long enough for him to think about what it was his new visitor saw.

Did she see how sparse the bedroom was? Did she notice there were no pictures within the room or trinkets on the dresser top? For all intents in purpose the room could have been a spare room that he had come to lay Bri down in. Who was he kidding; he wanted to bring more beauty into her life. So many years of hiding herself from the world he knew she deserved better. He wanted to be the man to give that to her. The how is where he was perpetually stumped.

The room seemed to fill with a stronger scent of lemon a testament to the presence of the seer standing across from him. She still had a look of irritation about her but he knew he too was past his point of patience.

"I don't know how much time I have so I will make haste. You and the Princess are to find the pieces of the Firing Sword that have been hidden from all worlds. The sword was broken long ago during the first great realm battle destroying the overlord who sought to destroy the peace among all realms creating havoc throughout the universe. Once the overlord was struck down by the Firing Sword the sword was broken and its pieces were cast out to whereabouts of which I do not exactly know, secretly hidden so if ever needed again it could be re-forged by the Blacksmith of the First Realm."

"What does this sword look like so we can find it?" The words came out harsher than he intended adding to the scowl on his face. He knew he was close to losing his temper. He just wanted to be left alone with his wife so she could have a chance to heal from the past two days. "All of this mystery stuff is really wearing on me so the sooner we find this sword, the sooner Bri can be free of this debt she believes she owes. Seriously Vakgdona I mean no disrespect but I'm a bit pissed off that the love of my life here"—waving his arm towards Bri then running his hand through his hair—"is paying a high price for everyone when all I want to do is take care of her. So if you don't mind stop with the long story and hurry up with the details."

"Patience warrior, your love for the Princess is evident, likewise is her love for you. You will have what you seek but as The Prophesy speaks of you will also have to pay a price along with her to gain the means to an end. You spoke to the Goddess of what you were willing to do in order to be the warrior the Princess needs you to be. You must not doubt yourself nor harbor doubt of her faith in you. Both of you will need to be united in heart and mind for you to accomplish the tasks set before you."

Sighing placing his knife back in its sheath strapped to his right thigh, he sat back down on the edge of the bed gazing at the other half of his soul seemingly oblivious to all that was going on around her. Her behavior was so unlike her and he was completely worried for her not to mention it pissed him off seeing her harmed right in front of him while he was helpless to protect her.

"Vakgdona, I don't want her to get hurt in all of this. I want to spend my life with her. I have so many dreams that I can only see her being a part of those dreams with me. The thought of her not being a part of them stabs my heart with so much pain it brings me to my knees."

Hearing her sigh brought his head up as she gazed up on him with understanding in her eyes. "Your belief in those shared dreams is what will forge an unbreakable bond between the two of you. This I have fore-seen and have come to share with you. As long as you both pay the price demanded by The Prophesy balance will be restored saving all worlds within the Universe. Your lives will be granted longevity and become fruitful. Peace shall once again be restored to all of Skaldanna thus saving the universe from despair."

Smiling now still confused about the sacrifice they would have to make he knew he was willing to stand by Bri no matter what the cost was. The seer seemed like she wanted him to believe he did have what it took to be the man Bri was going to need in order to fulfill The Prophesy. Seeing the second magical person in one evening tell him he had what it took to be the man she needed him to be made him feel confident he could be that man. It was a little bit of confidence, but hell, who was complaining. He needed to stop letting his doubts play havoc with his head. He knew, without a doubt, she was worth everything he had in him and it was time for him to man up.

Nodding her head knowing she had read his thoughts she went on, "Let me explain what you will need to do before you can re-forge the Firing Sword. The sword is long in length with a hilt shaped in a squared U. Three stones adorn each side of the hilt. In sets of two, the stones are in this order Thinking Stones which are Emerald Stones. Speaking Stones which are Black Pearls. Hand Stones which are Dark Amber and in the center where the blade meets the hilt is the Blood Stone which is a large Ruby Stone."

"You say stones, but don't you mean jewels?" Thinking of the last mission they had completed something was nagging in his memory but the thought kept eluding him so he brushed it off trying to stay focused on what Vakgdona was saying.

"Each of the smaller stones of the hilt is half an inch in diameter with the center Ruby being roughly the size of the center of my palm."

Looking down at her out stretched palm he thought about what Vakgdona had just told him. If what she said was true those were some serious jewels. The Ruby alone sounded just about the right size as the one they had recently lifted right out from under the nose of that fool servant for Lord Drakkoon. He knew he needed to keep focused so he started to speak but his question was easily forgotten when the seer continued speaking.

"It is exactly as I told you, but with more to it. The surrounding area the stones are set in is adorned in gold adding weight to the hilt. The handle of the sword was notched by the Blacksmith himself for easy grip. It is said he fashioned the handle after his own hand weaving magic into the handle of the sword so that whomever should wield it shall truly be one with the sword. The length of the blade is five feet in length. It is also said the steel had been forged by the breath of the Gods rendering the metal un-breakable."

Interrupting her shaking his head trying to absorb everything he had been told so far he opted to cross his arms over his chest and looked directly at the woman across from him doubt evident in his face. "This is where you lose me, if the sword is un-breakable and was forged by the

Gods, then why is it currently broken in pieces whereabouts unknown?" Sounding a bit smug to his own ears he waited for her to respond.

"The breath of the Gods renders the blade of the Fire Sword immortal."

Sounding completely frustrated what she was telling him didn't make any sense to him. "What the hell does that mean? The sword isn't living, is it?"

The lemon scent within the room intensified triggering what he believed were her emotions, filled his nose with almost an acidic scent he had no doubt would burn his scenes the more he pissed her off. That could be the only explanation as to why the lemon scent would grow stronger whenever he snapped at her. If he was ever going to be the man Bri needed when they went to Skaldanna then he had to get a grip on what flew out of his mouth. At least when it flew out, knowing when it came to his family they didn't react as much but he needed to remember to be her husband he had to be aware of how people were going to respond to what he said. He was a man of action, but it never hurt to know all the facts. He was after all a leader of a very formidable team whom over the years had rescued many people from the most obscene circumstances. So yeah, he'd learn to keep his mouth shut and be a better man no matter how bitter the taste seemed to him.

Clearing his wayward thoughts he knew he owed her an apology for being rude. Hell he was snapping at a hologram of a woman who had been held prisoner for thousands of years. Hell she still was. Sighing swallowing what felt like his own foot he was about to apologize verbally when she held up her hand preventing him from saying another word.

Snapping at him with her blue eyes flashing in increased agitation she pressed on. "You will have to be quiet if you want me to finish this before I go back into stasis. Apology accepted. You need to understand, Nathanial, the last time I was able to speak verbally with anyone was two centuries ago." Closing her eyes she reminded him of Bri when she lost her temper with him especially when he had irritated her with his famous Angelo charm.

Risking her wrath with one more interruption he felt he needed to tell her anyway. That was the way he was wired. If he was wrong there was no sense in keeping the knowledge to himself when he knew he needed to make amends. He believed stepping up to accept his role in Bri's life was part of the responsibility that made him a good guy. This was him, the man Bri loved and he always would be that guy for her.

"I apologize, Vakgdona. I am really trying to wrap my brain around all of this magic stuff." He hoped to appease her sympathy because he hadn't been raised in their realm or in their beliefs of magic. Hell he and his brother hadn't known there were other people in their own world like them until they ran into Bri and the twins a decade past. As far as they knew he and Stark were the only ones on the planet who had abilities other than what he read in comic books.

Opening her eyes she looked her composed serene self again. He could see how beautiful she was by the way she smiled at him meeting his eyes full leaving him with the feeling she could see right into his very soul. It made him a little uncomfortable to be under such a scrutinizing gaze especially from a beautiful woman, although he wasn't attracted to her in the same way he was with Bri. He just recognized beauty for what it was. Welcoming her thoughts on their conversation he nodded his head in acceptance giving her the respect she deserved, acknowledging her position in their lives. With that one act visually shown he had achieved what no man had achieved in centuries. Her respect.

"I wish we met under different circumstances you are truly a remarkable person. Your thoughts remind me we may be different in matters of birth origins, but we are similar in heart and mind. I respect that and admire you for it. You are a great leader and a good man, Nathanial. Your apology is accepted," continuing on with her story as if the interruption never happened. "The magic the Gods breathed into the sword made the blade immortal so that no matter if the blade were to be broken the true Blacksmith of the First Realm will have within him the tools and the magic to re-forge the sword to its original state."

"Why only the Blacksmith of the First Realm can re-forge the sword? Wouldn't any blacksmith do?" Still trying to understand the ways of Bri's world was hard for him to visualize but after his conversation with the seer it wasn't hard for him to accept.

"Many millennia ago prior to the First Great Battle; a promise was made to a man who befriended a God. This God gifted the man with the powers of both strength and magic over metals so his Realm would always prosper and be known for their craftsmanship with metals. The First Realm became renowned for their gift of metallurgy. They were sought out by all realms for their insight and craftsmanship for none were superior to the Blacksmiths of the First Realm."

"Wait, I thought you said there was one Blacksmith. The Blacksmith, yet now you say it plural as if there are more than one. Explain?

"The gift which the God had given was passed onto his son and his son's son for all eternity, always remaining with the firstborn of the royal line, thus keeping the promise of the God to the First Blacksmith. It was said the promise was made by the First God to his best friend, for a time, a simple man from a realm of Skaldanna whom became a legend due to his honor, strength and courage but most of all because of his faith in his best friend, for a time, the First God."

Trying to grasp all that she had told him he rubbed the back of his neck in frustration. "Where do we begin looking for all of the pieces? What is the name of the specific Blacksmith we are to contact?"

Seeming amused at his distressed tone she continued with her explanation showing a crinkling in her eyes as the corners of her mouth tilted in a grin. She knew she was testing the boundaries of his acceptance in the belief of magic. He could tell by the way she patiently told the story of the First God his brain was ready to revolt any second the same way a person's stomach felt right before they threw up.

"You already possess the Blood Stone. You accomplished the first part within this very world. The remaining portion of your quest will be with the lands of Skaldanna beginning by saving all which is dying. Find a way to save the land of Skaldanna and it will lead you to the path of your first mission, finding the Emeralds, but you will have to lose them in order to save those who have become lost thus regaining possession not only the Emerald stones but the next generation. Once you have the Emeralds you will set sail to the Sea of Topaz along Finn's Straight. There you must dive underwater to the giant caverns below where you will find the Black Pearls. Once you have those you will bring back to the Second Realm he whom was stolen that must be restored in order to return to the Second Realm healing the hearts of all the people within Skaldanna. After you have healed the people you will next travel to the Starr Mountains where you must save the Goddess restoring the heart of her warrior. There you will find the fabric of souls within the lands of the Third Realm in order to arm yourselves with the upcoming battle against evil forces sought to gain all through corruption and vengeance. Once you have armed yourselves with the fabric you will need to travel to the First Realm in search of Black Amber. The stones you need have been left lying deep within the mines of The Abyss. It will take the cooperation of all realms to achieve the last great feet for unity will triumph over centuries of mistrust. Your faith in one another will hold steadfast despite what your eyes may see or ears may hear."

She took a breath before continuing, "Once you have all the stones you need to bring them to the First Blacksmith of the First Realm where they will be safe in his possession as he and his families are still protected by the promise made by the Great God himself. Only he can find the location of the blade pieces and know how to recover them at that time. Nothing can be accomplished with the First Blacksmith without going through what I have told you. Everything must happen in this order so all that was lost may be reclaimed not only for you and Briksanna but for all in the universe. This was tasked by the powers that be long before I was shown the paths of those whom had hidden the precious stones holding the life of the blade. Once all pieces of the Fire Sword are in the possession of the Blacksmith he shall re-forge the sword with the help of the stones, thus breathing new life within the sword to be used by the Instrument of Peace."

Looking tired she began to fade. He knew she had revealed more to him than he guessed anyone knew about The Prophesy and he was very grateful to the Intel and for the opportunity to experience for the first time a bit of the magic surrounding The Prophesy. He felt good about knowing what he now knew and had a couple ideas already on who would be the best players for each task in what Vakgdona had just shared with him. Filing that information in the back of his head he'd wait to share that with Bri and Stark and get their feedback. Pushing his thoughts aside he once again focused on the present listening to what the seer needed to say next before she left him.

She looked lost her expression changed from stern to weariness. Her eyes no longer looked bright but droopy and tired. She kept rubbing her brow right below the circlet as if there was an itch along the underside of the object where it met her temple. Her focus seemed distracted as her eyes began to dart across the room like she was trying to memorize everything before she was forced back into confinement.

In that moment his instinct to rescue her from her prison became paramount. The familiar panicked look of a prisoner was all the same to him. He recognized it for what it was. Absolute fear in the loss of freedom. She was trapped and he could see it reflected in her eyes. It sometimes held people captive long after they had been physically freed, sucking the life from them years after they had been rescued. He wanted to get her out of there.

"Vakgdona? Where are you? Tell me about your surroundings, anything, no matter how insignificant. Do you see anything, smell anything? When we get to Skaldanna, we can arrange a search party to rescue..."

Dismissing his worry by shaking her head she closed her eyes as if the thought of where she was caused her pain. "I have done all that I can for now. I am losing power quickly and must conserve my strength if I am to be of any help to you or Briksanna. Know this warrior. Do not fear sleep for I know this well as I am held captive within my own mind. I am always with you and aware of all that goes on in both worlds, so shall you be with your Princess when the time comes. This will be your sacrifice and you will endure it for your love will not be lost only held apart from you for time. Believe me, you will know what I say to be true when the time comes and you must convince Briksanna of this for everyone to succeed in freedom from evil's tyranny. Look for the signs all around you, within the surrounding lands and within the people you meet along the way. I shall show each one of you what you will need to know as you follow along the path of this quest. This is not just for you but for all in your family as they each play a part in The Prophesy. It has been told long ago that many will aid the one needed to defeat the evil brought forth form The Master. Share with them your faith, honor and strength because they will look to you for guidance as well as comfort even when words cannot be said out loud, they will believe you for they will know your hearts and minds are connected always. The path has been laid before you and you all shall stand upon the same ground at one point deciding upon which choice is the proper choice to make. In this, all of you are one in the same. Be strong warrior, I have faith in you and the man you are destined to become."

He could barely see her silhouette while she continued to fade. She repeated the last words again. That wasn't what worried him except her last words she said before she disappeared left a knot in his throat.

"Be strong warrior, I have faith in all of you. I need you to believe in yourself, because by saving the Princess you save my life and that of your son."

11

"Nate! Dammit, open this door right now," closing his eyes worry filled his mind where his brother was concerned. He looked back at the twins holding supplies for Briksanna with worried expressions written over their faces.

"He just wanted a few minutes alone with her boss, we're sure of it." Harmony spoke up trying to reassure him looking over at her sister for confirmation. "Right Twin?"

"Right," Trinity responded with her own worried expression biting her lip trying to smile, for his benefit. "Besides he would have said otherwise if there was something wrong. Let's give them another minute and then we can talk about breaking down Momma's door."

Swinging the door open, ready to yell, Nate looked exhausted. "What took you so long?"

"What do you mean, took *us* this long. We've been pounding on this door for three minutes. H and T were ready to break the door down," Stark said briskly shoving past him to search the room for threats. Looking back at Nate he asked, "Why didn't you answer when we knocked?"

Harmony and Trinity quickly entered the room to see for themselves if Briksanna was alright. Efficiently hooking up an IV line, Trinity didn't even look up as she spoke, "Harmony and I agreed you had one minute left before we blew the door in. We've never seen Momma this way and we couldn't..."

"...get to her," finished Harmony in that ever present twin speak they shared. Eyes closed she was already singing, to the four elements, a familiar song of healing. Seconds after she entered the room, familiar smells of earth and pine began to fill the room from whatever herbs Harmony had brought with her. Filling the bowl in her hands she circled the bed never faltering in steps as she sang her healing song she used with whenever someone in the family had gotten sick. Familiar and calming was the scent, always reminding him of spring.

Looking at the twins, Stark reminded himself these two girls were Briksanna's babies and she was their mother. There wasn't anything she wouldn't do for them if it were one of them laid up on the bed instead of her. Stark sighed suddenly feeling older than his age. No matter what, these girls were her pride and joy; the children of her heart. She would have offered some form of comfort to them if it were them laying there sick, as she had been known to do over the years. He may not be the mothering feminine type but he recognized their need to offer the same type of comfort to their mother when she was down for the count.

"She loves you two as if you were her own children, never forget the depth of her love in everything she does or is about to do. What we are going to experience, real quick here, you are not to ever doubt the bond we both share for our loved ones. We are all first and foremost a family, is that clear?" Nate spoke up breaking the silence in the room with one simple direct statement. There it was the elephant that had been sitting in the room.

Waiting for the twins to look up at Nate when he spoke, he saw the need of acknowledgement his brother wanted, from the twins, for what he had just said. It made him realize he felt the same way. The depth of love Briksanna shared for them, believing the details of the quest he gleamed from his brothers thoughts, less all the details, was going to try all their endurances. Nate was right to make sure the twins, more so than the others, knew their love was felt by the both of them, but most of all, it was returned as well. This was something he and Nate both knew was important for the twins to believe in because they all were going to need this to be explained vocally because with everything they were about to go through there could be no dissension within the family. All doubts needed to be put to death right here, right now.

Harmony stopped chanting; opened her eyes and studied him for a moment then spoke frankly. "We are the daughters of her heart. We love her today and will continue to love her tomorrow." Looking directly at him completely focused on making sure he understood what she was saying. "Don't ever doubt what we would do or how far we would go in life for the mother of our heart. Now, *Dad,* if you have something else to do, Trinity and I could use the space to make sure all is good here with Momma." Dismissing him she went back to her chanting closing her eyes again facing the woman lying on the bed.

He knew he was hanging by a thread here with the twins emotionally, but they needed to know where things were between him and Bri. He didn't want to have anyone in the family to feel like they were bumped out of place because now they were husband and wife.

Testing the mental shared pathway for the rest of the family, he wasn't surprised to find the rest of the family's energy signature close by. With all the drama in the past couple of hours it was it was a no brainer they were waiting for any word on Bri's status.

Sighing, shifting in his position for the tenth time in a few minutes, staring at the love of his life, he knew he need to get this part over with. Sharing with the family their marital status wasn't the ideal way she would have wanted him to tell the kids about their relationship, but time had run out and they needed to know. His brother was standing sentry by the entry way knowing he was in charge of his domain, yet giving him the space to be the man he needed to be for Bri and the twins as her partner. God, he loved his brother for putting up with his shit for so long. How many times had he whined about wanting her but afraid if he showed her his feelings it would ruin their family dynamics. These past ten years have been more than he had imagined being part of a family could be. Something full and rewarding, scary and frustrating as everyone chomped on the bit with one another, especially during missions. Looking back, the way they interacted with one another was almost comical. They endured and pulled everything off professionally no matter what the odds were stacked against them or who was mad at whom within the family. Unconditional ties were the relationships shared by each member of the family. It was time for him to take the first step in changing the dynamics but not the relationships.

"I have an announcement to make. Seeing as the rest of the team is listening in telepathically I will let you know all at once. The goddess blessed the union of Briksanna and I earlier. We are now husband and wife or as she calls it mates. This is what we both want and what has been in our hearts for a very long time." Looking at Stark he said, *"You knew it and tried to tell me many times, brother, but I guess I was too pigheaded to tell her plain and simple. You were right all along, Stark. Plain and simple was all she ever wanted."*

Before anyone could respond he began to pace around the room. Feeling the hairs on the back of his neck rise, something was wrong. Quickly turning around he looked at Briksanna lying on the bed. All was fine there; Trinity was finished setting up her IV and had switch to checking her vital signs making notes on the notepad she carried around. Harmony was still chanting the healing song, quietly, but had exchanged the bowl for holding her mother's hand.

"Can anyone sense something off here? I hate to keep being the bearer of more craziness, but I feel like there's more going on here than meets the eye." Looking at Stark clearly agitated. *"Tell me what you're feeling big brother?"*

Nodding once Stark took up the leading reins telepathically addressing the group. *"Striker, Gabriella, Kenneth report?"*

"Gabby and I have finished our recon and are headed in now." Kenneth spoke. *"Shall we change directions or continue on meeting up with Striker?"*

"I am in command central, boss. Still running Intel on the earlier request Nate had asked." Striker added, *"Waiting on your command boss."*

"Nate, any changes you want to make to your original instructions for the team?"

"No, continue with the Intel needed for our trip." He calmly responded to the question, but I felt uneasy about the bad feeling in his gut. Maybe it was displaced worry over Bri's present condition. Honestly it could be everything that had happened the past several hours not to mention everything he had learned. Without having the opportunity to lay everything out to the one person he most wanted to, he needed to share what he knew with the next best person. Stark. He needed his big brother right now, like never before.

Telepathically he added, *"I want eyes and ears open everyone. Too much has happened in the past twenty four hours not to pay attention to what is around us at all times. Consider this full alert. I don't know for sure but something feels off to me. Is that clear?"*

"Crystal," they spoke unanimously.

Stark spoke calmly and assuredly knowing the team would protect everyone within. *"Alright boys and girls, back to work all of you. We'll regroup tomorrow, in the command room at twelve p.m. All of us are on watch tonight, two hour intervals. Striker, you and I will have first watch overseeing the perimeter inner and outer. Gabriella and Kenneth you take the second watch and H&T you two will to take the next shift. We will repeat the sequence until we meet tomorrow afternoon. Clear?"*

"Crystal!" Sounding charged they all agreed, mentally, with the mission they were given to protect their home.

He was quick to add again feeling the need to protect his family reminding them of what they needed to do. *"Every time you cycle out of rotation you're to get some sleep. We all need to stay on our toes."*

"Yes Captain," everyone replied.

"One last thing, Briksanna and I will share everything that that has transpired with all of you when we regroup tomorrow. Any questions?"

One by one Nate heard a clear, *No Sir,* from his team. *"Dismissed."*

After everyone mentally signed off, he looked around at those still within the room realizing he and Briksanna never made it to the dining hall to eat. They were right back where they had started a couple of hours ago. Sighing, he shook his head at how ludicrous the situation was, completely worn out emotionally with the evenings events, Nate looked at his older brother. "I need to get out of here for a few minutes. You game in keeping me company?"

Stark nodded not saying a thing just stood there waiting for him to lead the way. Looking back to where his wife laid on their bed he needed reassurance she would be taken care of in his absence even while knowing the twins would cut off their hands before they allowed anything bad happen to her, he just needed to hear the words for some reason.

"Harmony and Trinity, can you keep eye on Bri while Stark and I take a few minutes to get some food?"

Trinity looked up from what she was writing with a slight grin on her lips. "Only if you bring back a couple of sandwiches back for Harmony and I to eat? We're planning on going straight to bed from here once things are settled with Momma."

"Harmony are you good with this?" Making sure both girls were comfortable with him being the person to even question their willingness to stay and protect her.

"Yeah Nate, nothing will get by me and if anything should, by some crazy chance, Trinity, here will knock them down, right twin?"

"Right twin," Trinity responded sounding completely confident with her sisters' abilities as she resumed her writing.

"Ok, Stark and I will be back with the sandwiches." Both men turned to leave the room when Harmony piped up.

"Hey Boss, could you bring your favorite girl here back some chips? You know them barbeque kind you are always telling me to not eat. I could really use a salt fix right about now. Gods know when either one of us will have a chance to eat something like that again."

The last part was said almost to herself but Trinity must have caught it just like the rest of them had and reached across the bed for her sister's hand. "I know you are upset but Momma is just wiped out. She'll be fine, I know it and if I know it then it will be. Especially when it comes to matters of the body. None of us are going to let anything happen to her."

"Yeah, little bit. I'll bring you back the whole bag and a couple of sandwiches to boot." Stark spoke right at both girls knowing they were emotionally hanging on by a thread seeing the only mother they've known, a strong and powerful woman in her own right, weak and defenseless.

To him they looked every bit the nineteen year olds they were, daughters of his heart. He knew Stark felt the same way about them. They had said so to one another over the years.

Wanting to reassure them they were protected even when they were doing the protecting he decided it wouldn't hurt to push a bit vocally on the fatherly side. "We are all a bit tired so Stark and I will hurry up so you two can get some shut eye, ok?"

"Ok." They both replied sounding relieved to have someone take care of the basic needs such as provide food for them.

"We'll be back in a bit. Shout if you need anything or anything looks or sounds off, you let us know. We'll be here in seconds."

"Yeah, *Dad*, we hear ya!" Harmony said grinning as she reached for the bowl, crushing more of her herbs between her fingers releasing a fresh smell of pine in the room. "Go take a break and we'll see you in a bit." She raised her head from her task long enough to wink at him smiling at him effectively letting him know how much she appreciated what he said with words despite her verbal outburst.

Nodding at them, ignoring their sarcasm, not caring that neither one saw him do it, but doing it all the same he led Stark out of the room. He stopped one more time to look at Bri's resting body as he exited the door. He sent her the mental equivalence of a kiss on her right cheek along with his love. Turning around, his brother closed the door behind him effectively cutting off his view of her making his heart lurch while his fear for her safety was still very raw. Stark motioned with his hand to head towards the kitchen. If Stark hadn't closed that door right then he knew he wouldn't have been able to get the space he needed to recharge his dead batteries. There was only so much a man could do before he dropped and right now his older brother reminded him he was going to fall flat on his face.

What could he say, the two girls in there loved Bri as much as he did and knowing Bri, she loved them equally in return. He had been around for the past decade and knew the dedication those three women had for one another. Their love and their respect, but most of all it was the mother daughter relationship they had that scared him the most. With the girls, hell even with Striker, Kenneth and Gabriella, Bri held a place in her heart as mother to the entire Lightning Strike group with the exception of him and Stark.

Over the years, he saw everything she went through to bring Kenneth and Gabriella to the compound when the riots had hit Los Angeles. Both he and his brother were surprised she came back from a recon assignment at a museum telling them she had found two children huddled in the garbage dumpster outside the museum trying to stay warm. She dismissed the assignment calling it a 'silly paying job one they did not need money from' and brought the kids home. No questions asked, just won them over with her unconditional love and patience. All the kids saw her commitment to them as being another part of Bri. The unconditional love was freely given nothing expected in return. They were her children and she loved them, plain and simple.

When Striker joined the group, half a year before Gabriella and Kenneth, we were a little leery of her leaving this lanky surf loving teen with them and the twins. They were unsure of adding more to the family, but she assured the both of them he was meant to be there, end of subject. Striker's parents were killed by one of their assassin rivals, who had never been found by the police or any investigating team from the FBI. Bri believed it was the work of Lord Drakkoon, but we never looked deeply into it. Since no one had contacted or harassed them about it they decided to let it go, fully knowing the idea of an assassin terminating Bri's mission target was taboo in the mercenary field, especially once she had accepted the assignment. Even still they let it go. He always told Bri pay back was a bitch and the jerk who knocked off Stiker's parents would be dealt with in time. For some reason she dropped the subject but he could tell she had already made some sort of mental tally of bad things done by Lord Drakkoon and nothing anyone said was going to get her to take anything off her list once she made up her mind.

Instead of feeding the fears her instincts were driving, Bri went to the site of the crime, under cover as a favor for some government official who knows our team is good to deliver stolen goods, especially stolen lives, to investigate the matter privately. She found Striker hiding on their property in a secret bunker. Who would put a kid in a bunker alone? The world was filled with crazy people who did horrible crimes to kids every day. He couldn't figure out how she was able to find him when no one else had been able to find him. The crime scene had already been cleared by both local and federal authorities. 'By following his emotional anguish telepathically', she told them when she brought the boy home, acting as if it was no big deal to bring home a kid whose parents had been murdered. The kid had been hidden away for four days locked inside, according to Striker, 'for his safety'. This was what his parents had told him. He was fourteen years old when it happened and it was the last time he had spoken to his parents.

Stupid if you ask me, his parents put him in a bunker and told no one of its hidden location effectively locking him inside without showing him how to get out. Active assassins shouldn't be having families and still remain active in the field. Not only is it not good business, but it is unsafe for the family members. Even at fourteen years old, we could tell the kid was not only very intelligent but was a very tall athletic looking young man. He filled out to be the man we had expected him to be and so much more. He couldn't quit put his finger on it, but there was something more the kid wasn't sharing. Maybe he didn't know but something was defiantly bothering him of late. Mental note to self; talk to Striker next time he saw him. Time to figure out what was with the kid, because with the quest hanging over their heads he needed everyone running on full capacity.

They were all good kids deadly in their own right. They raised them that way, the three of them, the best they could. Showed them love and encouragement along the way, with a heaping of patience. Maybe teaching them the art of warfare may not have been what every family in the world did with their children, but for the three of them that was what their way of life required especially since each and every one of them had special abilities. They had to learn how to protect themselves at all costs and in every manner. The world would never accept them, just like he and his brother had never been accepted by their own father. No one in the world could handle people in his family like they had. All of them were better off together doing what they did. Accepting missions form time to time, rescuing the helpless form ruthless killers using ransom to fuel their race for greed.

No one messed with his family and his family didn't mess with anyone. They kept to themselves and he liked it that way. He knew there would come a time when each one of them would find the other half of their soul, like he had with Bri, but until that day came, when they'd turn that responsibility over to their partner, he would die protecting them.

Studying Stark as he followed him through their compound, hearing his stomach rumble he was glad to finally get some food. He remembered what they both had decided years ago when it was just the two of them, brother and brother.

He was eight years old and Stark was ten. Stark told him it was time for them to leave. Even at an early age, when he didn't understand why his brother was telling him they needed to leave, he just knew if Stark said it was time to do something they needed to get it done. Not like we were living under the best conditions as it was, but it was all they both had known up to that point. Stark told him it was better for them if they left that night only bringing what they could carry. He remembered being scared and had asked his brother did they need to leave everything behind? Stark told him their Father had sold them to the bad guys for lots of money because they could do special things. He knew what he meant by special things. Stark could persuade people to do things, reading impressions and emotions from anyone he touched. He had supernatural speed and was able to speak telepathically with his brother. He could run a mile in seconds if he really needed to. The only major drawback in doing all those crazy things were the psychic backslaps. It left them weak and drained, not gaining full strength often for days at a time. If they had waited for their father to make them do one more job for 'The Family', they would have been too drained to defend themselves from the bad guys. Stark was convinced they needed to leave that night in order to save their lives. No more jobs helping out Father. He was glad the day came he never looked back and put his trust in his brother completely.

Their father would pitch to them stealing from business owners, when they closed up for the night, several times a year, gave them enough money to survive on while never being caught for any of the crimes they had committed. They never considered the time living at home as a good life, they were constantly tired, drained and in fear. Looking back he actually thought at the time it was the way it was supposed to be for every kid who was special so they never questioned their fathers' seedy behavior. Father didn't work and we were homeschooled by mother until she died when he had turned eight. That's when Stark knew we didn't have anyone left who cared enough to protect them from their Father's lecherous behavior. With their mother dead their father had gotten worse, constantly blaming them, saying they were the reason she was dead. Never could it have been because he beat her one to many times and as a result she had died from massive internal injuries unattended by a physician because if anyone had examined her they would immediately have known she had been beaten. There would have been too many questions from too many people poking their noses into their lives. No it was to be their fault behind closed doors. Two weeks after Mom had died Stark woke him up to tell him they had to leave right then and there. Thinking back he hadn't known what to do but he had known Stark was the only person left who he could put his trust in aside from his mother.

Stark told him that night, "I trust you with my life, do you trust me?" To which he had responded, "I trust you with my life, forever Stark." His brother simply stared at him with those eerie hazel eyes of his that glowed whenever his power was building and nodded. "Let's go, you and me always, ok?

"Ok," he said. And that was that. They hadn't been apart since. Ever. It was the best decision he had made in his entire life next to loving Bri and their misfit family. Who knew there could be more out there in the great unknown called his future, but who cared. Every forward step he had taken so far had led him true. So far whenever he'd reflect on his life, he'd shake his head knowing he wouldn't be the man he was today or the man he could be tomorrow if he hadn't gone through all of those rotten moments of his life. Those moments shaped him to being the man he was today and he was exactly where he was supposed to be.

He couldn't believe Stark found them their own loft at the age of ten, using his influential touch. They stayed living in that loft until meeting up with Bri almost two decades later. He never questioned Stark, why they had to leave the way they did again. He simply trusted him. Turned out a few years later Stark told him, of his own accord, claiming he was finally old enough to handle the truth about the night they had left their father's house. Stark had overheard their father making a deal with the mafia selling the both of them for fifty grand. Stark figured dear old father had been made out by the cops and needed a nest egg in order to successfully escape from the police. Toting children along wouldn't be convenient for him or easy for him to remain unnoticeable, so he sold the both of them. Too bad the mafia came by as planned and they weren't there. They killed father for the lies alone and they had never been found. Seems Stark had taken father's existing nest egg figuring they were the ones who'd earned and they should be the ones to keep it. The rest was history, he bought them both bus tickets travelling from the east coast to San Francisco, California.

He trusted Stark with his life. It was simple for him to give unconditional love in exchange for trust, only now he extended his trust to more people than just Stark. He trusted their entire family with his life and in return they trusted their lives with him. This was what Stark had meant all those years ago.

"There is something better out there little brother, for the both of us, I just know it. We are going away simply cuz there's something bigger out there for us to do. We were meant to be a part of something greater than to grow up being thieves."

Thinking back on what Stark had said on that bus ride to San Francisco all those years ago, his brother was right, there was something bigger for them to do and now that time had come for him to share with Stark all that he had learned so far, brother to brother. Stark deserved no less than the honesty they've always had and he planned on giving him just that.

Walking into the kitchen heading directly for the fridge he began pulling fixings out for sandwiches while Stark went in search of the chips the twins wanted. A silence came over them as they put the meal together. Packing the girls their food setting it aside they decided to take a few minutes to eat and do a bit of talking. He didn't think he would be able to make it back to the room before eating, he was so hungry.

Plenty of chewing and drinking, he was ready to make a second sandwich before Stark decided to break the silence. "You gonna tell me what's been eating at you since we left the room and I don't mean the acid in your stomach, or do I need to touch you for me to find out?"

"You know me better than that Stark. Touching me is not going to tell you all you need to know and you've got more respect for me than that to start off this conversation with saying something as stupid as that."

"You're right; I'm just so wound up. Tell me." Sighing setting aside his instinct to question him, Stark went back to eating silently, waiting for him to share whatever was on his chest in his own time.

"It would be easier if I started out telling everyone at once, at least this part. Do you think you can link everyone telepathically broadcasting what I need to tell the team then when all is said you and I can talk brother to brother. That work for you?"

"Deal, but you keep your end of the bargain, Nate. I have never seen you so keyed up about anything and that has me worried. Do we have a deal?"

"Deal." Knowing he had made the right decision in speaking with the team he knew by speaking now about what Intel he had, regarding The Prophesy, would better prepare all of them for anything that could potentially come their way. He didn't like not having everyone on the same page. They never kept things that could affect the family a secret. Sure there were personal things everyone kept to themselves, like how he had felt about Bri all these years. Well Stark knew, but no one else did, because he never shared it with anyone else.

Closing his eyes, Stark tuned into his energy and after a few moments he opened his bright glowing eyes, *"Is everyone tuned in?"*

"All tuned," they responded.

"Listen up, Nate would like to fill us in on some Intel, so I am bridging telepathically so he can speak to us at once. You are all to keep your field positions as originally planned with your last confirmed instructions, always, safety first. We expect you to listen to the Intel Nate is going to share and we can have in depth discussions tomorrow when we meet."

"Go ahead little brother you are dialed in." Stark told him.

"Briksanna and I met with a Goddess tonight her name is Merridian. She is our Guardian and a Messenger of the Gods; daughter to the First God. She claims Lord Drakkoon is her twin and he had been sent to the Under Realm by their father, the First God, to bring balance to the universe by overseeing the Under Realm. This realm he oversees houses all the people who have been punished by the Gods; banished from Skaldanna. The Goddess said her father sent Lord Drakkoon there four thousand years ago and during the first two thousand years prosperity and peace had been held within both the Under and Upper Realms. My guess is something happened that either she doesn't know about or hasn't shared, but around the two thousand year mark Lord Drakkoon's actions began to turn dark. She described him as a man who had sacrificed the good in his own self for the balance of the universe.

To hear the Goddess describe her brother I don't doubt she has a great deal of pain she is holding inside, both for her brother and her father. It was hard to see and feel her pain and my empathetic abilities are on the low side, but listen up everyone, the place he had been condemned to oversee is no cake walk either. This son of the First God was sent to a place where, like I said earlier, is a place where every villain in the history of Skaldanna had been sent. There is this sort of parole hearing she called The Awakening where the Gods judge those held in Under Realm for permission to ascend into the Upper Realms of Skaldanna, for a second chance at life. Sort of reincarnation, if that makes sense. When they are first sent to the Under Realm their memories are wiped clean but it takes longer for the emotional trauma to dissipate from the individual so when they first get there Lord Drakkoon would absorb any remaining emotions releasing it into the realm environment essentially feeding their realm the negative energetic emotions. Sometimes those residual emotions were horrific and sometimes they were overwhelmingly depressing; never the less he did what had been asked of him so the people could have a better chance at life the second time around, earning their place of the redeemed. Everyone following my story so far?"

"Yes," they replied.

He continued, *"The Awakening occurs every hundred years, if you ask me, the correct question to ask the Goddess next time we see her is how often the people are sent to the Under Realm for punishment?"*

"Good question, boss what do you think?" asked Kenneth.

Stark was quiet for a minute with his eyes averted for some reason he thought he wasn't going to answer then he did speak. *"The Goddess visited the team in our family room prior to seeing you two"*—he held up his hand stopping him from saying anything until he was done with what he had to say—*"she told us it was important for all of us to support you in what you and Briksanna were going to go through and that all of us are a part of the Skaldannian Princess Prophesy. She also told us what The Prophesy was. She didn't go into detail like she apparently did with you two, but she did let us know she had been watching over each one of us guiding us throughout our lives so that we would be here together in this moment. She did tell us that each of us had been given these talents or gifts for a reason, by the First God himself. She said that each of our talents will gain in strength if not advance possibly branch off into new talents as we walk the path of the quest, whatever that means."*

He rubbed his hand across his eyes but kept them closed while he continued, *"When we asked her what we were to expect, she told us she could not read into the future, telling us what we wanted to know, but she would be there for us, helping to guide each one of us, every step of the way. All of us can get a hold of her by concentrating on her image then mentally calling for her. She promised to come, no matter what. She did tell us that she was heading to you and Briksanna's room to let you know she was here to help guide everyone through the Prophesy. I asked her why she didn't just tell us together instead of splitting the team up and she said there were things that were to be revealed to each member separately as The*

Prophesy progresses. Whatever that meant she wasn't very specific. She, also, said each of us plays a role right up to the fulfillment of The Prophesy and that you two, Nate and Briksanna, are the first to begin some sort of quest. She told us there would need to be a great sacrifice in order to bring forth the instrument of death and that we were all to be strong when that moment came and to trust our love for one another. Again she wasn't very forthcoming with the information other than she would be there for us when the time came."

He spoke then, *"That was where Bri became emotionally upset with the Goddess saying it was too much to ask of her, begging her not to ask this of her. I have never heard Bri beg for anything and I have never felt so much fear rolling off a person as I felt with her in that moment. Whatever she clued in on with the Goddess neither one shared what that sacrifice would be, so when we meet tomorrow that is another question to add to our meeting agenda."*

"Boss, could we wrap this up I need to get another bag of IV fluids for Momma and T and I need to eat before our turn at watch tomorrow," Harmony asked.

"Ok, Striker you and I will meet in ten minutes in the command center. If no one has anything to add then you are to return to your duties as assigned. Nate and I can't stress it enough, when you have free time you are to eat and sleep. We have a rough assignment ahead of us and we are all going to not be in our element so listen up. When you head into your rooms tonight or tomorrow, I want you to pack your gear for extended recon. You know the drill, nothing unnecessary. Twins, that means no beauty care. Gabby and Ken, no extra munitions and Striker no gadgets this is complicated enough plus we are about to all be put through a lot of strain so do what you need to do to get caught up now. Is everyone clear on what I am saying?" The last bit came out forcibly wanting to make his point with his tone of voice.

"Crystal," they shouted telepathically.

A very weak *"Yes"* was faintly heard by everyone.

"Momma!" cried Harmony and Trinity simultaneously while he shouted, "Briksanna!"

"I am well, rest easy everyone. I am very tired and will do as I have been instructed, by my mate and my physician, to sleep for a while and allow myself to heal. I heard all conversations just couldn't respond. Whatever has happened in the realm of Skaldanna is a hundred times worse and much deadlier to all within contact if I were to be rendered helpless here in the Earth realm. Do as Nate and Stark have commanded. Follow their words to the letter and remember; we are a family first and a team second. I am very tired so on this last note I will share with each one of you; I love you. Now rest, prepare and remain alert when needed because here on out everything we think, say or do will affect not only our lives but the lives of our loved ones."

"Dismissed," he spoke sending out the final command.

"Bri; baby remember the scaring ten years of the life off your mate I keep telling you about? You are not going to have anything left of a husband if this shit doesn't let up. I am ready to kill something for the pain you have gone through in the past several hours. Are you really alright?"

"Yes, I love you and No, you can't kill anything and Yes, I am resting and No, I am not hungry. I'm just sleepy. Take your time, Nate. The girls and I are fine for a bit."

"I will be with you very soon. Stay safe, Briksanna, I don't know what I will do if any harm comes to you, but I swear to all above and below not one hair on your head is to be touched or all bets are off. Everything will be hands on from then on." Shaking from the intensity of his emotions, the plates on the table began to vibrate a direct reflection of his emotions and his recently developed telekinesis.

"Peace my mate, eat. Let me sleep. Worry tomorrow," were her last words before shutting off her mental link with him.

He knew she was just drifting off to sleep but with his emotions so close to the surface, it was easy to imagine the worse feeling, the absolute quiet following her absence. He didn't want to feel this way ever. Life without Bri in it would render him an empty shell.

All the kitchenware and cupboards began to rattle around them.

He saw Stark close his eyes taking deep cleansing breaths effectively grounding himself out from holding the telepathic link before opening his eyes to speak up first. "What did you want to tell me that you left out from the team little brother or do you want to play ring toss with our dinnerware?"

He regarded his brother with his sarcasm cutting through his desolate thoughts of life without his wife in it realizing his brother was his best friend and knowing the telekinetic show was going to have to wait another day he reigned in his temper. Slowly letting go of his emotions he settled all the rattling going on around the kitchen. Stark was the first and last person on the planet whom he trusted to keep the information from the others until the right time came up for him to share it. He had to tell someone and Bri was just too drained to be dragged into anymore craziness tonight.

Pushing his empty plate aside he glanced Stark's way and decided right then and there he needed to upend his visit with the seer Vakgdona and the dreams he witnessed with Bri earlier. He had to get her instructions off his chest because the sooner he did, the sooner he wouldn't forget everything she had told him. Stark had amazing memory and so did Striker. Between the two of them they could solve any riddle set before the three of them.

After he told him everything he asked, "What do you think about everything I've shared with you? I plan on telling the others, but I want to know what you think before anyone has a chance delivering their input. Maybe Bri can add some input on this sword story, people had to have known about this story besides the conversation with the seer happened while Bri was still out so not even she knows of this quest we are all supposed to be on."

"I've got several questions about the quest," Stark pointed out looking at Nate with once again clear hazel eyes.

"Like..." Nate replied feeling better that he told his brother first instead of waiting for Bri to wake up.

"First off, who is this Tormentor and why keep this seer in stasis? I mean she sounds important. Sounds like our team is due for some research once we get there tomorrow. Second, what's with the pieces of the sword being scattered along with its jewels? After thousands of years no one would have thought to use the sword sealed with the breath of the First God to fight Lord Drakkoon's tyranny? How come this was kept secret for so long and then why hasn't this Blacksmith's family made a stand instead of keeping quit all this time? We are talking a whole realm out there that has been affected by Lord Drakkoon's terror. You know Nate, speaking of terror, what is it that he has done to everyone? I mean you've told me of her captivity but that was at the hand of her jailor. Who is this Master and what is it that he's doing to Skaldanna? There seems to be a whole lot more questions running around my head if I keep on this track so tell you what? You know me and how I function a whole lot better with some down time. Let me mull this over tonight. You go back to your woman and be there when she wakes up. Man if she were mine we wouldn't be here having this heart to heart. I'd be delivering some of that Angelo charm I keep telling you about." Rubbing a hand down his face he remembered a pair of green eyes that continue to haunt him. "I can't get her out of my head," he whispered.

"Who can't you get out of your head?" He spoke hating to see his brother stoked up over something thinking it was about what he just told him.

"Merridian, and don't you say anything or I will deck you."

He held his hands up defensively grinning, "You won't hear anything from me Bro. My lips are sealed." Bringing his right hand up to his lips he turned his hand mimicking a locked key sealing lips motion.

"I'm not ready to talk about this yet. Let's just say that there is one woman who could settle all this craziness within me. But it's more than that, she made the power inside of me hum and no one has ever done that for me, so yeah, shoot me. I sat up and took notice. You know what little brother for a minute there I could of sworn I felt me, really felt me for the first time in my life and in that one moment nothing else mattered. Not the mission not the kids and not even you. That really freaked me out to not think of you. I must be tired or something to be sharing this mushy shit with you. I have got to get out more."

Understanding exactly what Stark said he grinned raising his eyebrows deciding he would share one more thought with his brother before heading out. "Brother, I feel you on what you're saying. What you just described is exactly how I feel about Bri. When we are alone I swear I can feel her heart beat right along with mine that's how tuned in I am with her and I'm not just talking her body, I 'm talking her. I truly see her and she truly sees me. You feeling what I'm saying big brother?"

Running a hand through his hair sighing looking a bit rough around the edges Stark agreed. "Yes I do."

"Alright, I am pretty exhausted after all we've gone through these past few hours let alone this entire week." Clearing away the dishes they had used stacking them into the stainless steel dishwasher he continued to speak, "I will take dinner to the twins you go on ahead and meet Striker in the command center. Bri and I will be ok. Once I've made sure the twins have eaten I will send them to their quarters to pack and rest before their shift."

"Oh, and Stark, I can't get Bri out of my head too." He said last bit as he walked out of the kitchen weaving through the two long tables set up as their dining area heading out the door towards the direction of their room, leaving Stark to ponder on what he had just said.

"That's what I'm afraid of little brother. That's what I'm afraid of," Stark said out loud to no one but himself not realizing he heard him all the same as they were both still close enough sharing their mental bond as the two brothers they had always been with one another.

Turning the lights off Stark left the kitchen heading up to the command center muttering to himself. "It's going to be a long night, I can feel it."

12

After the twins ate their dinner and left, Nate went into the bathroom taking a quick shower feeling like he needed a few minutes longer to relax under the hot water. He couldn't stop thinking about what *the sacrifice* was supposed to be. He was really worried about the way Bri had reacted when the Goddess had mentioned it. He'd never seen her emotional as she had been in when Merridian spoke of The Prophesy needing a sacrifice. He couldn't get the fear reflected in her eyes out of his head. Bri meant everything to him. This woman was his mate, his life; the one who would be the mother of his children. She meant more to him than the next breath of air. He would do anything to keep the fear from returning to her eyes. He wanted to replace those memories with good ones. He could give her that.

Getting out of the shower he putted around the bathroom hoping the extra time would help further clear the worry he had in his head about *the sacrifice* and Bri's fears, but it didn't. He couldn't shake the feeling he was the key to all of this and that made his stomach clench. What if the sacrifice was a person? Who could it be? She was so upset over it begging Merridian for it to be anything else but this. Bri knows what the sacrifice is to be. She has to otherwise why be upset? He wasn't going to tackle that conversation tonight, but he was going to get to the bottom of it sooner rather than later. There had been enough secrets around his family long enough. He was going to find out what the hell had her so upset one way or another Looking in the mirror seeing the worry still etch on his face he decided he wanted to spend his time with his woman not bring up painful memories but create new ones with her. If there was going to be some heart wrenching shit they were about to face then he wanted to give her beautiful memories of their loving one another for the both of them to hold onto when times got rough.

He left the bathroom looking in on her still sleeping form. IV lines no longer connected her to her nutrition. She always seemed to recoup faster than anyone of them from any injury and this seemed no different. Her metabolism had always been the highest out of all of them. She once explained to him, Stark and the twins over dinner what it meant for her to have a high metabolism. "It is because I come from another realm, time passes slower there than over here. Likewise, my metabolism runs faster here too. It is like this, for every one year in Skaldanna ten years pass on the earth plane. This is why I always have to eat and drink so much. If I do not pay attention to my body's physical needs then my energy will try to compensate and that is not good for anyone."

"What happens when your energy becomes involved?" asked ten year old Trinity, always the scientist.

Looking down at the little girl her expression changed. She became very serious, "My energy will always do what it feels it needs to do in order to protect me. In this case it will take what I need in the form of energy off any living source within a certain radius surrounding me. I had trouble with that when I first came to your realm but quickly mastered keeping my metabolism feed just like all other things in my life."

Her voice dropped noticeably, "If anything should ever happen to me while in this realm and I cannot feed myself, you will have to do it for me. I speak to all of you or your lives could be in danger possibly forfeited if not taken seriously. It is not something I am proud of, but in the type of business we are in, this is the first time in all of my existence I am living with people. The twins were easy to raise but I have a feeling our family will be getting larger and the four of you know me well enough to understand what I am saying."

All heads nodded, "Good then if I should ever ignore what I already know to be my responsibility"—lips twitching looking at the twins again—"I expect the two of you will put me in a time out and make me eat my food like I am supposed to." Giggles erupted around the room and the joking began.

Looking back on that day, Bri had always shown her love for those two girls more than the rest. She had raised them from infancy; he could understand the bond she had with them more than anyone because he felt the same way. They held a key place in her heart even he could tell by the way she was when she was with them. Bri was a proud, wise, strong woman who could also be caring and gentle when needed. She had demonstrated time and time again with all the kids how she could connect with them lovingly, but he needed to know if she could connect with him in the same way?

Looking down at the women of his dreams with her hair spread about the pillow tugged on his heart. The need to run his fingers through her hair while he wrapped himself around her was overwhelming.

Slipping off the towel he had wrapped around his waist he padded closer to the bed. Having already secured the room for the night he pulled the blankets back careful not to wake her. He slipped underneath them holding his breathe not wanting to wake her. He didn't sense any changes in her breathing as he slowly slid closer towards her lifting his arm in the process gently laying his palm on her back never taking his eyes off her face when all of the sudden he froze. "You plan on doing something with that knife you have pointed in my gut Mrs. Angelo or are you just teasing me?"

Opening her eyes it took a few seconds for Bri to recognize who she was staring at but he saw the moment recognition hit her. "I did not know who it was who had grabbed me." She said with a hitch in her breath. She must have noticed they were both without clothes.

"I awoke when the girls where here and told them with all that had happened how I had appreciated their help and just needed more rest. This is Harmony's blade. She said I was much too tired to worry about whose blade it was as long as it was sharp." The last bit she said bighting back a laugh. "Those two worry too much about me," she grinned while placing the blade back under her pillow where her hand had been resting on it earlier.

Not letting her go too far he held her possessively relieved she sounded more herself after a few hours of rest. "I wonder who they get that kind of thinking from?" He said tugging her slightly back towards him, "Come back to me, Bri. I need you right here, right now. I want to show you how much I love you."

Cupping his face with both of her hands she studied his face a few seconds before she replied, "I trust you with not just my heart but my body as well. I trust you to hold me and caress me. I trust you, Nathanial, with all my heart."

He leaned in on those last words and kissed her on the mouth. Circling his arms around her back pulling her closer as the kiss deepened. Consuming were the emotions he felt for her like flames stroked over a fire, he was done. Cooked. Their mouths danced in tune with her hands; reaching, seeking, constantly exploring; setting his inner fire roaring higher. Her hands roamed over his back, chest and legs. She was desperate in her touch like she was just as hot as he was.

Her skin felt like it was burning up. He was a writhing mass of fire while their lips continued to seek relief in the wetness of their mouths. Her hands slide up from his chest to rake through his hair demanding more from him as if she could crawl into his mouth. She was took from their union as much as he was gave. She closed her eyes giving in to the emotions his love his heart demanded of her. She immediately stilled when he moved again.

Pulling back he looked in her eyes noting she looked anxious instead of excited. "What is it?" Nate cautiously asked looking from her mouth back up to her face hoping he had the strength to set aside his raging hormones to bring the warrior he was up to the forefront of his brain.

"You have never mentioned the scars. I know what they look like and they cover my body. I felt my body that had been disfigured so long ago was not worthy of your touch because I want it to be perfect for you. That is why I stilled in your arms," casting her eyes away from him as if she were embarrassed by her admission. "You mean everything to me as much as the children do and I do not want to disappoint you."

Lifting her chin with his hand he looked directly into her eyes, "You are never a disappointment to me. Do you understand me? I want to worship your body right now and am hanging on by a thread Bri. Can you not feel my desire for you in this moment? Your scars are nothing but a part of who you are. They do not define who you are. Do you understand what I'm saying to you? I love you unconditionally." He poured all of his love for her into those last four words in hope he could banish any and all remaining insecurities she held onto about herself.

Without any warning she fisted her hands into his hair pulling him down for a searing kiss. Her kiss was consuming, so full of love she felt it flow from the tips of her toes to the top of her head. Pouring her joy at his proclamation and with it her unconditional love back at him, showing him how he truly was the warrior of her heart.

"I want you right now more than I want to take my next breath, but baby, I want to take this slow."

Peppering his mouth, face and neck with kisses she replied, "I don't want to do slow, I want you right now. I have waited too long for this. I need you Nathanial, I need you now." The last part she said in a growl.

She didn't have to say anything else. It was like something in him snapped when she growled in his ear and then it was his turn to burn up from the inside out. He crawled over her moving his lips from her mouth kissing down her neck and shoulder, pushing the sheets further down the bed granting him better access to her body. He began to make love to her showing her how beautiful she really was, her breasts, her stomach, her legs then back up again, raising the fever of excitement with his touch. Time held no meaning in how long they took exploring one another she just needed his brand on her and hers on him.

Feeling tongue and teeth sent electricity through her veins bringing the energy within the room to a higher vibration. Her eyes began to glow a deep violet something he had never seen before. It was as if the glow was contained within her not expanding out of her like it normally did.

"You are so beautiful. Your eyes are so beautiful when you look at me like that." He whispered in her ear as he slipped partially inside of her for the first time and held still extending his arms so he could look down at her splayed underneath him. "I don't want to hurt you."

"You will not hurt me"—cupping his face—"Nathanial, you are loving me." Speaking from her soul awaiting for his next move she held his gaze and looked for any clue if he did not share the same depth of feelings she held for him.

Watching her intently for any signs of pain he pushed himself further passing through her maidenhead, all the way to the hilt, then stilled once again allowing her to accept all of him. She was so tight it was all she could do not to move knowing he was bunched up ready to spring like an animal in heat with its mate. They were so consumed in the moment she didn't know if she could wait any longer. There was no pain just a need to move. Wrapping her fingers in his hair she pulled him down to her mouth raising her hips up in encouragement.

No need to say more, he was all over her.

She knew she was lost in a sea of emotions once he began to move faster lifting her desire higher and higher. She truly felt like she could not get enough of him. There was a burning sensation in her abdomen, fanning the flames of her desire until she was afraid she would burst from it. She was assaulted with her desire to be one with him. Their lovemaking brokered no room for thought, just the two of them tangled within a storm of feelings they were creating with one another. She was blinded with an old age instinct of her kind to claim him for the mate he was. It was more than she could do to keep her energy at bay.

Grabbing his hair she pulled his mouth close hers breathing some of her life force into him. His mouth crashed down onto hers in a frenzy of need and want. She sealed her half of the mating ritual, allowing Skaldanna's core energy to blend with the essence of her mate as was custom of their kind

Nathanial instinctively drew her breath into his body and fireworks went off in his head. She could see the drive to claim his woman, branding her to him for all time, was becoming more than he could sustain. Pulling away from his mouth seeing the strain in his corded muscles as he continued to hold himself above her while she laid beneath him panting for breath. Fists tight on his arms eyes heavy lidded she saw the need he had to claim her as his mate. His eyes were a bright mesmerizing green capturing her attention. She held her breathe not knowing what to do.

She closed her eyes afraid of what would happen next, knowing her heart was beating a rhythm she did not want to let go of. He had her whole heart given freely in the act of love. Could he do the same for her?

She was afraid to know the answer.

It was time to for him to claim his mate. "Baby, open your eyes fully for me. I want you to see who your chosen mate is, the man who gives the other half of his soul to you freely."

Instinctively reciprocating the passion she had just given him, he leaned close to her mouth taking a deep breath and exhaled his love into her waiting mouth giving her his life force in return. In that moment she knew he loved her for everything she was. There was nothing that could keep their love hidden any longer. Not themselves, any person, or any obstacle. Their love transcended all time. In that moment she discovered no longer would she need to question the depth of his love or what it was he would be willing to sacrifice, not the other way around. This was the lesson of the sacrifice she recognized in his act of reciprocating their energy sealing their kiss with a piece of his soul freely given.

She did not know if she was going to remain alive the pleasure was so intense. She released his arms gripping the sheets for purchase as he pounded into her, screaming his name she let go of the sheets pushing off the mattress claiming his mouth in an effort to seal their life forces wanting to hold onto the moment allowing the strongest source of energy she knew to settle. She had claimed her warrior for the life mate that he was sealing the bargain to love and cherish one another during the act of consummation in its most primal sense.

She had finally claimed her mate. The man she had waited to claim for two thousand years.

Nate pulled away from her mouth roaring her name he was so overcome with emotions when she had kissed him. They were one. He could feel the shift within him. His body was molding itself to be her other half as she thrust her hips up clenching her inner muscles forcing them to milk him while their bodies became slippery from the sweat they were expelling. He yelled her name again pulling her closer lifting her leg up higher giving him better access to drive into her all the while keeping the rhythmic pace of their lovemaking never breaking stride. God, he felt like he was going to explode literally.

She arched fully off the bed head imbedded into the pillow when she screamed his name. He felt her body fly apart in a million pieces sending lightning bolts outside releasing her energy as she came. He followed her over the cliff of climax, yelling her name long and loud.

He held her while their bodies remained intertwined for a while giving their breathing a chance to return to normal. Looking down at her he rubbed several strands of hair out of her face and asked her, "Are you ok? Did I hurt you?"

She smiled slowly staring at him before responding, "Did that feel or sound like I was hurting? Silly man, you have made my millennia"—leaning towards him for a kiss—"I loved every beautiful second of it."

Breaking the kiss he held her closely enjoying the physical closeness. Seeing her cuddled up to him resting her hand protectively over his heart she opened her once again green eyes. She just stared at him and he was in no rush to ask her what was on her mind because he was staring at her beautiful face just the same. "You are everything to me Nathanial." Slowly grinning she smirked at him sounding a bit too confident for his tastes. "I am ready for your pillow talk now."

He laughed out right kissing her soundly on the head squeezing her tight. "Yes woman, you are most deserving of pillow talk. Let me see..."

"This should be interesting, may I go first?"

"By all means"—waving his free hand in a circular motion—"go right on ahead, my lady."

Swatting his hand back down playfully, "The energy exchange we experience did it scare you?"

Rubbing his neck, clearly forgetting what happened earlier. "I figured you had given me the most intense kiss. Fireworks woman, there were explosions going off in my head, so no, I wasn't afraid. I was too caught up in our lovemaking to feel anything else. There was no pain Bri, why do you ask?"

"It is customary for mates, when they first come together, to seal their marital covenant with a mutual exchange of their life force. The purest source is through a kiss and it is not something that happens repetitively;

it is sort of like what I have heard humans call the Wedding Night. Where I come from that is how it is done between mates, we seal our bonds of promise to one another within the privacy of our first lovemaking when we are the closest to being one person. Only once in our lifetimes can we do this with the person we have chosen unless our chosen mate has died and we take another. When this happens the energy core accepts our claim for another mate allowing us to complete the transfer sealing the love of the next chosen mate together. Does this bother you?"

"No, but I'm not Skaldannian, but my seal on the marital covenant has already been made. I choose you. I breathed my promise into you just the same Mrs. Angelo." Kissing her eyes, checks, chin and neck he began to stoke the fire which had just been banked.

Raising her hand pushing on his chest stopping his lovemaking, "Nate I have to tell you something before we continue, please give me a moment longer?" she looked up to him pleadingly.

Sighing Nate eased back to listen wrapping his arms around her, "I'm listening Bri, what is it."

"Women of my realm often get pregnant right away and with this prophesy hanging over our heads I figured we should at least agree on a few things. First, I do not believe in birth control, nor do I believe it could work with my physiology. Second, if I were to become pregnant, where would the child be born and raised? I have come to know your realm as my home. Even though I have spent most of my life in the Earth realm, Skaldanna is my home too and I go there often. But where would our children be safe from all of this turmoil? Our lives will change and I want us to be open about this always. Third, our life spans are different. I am two hundred years old in Skaldanna terms, but in the Earth realm I have been living in this realm for two thousand years. Time passes differently here. For a Skaldannians, we have very long life spans. Katerina and I are the same age yet in her memories she has been alive for only two hundred years where I have memories spanning two thousand. Does this make sense to you?"

"Go on, you sound like there is more," nudging her gently on the shoulder with his hand urging her to continue. "So far none of this bothers me. I love you for who you are. This will all work itself out and doesn't need to be solved today and before you begin; I am not taking this lightly. We have this prophesy to deal with first then us. And Bri, there will always be an *Us*. Do you understand me? I am not going anywhere and neither are you. We will figure this out together."

Turning her head away from him, "I don't want you to think less of me because I am different from you. I want to be worthy of your love not as a person from a different realm but as a woman. I want you to believe me when I tell you, you mean everything to me and as far as my having had a long life; you are the man I have waited for in my long life"—looking back to him—"you are everything to me and have been for a long time now. I have finally put voice to what I have been fighting in my heart for quite some time." Raising her hand to cover his heart again, "You have my forever."

She waited for his response while he continued to study her before he spoke. She laid it out there and was hoping he would understand her worries and talk through anything, but most of all she wanted him to know that no matter what the obstacles were in front of them she had seen him as the other half of her soul, her companion, her mate in every sense of the word on both realms. He understood this. He thought she knew, already, what he was willing to do for her. How far he would go for her? Knowing her insecurities were thousands of years in the making made it a little easier for him to accept her questioning mind but he was not going to waste another second allowing her to keep feeding those insecurities. She needed to know how he saw her in words not just in actions. He understood she needed both, the words and the actions to soothe so many years of doubt. However long it took for her to let go of them, he was willing to be there every step of the way to remind her he was going nowhere.

"Bri, first and foremost you mean everything to me and any children we are blessed to have will not be raised any differently than how we raised the children in our care now. They are good children, Bri, raised in love, honesty and with the gifts they each have they have been raised to believe in themselves. I don't believe for a second the world we live in could have done better than what we've done. If you were to get pregnant right away I would be happy. If you were to get pregnant a couple of years from now I would still be happy. I have faith in the both of us when it comes to parenting. As far as where would you give birth when the time comes, that is completely up to you. I haven't been to Skaldanna; no one has from our family. So my only condition is that if you choose to have the child there, I am with you"—holding his hand up—"hear me out first before you say anything. We are two very strong leaders and I told you ten years ago I would follow your lead. Well in this"—waving his hand back and forth between them—"I will follow your lead. I only ask that we continue not to keep anything from each other no matter how bad it may seem to the other person and that we keep our family together. So if you want to raise our children between both realms, I think it should start with the ones we already have."

"I know there isn't always a happy ending out there Bri, hell for most people it can be very bad, but for us I'd like to hope that we have a chance to have a true happily ever after. That is what I picture for you and I in our lifetime. As far as a long life, no one's life is guaranteed. Not your life, not my life. I want to take the time I have together with you as your mate and spend every minute with you in the present, not constantly worried about the future so much that I lose the ability to live in the moment. If that means right now we're helping out the people of Skaldanna, then so be it. It doesn't matter to me, Bri, as long as I am spending my time with you, I'm happy."

Swinging her arms around his neck he felt complete for the first time in in his life saying those words to her. He realized he needed to hear himself say the words as much as she needed to hear them. He found his home there in her arms.

"Where I go, you go. Where we go, our children go. I will always be true to you. I love you forever Nathanial."

Reaching around he pulled her close and spoke of his love for her until she heard his whispers deep into the night then he did the next best thing, he spent the rest of the night showing her how much he loved her.

13

"Stark, you with me here?" Striker's eyes were drawn down in concentration while he looked genuinely confused. "Briksanna goes to Skaldanna twice a year. Once in November for Samhain and then later in May for Beltane."

"Any changes or deviances to that schedule that you can see? I know you've looked at this stuff sideways, but we have to be missing something. This is all she took with her, you're sure? I don't get it." Running his hand through his hair frustrated at what Striker had told him.

Shaking his head, Striker reminded him, "She only took food and few medical supplies all organic nothing pharmaceutical. Other than it's like I told you; no ammunition, clothing or hardware of any kind is missing from our inventories during the times she left. I double checked our inventory prior to and after each of her trips and the only things I can see missing are staples like flour, salt and spices along with common herbal pain killers like valerian, turmeric, poppy, willow bark and lavender. She didn't even take an antibiotic with her. Nothing comes back into inventory either. Boss, you know if you were going back and forth from home wouldn't you at least bring back mementos or something? Nothing comes back into inventory. I checked, what goes stays gone. I guess Briksanna will have to tell us what she does when she goes later today. She's the only one who knows."

"Ok enough, there is nothing more for you to do on this. I want you to grab something to eat. I'm going to check with Kenneth and Gabriella briefly and then you and I will meet up at the main entrance in twenty for first watch."

He left the command center in Striker's capable hands and headed to the nearest exit. Maybe a few minutes outside will help clear his head. At this point it seemed more like a nightmare to him. Having all of this craziness this close to home was not sitting well with him. Since he left home taking, Nate with him, life had been solid and no one interfered with his family on their home turf. Ever. Stepping outside, Stark was immediately tense. There was too much static electricity in the air. Something he knew from personal experiences over the years with Briksanna to recognize Skaldannian activity when he felt it. Closing his eyes he reached out for Kenneth and Gabriella, worried they may be in need of his help. Nope, they were walking towards the kitchen and Striker was already there. Nate and Briksanna were locked up in their quarters. "What is going on," he mumbled to himself as he turned around to head back the way he came when he heard her voice.

"Help us, please." Came a voice not thirty feet off to his left.

Running towards the sound of her voice he was prepared for anything. Throwing knife in his left hand Glock in his right he was ready for an attack, except for the one thing that had appeared right out of thin air.

The Goddess Merridian and another lady he had never seen before appeared before him. The Goddess smiled in relief then her eyes rolled back in her head as she started to collapse away from her companion when he put on a burst of speed, he didn't know he had, to reach her, picking her up pulling her close to his body cradling her head with his gun hand. She looked so worn out since the few hours when he had last seen her. A sheen of sweat covered her face. She was pale, lips turning blue. She looked like a lady who had just made it out of hell with barely enough time to escape. Escape from what exactly he damn well wanted to know.

Emotions starting to rise near volatile in direct response to her state of being he turned glowing hazel eyes and barked to her companion. "What happened?" When he looked up at the lady first thing he noticed was she was pale, lips turning blue like Merridian's had and she appeared to be hanging on by thread herself just to remain upright.

"I am the Princesses companion, Ellena, sent to her by the First God. I come in peace. We were in Deepsong when we were hit with the most malevolent psychic energy we had ever encountered. She brought us here for safety for she is not well from what from what had happened. We both are not well from it. Please sir, may we seek sanctuary here?"

He nodded towards her looking back at the Goddess afraid to take his eyes off Merridian. Those were the last words she spoke, because there was no other way to describe what happened next, she simply collapsed. He was barely able to catch her with his knife hand.

"Kenneth, I need you stat, north entrance of the compound, you hear me I mean stat. Gabriella and Striker, I want you in the command room. You make sure all eyes are on our home. Nothing gets in and nothing goes out. H and T, I want the infirmary set up to receive two stat. Move everyone!"

One by one they answered their compliance, but he couldn't acknowledge them he was too busy consumed with worry for the Goddess. Kenneth burst through the doors with his Glock in hand looking for the threat.

"Over here, I can't hold them both much longer without hurting them, pick her up"—nodding to Merridian's companion—"and let's get them to the infirmary," he said indicating the Goddess's companion. "We better hurry, whatever happened to them, I'd feel a whole lot better secured in our compound."

Picking up the stranger, Kenneth was keen on his task to retrieve and deliver; until he caught a glimpse of the package he was carrying once they were inside the compound walls. "It's you." He said stopping in his tracks. "Stark, it's her; the lady that was telling me where to go with Gabby when Briksanna found us. She's real," the last part was spoken more to himself than to Stark.

"We can deal with that later, son. Right now we have to get them into the infirmary and make sure this place is secure. Get a move on, now!"

Clearing his head of memories Kenneth heard his command shaking his head as if to physically remove the distracting thoughts. He kept pace alongside him heading to the infirmary where the twins were preparing in emergency response to his earlier distress call.

Entering the room quickly avoiding the handful of carts laden with supplies he noted they had been in the middle of packing their medical supplies for the trip which lead to the assortment of medical packages strewn about the counters. He placed the Goddess on the first bed careful not to jostle her.

Trinity ran over to examine her patient. "Kenneth, put the other person down over there"—indicating with her head to the next bed over—"I want to get a better sense of what is wrong here."

Laying her hands on the Goddess forehead Trinity glanced at him briefly before returning to her task, "What happened?"

"I went outside to check the perimeter one last time and get some fresh air. As I was heading back in I heard a voice asking for help. I went to investigate and saw nothing, when they just appeared out of nowhere. The Goddess looked right at me, smiled then immediately passed out. I had just a second to catch her before she hit the ground"—waving his hand at the other bed—"she didn't even have the energy to catch her let alone keep herself upright. She says she is the Princesses companion and that they were in Deepsong when the same psychic wave of energy that put Briksanna out hit them. They look worse than Briksanna. She kept asking if I would grant them sanctuary. I told her yes and then she passed out."

Looking up from her patient, Trinity walked over to where the stranger was laid and repeated the process. After a couple of minutes she let go. Yelling for Harmony. "Harmony, I need IV set up for both to include a bolus of nutrients we gave Momma. Better yet, double the dose of nutrients for each bolus as they are ten times worse off than Momma was. They have depleted their stores of energy, just like Momma but at this rate their cells aren't regenerating. It's like their life force was ripped out of them by force. I've never seen a living life thread pulse so faintly. We need to hurry; I have a bad feeling about this."

Suddenly unable to stand on her feet Trinity began to list to the left like she was going to fall over, he leaned in and grabbed Trinity by her upper arms. Holding her upright he briskly told her, "You need to rest. Come on sit down over here. You can tell us what needs to be done, but you are going to do the leading while you rest."

Trinity let him lead her to a nearby stool without complaint. A testament on how worn out stabilizing her patients had been on her system. This kid can't take much more in one day and he knew it.

"Kenneth, work with Harmony to get everything set up. You know the drill. Trinity I want you to sit tight and I am bringing the cot over so you can rest while your patients re-charge"—putting up a hand to ward off any complaints—"that is not up for discussion but an order. Do you comply or do I have to babysit you?"

"I hear you, boss. Maybe I will rest for a bit and let them watch over my patients. I just hate how I tire easily. Why do I have this gift if I can't maintain a charge of my own energy? That alone frustrates the mess out of me."

Frustration lit all over her face when she looked up at him from where she sat waiting for his answer. His heart went out for her.

Leaning over he gave her a brief hug, "I don't know sweetheart but you do great things and I don't want you beating yourself up any more than you already have. We all have to conserve as much energy as we can." He kissed the top of her head, "Thanks for saving her, baby." He said quietly wanting to let her know how much her selfless actions were in saving a woman he couldn't keep out of his mind from death.

Leaving Trinity resting against the counter, Stark checked mentally with Gabriella and Striker. *"Striker, are you and Gabriella clear in command?"*

"All clear here boss. Gabby is with me and we have the com. It's quiet both inside and out. Nate and Briksanna are still in their quarters and haven't contacted us for any Intel to the resent events. I assume they are otherwise occupied."

"Watch your tone there Striker this is no drill and yes I agree their energy reads a bit on the occupied side and with Trinity declaring our patients stable, I thought you two could meet us in the infirmary. Set the compound on red alert. I don't want anything approaching us from two clicks out without our knowing it, let alone within the perimeter. Do you read me?"

"Loud and clear," chimed both Gabriella and Striker.

"Set your toys, Striker then bring your sister down so we can all chat as a team."

"Wrapping it up as we speak," Gabriella interjected.

Chancing a glance at Harmony and Kenneth working together while he headed over to the closet to grab a cot, he noticed the serious expressions on their face while they worked. Normally they were nipping at each other about one thing or another. It's was always a challenge having Kenneth and Harmony do the littlest of things like set the table before they got into an argument. He didn't know why but they were oil and vinegar. Trinity and Kenneth act more like biological brother and sister than H and T did. Briksanna made mention a couple of years after she brought Gabriella and Kenneth to the compound, how close they had become. He and Nate were waiting for Harmony and Gabriella to explode, but it never happened. For some reason those two seemed to not speak about it directly to one another except for the teasing.

The teasing would sometimes go on for hours. Never getting too far out of hand, but not letting up either. He knew firsthand how much Trinity's relationship with Kenneth had hurt Harmony. He didn't know how she hid the pain from her other half, but she did and had kept it that way all these years.

One night, several years ago, he caught her outside looking up at the stars crying. Harmony never cried, at least he'd never seen her cry until that moment. He sat down next to her eventually lying beside her looking up at the same stars she had been watching waiting for her to say whatever it was that had her so upset. She told him how much she just wanted it to be the five of them again and that even though she understood with her mind, sometimes her heart hurt because now she had to share her sister. She went on to say it wasn't so much as having more kids around when there hadn't been anyone their age before, it was the fact that Trinity, her twin, liked having them around to talk to as much as she liked talking to her. At that statement he had to hug her. In his eyes all he could see was the little tyke she used to be and here he was holding a gangly teenager in his arms under the moonlight while she poured her heart out crying in his arms. Got him thinking about his relationship with Nate. How much Harmony reminded him of himself. How sacrificing for the other sibling was what he had done so the other sibling could have a fuller life despite the hardship. In that moment he understood her pain and tilted her chin up so she could look him in the eyes.

"You are very important to Trinity. I know she loves you not just up here, but in here"—he pointed from her head to her heart.—"you came first in her life and will always be a part of her life. Things just shifted a bit, but one thing never shifts out of a person's life and that is the relationship of a sibling. Nate and I know this without ever having to think about it. It took me awhile to come to grips with that when we were growing up, but now I don't ever have to question it. We will be loyal to one another to the grave as I suspect you and Trinity will be when you get older."

No longer crying, Harmony thought about what he had just told her then looked back at him saying, "I'll have your word that no one will know how weak I became by crying here?"

Grin starting to spread across his face because she sounded so much like Briksanna, "You have my word little tyke. No one will know from me we had this conversation. This is just between the two of us, unless you say otherwise, deal?"

Relief flashed on her face as she broke out into her own grin, "You know you are the only father figure Trinity and I have ever known besides Nate. Is it ok if between us, I call you Dad?"

Suddenly very still he stared into her eyes and prayed to God that his powers didn't kick in betraying what he knew was one of those important moments a person never forgets about in their entire life. This was that moment for him and Harmony.

She began to look nervous; the smile that moments ago lit up her face began to disappear. "If you don't want to I understand. It was a dumb..."

Putting his hand over mouth to silence her, "You are the daughter of my heart. I would be most honored for you to call me Dad on one condition."

Nodding her head he could hear a muffled voice when she spoke into his hand. "Yes"

"I get the honor of calling you daughter."

Her eyes immediately filled with tears, spilling over running down her face. He moved his hand allowing better access to give her a hug. She grabbed him around the neck so tight, he thought this little bit of a thing was going to choke the stuffing out of him but he would never tell her that so he kept on hugging her as long as she needed it.

By sharing her fears with him he thought from that moment on Harmony was able to compartmentalize her fear of losing Trinity, someplace where no one could see it, not even herself. He could totally relate to how she felt and her love for Trinity. He always had and always would. She held a special place in his heart

Walking back to where Trinity sat on the stool slumped over the counter, he proceeded to set up a place for her to sleep while Kenneth and Harmony finished setting bags of nutrition and fluid for their new guests. Striker and Gabby entered the room with some blankets and snacks. Setting the snacks on the counter they both proceeded to make up the remaining two beds in the infirmary so no one would ever have to be alone with the patients. Made sense, seemed efficient seeing there were only six of them and two would always have to be on duty to monitor the patients and the ones sleeping while two were on patrol.

"Listen up everyone; I want two people up at all times here in the infirmary until I say otherwise, which means two will be able to sleep, while two will be on patrol. Striker you and I have the first watch, Kenneth and Gabriella you have the second watch and H and T you have the third watch. Gabriella, I want you and your brother here watching the patients while the twins get some shut eye. I want eyes, ears and minds open. Keep your wits about you and no one is to leave the compound building let alone the premises period. Is that understood?"

Various heads nodded while he continued on, "Nate and Briksanna are not to be disturbed tonight. Remember what the Goddess said, this is about them and I want more than anything to give my baby brother the chance to be happy if only for a little while. So we are going to run this campaign from here with just us involved until those two poke their heads out of the room. Understood?"

Again, various heads nodded. He looked around for any objection and when he didn't find any he continued. "H and T, you are to get some rest first. You both have put out a lot of energy healing Briksanna and now these two patients. I have a feeling we are going to need your special abilities where all this is heading tomorrow. I want all of you to drink one bottle of water before you get some shut eye and grab a snack off the counter while you're at it. Remember to hydrate and keep the calories coming. We all know we tend to give off more energy than the average human so keep up with yourselves while we are going through this."

Looking around at each of their faces making sure they were really hearing him, he wanted to get his point across. "You are all responsible for not just yourselves but that of the person next to you, and the one next to that person. We are a family and family watches out for each other. So if I mess up you guys can let me know. If you mess up, you can count on it I'm going tell you about it. Understood?"

"Crystal," they spoke unanimously.

"Trinity, how long do you think our patients will be out of commission and what are they going to need while you sleep?"

Easing down off her stool Trinity glanced at each of the patients with that faraway look in her eyes before she replied. Everyone knew to give Trinity some room to formulate her opinion on any health related question. "Anywhere from eight to twelve hours, maybe longer. Stark, they both were severely drained of their life's energy more so than I have ever seen Momma's drop. When I tried to access the source of the drain in hopes of better treating the problem, it appeared as if something had ripped it out of them. I know that makes no sense, since we are humans but all of us in here is familiar with who and what is a Skaldannian."

"Can you be more specific, T? I didn't see any defensive wounds setting up her IV. Did you Kenneth?" asked Harmony.

"No, I never would have guessed they were assaulted by their appearance alone." Kenneth responded frowning as he thought about it.

"Think about it, everyone, that psychic wave Momma felt in this realm was intense enough that it zapped all of her energy. Remember the incident occurred on Skaldanna, but it attacked her in this realm. I know she was tired and on her way to the kitchen to eat when it happened, but think. Momma is tied to Skaldanna not just a person from their realm but literally tied to it. She explained it to us once as if something were to ever catastrophically happen on Skaldanna, she would feel it psychically here because her life's energy is tied to the land as well as the people. That is why she has to go back twice a year to ground herself out energetically during Beltane and Samhain. It takes only a few hours there for her to achieve that then she has a meal with Aunt Katerina then heads back."

Looking around at all the astonished faces he noticed Harmony's and Trinity's faces were the only ones who weren't surprised.

Harmony spoke up first, "Didn't you all know what Momma did when she went over to the other side? Trinity and I had to learn from an early age not to move when she left or we would be without a parent if we did, because the bad man could find her if she didn't give back to the land all the energy she stored up. Trinity and I asked her what happened to the land when she gave her energy back, she said the land soaked it up and was grateful. Later on when we got older she told us of how the gardens always produced abundantly and that the wells never dried up, like they were usually prone to because of her generosity in giving energy she had stored up while living here in the Earth realm. See Momma wasn't ever not to be on Skaldanna. It is Momma's choice so she doesn't have to fight the bad man starting another war on her homeland, so she fled to our realm."

Trinity picked up the story from there, "Skaldanna must always have a ruling monarch for the realms to remain habitable for the people and for the land. So she has to go back and give enough energy to sustain the land. What she found out is that the energy here on Earth is much more energetic, running on a higher frequency. That's why her metabolism runs faster here and so does time in comparison with Skaldanna. By giving back the energy she has acquired here on Earth she is able to feed their realm tenfold, kind of like a virus. She explained it once, what it looked like to give back her energy. She said it was like a great wind for a period of two hours as she gave her energy to the land. This wind would pick up the energy and carry it in the air spreading her gift like a giant wave of the sweetest nectar feeding all living things tied to Skaldanna, giving reason for Skaldanna to want to give back in its spoils; sometimes they see it in the crops where the food grows or in the lakes where the fish are, or in the livestock where their numbers never seem to dwindle, thus sustaining hope throughout all the land."

"Who watches her realm while she is here?" Kenneth asked her quietly.

"Uncle Fenrir. Trinity and I used to tease him through Momma's mental link when we were younger. He would help bridge a link to us through Momma when we were real little so he could keep an eye on us while she was there giving back to the land. Personally I like Uncle Fenrir. It always seems like a holiday for Trinity and I to talk to Uncle Fenrir or Aunt Katerina during those times because we couldn't any other time of the year. We both have never seen either Uncle Fenrir or Aunt Katerina because we weren't allowed to cross over. Momma said it was too dangerous for us to do that and we would have to wait until we were older."

"You mean a human can travel to Skaldanna?" Striker chimed in clearly interested.

Looking at all the stupefied faces, Trinity tried to hide her laughter, "Duh, yeah. What is wrong with all of you? Haven't you heard the bedtime story from Momma?"

Heads shaking no all around, he noticed Trinity getting nervous by the way she began to fidget with the ends of her sweatshirt sleeves. Maybe judging her family a bit too carelessly with her last comment was not the way to go.

"I'm sorry, it must be because Harmony and I have been with Momma since we were babies and maybe she did what she had to in order to keep us safe without risking her realm in doing so, trying not to start a war inviting the bad man to play war with her. I don't know why she didn't tell you."

Looking a bit uncomfortable and sad Harmony looked up, "I'm sorry Stark. I know how much you hate having secrets within the family and this must have been a blow to you. Trinity and I would be more than happy to relay any information we already know with all of you. We just never thought about it and we're taught from the cradle never to speak about this to anyone. Having a mom in our life was dependent on our keeping this a secret. We assumed all along that if Momma allowed all of you into our family that you too were keeping her life on Skaldanna and all that she had sacrificed a secret too. That's why we never spoke about it with you, we thought it was a given."

"Tomorrow, we will go over this as a group, no more missing pieces to the puzzle. We know all or we don't step foot and help. I will be damned if my children are going to be put at risk for some realm we had no idea we could be a part of let alone know details about any war if we did step foot on it." Wiping his hand down his face he kept his eyes closed and counted to ten, while he reigned in his swirling emotions. He did not want to explode at everyone unintentionally. "If we are all done here for now, Trinity what will Gabriella and Kenneth need for infirmary duty?"

"Two more bags, each, nutrition and IV fluids," yawning sleepily, Trinity responded padding slowly to her cot. Abruptly looking very awake and in control she spoke to all in the room, "I will go to sleep on one condition. If anyone needs medical assistance, you are to wake me up immediately. Is that understood?"

Stark nodded with a slight grin on his face as the rest of the team assured her they would wake her if she was needed. Harmony on the other hand went to the counter retrieving two waters and snacks for the both of them, talking Trinity into drinking her water before passing out. Gabriella and Kenneth both checked on their patients and were talking quietly from a vantage point within the room to keep watch over everyone as well as the only entrance he and Striker were about to head out of. Feeling secure the Goddess and his family were going to be taken care of he signaled Striker that it was time to head out. It was time for him to do his job and keep watch over his family.

"This has been one hell of a long night." he mumbled striding behind Striker.

14

Sending out the mental command; he let everyone know, *"There is to be a meeting in the family room beginning in one hour. Everyone is to have their bags packed and since the perimeter has been quiet since last night for the duration of the meeting we're going to rely on Striker's toys to alert us of any additional unexpected visitors whom I have recently learned we are now housing. I have faith in Striker's talent with gadgets so not to worry everyone, we are safe. Bri and I are up and about, currently dinning in the kitchen, extremely hungry from last night's activities no doubt."* Giggles erupted mentally all around, *"All right boys and girls let's get serious, we are all looking forward to our round table discussion so saddle up. Do what you need to do to prepare. No weapons, no gadgets of any kind. We will go over specifics during our meeting. Understood?"*

Acknowledgements were heard from everyone through the family mental link. Using a private channel with his brother, Stark told them to meet him in the infirmary. He had some information to share with him privately prior to their meeting.

"You ready to do this?" Nate asked worried about what he hadn't shared with Briksanna about the seer Vakgdona. She wasn't going to probe him about details counting on him to reveal them to her.

"I am." Blushing she moved the hair out of her face as she had yet to put it in a braid. Flustered from their lovemaking and the closeness she had yet to figure out how to be around Nate outside of their bedroom, so she hurried with cleaning their dishes in the sink and turned around to face Nathanial. "I had hoped we could talk privately about what I have been thinking with regards to all that has happened prior to our meeting with the team."

Looking at him closely trying to judge just what to tell him she realized how difficult it had been all those years keeping her secrets to herself. Outside of the twins she had always kept her knowledge of her role on Skaldanna to herself. Afraid of involving anyone in her dangerous life she loved Nathanial too much to keep anything from him one more second.

"I wanted to share with you what it is I do on Skaldanna when I leave and why. It is important to me that you hear me out fully before you ask any questions."

"I'm all yours babe." Sliding closer to her but standing enough out of her way to give her the space she needed in order to feel comfortable. Clearly it must be bothering her enough to make her visibly nervous. How absurd it was the way she was behaving? She never fidgeted, but the way she was twisting the dish towel right now mimicked how she felt inside.

"Bri, whatever it is you have to tell me you can trust me. I am your other half and being that person means your comfort is a priority to me. Whatever it is that has you twisted in knots you can share with me so I can help you here. Do you trust me?"

"Absolutely."

She let out a breath she wasn't aware she held closed her eyes and regained her composure only to open them again. This was Nathanial, her honorable warrior. The man she had taken to mate. She knew he was right in telling her to believe in their trust. As a Skaldannian she knew her bond with her mate was impenetrable. She remembered her parents and how they ruled of all the realms with utter calm, resolution and grace. They loved each other never keeping anything from one other carefully listening to their advisors but never making a decision without consulting one another. Their relationship as King and Queen was admirable to all who witnessed it. Their relationship was what she had dreamt for herself years ago.

"Let us sit for a moment so I can share what I want to say with you." Walking back to the dining table she sat across from him.

"When I was a young girl I was a princess but more than that, I was a sister, a daughter, a friend and soon to be a betrothed to the prince of the Second Realm." Looking up to see his reaction she knew he was absorbing everything as his posture had stiffened. She could see his knuckles growing tighter in his right palm as he squeezed his fist closed. Continuing on not feeling too concerned with his immediate reaction.

"Our marriage was a planned marriage. Our parents believed an alliance between both realms would strengthen the people's belief of my father's rule within all realms on Skaldanna and would secure future heirs from our family in the future."

"What is the ruling status of the person you were to be engaged with have to do with you? I mean you were all equals, right? He was royalty, you were royalty. Why the need for an alliance if there was existing peace within your lands?"

Shaking her head slightly, "It was different. My father was the High King, meaning he was the ruler over all the realms and with that status he had the role as overseer of the entire realm of Skaldanna. He maintained all the energies that supported each individual realm. Energy is what supports life on Skaldanna. It has always existed and its balance is maintained by one bloodline, that of the High King & Queen. The collected energies from all realms support plant growth, animals, water and all living beings within it above and below. Energy is the essence of Skaldanna and my father was the High King. The responsibility of maintaining the balance of energies within all of Skaldanna can only come from someone powerful enough to withstand its flow."

Opening her hand she allowed a little bit of energy to build within her palm allowing the energy to fold on itself over and over again until it formed the shape of a purple ball. Holding her palm a little higher she gave the glowing ball a mental push and it floated slowly over to him.

"Can I touch it?" Trying to keep the little boy wonder out of his voice Nate reached out to touch the flying purple orb.

"Yes, but be careful not to close your hand. Human energy and the energy I expel are different and I have never known the true particulars other than the Human body cannot withstand the force in which Skaldannian energy flows. Closing your palm would be the correct course of action when wanting to reabsorb the energy effectively extinguishing the light."

Looking at Nathanial study the purple ball of light in the palm of his hand reminded her of her sister. The way she would laugh at their antics when they were alone in their rooms playing with their energy. No matter how much time had passed the sharp reminder of her betrothed's betrayal cutting down such a beautiful life brought a painful reminder of all that was at stake with her return. It was then she realized she had never felt such passion for another person, not even for the children. Their love was strong and unbreakable but the feelings for Nate ran deeper, straight to her soul intertwining with her own life force. He was her other half.

This moment was her defining moment. How she would make her choices from this point forward were entirely up to her and would effect not just herself as in the past two thousand years but that of everyone around her she loved. He was an integral part of her being now. Like the air she breathed. Life would cease to exist without him in it. She did not want to let go of Nathanial, but knowing what the Merridian meant she needed to do was to have trust in what fate had been prophesized of her long ago. She had to believe not only in the people around her or in her future, or the person beside her but she would have to believe in herself. That was something she had not realized she had done while hiding from Lord Drakkoon. She had only managed to hide from herself.

"Did you hear what I just said?"

She imagined her thoughts of the past had pulled her away from their conversation visibly showing her emotions on her face. It must have looked like every drop of emotion had given her a different expression.

"Where were you a minute ago?" He inquired without anger gently moving his hand towards her, pushing the ball of light back towards smiling at his actions.

Closing her palm essentially willing her body to reabsorb the energy, she looked back up at him. His face did not show censure but compassion the way his eyes melted with understanding. He smiled at her as he squeezed his palm over hers gently patting it signaling he appreciated the display of energy as well as encouraging her to continue with what she wanted to say.

Smiling back at him thanking him with that single gesture and his understanding did her in. She would hold nothing back from him ever.

"With energy a person can heal, grow, move objects or substance and even use energy to help create. I noticed similar uses of energy in the twins. Each girl can use her energy in the same manner as my father could. That is what I am trying to explain and maybe not doing a good job of it."

Fiddling with the napkin in front of her, she seemed so lost. She wanted to crawl over the table and climb into his lap put her arms around him despite knowing it was not the time for comfort. If she did she would never want him to let her go and she had a bad feeling that everything was starting to head in a direction of being lost.

Reaching across the table he laid his hand on hers, stilling her fidgeting fingers. Startled out of her panicking thoughts she looked up. Green eyes instantly captured her attention. Her love was mirrored in his eyes, reflecting the depth of his commitment to her. In that moment she knew with him all could be accomplished, even the happily ever after. She just had to believe in herself.

He smiled revealing deep dimples. Her heart stopped completely. This man, this warrior was completely dedicated to her. How could this be? What had she done to deserve this? She was drawn to his dedication, attracted to his cocky attitude, his strength and prowess in battle, whether in guerilla warfare or single target missions. How could he be so committed to a single person forever? Could he be that committed to her? Feeling so out of depth, she tried to think of any relationships she knew of comparing them to what she felt existed between her and Nate. Her mentor and champion had been her father but those were only memories to draw upon for reference. Frankly after two thousand years some memories were very distant. Nothing concrete or recent to compare to, she had avoided relationships at all costs, throughout the millennia, with the exception of the twins coming into her life. She had always kept everything and everyone at a distance.

Staring at Nathanial knowing the feelings he inspired within her were so intense she felt like she could go up in flames all the time. She felt the flush of attraction color her face, making how much he affected her obvious. Quickly averting her eyes from his beautiful face, she looked back down at her hands, wondering if they really needed to meet everyone or was there enough time for her to explore this feminine side of herself that wants to share her body with the sexiest man she has ever laid eyes upon.

"If you keep up with those thoughts I'll have you on this table under me and where will that leave us when the family comes looking, because I guarantee once I get you there we're not doing a damn thing for anyone." Confidently he grinned winking at her with a hidden promise of intent.

"Oh, my." Was all she could say forgetting he could read her mind. She pulled her hands from his grasp, took a deep breath, and continued on with what needed to be said. They were running out of time.

"Trinity can heal the living body. Harmony can heal the earth; even create new growth by coaxing life to begin anew. Gabriella can shift, but I haven't seen her yet, however I can smell the energy signature of a shifter growing strong within her. It is almost time for her to change; this is what makes her such a chameleon in the field. Kenneth is stealth and skill at everything he sees, he memorizes everything. His hearing is that of Vampires. He too will shift soon just like his sister. Striker is faster at strategy more so than anyone I have ever known and his gadgets coupled with the ability to surprise the enemy astounds me, not to mention his telekinesis is getting stronger. There is more there but it is as if it is lying dormant, not even I can figure out what it really is. Stark can pull energy and channel it into something powerful and yet beautiful. He is a very strong conduit for energy. He would have been made General of my father's armies and most loyal confidant, this I do not doubt. I may have brought us all together but it is he who is the glue holding us.

Then there is you. You have such speed for a human that there have been times when even I cannot track you and I am good at that! You are the surest person I know running a click per second, I blink and your there suspended from any surface I have seen so far. What you can do with your hands and feet completely defies my understanding yet remains absolutely incredible. To be able to wrap your energy around any surface molding yourself to that frequency, as if you are physically apart of it, is amazing. I would not be surprised if you begin to walk through walls. I do not want to figure out why we can do what each of us can do, I just accept everyone as they are."

"And this bothers you?" Frowning he held a wounded expression on his face like she had offended him with her assessment.

Wanting to assure him she would never be ashamed of her family. "Quite the opposite in fact, all of these abilities within Skaldanna are only found within a royal bloodline. Never all within one family, but the High King would have the potential to house more than, let's say four abilities, in a given lifetime residing during his or her reign. And that is the most abilities the royal family has ever had in our history. Some family members may be stronger than say brother and sister who share the same ability. The brother may be stronger in wielding an ability than the sister, but with the High King or Queen, he is master of all four abilities. The High Royal family does not have, collectively, more abilities than the four mentioned, including the High King."

"Skaldannian's live hundreds of years. We do not recognize children being in their prime until they reach their thirtieth year. My father was two hundred years old when he was murdered. He and my mother only had 150 years together. It was the eve of his two hundredth birthday that my royal engagement was to be announced. The wedding was to occur two months hence the announcement. Our family contains all the abilities of Skaldanna and more with the exception of Fenrir."

"Fenrir? Who is Fenrir?" Still sitting at attention holding her hand she noticed he squeezed it a bit tighter at the mention of another man in her life.

"Fenrir is my acting regent while I am here and one of my most trusted friends. He has been invaluable to my kingdom and to me all of the years I have resided on Earth. I could not have separated myself from the twins if it was not for Fenrir's active role linking him telepathically to guard the children. Albeit I think the correct word to use is entertain the children. Fenrir is a prince of his own realm but not that of Skaldanna"— holding her hand up to ward off questions from Nate—"suffice it to say, for now I trust Fenrir with the lives of my children. We can talk about the particulars of his existence later."

Smiling now at her aggressiveness, but still feeling uneasy about Fenrir he let it go. "I like it when you get all bossy with me. It turns me on," wiggling his eyebrows.

"There is so much to share with you, Nathanial. I feel like there is not enough time to get to know you with saving the realm hanging over my head." Sounding exasperated she looked desperately to him for support. Wanting him to wrap her up in his arms filling her heart and mind with warmth and security was becoming harder and harder to deny. She realized she not only needed him to hold her, she wanted it more than she had imagined she ever would with another person.

Tugging on her hands pulling her around the table she sat in his lap. "Don't borrow trouble from tomorrow, lady. I believe there is a reason for all of this. You, the kids, hell even Stark and I. In the end we will do what is right and what is expected to get the job done regardless of who we piss off or how much it hurts. No one is immortal, Bri, there is no avoiding death. We just accept it and move forward meanwhile I will enjoy every second I have been given with you. By my side, enduring all that is put before us. Do you read me lady? I love you and with that love is my unconditional support and understanding."

"Is this mixed family of ours a bad thing, I mean you make it sound like we are all freaks or something because we aren't royalty?" Brows beginning to furrow he looked agitated over what he had vocalized.

Grabbing his hand she glimpsed at the wounded expression on his face, just before he closed off his emotions from her. She had put that expression on his face. She had put that seed of doubt in his mind that caused him to close off his feelings from her.

Not acceptable. She was not going to let him go another minute thinking she viewed any of them that way. It was really quite the opposite.

"It is not that I have considered you freaks, Nathanial. I want to say I consider you family and for all of you to have been born from separate family lines it is unheard of from where I come from. We on Skaldanna only see this kind of power from the royal lines. I love you Nathanial and I really need you to understand what I am sharing with you. It is a deep concern of mine but not a thought I would keep from you. I believe this is very significant information we must share with the rest of the team before we depart."

Considering what she had just confided and how much Bri wanted him to understand her, he thought for a minute staring into her beautiful violet green eyes. Lost in a moment of utter wonder, he knew she was right. Their family was different. Always had been close, like true blood siblings even after a short while of living together. That was what he and Stark had always talked about being the best part about choosing to make this home. They were all tighter than any unit they had ever known. They didn't worry about anyone's back it was understood it would be covered by the person next to you. They were all covered whether on assignment or off. Yeah he noticed all those things she had pointed out knowing he had to say something to her was a no brainer. Bri was his world and what she believed he believed as long as they were honest with one another enough to listen, never acting without full consent from one another then he was all good.

Mind made up he leaned forward and kissed her startling her from her thoughts for a moment until he felt her arms wrap around his neck. He deepened the kiss pouring his love and reassurances of his solidarity with what she had just shared. He was on board one hundred and fifty percent.

Pulling back knowing they had somewhere to be, "I believe you and I believe in our family. There is no team I would rather be working with and no relationship I would rather be in than with you and our family. We all belong together and I believe this prophesy is our next assignment. On that note we need to head them up and move them out."

Kissing her again lightly before releasing her, Nate spanked her on the butt to get her moving. He was watching it closely. She could feel his emotions go from his head to his groin in two seconds flat. He wanted her again. Right now, on the table, on the counter, against the wall. His need to touch her was eating him alive.

"Mate I would watch what you do with that hand of yours at all times, because if you were to continue with that train of thought I would be forced to evade your company for several days as seems a proper punishment for touching me so." Climbing off of his lap trying to keep a serious look on her face he saw her almost break her concentration giving into the laughter that had threatened to bubble out of her. That was when she noticed he still sat in the same spot and had not commented on her last statement.

"What is it?" He caught the wariness from her tone.

Playfulness forgotten, "I forgot to tell you I had a visit from the seer Vakgdona last night while you were sleeping. She explained what we would need to do in order to free Skaldanna from the grips of this prophesy."

"How? I mean she has been missing since The Prophesy was first foretold. I was there when she first spoke to my father. I was in the room. Nathanial, I have never forgotten her or the mystery surrounding her disappearance."

"She said she had been captured by the Tormentor and put into stasis, but was been able to see everything that had happened with Skaldanna and with you over the years."

"She's alive?" She blanched at what he just said looking like her legs were about to give out. She held her ground by gripping a chair to steady herself.

"Did you just say Tormentor?" Turning away from him plopping in the very chair she held onto, she put her head down on the table for a moment in a gesture of defeat laying there no doubt trying to collect her thoughts she believed had been buried long ago.

He knew she never wanted to relieve that hellish torture again in her mind just like he knew she would never wish it upon another living soul. Being tortured then learning it was by the hand of the one person you were grieving a loss of future with was utter betrayal in her mind and in his too.

"*Yes,*" he spoke to her telepathically knowing she was beginning to crumple. How she could hold herself together with all of her fears evident in just a few moments, made him proud. For her to work so hard to bury them deep within herself so no one knew the horrors she had felt and experienced when they haunt her to this day amazed him. This was his woman and he was proud of her. Whatever she needed, to get a handle on this, he would give her all the time in the world to work out. By her side he would be her strength when she felt week. He wanted to be her champion if she would only let him.

With her back turned he saw her take deep even breathes waiting for the reasonable response she would give to explain her actions. She knew he had been inside her head but did she know how much those memories still haunted her? She had to let him know verbally, he knew this was the only way for her to let go of the chains her torture still held around her. No more secrets. No more wasted time between them. He was right, this was the only way they were going to be able to defeat the threat to Skaldanna and fulfill The Prophesy.

"Nathanial, my nightmares, you've been in my head. You have seen what I have experienced, yes?"

"Yes," he answered her quietly.

Turning around she spoke to him out loud. "The Tormentor, was my betrothed. He was overtaken by The Master. Killed many people within his own realm for no reason other than to destroy and prove a position of power on behalf of Lord Drakkoon. He killed my family, my father's entire personal bodyguard. He captured and tormented me for three months daily. The name Tormentor is the name I gave him. She had to of been watching me to know that name."

Wondering if she was more upset about the fact someone witnessed what had happened to her or if she was worried someone else had been tortured by the Tormentor too. Likely the latter.

"Oh, thank the Gods she is still alive. Did she say how we can reach her or where to find her? We have to hurry now there is so much to do." She spoke out loud, but he knew she was really talking to herself not really realizing what the most important question should be was.

"Bri, what a minute, she told me what we would have to do. I need to tell you. Besides when she came to me she was more apparition than a breathing person. She is still in stasis. The same energy drain you felt helped her to break through and contact you since her capture. You need to hear what she said then we need to share it with the team. We take this one step at a time, together, with the family, Okay?"

Getting up from where he was sitting he stepped closer to her, stretched his arms around her shoulders and offered the best assurance he could manage without letting his own anger show. Scaring his woman two thousand years later, really? Made him want to hunt up the spirit of the Tormentor in the afterlife, bring him back to solid form then kill him again, slower, much slower and he'd make sure there was a lot more screaming involved. Yeah, make his woman upset. Shit, we could repeat the whole damn process over and over, he didn't care as long as the guy suffered as his woman had, then maybe he'd feel a little better.

"It will all work itself out. Try not to borrow trouble, baby. I am not going anywhere and neither is the rest of our family"—pulling back so she could look into his eyes—"we are one family. Our own royal bloodline and there is nothing out there in the big bad world that can break that. Maybe what you need to be focusing on is the future and only remember the past when you need to. Don't dwell there. There is nothing you need by going there in your mind. Haven't you ever heard of the phrase, 'Been there, done that and don't need to do it again?' Well that's you, sweetheart. You can mentally move forward and anytime you feel like you are stuck in a way of thinking, then you can remember the thought. You not only have me but our royal family beside you, all around you. We will hold you up when you feel down."

He could sense part of her still wanted to run and hide because that one word, Tormentor, had more power over her deepest fears for so long more than anything he had ever seen. He could feel parts of her felt charged and battle ready to cross over into Skaldanna with her family by her side, yet there were still parts of her that was the scared young woman who was helpless chained in a dungeon. Looking at her mate, the man she loved, he knew he was right and she saw that for what it was. He felt it in his heart when she conceded to what he was telling her. The concern on his face was for her benefit.

Clearly she had done what the twins were always teasing her about; she had gone and lost her head. "You are correct, of course. Did I tell you I love you today?" She released the tension in her posture and looked up at him.

"Yup, but you can do it again. I will never get tired of hearing those words from your lips, woman"

With a light spank on her behind he released her and turned her towards the door leading to the hallway.

"Stark is waiting for us in the infirmary. Let's get this show on the road"

— —

He wondered, checking his gear bag for the last time, if Merridian was healing. The last time he checked with Trinity she said as far as she could see they were recouping as well as could be expected. Each trip he made to the infirmary to check on everyone he felt himself becoming more and more possessive of the Goddess and he didn't know what to do about it. He had never felt this way about a woman before.

Hell he didn't need any distractions. It was bad enough that Kenneth couldn't keep his eyes off her companion. He couldn't afford to be distracted. With everyone involved in this prophesy he designated himself the man in charge when it came to being the objective voice in the group. Hell he had to be the leader especially with Nate and Briksanna being put to the test first there weren't any other options. The sooner he let everyone know the better off they would be able to utilize resources available to them and plan their mission like the team he knew they were.

"Snap out of it, Stark," he said to himself more than to an empty room. He left the room and headed out to meet his brother and Briksanna in the infirmary. He wanted to get there first so he could tell them himself about their new visitors and all details he had learned from last night.

Arriving prior to his brother as planned he stepped into the infirmary relieving Kenneth and Gabriella of their watch so they could take care of their needs in preparation of the meeting. He watched them leave the infirmary knowing it was for selfish reasons he was there with no one around. He wanted to see her again, alone. He didn't want to clue anyone in on how much he had been affected by her presence. He couldn't get her out of his head. He hoped she felt the same way about him as he felt about her.

"Get a grip, you sound like a teenager all over again." Mumbling to himself he walked over to where she laid for the past twelve hours. He felt like he she was the one woman he could connect to unlike any other person he had ever met or would ever meet. He knew she could be the one person who was made just for him. His other half. She alone had the one thing no one else had. She could calm his swirling vortex of emotions that he struggled with on a daily basis. That made her unique and hell if he didn't stop and take notice.

Reaching for her hand he hesitated for a split second, reliving his fear of starting something that could potentially be one sided feelings. Quickly squashing his troubled thoughts he gently held her hand. Closing his eyes he focused on clearing his mind of all activity and reached for the thread of life he knew belonged to him. He was always amazed when he first began to meditate how his perception viewed his energy as a rushing river, crystal blue like the sky above but turbulent full with raging emotions at war with one another. Reaching for his thread of energy he noticed right away the water in his mind was calm not rushing like it had appeared to him for his entire life. Checking his mental state, he didn't feel stressed even in the deepest regions of his mind. He sighed, knowing it was due to the contact he had with her right now.

Mentally thanking her for her kind gift, he decided he wanted to do more than just give her the mental equivalent of a few words. He wanted to share his inner peace with her. He focused on his energy, reaching physically into the river with imaginary hands mentally scooping up the water holding the precious liquid in his palm then in his mental state he willed what he held directly to Merridian, along with a wish for a speedy recovery combined with his heartfelt peace she was still alive. He wanted to give a piece of himself to her just because he wanted to. From his hands to hers he gave, sharing his desire for her in the end, not meaning to, but not stopping himself from doing it. He knew he was deeply attracted to her.

Immediately her grip tightened within his hand and she took a deep breath, opening her eyes in a flash not saying a word. She stared for a full minute while he stood holding her hand. His eyes were still closed. He did not realize she had awakened.

He desires me as I desire him. Father, what am I to do? I have never felt these emotions for another person before. Is there something wrong with me? Father, I am worried. He is mortal and I am your daughter. Help me Father make good choices; guide my path with truth, honor and compassion for all those seen and unseen. I respect your will and always shall do what is right and just, yet I have feelings for this mortal and I am afraid. Please hear my prayer send your reply as swiftly as the wind blows.

Looking at Stark Angelo was like looking at a reflection of her heart. She knew she should turn away, yet at the same time she had been longing for this moment for thousands of years. Licking her lips she started to speak but realized her throat had gone dry. That was strange, she was a Goddess. Her throat never went dry. What was going on? Trying to speak, she looked around her and noticed Ellena was in the bed nearest her and they both were in some sort of medical facility.

"You are safe Goddess"—placing a cup of water, for her to sip from, close to her mouth—"you both are safe here under my protection."

Sipping her water slowly to clear her throat she replied, "Assemble your team soon Stark Angelo. Your team is needed now more than ever. I have rested enough."

Attempting to sit up, she was surprised how week she was and fell back in the bed appalled at her weakness. "How long have I been asleep?"

"Twelve hours Goddess."

"Merridian."

"I beg your pardon?" Clearly interested in where this conversation was heading, he smiled at her knowing fully where he wanted the conversation to go. Mortal assumptions.

"I give you leave to call me by my given name. It is Merridian. I want to thank you for your generous hospitality and your protection. What is this attached to my arm and what have you been putting in us?"

Looking curious and not a bit angry she turned to look at the IV bags, both hers and Ellena's then returned her gaze back to the man standing beside her. "I am not upset, just curious."

"Stark, you can call me by my first name too. Nutrition and fluids, Meridian, all things necessary for you both to heal properly while in our realm. When you both arrived you were near death with energy loss. My medical officer has looked you over, thoroughly, and has deemed both you and Ellena fit to return to wherever you need to be once you have regained your strength. The IV fluids being pumped through you is the same formula Briksanna uses from time to time when needed. Truly, you are safe while you rest here; I promise you nothing will happen to you while you are under my protection."

Reaching for his hand, resting on the bed, she threaded her fingers through his palm. Squeezing gently reassuring him of her gratitude she looked from their joined hands to his beautiful face mesmerized by the changing colors of his eyes. They were a light green with flecks of yellow scattered throughout.

"I believe you, Stark. I also, believe that no harm has befallen my companion. There is much yet to do. I have come so far to be encumbered with illness." Eyes flashing, beginning to spark, "I just want to beat my brother into a pulp sometimes. His games go too far and hurt too many. Look at what has happened to me, Stark? The brother I knew before would cut off his own hand before harming anyone especially his womb sister."

He studied her while leaving her question unanswered. Her eyes and face went from angry to grief in a flash of a second. Her eyes filled with tears spilling over sliding slowly down her cheeks. She looked so lost, so overwhelmed and very, very human. This reaction was what he would expect from any person given the amount of trauma she had to deal with. She knew that in her mind but her heart had other ideas and right now it was broken. The turmoil of knowing the source of pain came from her twin brother was apparent by the way she tried to contain her grief he imagined bubbling just under the surface. How she had sustained herself so far, was beyond him. If it were Nate in the place of Lord Drakkoon, he knew he would have one hell of a time reconciling the insidious behavior with the boy he raised and loved.

Nate wasn't just his brother, he was his best friend, his confidant, the person he could always count on and the one he never had to think twice about. It was the same for her and her brother. If they didn't agree, they would just hash it out and deal with it. Never did things go left unsaid or not dealt with. You just kept on going until you agreed on a solution.

Seeing her in such a state reminded him of Harmony back when she asked if she could call him Dad; she looked lost and vulnerable in that moment and he wanted to reach down, scoop her up in his arms and whisper his reassurances hoping his words calmed her fears. He didn't know she would accept him let alone his touch.

She held her breath trying hard to gather her resolve not wanting to breakdown, yet despite her efforts her emotional wall began to visibly crumple around her. Decision made, Stark leaned over careful to reach around because she was still hooked up to an IV line he pulled her gently into his embrace.

"What do you t-think you are d-doing?" She stuttered trying to push out of his arms all the while sniffling harder into what sounded like the path of good cry.

"Doing what I should have done from the beginning. Doing what I've wanted to do since the first moment I laid eyes on you. Hold you." He said with conviction as he held her feeling her struggles turn to sobs while her body's desire to be held won.

He held her knowing with this woman he just might not be the right person to lead the team in this battle, but he didn't care because loving her might be the best thing he'd ever done in his life and that scared the living crap out of him. He buried his face in her hair and held her a little tighter when she broke down completely sobbing her heart out. She reminded him that the strongest person still bled and right now she was a Goddess who was bleeding straight from her soul.

She cried harder holding onto his arms with a grip of steel letting free reign on her emotions grieving for what her brother had done and what she would have to do. He felt all of this roar through his mind without the details but with the force of her emotions. He turned his head burrowing as deep as he could go and sniffed her hair effectively breathing her essence into him.

Her hair smelled of lavender and rain. She knew because she and Ellena had washed it with her special shampoo in honor of the visit she planned to have with her brother. She slide her hands to the edge of Stark's shirt and gripped it tighter where she had intended to push him away earlier she held on for dear life. Despite her state she could still hear his emotions and thoughts. The most startling was the thought he projected right before she realized they were no longer alone in the medical facility.

He didn't know if he could be the man in charge that everyone needed him to be while he was fell in love with her and that really scared the hell out of him.

15

"So this is what you have been doing with your time, big brother?" Breaking apart abruptly Stark released Merridian careful of the IV lines still connected to her, "Watch what you say little brother. You might not like what's said in return." He responded quietly letting go of her hand.

Not wanting to be far from the Goddess he crossed his arms over his massive chest and scowled down as his brother and Briksanna approached the bed. Briksanna looked shocked by the pale look on her face and the grip she held onto Nate's forearm. Nate on the other hand took everything in at once and decided the first remark that was going to fly out of his mouth was going to be an A-typical Nate response. Tease first asks questions later. Judging by his body language he appeared all business like, but his crooked smile and the glint in his eyes, he knew he was daring him to say something about his earlier comment.

"Keep it up little brother. With the night I've had a little beat up brother time would be just about right for me. You look like you need an as whooping to wipe that stupid smirk from your face."

"Stark, my man, you know if you needed privacy. You could have used a room. Hell, you could have used our room as you are flying solo these days, or are you? What was that we heard

when we walked in, 'Doing what you wanted to do all along'? Man, I taught you better words to say than that sorry line."

"Boy, you don't know when to keep your mouth shut, do you?" Feeling his temper rise right along with the need to cause damage, a direct result of his anger about Merridian's emotional pain, he was hanging on by a thread and Nate was going to push him one smart ass comment too far. He had to keep calm or all hell was going to break loose. He felt his hands clench and unclench squeezing his arms tighter raising his need to hurt his brother a little more than the minute before. A fight between the two of them never hurt anyone before, did it?

"What would you know, you haven't been around. You didn't catch your woman from falling not knowing if she was alive or not. You didn't deal with the kids trying to keep them moving forward as we managed the crisis; keeping the compound alert and safe. You didn't see the way Kenneth was consumed with worry for Ellena, which we will have to deal with and no I don't know when we will have the damn time for that. And you didn't see Trinity almost drain herself into a coma trying to stabilize these two so we could get them to a point of nourishment and rest where they could heal. Then set up perimeter watch both inside and out along with everyone's details in complete preparation for our team's insertion point on Skaldanna. No you wouldn't have a dam clue. I know you think you are all smug because you two are newly married, but brother one more smart remark, just one and it's on. You read me boy?" growling out the last few mentally he felt his temper peaking just as loud as his mental tirade.

Briksanna was not only at a complete loss for words after seeing the state of the two women lying in the infirmary, but to hear the venom in Stark's voice was a sure testament to his rising anger along with the amount of restraint it took for him not to act on his instincts to cause damage. She had not seen Stark this angry in a very long time. Looking between both males she did not know what to make from either expression. Stark's fury or Nathanial's aloofness until the last statement settled into Nathanial's brain. She could almost pin point her mate's moment of forfeit. He stopped walking and she tugged his hand a bit to bring his attention back to the moment.

Looking between the males in the room, Briksanna wanted to quickly diffuse what she knew was going to be male, beat on my chest like a caveman, moment. And like all good little boys who liked to play, a fight was brewing. So typical for this lot, it was no wonder Kenneth and Striker jumped in any chance they could get once a brawl got started in the house. Look who they had as examples.

Turning to her mate, "You will apologize for that"—looking at Stark—"You will work on your breathing technique to bring that which you are losing back under control."

Looking between them both; "Have I made myself clear? This problem is bigger than all of us and if I have to keep reminding you both of this then it may be best that the two of you stay behind from this mission so you two can figure out how to behave as warriors should." Letting go of her mate's hand she approached the Goddess and looked between her and the other lady within the room. "Care to share what happened, Merridian?"

Merridian was reeling from Stark's revelation, 'His woman?' She could tell by the way she mumbled that statement several times in a row under her breath. Hearing that about her, spoken out loud, must have been a shock. She could relate as she had not been claimed, directly or indirectly, that she had belonged to anyone over the many years spent in the Earth Realm. She did not know how she felt about Stark and Merridian feeling that way about each other, but she quickly put those thoughts aside to deal with at another time. There were more pressing matters to deal with at hand. Focusing her attention back on Merridian, she waited for the Goddess to respond.

"Aye, I agree we have much to discuss. I am feeling weak but if you can connect with me I can transmit what transpired yesterday prior to waking up here. Your mate along with Stark can connect psychically onto our energy waves to gain the information. Grab my hand Briksanna and hold it close to your heart."

She did as the Goddess bid, briefly thinking how coarse her hands were for a Goddess. She thought that odd for she had expected her hands to be soft as a newborns skin, unharmed by the toils of life. How odd that her hands were chaffed, not smooth was the last thought she had before she was assaulted by the images and feelings pouring through her mind and heart, as if she were the Goddess herself. The assault lasted seconds, but the emotional toil was astounding ripping a scream from her throat in the process.

To say when she pulled her hand away left her reeling was an understatement. It was reassuring to see Nathanial grabbing the frame at the foot of the bed to steady himself when she disconnected her hands. That was when she heard it.

A loud roar, like a lion challenging his enemy to a fight, left chills racing along her arms and legs. The sound came from Stark's direction. The Goddess had visibly blanched when she noticed there must be a private mental conversation going on between the two of them, because obliviously someone had to calm him down. At this point there was anything she or Nathanial could have done other than to let him have his temper tantrum in any form he needed to as long as he did not hurt anyone in the process.

He looked like he was completely ready to explode.

Gritting his teeth turning his sparking hazel eyes towards the bed she could hear the conversation flowing between the both of them through her link with Nathanial.

"Let me go Merridian, you know it has to be done. He almost killed you. If you don't let me go this minute I will explode right here, right now and no one wants that. Now let me go." He said enunciating the last few words clearly struggling not to harm the woman in the bed.

"You will calm yourself warrior for I believe you need to hear what I have to say. The team needs you. Nathanial and Briksanna need you. I need you. Do you hear me? I-need-you-to calm yourself. I don't know where this, that which is between us can go, but I will tell you truthfully, you build a fire within my soul that I have never felt before. In all the millennia's I have been alive I have never felt desire for another which burns within me as I have for you. I cannot know where these feelings may go if you get yourself killed on impulse. I know you to be stronger than to act like a child but if you go after my brother in this manner you will be acting very much as a child getting yourself killed in the process. Please Stark, if anything I may say to you right now to convince you of your importance in all of this; is this one thing, stay with me Stark for I am afraid. I have always been worried, yet never afraid."

Holding his breath, Nathanial did not make a sound. She knew that he normally did not listen in on his brother's thoughts, but when they heard that roar, anger mixed with so much emotional pain, he did not hesitate to connect with his brother's thoughts bringing her right along with him. She could tell he was glad the Merridian was able to talk to his brother, and knowing how close they were as siblings, she felt the same relief he had felt listening to her words. By the looks of it what she was saying looked like it was going to work because he did not appear to be as angry as he was a minute ago. She could tell he did not want to know the details of their conversation and felt guilty for being privy to what should have been their private thoughts.

Leaving the link he mentally shared with his brother alone, he turned his attention to her instead. *"Did you get all of that?"*

"Yes, I was already linked with you when you connected with your brother. I am glad for the both of them. If there was anyone I would want to have peace and contentment in their life, it is your brother. It is Merridian I am concerned with. She will have to say and do plenty to convince me of her loyalty to Stark. Was she not here recently pleading the case of her brother and then in his castle directly from leaving us? I do not know what I am to think about all she has spoken; however I do know this, she has explaining to do. What was she doing in the Under Realm? In Lord Drakkoon's castle no doubt, sisterly visit to catch up on times past? No, what she planned to do is what we need to know especially now that she knows her brother has done something that almost killed her and her friend. I do not like having my family, my mate and my children dragged into this battle so that she can have what I believe will never be again. A family with her brother. The sooner she believes this the better I will feel about our role in all of this.

She was so caught up in her tirade she did not notice that Merridian had calmed Stark down and that the rest of the family was in the room hanging close to the door, obviously present due to Stark's outburst. Looking at the kids who were standing with their weapons held at their sides they appeared more worried than angry.

He did not blame them one bit for their fears. Stark ready to explode was not a pretty site and no one wanted to bear witness to the person on the receiving end of his fury.

If he had known that there was a threat to his family and they were about to face, God only knows what, he would have had a worried look on his face no matter how skilled of a warrior he was. On top from what Stark had shared, last night must have been one hell of a stressful night for everyone. He would be looking just like they looked, doubtful witnessing the faces of their leaders looking so pissed and completely confused all rolled up into one hopeless expression. Bri was going to be feeling completely embarrassed knowing everyone was watching her build up to a major snit. He decided he needed to step in and deflect.

Looking at Stark seeing his eyes no longer held their otherworldly glow he did what he did best. He spoke up and led the team.

"All right boys and girls gather around and cop a squat. We had originally thought to have this meeting in the main room but with the Goddess and her companion still laid up we are going to accommodate them here. They have as much invested in this quest as we do. So grab your paper and pencils folks and come closer. Striker, I want confirmation that our perimeter both interior and exterior are set with a green light on your gadgets. No one is to get in or out; consider this meeting live and hot. Take Gabby with you, she can manage the interior and you can deal with the exterior." Striker glanced at Gabriella nodding his response. He knew despite their constant bickering they would have each other's back without a word needing to be said from him.

"Kenneth, I want this room sound proof once your brother and sister are back from setting the perimeter; I want this room sealed tight. No Intel is to be leaked from this room, understood?" He nodded acknowledging what had been asked of him.

"What we are about to say is of utmost importance and if leaked can kill all of us and possibly that of both worlds. It's up to the ten of us to see this to the end; until you hear otherwise from Stark, myself or from Bri, not a word is to be shared with anyone. Where we go from here will entirely depend on what phase of this quest we are on, but one thing I want all of you to remember; first and foremost we're a family and nothing can break that bond. Ever. So if you have any problems with your teammates we need to air them out right now or you can consider yourself off this mission and out of this room before Intel is spilled. No if ands or buts about it. Any takers on the easy way out?" Looking at each member of his family not realizing he was holding his breath praying everyone understood the seriousness of what he believed to be the mission of a lifetime he waited for the smart comment to come flying from one of them like they usually did to lighten the seriousness of the mood whenever their meetings got tense.

No one said a word.

"This is the kind of mission that could make, break or even kill a person. Again I ask, any takers on the easy way out?"

"No, sir." Not a face in the room had lost its intensity. He could tell they were all on the same page and at the very moment he realized the kids he had helped raise now stood before him as men and women each a warrior in their own right. He was proud of them in that moment.

"Second thing, if for any reason we decide to split the family up, know it is because of efficiency and only efficiency is what will be needed to succeed with this mission never because one team is better than the other. I don't want any words, arguments about who can do better at what on this mission. The three of us decide who goes where and does what, not you. We are to trust each other with our lives and that includes the decision makers. I have complete faith and unconditional trust in each of you. That is what will be needed of each of you; your skills and assets are second to that. You must hold strong to what I am saying to you because I have a feeling what we have known in our lives up to this point will be put to the test. If you, for a second, don't have complete faith and unconditional love for any person in this room remember this; your doubt in the person across from you could be their downfall and no matter how much the person across from you pisses you off, you don't want them dead, ever. So put all the childish antics aside and step up your game. This is the big leagues we are playing in right now and nothing, I mean nothing, is more important to me than my family. So button down the hatches and let's dig in."

Striker and Gabriella headed out with a nod of their heads to secure the perimeter while Kenneth went to Ellena's bedside and sat down to clear his thoughts beginning to do as requested, he was going to sound-proof the room.

He still wasn't sure how the boy was able to do what he did. Kenneth had explained it once saying he was able to send an energy thread around an area and that thread would weave its way throughout the perimeter he selected similar to a web. For the ones within his soundproof ring no sound could get through the weave of energy but sound could be heard outside the web allowing those within to remain in control of their surroundings but no one on the outside would be able to detect anything different than what he led them to believe, simply an unoccupied area. It made it impossible to detect Kenneth's location when he used it in the field. He and Stark believed they needed to continue working with each other using their talents along with weapons training. This way they were most effective in any situation they may encounter. It was something Bri was adamant about with everyone's training. All of them had to learn how to use their psychic abilities combined with combat training.

By the time his thoughts had drifted off and back again, Striker and Gabriella had returned and Kenneth opened his eyes, telling him with a slight nod the room had been secured.

"We feeling good here?" Feeling a bit sentimental over his own reminiscent thoughts regarding the people in the room, Nate took each person's measure. Seeing them as attentive and confidant, not a trace of doubt could be find on the face of any member in his family.

Looking lastly at Bri, he noticed her rapt attention was on him. He took a bit longer staring at her eyes looking for any hint of displeasure because he had addressed the family this way. Yes they were a team but he knew she believed like he did, family came first before being a team. He could get lost staring in her eyes, more violet in color than green right now, a true testament of how high her emotions were riding. Her brow was straight, eyes focused. Her mouth firm not pressed too tight like he could tell whenever she felt anxious. She looked poised, almost as if she were holding her breath for something. Her overall stance was straight and now that he thought on it he remembered she could read his thoughts as he was taking her measure. Without reaching for the answers telepathically, he wanted to see for himself, how his mate viewed him. Glancing at her mouth again wondering if he might have misread her emotions, he took a chance knowing he had to get his self-doubt under control. Wasn't that what he was preaching to the kids a minute ago? Shaking his head mentally he knew she was waiting for him to speak. Checking himself mentally for any doubts on what he was going to say he discovered he didn't feel too worried about what he was going to say.

Glancing at her again he saw pride in her eyes or was that anxiety for enticing the kids with his hint of a dangerous mission knowing each one of them were just plain adrenaline junkies when it came to a good fight; especially one that included saving people and this one hinted at saving not only Skaldanna but their world as well.

"I am proud of you. Do not doubt your worth to me; especially your position with our children, I trust you with their lives. You spoke exactly as I would have spoken only you spoke prior to my having formed the words in my own head. You are exactly what this mission needs. You are a leader. Together with Stark and I, the three of us will guide them along as we always have; knowing the risks today are no greater than what we have taken numerous times in the past. I trust you, Nate, unconditionally, to be the King this family will need you to be. The King I know you are right now."

Finding it a bit hard to hide the prideful grin ready to split his face from her praise, he did what he believed to be the best course of action. Keeping his eyes on Briksanna; his family's observation in his peripheral, the conversation with Bri passed in a matter of seconds but it was longer than usual to hear a response from the team.

Breaking eye contact he looked at Stark and raised an eyebrow as he passed the reins of the mission explanations over to Stark, mentally letting him know, *"Your turn, Bro."*

Not hesitating for a second he picked up the role of leader exactly where Nate had left off, "You heard the man, are we all feeling good here?" repeating Nate's question for the second time.

"Yes, sir," they replied not voicing the response with the enthusiasm his family normally carried.

"I don't think I heard you," challenging them to readiness. They needed to listen to what both Nate and Briksanna had to share regarding the quest and sketch out a game plan on handling it all. Running his hand down his face so much had happened since everyone had debriefed thirty six hours ago. It seemed like longer than that with all that they had been through but he knew, in his gut, there was so much more to come. On that thought he took a seat next to Merridian's bed.

"Stark, can I ask a question I bet everyone wants to ask and maybe the question is what has been delaying some of our responses." Harmony spoke first breaking the tense silence filling the room.

"Where all ears H," gesturing for everyone else to grab a seat where they could.

"I don't mean disrespect to your authority here nor do we"—waving her hand around the room to include the rest of the team—"think any of you carry mistrust for us, but what does this mission have to do with us? No disrespect to you either Goddess but why our family? Each member of this family is nothing but a bunch of misfits from different families and backgrounds who have come together by a fate driven only by our mother, Briksanna; again no disrespect. Briksanna is the only person here who was driven to find us and find us she did. She has given up everything to bring us together, raised us as her children and brought us something we never had before, a family. She has taught us everything she knew even taking time with each of us, boys and girls separately knowing a little girl or boy time was exactly what we needed at the moment from a mother; reminding each of us to never give up that little bit of ourselves making us who we are today. To not lose that sense of identity she strove so hard to instill within us until one day we all grew up realizing we are a part of the closest, faithful and without a doubt, sir; trustworthy, unconditional family unit on the planet." Pacing now back and forth as she continued to ticked off her reasons clearly getting angrier as she voiced them out loud.

She avoided looking at Briksanna not making any eye contact. Whenever that happened nothing could stop her from her tirade until she got it all off her chest before losing her nerve. Briksanna was the one person in the room that could get Harmony to toe the line with just one look when she was wound up like that.

"So that quest you say which is detrimental to both our worlds? The one to save Lord Drakkoon who has hunted our Mother, the very woman who has woven the most beautiful of songs I have ever heard; threading our essence together as if we are one? We are supposed to save the one person who has had her in fear for her life for all of her two thousand years on Earth that she cannot return to her own land for nothing longer than a few hours only to selflessly restore the energy so depleted in the realm by said Lord Drakkoon's rein? This is the quest you want our family to sacrifice for? I know I am speaking for all young adults here and me, personally, am not about to sacrifice our Mother's life for the sake of saving her enemy no matter who he is to you or any God. I love my Mother unconditionally. I love my family unconditionally and I am sure as hell not about to let you or anyone else sacrifice anyone of us so you or your God can try and have what we already have." She tried to rein in her temper as she yelled the last few words out.

Looking at Merridian's blanched face feeling the scowl on his own face, Harmony had better wrap up what she feels she needs to say or he was going to lash out at her for sounding so cold hearted. He hadn't raised her to be so disrespectful.

"Love doesn't work that way, Goddess. Love is earned through faith and trust but most important it is held together with understanding, patience and practice. I learned that the hard way, Mamma would always say, 'Practice will save you every time faster and without harm than over thinking a situation'. So I ask all of you leaders, why does this family need to do this?"

He didn't know what to say to that. Everything she had said were the same thoughts that had run through his mind over the past two days. Looking over at Briksanna who appeared just as stunned as Nate was.

"Want to give it a try big brother?" Nate asked.

"I will address this. Just give me a moment. Do not say anything as I believe everyone needs to absorb her words. A few minutes of silence will do each of us some good." Briksanna interrupted.

"They are all yours, Briksanna" he replied.

He hoped she knew what she was going to say, because after that speech Harmony gave, even he had doubts. Why did they have to be the one to sacrifice more of themselves after what he did to his own flesh and blood?

Family didn't treat family that way. This man needed to be taught a lesson and he was the perfect man to dole it out for himself, for Merridian and for everyone he had hurt along the way. When he got ahold of him, not if, when he did catch up to Lord Drakkoon he was going to beat the shit out of the man.

While some remained standing as Harmony spoke others had taken seats, now everyone took a seat around the room and no one commented on Harmony's tirade. She had a point and it was well made; although sensing rather than speaking, she knew each one of her children felt the same, one hundred percent. She looked carefully at each member of her family. Although, Nathanial reminded her that these were her children, she also knew them for the individual warriors they had grown up to be.

How many times had the twins gone after an opponent on a mission only to impress her more with their combined fighting techniques, regardless of the weapon? Hundreds of times. The way they use their knives in tag team effort not only impressed her the first time she saw it; she grew to envy it every time thereafter. This was what she and Katerina used to do when they were younger, allowing their energy to weave its way into whatever form of combat they chose to use enhancing the movement enabling the fighter to hit harder, slice deeper and move faster. This was how it would have been if they would have been allowed to continue with their training as royal children of the realm. She knew it every time she watched the twins fight and she smiled because she knew she taught them the right technique for combat training.

Both she and Kat were trained in the art of fighting in one on one combat and in back to back strategy with a dozen guards for opponents. They had to have the utmost faith and trust in each other to work in tandem against their foe during battle not to mention having Lysinious as an older brother. Kat was always writing to her in detail about what new fighting technique she had discovered while observing his combat training. That way they could incorporate their new founded knowledge into their next training practice.

It was like looking in a looking glass of her history while watching Harmony and Trinity fight. Remembering when Kat and she used to train in the solar away from the palace guards. Her father used to peak in from time to time teasing them both on their skills first but always instructing them on their technique before he left saying, *"No matter how many times you twirl around your opponent, Briksanna, you must never take your eye off of them, not for a second. The moment you do that very second could mean the end of your life and the lives of those you protect."*

She taught the girls those same principles; from the cradle and the rest of the children as they came into the family fold, applying that knowledge in their personal fighting techniques, honing their skills making hand to hand combat an art. It almost appeared as if both girls were dancing with their opponent.

The only thing scarier than Trinity and Harmony with their knives was Kenneth and Gabriella with their bow and arrows. Smiling at the thought, chuckling mentally, she knew she should not have ever shown those two how to wield a bow. Having never liked modern technology herself on most weaponry in this century, the cross bow was not for her but she did love the compound bow. It was easier to carry around and she was used to reloading in one fluid motion never having to take her eye off her target. With the cross bow she just never had the patience to train herself for shooting an arrow and then having to restring the bow with two hands. She had mastered how to use a long bow centuries ago. Plus it was easier to pack two babies along with knives strapped to her body when on missions. That did not say for what she had loaded in the diaper bag of a back pack nor did it say anything about the trunk of the car she drove. They all grew up with weaponry such as knives, bows, swords and guns with respect for each and every piece of weaponry as it should be.

Sighing she allowed herself to continue with this path of thought. Suppose this mission was good, then what did she say? Did she push too hard leeching her fears and anxieties of her role in the prophecy onto them unknowingly? Mentally taking herself to task for doubting herself, she tossed all of her doubts out of her head and closed her eyes for a second. Clearing her head always allowed her to focus. Focusing on the task at hand was important right now.

The questions Harmony brought to everyone's attention was the elephant in the room and it took her child, to reveal them to everyone. Opening her eyes she wanted to be the first to respond before Nate or Stark said a word because it was her that placed the seed of fear and hate into everyone's heart. Harmony's revelations were exactly what everyone has had on their minds these past two days. Those questions were the very same ones she had running through her head over the past two millennia. It was what kept her from taking a mate or having children all this time; but in the blink of her life span here she was mated and in a room full of what she knew in her soul to be the children of her heart with the promise of more children between her and Nathanial. She could not hide in fear any longer and everyone needed to know this.

"Stand down, both of you. I will address this," she sent the message telepathically to both men. Ten years ago she would never had thought, when she first laid eyes on them, they would equal her in leadership, but they do and that was what made this meeting about family first, team second.

Looking directly at Harmony first then to each one of her family members before she took their measure once more trying to determine if this was a family opinion shared by all or by a select few in which case she would address them in public regardless. One big rule in their family, almost a non-negotiable rule, was nothing was private. Being truthful was what had kept her family strong and safe. She should have known the time would come when she would have to share The Prophesy with them. She had hoped that with Skaldanna being so quiet over the centuries that she could become complacent. Time was now precious to her where for centuries she had simply existed knowing there would be a day she would retaliate for the damage done to her and the people of Skaldanna. She knew, now, she had something to lose and they were all there in that very room.

16

"Survivors of the fittest," Kenneth would always say to her while he trained. She thought it was cute but cute was not a manly word to use he would tell her. First time she said she thought his words were cute was right at the end of his first year in combat team training. He had worked so hard at controlling his temper all year long wanting to be just like Stark it was almost hard to watch. As his mentor and impromptu mother, she knew he had much potential stored within him, if only he could have faith in himself. It took time, patience and many hours of practice. She was so proud of him on that last day of training she was not paying attention to anything or anyone around but him in that moment, so when he walked up to her with that proud face of his chest puffed up and head held high she had blurted out like any other mother on the planet had done with their young and told him how she had thought his mannerisms were cute and reached to embrace him in a tight hug.

She did not know his natural tan could visibly blanch a ghostly white in direct sunlight. His did in that moment and she knew right then he was becoming a man not the fifteen year old boy he was at the time. Knowing the word cute did not fall into her Kenneth vocabulary any more. She had just humiliated him and in front of Stark, his one and only idol, not to mention the whole family.

Thinking back on that moment in time reminded her that all of the children had grown up and with their maturity they too had felt the burden of The Prophesy, albeit indirectly; no matter how hard she tried to shield them from it. Realizing now keeping the truth and her own fears from her family was the most selfish thing she could have done.

Looking back at Harmony she knew more than anything she had been right. She needed to come clean with her family once and for all, but she wanted to do this mission her way.

"I want all of you to listen to what I have to say, here and now. I know you have heard bits and pieces of what has weighed on my soul throughout my life and as you well know that has been a very long time. I want you to know I did not share everything with all of you at first due to the simple truth, I believed by not sharing anything with you I was protecting you; the most important people in my life aside from those still living on Skaldanna and by not sharing I might minimize the potential risk of backlash from Lord Drakkoon. I kept the knowledge of my life close to my heart all of this time not allowing you, my family, the opportunity to truly know who I am."

She gathered her strength and looked into the face of each family member, "Let me tell you a story I should have told each one of you long ago. When I was your age I lived with my family on Skaldanna. My parents were the High King and Queen of the High Realm; meaning they were the ruling monarch over all the Realms in Skaldanna. As the eldest princess of the High King I had every privilege due to our station as royalty. I had a very loving family and friends from every realm. Our lands were at peace, there were no wars nor were their dissension within the lands with the exception of political disagreements. I was young and my parents had just planned my engagement to my best friend's older brother Prince Lysinous of the Second Realm. I believed him to be a magnificent man, see you have to understand, as a princess of the High King our bloodlines were obsolete. On Skaldanna this was why our family was the only family who could manipulate the energies supporting all of Skaldanna. My father would channel the energy from the other realms and infuse each stream of energy into one sphere held within the grounds of the palace. There was no need to constantly oversee this process as long as he maintained the sphere's dispensation of energy back into Skaldanna like an infused source of fuel for the lands. This infusion of different realm energy not only sustained all realms energies but the people as well. The harmony of energies combined fueled the people and enriched their lives."

"The infused energies would literally feed the land, grow the crops, feed the animals and trickle in our waters; thereby feeding us the habitants on Skaldanna. All people within the realms depended on this energy infusion to keep them alive. My mother was daughter of the High Lord in the Third Realm. They were the keepers of the merchants. All trade in Skaldanna was routed through my Grandfather's House. My father was Prince of the High King of Skaldanna. Their marriage was not only a loving one but an alliance of energies settling throughout the realms strengthening the High Kings energy pattern literally infusing the love they shared with one another back into the lands.

My marriage to the Prince of the Second Realm was a hope to continue with the tradition of aligning the realms with the family of the High King; further strengthening the foundation of the High King's royal bloodlines, with future airs to the throne and in the management of the infused energies. Remember this concept is essential to the overall maintenance within all of Skaldanna. Each realm managed by the royal bloodlines had their own energies they mastered the psychic abilities that were indicative to their realm and collectively as a whole brought together the infused energies feed all the lands of Skaldanna."

"Everyone following me so far?" she hoped she could keep spilling everything, realizing there was so much she had not shared with them.

"Good so far, Mamma." Trinity spoke reassuringly.

Taking a deep breath she forged on and hoped she did not offend nor surprise anyone with her open declarations, but the time for secrets was over.

"Trinity you can heal the living body. Harmony can heal the living earth, even create new growth by coaxing life to begin, both of you have this gift. Most healers are common to the First Realm, why, I am not sure of. It has been a very long time since I have considered all of this.

Gabriella and Kenneth you are both chameleons in the field and you have recognized some things are changing in your physical bodies, but I can tell you right now what it is both of you will encounter and that is you are shifters. Of what clan, I believe wolf, but we shall see when your time comes. You may not see it yet but give the idea time and the thought may not be too far off from where your own personal thoughts were heading in the first place. I can smell the energy signature of a shifter growing stronger within the both of you. This is common for Third Realm inhabitants so I am accustomed to shifters. Do not be afraid of yourself nor think you are a danger to this family or mission. You are invaluable to me. I love you regardless of your heritage and should have told you what I suspected earlier. I had hoped you two would come to me first and wished for discretion; however I now see where secrets have brought so more harm than good.

Striker you are the fastest person I have even known at strategy coupled with your gadgets you always seem to retain the advantage of surprise with the enemy; it is astounding, not to mention your telekinesis has been getting stronger. There is more to you but honestly I cannot figure out what it is. It's as if there is more energy buried within you lying dormant almost hidden on purpose. Not even I can figure out what it really is or what you will be able to do once you can tap into it. I do know one thing. You are a very strong talented man who given your own leadership you may even take Stark for a run at being General.

"Hear what she said Old Man? Watch out I'm gaining on you. You might even be a little afraid," Striker said teasingly to Stark. Everyone held their breath wondering what Stark would say.

Suddenly appearing as if his teasing Stark may not have been a good idea he said, "Sorry man I was only…"

"Gotcha! See that is why, my boy, I will always remain the master and you the pupil." Chuckling to himself shaking his head. "I am the Master!" Flinging his arms out wide like he always did when he was playing with the boys.

"Dude you are so going down, right Kenneth? It's you and me Old Man in the arena, any day. Let's see who will be the Master then."

"I am so down for that one man, can't wait to rip me a can of whop ass in there," Kenneth added.

"So you say, boys. So you say, but let's get one thing straight. You two knuckle heads try every time to beat me and I keep servin' it up to you. You'll get tired one day and realize your place as the pups in the family is where you belong."

Laughing hysterically now, Trinity leaned over to Kenneth, "You are so in for it now little boy."

Harmony high fived her twin, "Striker doesn't have a chance, ten bucks he's the one going down first. You in Gabby?"

Gabriella looked at them both seriously before the silly grin broke over her face, "Twenty and you're on, but on one condition, twenty bucks Stark can knock them both out cold in one shot. You twins game?"

Whooping loudly, Harmony spoke up this time, "Accepted and agreed, but if only one person is knocked out you pay up ten bucks to us each."

"You're on."

Various comments were being said around the room wondering who was better than whom and what they could make of Striker's unknown energy. Voices were starting to get loud, which seemed normal for their family. They felt comfortable talking about one another, as it should be. This was what she should have done long ago.

Raising his voice Nate commanded, "Calm down everyone, Bri isn't done. Pay attention and let's continue."

Looking at everyone settle down, she chanced a look at the Goddess. She seemed deep in thought but attentive not overwhelmed and with the open bantering the kids were displaying. She was very grateful she didn't interrupt or dispute all that went on with them out loud or about how the family was behaving now; however she was curious as to what she will have to say once given the opportunity.

She looked almost envious in the way she was watching each of the children interact with one another and in how they, the adult role models, managed them. How lonely her life had to of been not to have a family in her life for thousands of years. She knew she did not really know how much she had been missing by keeping to the shadows always watching in on families over the centuries instead of becoming a part of one. Now having this tight group in her life she did not know what she would have done without them.

She picked up from where she left off forcing her thoughts about Merridian to the back of her mind she continued to address her family. "Stark can pull energy and channel it into something powerful and or beautiful given the opportunity and creativity. He is a very strong conduit for energy. Stark you would have been made General of my father's armies and most loyal confidant, this I do not doubt. I may have brought us all together but it is you who binds us to one another. I have come to admire you in our short time together, thank you for all that you have done and continue to do." Looking at Stark head on hoping he could read the genuine gratitude not just the words she had spoken. Seeing his nod she felt his praise send a warmth feeling of relief throughout her entire being.

Turning towards her mate, she knew she could hide nothing from him and no longer needed to. He was the person the Gods had sent to complete her. With this man she could accomplish the quest set forth by The Prophesy; she believed this with every fiber of her being.

Smiling openly showing her love for him, "Then there is you, Nathanial. You have speed and stealth, faster than any person I know. What you can do with your energy, wrapping it around surfaces, molding yourself to the structure is amazing. I have never seen the like in all my two thousand years. Like I have said before it will not be long before you can walk through walls. You are a major asset to any mission we have been on or may come up against."

Looking around the room at everyone she hoped her conviction of her admiration could be woven into words as she continued to explain her thoughts. "I do not want to figure out why we can do what each of us can do, I just accept everyone as they are. You are my family; my Royal Family and as such, entering the realm of Skaldanna, you will be presented as such."

"It is my understanding you have been brought up to speed about what it is I do when I take my leave on Skaldanna; what you may not understand is why I continue to do it." she asked them.

Looking around the room she saw she held everyone's attention. "It is quite simple, if there is no ruling member of the High Royal family alive the inhabitants on Skaldanna will die. I am what remain of that family line. I suspect by my accepting you all into my family by words of honor and the energetic familial bond we share, you will automatically be accepted as High Royalty when we arrive as well."

Recognizing her anxiety anticipating their response to the bomb she had just dropped, Nate spoke up cutting her off. "Any questions you have you will have to keep them to yourself at this point. We can have open discussions, in private, once we arrive at our destination. As it is Katerina will be wondering where we are."

"You all should have your standard gear prepared and packed, remember folks, no weapons are to be brought over. What you need will be provided for you at the time of departure. You are trained soldiers as well as family members. You will be expected to behave as Royalty at all times unless you are within the confines of your room or within closed family discussions. Understood?" glaring at the team Stark made sure everyone knew the penalty if his edict was disobeyed. They would have to deal with him.

No one wanted to piss Stark off.

"Yes Sir. Understood Sir," was the loud response.

"I have something to add, if I may," said a soft request from the corner of the room.

She did not know what to think about all that had been spoken yet she did know she owed this honorable family all the help she could offer to stop her brother and only the truth would do from this point forward, even if it hurt her in the end.

"Each of you need to understand that my brother will detect Briksanna once she enters Skaldanna. He has always searched for her in the past then go into hiding, but with events from last night, I believe he has done something, I do not think even I can forgive. Directly after it happened I kept thinking there was something familiar about the way the energy being ripped from us felt but the memory did not correspond with the present moment. The experiences did not match."

"You are not making much sense Goddess." Emphasizing on the *Goddess* part, Harmony asked waving her hand flippantly. "What do you mean by the memory and the experience did not match?"

"Mind yourself Harmony," flashing her eyes at the young girl who obviously did not like her hand in Starks by the way she kept sneaking glances at their joined hands. "That attitude will not gain you the respect you will need within the realms of Skaldanna nor will it assist any member of your family in their acceptance as adopted High Royalty. I believe Stark said 'You will be expected to behave as Royalty at all times'. I would practice that if I were you."

Clearing his throat hoping to dissolve a conniption fit he could feel Harmony building up, Stark jumped right in. "That goes for everyone in this room. Start practicing now. How you speak and how you carry yourself about is what will gain the support for our cause and lesson the problems for Briksanna and Nate once there."

Looking back towards her he indicated with his non-joined hand waving it around the room, "Please continue."

Sighing her resignation at Harmony's display of complete disrespect, "Harmony is right I may not have explained myself well. What I am trying to say is the energy drain was negative. I have experience positive energy pulls from my brother all of our lives. When he needed my energy to heal an animal or person on Skaldanna in the past or when I needed his energy to attempt to do the same; it was always a mutual give and take between us and a familiar pull of positive energy freely given and taken with consent. That is what triggers and inspires the act of healing weather it is land, animal or person. What I felt yesterday was the opposite, a negative pull on energy, to create something forbidden by a forbidden act. I do not know what he has done or what the act exactly was, but I do know that whatever it is bodes horribly for this quest."

Turning away from the young men and women she looked directly at Briksanna. "There are no hidden agendas between us, Briksanna. I know you believe I have a secret agenda to save my brother, I may hope for his salvation; however I know and do understand that this may not happen. My brother is lost to me for that I am truly sorry for all the pain he has caused you, your family and those on Skaldanna above and below."

Becoming completely emotional at this point from the words she had just spoken she did not know if she was going to be able to get the last part out knowing it was absolutely crucial to the mission before them all.

Wiping the tears leaking from her eyes with her free hand she knew if she let go of Stark she would not be able to hold her head up in front of everyone. She was completely humbled within their presence knowing all she had ever wanted was the closeness of having a family represented by these warriors who have had freely given by the one woman her brother had hunted without remorse.

"My brothers confinement as overlord of the Under Realm was never meant to last this long. We both were never told his length of servitude would be four thousand years, yet it has remained so. Our father is not open for discussion on the matter, if I may be frank, he has not been around for either one of us in centuries. I have searched for him, prayed to him and begged for Drake's release from his obligation and am met with silence. I am worried what that means for everyone; and at the same time I am not. I can feel his existence is still tied to us just as you, Briksanna, can feel that bond with your family and they of you. Family connection is the same for us as it is for you; we are one in the same you and I."

She continued on, "It is this connection of sharing energy that triggered the memory of Drake and I when we were younger, we shared energy all the time before he left for the Under Realm. This time it was negative but it was more than that. Something attached itself to the energy signature warping the energy intended for the recipient. The outcome was deadly and connected it to something or someone other than my brother. Whatever my brother has done something else has happened to make it worse. This cannot be good for anyone or anything, in fact I fear what has occurred has made our quest worse if not deadly. It is this that has made me very afraid. I absolutely do not know what to make of it and if I do not know what this thing is, there is no one but all of us to find it out and eliminate that threat."

Feeling desperate thinking maybe she had not gotten her point across with how committed she was to the success of the mission for their sakes and for the sake of all the living in the Universe. She needed to get her point across. She was desperate for all of them to know it would go against everything she believed in to betray their trust. The unity they displayed this evening was more beautiful to experience than she had imagined. What she would give to be a part of that.

"I am with all of you on this completely and with that you have my complete trust. I give this to you freely. Never will I forsake you nor will I keep anything from you. Each of you represents the love of what was originally intended for every person man or woman; an example of a united kingdom and how it should be managed; with love, commitment and teamwork. I have always represented and fought for the preservation of all living things. It is simply the right thing to do and I refuse to do anything less than that. It is what drove me to visit my brother continuously hoping by doing so he would remember we both used to share those same dreams of always doing the right thing, to preserve life."

Shaking her head she felt helpless. Everyone held the same expression as she did, they waited to hear what their leaders thought of her words spoken without the merit of earned trust. Earlier she had believed she needed to only speak the words from her mouth and that was what she had intended to do but now she knew she would need to play an active role in all of this from their point of view. Right alongside them as an active participant not as a watcher or guide. She knew she had been hurting for the brother who was left behind to suffer the horrors of his confinement. She hoped they were thinking if it had been their family member who was left for several millennia in the Under Realm, century after century lost to the depravity the environment withheld, would they have given up on one another? Would they continue to have hope for the family member that appeared lost who was hoped for salvation like her brother had? She did not know if she could continue being strong if they did not believe her.

"What would we all do, Bri. The same as the Goddess here; we'd fight to get you back. The ends of the Earth and you know it. Go easy on her."

She heard the words spoken from Nathanial to Briksanna as if the words were directed to her. Her eyes snapped to attention from where they had wandered in deep thought, brought back to the one person whom she knew the acceptance within their family depended on for this mission to succeed and The Prophesy to be fulfilled. Briksanna held all the cards.

"Goddess, I speak for all of us when I say this; I know what you say in regards to your commitment to us and this mission is truth. I also know that in doing so you feel you are betraying the love of your brother, but you are not. You are saving him and all those who are affected directly and indirectly. You are saving your brother."

Looking up at everyone, she took the measure of the woman fate had picked long ago to be the bringer of salvation. Could Briksanna be speaking the truth? Could all of this be solved simply by doing the right thing starting right here in that room? It seemed like a mountain of problems for such a simple answer.

"No one said doing the right thing was easy. Sometimes you have to bleed a little and that hurts. Hurting is exactly what it means, Merridian, a painful feeling that stays with a person sometimes because that is how much it hurts yet in the end you know you've done the right thing regard-less of the pain doing it causes. You just do it until whatever it is, is done. That is what it means to be that kind of person; the one who does the right thing."

Turning her wet eyes towards Stark she was surprised at the level of wisdom he possessed. Her heart beat faster knowing he had heard her thoughts and read her heart. He spoke true and her fear had disappeared as a result of it.

He was her other half. Squeezing his hand hoping the gesture was interpreted as she had intended, a sign of her appreciation of the words he had spoken. Smiling at him behind hooded eyes she knew her emotional state was erratic towards this man. She cut off her wayward thoughts before anyone could pick up on her erratic energy right now. She did not want to give herself away until she had more time to think on it. Certainly not in a room full of people, that was a bit much to ask.

Nodding her head in acceptance, she vowed she would do everything in her power to make sure any pain caused would occur to her or at the very least everyone affected would hurt minimally, this she silently vowed. She felt they deserved more from her.

"I will endeavor to hold your words close to heart." She just did not know what else to say so she bowed her head for a minute to gather her emotions once more then raised her head and looked them in the eye before turning her head to Nate and Briksanna.

Seeming to break the solemn mood, Nate stood up and gestured for everyone to get moving, "Time to suit up boys and girls, its play time. We gather at the south entrance in one hour. Consider yourself dismissed."

Everyone stood and was filling out of the room except Harmony and Trinity. Trinity headed to talk to Briksanna and Harmony headed directly towards him. Looking at the girl that held the biggest piece of his heart he waited for her to approach not letting go of Merridian's hand. He saw the way she kept looking at their joined hands and the scowl present on her face got deeper the closer she walked toward them until he thought her brow creasing had to be causing her a headache.

"What's up little bit?"

"I just wanted to tell you I don't regret speaking up like I did, but for a minute there I thought you were disappointed in me for doing so. In good conscience before going on this mission, I am choosing to do like you said and air things out before we leave."

She turned her attention directly to the Goddess as she spoke next, "This man is the only father figure I have known and I love him with my whole heart. I have known him longer than you have watched him from wherever you came from, this I feel in here"—raising her hand over her heart—"I can see how much he cares for you and not in the same way he cares for me, so this thing going on between the two of you looks pretty serious and I am not sure how I feel about that, yesterday, today or tomorrow"—holding up her hand to ward Stark off from speaking—"but that doesn't mean I didn't read the honesty in the words you spoke or in the way you look at him. I love Stark unconditionally and until you can prove to me you feel the same way about him as I do, I will be watching you."

"Are you about finished?" getting more irritated by the minute. Stark reached out and grabbed her hand, "First off, you are my daughter never forget that. If you do I will be there to remind you every time you do forget. Second, times might change, places may change but us, we are forever. You read me kid? Come give an old man a hug."

He didn't give her a chance to argue; he just pulled her into an embrace letting go of Merridian's hand in the process. He held the daughter of his heart tight against him smelling the familiar scent of her strawberry shampoo.

"I love you Harmony, you stay alert on this mission you hear me kid. My life depends on it, understand?" Pushing her away to read her eyes, she nodded blinking furiously to clear up the tears that threatened to fall.

"You have my vow not only as a Goddess but as a woman; I tell you the truth in what I said earlier. I care deeply for Stark and that caring is not limited. It is for you all. I will do what must be done when the time comes. Please believe what I say. If there is anything I want you to understand it is this one thing, your family is something I envy with every fiber of my body, not in a hazardous way in a loving way. I want to be a part of that bond; however I will never jeopardize that love to save one individual. Do you understand what I am trying to tell you?"

He could tell Merridian silently prayed Harmony would believe her. He could hear her thoughts and was waiting right along with her for the response he wanted to say himself. He waited in silence for Harmony to say something and he saw the hope in Merridian's eyes fade when she didn't answer right away. Harmony just stared at her not acknowledging in any way. It was nerve racking.

Before he could say anything to break the anxiety Harmony spoke. "We're good you and I. Time will tell, Merridian, time will tell about all the rest. I have to go get ready," she pulled away from them and started to walk away.

He knew from his mental tap into Harmony's mind she didn't tell the Goddess everything. Deep down she knew that he had love for the Goddess and that was all that counted with her. If he believed for a second that the Goddess was hiding anything he wouldn't give her the time of day. Maybe he should have gone a little easier on her? He didn't know, he guessed time would tell for all of them.

Looking back over her shoulder he read from Harmony that she could see how upset the Goddess was over her brush off reply and that he was trying to console her by picking up her hand again kissing the back of it. Sighing he looked up as she turned around and walked out of the room and knew she had seen what he had done.

The last thoughts he read from his favorite child was she needed to get her head in the game and that right now was not the time to worry about other people and their feelings. She had her own agenda and no one was going to get in front of that. Whatever the hell she thought her agenda was he wasn't going to let go anytime soon. He was going to make sure all of his children came back home safe especially Harmony.

— ~

Not knowing what was being planned in the Earth Realm, Jackson walked through the main eating hall as if he owned the place. No longer was he just the team leader, he was Tarmac the Realm Keeper and everyone knew it. No one would look him in the eyes anymore, they looked away or down in the same submissive position he had practiced centuries ago. He slowed his purposeful stride exiting the main dining hall when he looked around at everyone as they went about their business. The thought of the time when they would bow down to him outside the walls as they were doing in here made him feel good inside.

Picking up his stride he knew he needed to keep on task and not lose his thoughts along the way. Anticipation at what the Mistress had planned was what he woke up to this morning. He couldn't wait to get back in the field again so he could fight using his new body.

"I've finally got skills that can bring down that damned bitch of a girl, Harmony, not to mention the whole damn team." Thinking out loud pounding his fist onto his open palm; he wanted to cause them pain. Too many times they had made him look like a babe in battle. He was no child. He was a hardened warrior taken from the field of battle and had existed in hell for centuries under the rule of an obsessed love sick overlord prone to tantrums. His time of penance was up and no one was going to be the master over him ever again.

He had been called a seasoned warrior by his clan when he was alive. He spent centuries within the Under Realm and learned all he had from the world each time he had been sent on a mission, over time coupled with determination, he became well trained, and well versed in doing the Lord Drakkoon's bidding. He had been dragged into his place, in the Under Realm, against his will but had suffered like everyone nonetheless because Lord Drakkoon willed it so. He never had a chance for redemption as was promised when he had first arrived. He was trapped here like everyone else had been. All the lies for a chance at being chosen during The Reckoning never happened not only for him but for no one else sentenced to hell. Some of the old ones talked about The Reckoning as if it had been a second chance at life after have served Lord Drakkoon's bidding within the hell hole and they still believed in that hope. They kept to the old ways of not doing anything to disrupt their chance for redemption. Let them be the Lord Drakkoon's lapdogs. He would never believe those lies again.

He knew different; one hundred years passed, two hundred years passed then three. How long must a person wait to see redemption? It was all a pack of lies told to keep everyone in line. Nothing happened; no Awakening, there was no redemption for anyone sent to the Under Realm. All the souls sent down have been left to rot, forgotten by the Gods. The land is overcrowded like the prisons he found on the Earth Realm. Everyone was poor scrambling for food at every turn. If it wasn't for the strict enforcers of Lord Drakkoon's armies, havoc would reign supreme in this place of unforgiving servitude. How could they still believe in hope for redemption when they had been forgotten and their overlord did not care for his people?

He needed to get his head in the game. From what the lady in his dreams told him he needed to keep his focus on the mission in front of him. Let Lord Drakkoon think he was in charge. For now he was, but not for long that he vowed. The lady had never steered him wrong in what she foretold. Everything she had said to him had come to pass and he believed actions spoke louder than empty promises sung from a dictator hung up on some bitch from another time. Hell, he couldn't even leave this place to get her himself without Lord Drakkoon's permission. It was infuriating.

He was sick and tired of believing he could earn his way out of this place to be shot down when nothing happened. Not one damn thing happened to indicate he could earn his chance at a second life. Each year had passed and kept right on passing while he was kept in a constant mental prison of hope to live freely once again. The lady was his only ticket out of there. She was the truth in all of his chaos called life. If he was going to believe in anything again it would be her. She wouldn't lie to him down.

Shaking off his thoughts he headed down the corridor to the Lord Drakkoon's study. Quickly knocking on the door, he waited a moment to allow for the customary time allowed before he opened the door. Lord Drakkoon sat in a chair facing the empty fireplace. That was odd; whenever he was in this room the fire had been lit.

"I am here, My Lord, as requested."

The room was quiet no noise and no response came from Lord Drakkoon. He just sat there starring forward. It must have been a few minutes while he waited for a response, when he thought maybe he might have done something to tip his hand at is true intentions. You never knew with the Lord Drakkoon, yesterday was the worse he had ever been treated by him and that was small display of his temper. He had seen him conduct worse.

"Master, is there anything you need or that I may do for you?"

"Realm Keeper, I want you to gather your Shadow Riders. Pick them for loyalty and efficiency. I want them to respond to your command and your command only. Pick your Riders wisely as they are not to think for themselves they are solely to be put in your command to obey. Once you have your Riders assembled, ready yourselves for a journey to the Second Realm. This is where you will find your adversaries. I want Briksanna captured and brought to me unharmed. You will alert me prior to engaging the Lightning Strike team and once you have Briksanna. I want to know what your plan will be once you have set eyes upon my prize before you proceed with her capture."

Speaking quietly he noticed Lord Drakkoon had never taken his eyes off the empty fireplace. "Yes Master, at once. How do you know they will be in the Second Realm?"

"She is coming today, I can feel her intent. It is the closest I have felt to her in two hundred years. She wants me to know she is coming back. She has hidden herself well, but no longer. You would do well not to question me often, Realm Keeper. Your ascension as Realm Keeper can be dissolved at any given moment. May I remind you if you displease me or I find your insolence intolerable you will be instantly dispatched no matter where you are. Have I made myself understood?"

"Perfectly, My Lord. May I live to serve you," he bowed as he spoke and awaited his approval.

"You may go," effectively dismissing him without further word.

He turned around and strode to the door feeling his anger build with every step at the dismissive manner in which he had been treated. It was insulting and degrading in the manner after all the years of absolute servitude.

"Realm Keeper?"

He stopped dead in his tracks and realized he let his thoughts float freely within the presence of Lord Drakkoon. Nervously he turned around to find his overlord had turned to face him with piercing green eyes. Swallowing a lump in his throat he responded, "Yes, My Lord"

"I treat you with better respect than which you will treat the Shadow Riders. Do remember that in the future; when you find yourself in my presence complaining in thought?"

"My apologies, My Lord, for the disrespect. I am learning to..." Allowing his true nervousness to rise to the forefront he knew he had made a terrible mistake by giving into his anger within the presence of Lord Drakkoon.

"I do not want to hear another word." He spoke absolutely and with venom.

Rising from his chair he walked slowly towards him with not an ounce of intent on his face. He stopped directly in front of him studying his face or hair, and just kept on staring like he was looking for something. The more Lord Drakkoon searched his face the more nervous he became. *Do not think of her. Do not think of her, Do not think...*

"You seem different from last night. There is something different about you that even I cannot see what it is. Are you hiding something from me Realm Keeper?"

Gulping the scrap of spit left in his mouth, he tried to clear his throat before responding. It wasn't working well, he coughed instead. "No Master, I am the same as you saw yester eve. I hide nothing My Lord. My deep apologies for having offended you."

"Hmmm," he looked for a minute longer then dismissed him again, already returning back to his chair. "You may leave."

"Thank you, My Lord." He abruptly turned from where he stood, and all but ran out of the room. He closed the study doors and leaned back to catch his breath. He turned around to face the door so no one could interpret his time outside Lord Drakkoon's doors as a sign of weakness. He took a deep breath to steady his beating heart hating how weak he felt a few minutes ago in front of Lord Drakkoon. Stretching to his full height he turned around and headed towards the outer training yard to assemble his Shadow Riders.

Halfway to the yard he reached into his tunic and pulled out the necklace he found around his neck this morning. The Lady had told him she would leave a symbol for him to recognize her commitment to help him. The symbol would represent their agreement binding his energy to her and would grant him access to her power when needed. Aligning himself with the lady would make him stronger than Lord Drakkoon and would forge a way for her to channel her energy through him giving him the means to defeat Lord Drakkoon when the time came. The only way to defeat Lord Drakkoon was to cut off what he valued most.

He valued Briksanna and Merridian and they were the ones he would strike at first.

17

Gathered outside at the south side entrance of their compound, everyone appeared battle ready minus the normal gear. It looked different not to see everyone with their normal packs slung over their backs but he believed they would be just a successful without the munitions, gadgets and arms. Knives and bows were all Briksanna said they could bring and that nothing else could be brought into Skaldanna through the portal. He assumed she had tried over the years so he didn't feel the need to question her judgment.

His impression, from what little she had shared over the years, was that Skaldanna for all appearances was like a blast from Medieval England with psychic perks and some modern conveniences like plumbing. Might be seven centuries blast in the past for him and he felt clueless in what to expect from the political hierarchy, but hey, he could totally handle this, right?

He wanted to make her proud when he stepped into her world as part of her Royal Family, most importantly as her husband. He didn't want to embarrass her but he did have enough faith in himself to believe he would be the best partner intent to stand beside wherever she had to go. Being the mate of the High Queen had even more responsibility then if they were to be man and wife on Earth. He understood that, especially now that he knew she was the Queen of the entire realm. There he thought it. That was the biggest issue he had with the whole damn thing. Here he and his brother came from a poor excuse of a family, not to disrespect his mother whenever he thought of his past, but she could have left that bastard of a father they had long ago, for him and Stark to land in a relationship with what he believed, without a doubt, was the other half of his soul to find out she was a Queen. Good God, what did he get himself into?

What would he know about being the husband to the High Queen of Skaldanna? He was going to have to eat dirt on this one and ask for help. He knew it was going to be inevitable and that he'd have to learn patience. He had it in spades for his family, strangers he didn't think he could to it right away, but for her he would step over coals just to be the man she needed him to be and that thought gave him hope he could be the King she needed him to be. Sure he wanted to impress her with his understanding of her traditions and customs, but on his own terms and in his own time and for now that would have to wait. Their completing this quest was a priority along with keeping the family safe and together coming in a close second. He had gleamed bits and pieces of information from her memories when they were talking to the family knowing it wasn't enough for him truly grasp what it meant to be High Royalty. He planned on paying close attention to everyone once they arrived taking his que from the important people in her life, starting with Princess Katerina. He would have to determine who else he could trust for information once he got there.

There were times when he felt way in over his head around her because she had lived for so long, seen and done so much, but in this instance, despite the unknown, Bri had a way of calming his inner demons despite his fears of the unknown. He believed deep down no matter what they might encounter on the quest, as long as they were together, there wasn't anything they couldn't do together.

He turned his thoughts back to the present moment and towards the woman in question; she truly was the most beautiful person he had ever seen. Standing in her battle gear; metallic lavender leather bodice with matching long strap skirt complete with bracers and leg guards she was stunning. Her hair was braided with matching lavender ribbons woven through the long braid hanging below her waist taunted him to pull them loose just to see her eyes darken at his blatant desire run his fingers through each strand just like he wanted to do with her body. Her boots were knee high wrapping her beautiful calves protectively reminiscent of his hands running along the length of them like he had done earlier that morning. Seeing his woman dressed for battle tied him in knots.

In the past when he watched her from a distance he admired her beauty locking his desire inside of him not wanting to disrupt the family dynamics, but today, seeing her standing in the twilight she was magnificent. He loved her deeply and his soul filled with passion for the woman she was to him and for the first time he let it show for the world to know. He loved her and in that moment he knew it didn't matter what she wore on the outside or who she was politically to everyone else. To him, she was beautiful just as she was and she belonged to him.

Both of her swords were strapped to her back knowing how she liked to intimidate people with the sight of her dual swords when on missions. He didn't know what impression she needed to emit once they were in her realm so he just figured he'd go along with her que. He imagined she would want to engage the role of High Queen and that of warrior, which was fine by him; hence the light cloak she had draped over her shoulders and the whole picture Zena the Warrior Princes she had going on with her appearance. As far as he was concerned she was his Queen and he would do his damndest to be her King.

Seeing the girls were dressed similarly he smiled. All three girls had on matching outfits with the exception of color, Trinity dressed in blue and Harmony in green while Gabriella wore red. They each wore bracers and leg guards but had only one sword strapped to their back. Daggers were placed strategically throughout their body and in some hidden places like he had seen Bri put on earlier. No doubt the girls were just as deadly wielding them as their mother figure. Any man should be wary of the girls if they ever chose to pursue them with the intent to harm.

He and Stark laughed about it several times in the past. He frowned, the girls were no longer girls. He should stop using that word. He looked closer believing he needed to view them more as who they were today, beautiful women who if were to be engaged in battle he and his brother had no doubt they'd handle the situation to the death on their own. He knew all three of them had raised girls well and he was proud of the women they had become.

Turning to so he could check out the men he almost laughed because they looked just as deadly as the women had. Dressed in loose white tunics with leather covering their fronts with shoulder straps to hold their swords along with various daggers placed on their belts except for Striker. He knew his legs wouldn't carry him unless he had several more knives along his arms, chest and back. Chancing a glance at Stark he took his measure wanting to be sure whatever was running through his head he was still in the game. Hell they all had to be and that included him.

"Stark, you ready man?" He walked up to him and stopped a few feet from where the Goddess and her companion stood, whom he noticed, hadn't left his side since they had gathered at the designated site ten minutes ago.

"Spot on, you?" came his response.

"Ready as I'll ever be. Think the team is ready for what we're about to do? I don't want to see any of them put in unnecessary positions and at the same time I know they can handle whatever it is that's waiting for us when we get there. I know in my head they're not little kids anymore and I know they have my back in any battle just as I trust you, Stark, but it's more than that. I don't want anything to happen to them, all of them, and for some reason this quest, us going to Skaldanna, it feels different and final all rolled into one giant ball of nervousness. Shit I don't know. I just feel like life as we know it as a family is about to seriously change and that is what has me worried. Not in a bad way, just worried."

Rubbing the back of his neck trying to loosen the tension he felt tightening, "I have a bad feeling already sitting on my shoulders about this quest but, I trust Bri and I trust Merridian, so forward we all will go. Just wish we had a little more Intel. You know what I mean?"

He glanced back as Bri stood with the women and noticed how beautiful she looked in her courtly armor. He knew by the way his thoughts of anxiety flew out of his head when he saw her standing there talking to them. He must have had some stupid dreamy look on it because that was just how dumbstruck he felt watching her in the moment. It wasn't the first time in the past couple of days he had thought of her as his. The difference was he wasn't afraid to show it in front of everybody now and that suited him just fine.

Clapping him on the shoulder Stark snapped him out of his thoughts. "We're in this together. We're family and no one messes with our family. We treat this as any other mission, we assess, strategize then we attack just like any other mission we've dealt with in the past. The kids are good, better than most merc's we've come to know so is Briksanna, you know that. We are winners Nate, nothing else will do for any of us and you know that. We will win this thing I have no doubt in my head or in my heart."

Turning his gaze towards the Goddess tipping his chin in her direction, "What about our added companions? Who will protect them while we are off being Rambo?"

Looking away from him to the women in question, "Merridian is her own warrior. She will take care of business when the time comes. I have no doubt in how far she is willing to go to achieve peace in both our worlds. I trust her Nate, and trust is something I don't give without careful consideration and a boatload of Intel. She has let me inside her head regarding this mission and what she thinks might be going on and it's no different from what she said to all of us yesterday." He said tapping his fingers to his temple, "That took a lot of trust on her part letting me look in her head like that. I wouldn't take any information I wanted from her or betray her trust because curiosity killed the cat just to know how she felt about me. She can handle more than everyone here believes. She really is beautiful, Nate, more beautiful than I remembered."

"You are hung up, my man." Grinning madly over the way his brother spoke about another person let alone a woman he was interested in. Stark never spoke that away about a woman period. "Let me help you."

Stark turned back around to him with a questioning look on his face tilting his head to the side to study him before looking down at his gear, "Nothing is hung up on you or me, what do I need help with. I grabbed everything, right?"

Not able to hold it in any longer, he knew they had a couple of on lookers so he went in for the kill. Thumping Stark on the back of his head, "Right in hear man"—leaning closer speaking lower—"don't wait as long as I did, God knows what we are up against and one thing I've learned is I wouldn't trade a minute of it waiting for the right moment. I have your back man; go for it with both feet in."

He pulled his brother in for a tight hug pounding on his back in a manly fashion that men loved to do reminding him of their unconditional love. He let go and stepped back while Stark looked at him for a couple of seconds stunned by his speech, then he picked up his gear turned around. Before he left he saw Merridian had scooted to the spot he vacated knowing it was time to give them the privacy they needed to talk.

Looking for his wife startled that she wasn't in the same vicinity she had been a couple of seconds ago he turned around and felt panicked when he noticed everyone around him appeared calm and in good spirits, not stressed as he felt inside. Maybe Stark was right about all of this, he was worrying too much and needed to let the stress go. They weren't just The Lightning Strike team; they were first and foremost a family.

Bri, stepped from behind Gabriella holding her short bow. She had several quiver of arrows in her other hand and began handing them out to the women, gaining smiles while she did it. Feeling comfortable watching her a little longer content to be in the moment he was reminded of what attracted him to her in the first place. The way she brushed her hand down Gabriella's hair or gently squeezed Trinity's arm and winked at Harmony before they all burst out laughing from whatever it was that was being said. He could see how much of a mother she had been with the girls. The way she touched their shoulders while she helped them adjust their swords to better fit the bow and quiver or the way she held their attention and affection with simple gestures and a few words. There was the way she moved Gabby's hair out of the way carefully so she could cinch her shoulder straps or the way she instructed the twins to mimic what she was doing so they all would know how to repeat the process on their own. He observed the way she laughed when Trinity teased Harmony about something because not soon after every one of them were laughing loud. For a split second she looked at them as if she were memorizing that very moment and then a mask fell over her face and the look had disappeared while she nodded at something Gabriella had said.

Frowning he looked hard at his woman knowing his eyes hadn't played tricks on him. He saw her expression and knew it meant something. Memorizing what was exactly what he'd like to know.

Letting go of Gabriella Briksanna knew her mate was observing her with the girls. She could feel his eyes boring into her from a distance. She also knew that the Goddess and her companion, Ellena, were watching as well. Did she have something hanging off of her? She almost chanced looking down to see if her leggings had come un-laced. The best course of action was to begin explaining what they should expect with regards to travelling between realms. It would take the tension off of her and distract her heart from the worry of her loved ones safety. For a split second she thought of the pain she would feel if anything were to happen to the girls, but quickly brushed it aside banishing the horrid emotions the thought had brought with it.

She knew they were no longer children but young men and women fierce in their own right capable to cut down hardened enemies. She knew it in her mind, believed it in her heart, but when she looked at them interacted with them, in moments like this, she was reminded they were still her children regardless of their age or their skill and she loved them with every ounce of her being. Sighing, knowing she needed to move forward with her task she stepped away from the women nodding to them as she walked by knowing it was not to be for the last time she would smile or laugh with them. Clearing her throat she gave a quick two chirp whistle letting everyone know it was time to listen up. That was her signature call to get their attention.

"It is time for us to travel through the portal. You will be fine going through the energy portal with what you have on you. I will hold the connection here and Katerina will maintain the portal on Skaldanna. As long as there is an energetic connection on either end the portal will remain balanced and whole for a duration of time. I have traveled by these means for centuries, so do not over worry yourselves about the semantics of the portal. Any questions before we leave?" No one spoke or gestured for her to answer any questions so she continued.

"Is there any special way we are to speak or behave once we arrive? Any customs we should be observing in particular to Skaldanna that should immediately concern us?

She could always count on Gabriella for the proper way on approaching a situation or bringing to attention the elephant sitting in the room no one wanted to talk about.

"Think of it as being at court during the reign of Queen Elizabeth but without the excessive wardrobe and the continuous bowing. We can talk more on the subject when we arrive. Just follow my lead and remember always speak and act formal in speech and in mannerisms. Respect is given and shown in everything people do so you need to keep in mind to watch your language. No slang words are used so try to be direct in speech and you will be fine." Keeping her tone matter of fact she did not want to alarm them any more than they already were feeling regarding her status on Skaldanna and what that would mean for them as being part of her family.

Stepping further away from the group to where she wanted to create the portal, she wanted a space where there was enough room for her to make as large as possible. Turning to Nathanial she spoke telepathically.

"This is the place where I will create the portal. Be sure to guide them in and Stark can take the rear. I will be last for I need to remain here making sure the portal stays open and so I can close it once everyone has passed through. Only a person with the energy level equivalent to a Skaldannian can open, maintain and close a portal between both realms."

Closing her eyes knowing her orders would be followed to the letter she focused inward and reached mentally for that familiar pulse of violet light she carried deep within her always reminding her of home. She found the thin thread and imagined it coiling around in a tight ball as she allowed the energy to build growing in size as it did. She believed in its strength, the strength of her forefathers and of those both on Skaldanna and within the Earth Realm. She pulled harder on the energy commanding the formation of the portal walls to bend to her will. The wind picked up as well as the static electricity surrounding the area. She heard no voices, no sound. She was one with her energy, her life force feeding the command to see her family travel safely between realms.

Her energy was what held her together both inside and out. It was the only constant she had held close to her for thousands of years. Years where she had been so lonely her memories where her only companions until she held the twins in each arm. Then came Stark and Nathanial followed by Striker then Kenneth and Gabriella. All of them were her family and she would give her life to see no harm befell them. They belonged together bound by tragic circumstance, and yet they no longer held themselves by their circumstance but with the unconditional love that has shaped and bound them to be the men and women today. She felt the energy build attracted to the people standing close to her recognizing them as one family belonging to her heart pushing at her mental wards wanting to reach out and connect with them, but she held strong and true forcing her will only for a portal to appear. Skaldanna would meet her family soon enough for the High Royalty they were.

She channeled energy into a large circular portal and thought it was the largest portal she had ever built. She wanted to make sure her family was safe because for the first time in her very long life she had a lot to lose.

"Kat are you ready to connect?" Holding her breath not knowing what to expect once she had made contact with her friend. She did not want to let her worry get the best of her keeping her focus on the task at hand.

"I am here waiting on you as usual, your highness." She heard the excitement in her voice despite the sarcasm and it was a relief to her heart.

"Let us connect, you and I. My family and I are ready to come home."

"Reach for me, Briksanna like we used to do as little girls. Hold fast to our bond and know I will remain steadfast for your travelers are very dear to me as well."

With just a thought she reached for her best friend finding the familiar energetic connection between them whenever she connected with Katerina. With a loud thunder clap and several lightning bolts later she had accomplished what she set out to do. She opened her eyes and saw a massive portal staring back at her. Mentally testing the structural integrity for any flaws noting there were none she declared, "Simply amazing."

"Are you ready to meet my family, Katerina? I am ready to bring them home."

"I have been ready to meet them for the past several months," sounding excited.

"I will send them to you in pairs."

"My guard and I await you. All is well Briksanna, truly you are safe and welcomed here."

"I will begin sending them now." Yelling over her left shoulder she began to instruct everyone to proceed through the portal.

"Nate, I want you to enter with Harmony first. Katerina and her guard wait on the other side. Trinity you and Kenneth will go next.

Gabriella you and Striker followed by the Merridian and Ellena. Stark you will step in with me but hold onto my hand as I will need to close the portal behind us and you will need to be in direct contact with me while we travel through."

"Stark can lead with Harmony. You and I are one Bri always. Better get used to it Lady."—looking over his shoulder he motioned with his head for his brother to take his place in lead—"Brother you lead I'll watch your back." Putting on his fiercest facial expression he wanted them to know he had all of their backs.

Stark took one look at her and nodded then grabbed his gear Harmony's hand and walked with her through the blaze of purple light, trusting Briksanna with their lives into the great unknown setting an example for everyone watching. Each group walked through grinning with Gabriella and Striker sounding a loud whoop as they jumped through grins on both their faces. The Goddess looked over briefly at Nate smiled then grabbed Ellena's hand as they gracefully entered for all intents and purposes the royalty that they were.

"Our turn," she looked at the man she loved and reached for his hand. "It's you and me forever lady."

Not willing to chance breaking her concentration with a portal this large she smiled squeezing his hand knowing Nate could feel her love for him. "*I love you,*" she thought.

"I love you, more." Tugging her hand towards the portal he glanced back and winked before he turned around and entered the portal.

He made her feel as if she was the most beautiful woman with one look and a couple of words spoken wrapped with love given freely. He was proud of her right now and she felt his emotions when he grabbed her hand. How he had marveled over what she had created. Her confidence he felt from their family and how brave he believed her to be. She felt all of it in a swirling rush of thoughts and emotions right before stepped through the portal and by the way his eyes twinkled with love when he winked at her. He knew sending her family to the one place she was afraid of going to for so long was the hardest thing she had done. She told him that yesterday and again this morning when the hid the Blood Stone in the center of her scabbard sewing it closed where the two strips of leather met with enough room for her swords to fit over it concealing its presence yet not making the overall appearance as if something had been hidden underneath.

Hoping Skaldanna would receive her family well was another concern of hers something he said he understood. He reassured her he would be there to help shoulder the burden she had carried alone for so long, but she knew a large part of her fear had been fed with the belief her long life had to been surrounded by solitude in order for her to evade the man she was convinced had been the reason for her pain both inside and out. It was not so easy for her to forgive and forget what she had experienced or what she had endured in her captivity. The atrocities' had been directed at her and her family. She never understood Lord Drakkoon's obsession with her. What she did know was she no longer feared him and that was what gave her hope she her family would succeed what she could not do alone. Settle her fate that was tied in The Prophesy.

When he stepped through the portal his first instinct was to close his eyes but he kept them open wanting to see everything that was going on around him more. He didn't want to miss a thing. Right now he wanted to whoop like Striker and Gabriella had excited in trying something new and crazy. He felt Bri turn away from him holding his hand in the process. He looked back towards her sensing her focus shift on pulling the energy back inside of herself, literally. It was surreal to see the area they had been standing outside of their home on Earth close in on itself like a picture screen getting fuzzier and fuzzier until that picture faded into nothingness all the while a stream of energy from that end of the portal found its way back to the small of Bri's back.

She turned around and took steps towards him. Earth was their home and even though they were leaving it behind that didn't mean where they were going could not be home for them too. He meant it when he told her, wherever they were was home for him as long as they were together. Walking beside her, for what seemed like ten feet, he noticed firelight shining ahead of them. They walked for about twenty more feet and stepped through the portal end. When they passed through he noticed two things, first, there was a lot more static electricity going on this end then when he had entered the portal and second, their family's faces didn't appear happy.

Yup, stepping through the portal stung like hell. It felt like being shocked by an electric toaster when you wiped it clean with a wet rag while plugged in but all over. He did that once and never did it again. It felt worse because every inch of his body had been shocked at once. As quickly as the shock hit his system spreading all over his body with an intense stream of pain it ended. He wanted to scream, that's how much it had hurt.

"Holy crap that hurt, Bri!" Frowning he let go of her hand to brush his arms and stomach trying to determine if there really were any wounds on him.

"What happened? Are you all ok, anyone else feel that sting coming out of the portal?"

All nodded except Merridian and Ellena. Were they trying to hide a smile at his discomfort? Seriously?

"Yes and no, Mamma didn't say we should to expect that." Again always count on Gabriella to state the obvious, where everyone else just grunted rubbing themselves like he was doing.

"You must have felt the shift in energy frequency when you passed from one realm to the next. I have been travelling through portals for so long I had forgotten that first jolt where the body acclimates itself to a new realm. I no longer feel it when I pass through portals. Suffice it to say you may expect the same when you travel via the portal the next time but not much after that."

Looking at everyone making sure no one had any true injuries due to the energy shift. He was worried at first but seeing everyone shaking off the effects no longer briskly rubbing themselves he felt relieved. He turned to face Bri and caught a streak of blonde hair fly in front of him barreling into his wife.

"Katerina!"

He watched Katerina hold Bri tight as she closed her own eyes obviously feeling the familiar embrace of her longtime friend. He noticed Bri open her eyes widening in surprise. Following her gaze he spied a pair of blue eyes belonging to a very tall man standing directly behind Katerina.

He quickly checked his mental link with Bri to see if the stranger was a threat to them. By the shocked expression on her face what he gleamed from their mental link was impression of an important man from her father's past she had not seen in thousands of years. He looked back and took a close measure of the stranger.

A fair face held eyes that looked hardened from life, not too bad on his looks, straight nose square jaw where blonde hair fell to his shoulders framing his face. He held his massive arms across his equally massive chest and scowled down at both women. He picked up on the gasp of shock as Bri mentally traced the tattooed armbands that flashed the torched firelight. She recognized the tattoos along with the pair of blue eyes that stared back at her. He wanted to know who the hell the man was that his woman would recognize something so intimate as a tattoo.

"Hawk!" She screeched his name and launched herself into arms of the General of the High Royal Guards; her father's personal guard and best friend.

His jealousy reared its ugly head right next to its best friend anxiety. Something about this whole scene seemed off to him. Why would Katerina not tell Bri of this blast from the past when she had the opportunity? And why keep it a surprise knowing how scared Bri was about coming back to her home realm in the first place? Something defiantly was off.

Turning his attention back to the two people in front of him he saw the giant of a man scramble to unfold his arms before Bri slammed into him.

"Where have you been all this time? I have not seen you since the night our castle had been attacked. I thought you long dead all these years."

He knew she felt ashamed at her behavior but didn't care at what people thought. This man had been an uncle to her and a brother to her father. He felt his jealously dissipate when her thoughts passed through his mind. He saw them pull back from each other and noticed Bri seemed hesitant to let him go by the way she grasped his shirt at his waist and looked into the eyes of the man she had once idolized.

He noticed the man's eyes were just as wet as Bri's. Seeing his emotion over their reunion helped him to banish whatever shreds of jealousy that remained. This man clearly had been a person she had respected and still did.

"Where have you been hiding, Hawk? Are there more survivors? Is Rissa alive as well? Oh, Gods, I thought no one had survived all this time and here you are. Please take me to her Hawk, I must see my sister. Take me at once."

She stepped away from him fully prepared to march off casting away all thoughts of what she was supposed to do and everyone who was with her. Her actions shocked her filling her with the much remembered desperation she felt searching for her sister centuries past. His heart went out to her knowing she would hate herself the moment she realized what she had said.

How easy it had been for her to step into the role of a spoiled Princesses with just a few words and a familiar face. He had never heard her speak to someone like that before, but then he had never seen her come face to face with members of her pas.

"I want to see Rissa immediately, please take me to her Hawk. You have no idea how long it has been since I have felt the embrace of flesh and bone instead of distant memories."

He watched her search the face of the man he couldn't mentally read. He just stared back at her not speaking a single word or hinting at his thoughts through facial expression. Man he could take notes on that stoic expression the General kept. Just moments ago he witnessed the same man wipe tears from his eyes over their reunion.

He gently placed his arms around Bri's waist as he came up behind her. The moment he moved closer to her everything exploded all around them.

Hawk quickly grabbed Bri and threw her behind him simultaneously he pulled his long sword out from his scabbard. Before the sword was pulled completely from its sheath the twins had their daggers pointed under his chin at each side of his major artery in his neck. He sped over and pulled Bri from harm's way so the team could do what they did best. Striker had grabbed Princess Katerina safely to the outer rim of the firelight along with Gabriella and Kenneth was behind Hawk sword out pointed at the General's kidney. Glancing at his brother, Stark had pulled the Goddess and Ellena out of the way to the edge of the clearing. Everyone was safe.

"Cease!"

Out of fear for her family's safety she shouted while lightning bolt after lightning bolt crashed down around them and still no one moved or seemed afraid. All eyes were on the quartet in the middle of the forest circle.

"I would leave your wee blade where it lay sir and remove your hand from its hilt slowly. That's it"—he pushed the sword back into its scabbard slowly—"now my sister and I would like nothing but to carve you up into tiny pieces, but considering how Mamma was taken with you I'm guessing she wouldn't appreciate it one bit; isn't that right twin?"

Harmony had spoken not giving a hint to the venom she knew her daughter harbored in the sound of her voice nor had she taken her eyes off the man who had threatened her a moment ago. She knew that was how her family had perceived him at this moment, yet she could hardly believe Hawk would hurt her or her family. He taught her the concept everyone was a threat until proven otherwise. She waited a few minutes to see what would happen next knowing Hawk had to believe the people around him were not a threat to her especially after he heard Harmony's declaration of her being their mother.

Looking equally calm Trinity slowly pulled one of the blades she held next to his heart away in her belt. "Sounds about right to me twin; I think he needs a lesson on manners. Something his mother should have shown him long ago and seeing our mother had recognized him means he should have had lots of time to practice it. Maybe he just needs to be reminded of the proper way to greet guests due to their station. Why don't we give him a hand with that?"

"I got your back ladies, or should say his back seeing he feels a bit cocky assessing our intentions towards our own mother. Maybe you should help him out a bit Trin, seeing he can't seem to remember where the hell he's at or who he's dealing with."—leaning close to the back of his head—"word of advice, I wouldn't push the twins on this. They can be a tad bit sharp on a man's blade when they get all protective and such over family."—stepping back to where he originally stood he added—"Oh and another thing, you just threatened our mother over there so I'd say you lost a hell of a lot of points right off the bat with those two, but what do I know, you may like a challenge. I'm game; I'd love to see what you've got just to loosen up a bit after that portal joy ride."

Trinity placed her palm on his chest in hopes to read his true intentions which were one of her many talents in healing; she could assess not only the physical state of the body but the emotional side as well to include the energetic intentions of an individual.

She held her breath and knew her family had tried to protect her yet in the same breath she wanted desperately to believe her sister was still alive. Hawk was the last person to be with her sister when her family had been attacked all those years ago. She did not want to look her daughter in the eye if his intentions turned out to be false. It would kill her, yet she knew her children would do anything to spare her an ounce of pain even kill the man she once worshiped the ground he had walked on.

She watched Trinity hold her palm against his heart for a few moments, but it must have been long enough because she looked up right at him and said, "He is no threat, he reacted to Nate coming up behind her and his immediate response was to put Momma behind him. He is quiet because he is assessing us."

Harmony was far from convinced that the huge man in front of her was no longer a threat. She was relieved over Trinity' assessment and irritated with her children's prolonged hesitation apparent in Harmony's reaction towards him. She was her mother, of course she knew her daughter. She was slow to accept but generous to a fault. Once a person made a bad move against her family it was hard for Harmony to relinquish her trust again. Her knife was still in her grip close to his artery with her other hand held towards his side more than likely between his ribs in hopes to access his heart.

Smiling mentally she wanted to laugh. The girls really were dangerous with their knives and very protective of her. It was beautiful to witness and made her proud.

"Stand down the three of you, now." Coming around Nate she shook her head slightly at her mate indicating she did not want him to interfere.

"I need for you to let him go Harmony, he was doing his job and from hundreds of years of training it was instinct for him to protect me not knowing who you are."

"Seems to me we all just came through here together and with him being here with Aunt Kat he would have known who he was to be expecting." Shaking her head slightly clearly not agreeing with what she was being told. "There is too much danger here, Momma, to let this one man make an obvious threat to you as soon as we enter the realm. I don't like it at all, so I'm going to ask you once mister, why did you grab my Momma like that? What's your purpose? Like she said earlier where have you been all this time? Seems she asked you a number of questions and you just stood there."

He finally blinked his eyes and stared down at Harmony then turned his head to look at Trinity. He swallowed and looked around at the men and women around everyone most likely realizing the majority of them where children entering maturity. She knew he could escape where they held him, he more than likely had counted the moves, seen the act of escape in his minds eye like he had trained both her and Kat; yet he did not want to hurt any of them which was apparent by his lack of action.

He looked up at her he and swallowed before he spoke with a face of weariness than the stoic expression she had witnessed earlier.

"Is what the lady says true, Lady Briksanna? You are their mother?"

"Yes, sir Hawk it is truth and a story which we can best explain over a tankard of wine beside a warm fire."

He nodded to her then turned back to Harmony and spoke. "I grabbed her because the man came at the princess from behind. To me that is a vulnerable position for her to be in and a threat to her safety"—shaking his head—"a non-negotiable move of protection with Royalty especially High Court Royalty. My purpose is here tonight was to see to Princess Katerina's safety while she was to greet an emissary of great importance to aid us during this travesty. Where have I been all this time, looks like if you want that answer you will have to lower your weapon kitten and have a sip of wine, because that my dear lady is a long story. Now step aside or I will remove you of the weapons in hand within five moves."

Trinity had already sheathed her dagger along with Kenneth and they had stepped back fully expecting, with the challenge Hawk had given Harmony, she would not be able to resist taking him up on his offer.

"We do not have time for this game. Harmony sheath your weapons immediately and Hawk please join us in Kat's solar so we may speak of all that has transpired since we last met."

Not seeing Harmony move she felt herself lose her temper. Sending out a tendril of energy towards Harmony she gave the equivalence of a sharp flick on her arm, zapping some sense into her stubborn child. "Do not make me repeat myself, young lady. Let's move towards the castle. The sooner we are indoors the safer I will feel. Remember our enemy is Lord Drakkoon and his minions not one another."

Reluctantly Harmony removed her blade. It took a lot for her to not take up his challenge she knew that for a fact. Her daughter was the most protective of everyone in the family. Using the mental family link she asked Harmony what was the real problem. Everyone was waiting on her to proceed and she knew it was so unlike her to behave this way.

"There is something about him that seems familiar and it is creeping me out more than what I had felt when I initially thought his intention was to harm you. It's as if everything within me wants to get away from his piercing blue stare, but at the same time I feel like I know him from somewhere. He seems just as intent looking at me for some reason. Like he's just as shocked to see me and Trinity as we are to see him. I don't know what is going on, I'm mostly creeped out about the familiarity thing, ok?"

She glanced at Nathanial for his input. He shrugged his shoulders not adding anything for her to work with then tapped his wrist to let her know they were now risking exposure outside castle walls. They did not have time for all of this animosity and she was getting irritated.

"I accept your challenge Sir Hawk and will be happy to charm you with a blade or two in the morning unless you need your beauty sleep due to old age."

"Harmony, that's enough!" She yelled at Harmony knowing her eyes were glowing violent feeling her tumultuous emotions leak out of her in the form of energy. Energy which she had just manifested in the form of a powerful voice. Judging from the rest of the members surrounding her and the shaking of their heads she had surprised them too. She had used a sonic voice with her command. The only two people who did not seem affected were Merridian and her companion Ellena. Merridian smiled at her nodding her head slightly in reverence to the revelation of additional power like she had predicted. She had said that would happen to all of them, she happened to be the first one it had happened to.

Startled at her mother's tone of voice, knowing she pushed her too far with that last comment simply because Hawk unnerved her. Harmony replied, "Yes ma'am."

Harmony forced herself to turn away from Hawk and sheathed her weapons while she grabbed the gear she had dropped earlier. In a few seconds she was ready to go expression of curiosity and anxiety gone. The warrior daughter she knew her to be stood before her once again. Would they be able to shake off the anxiety haunting all of them in order to save the future? She had no idea, but was willing to give it a go for the first time in her life.

18

Stepping away from the mountain of a man who had stood in front of her the moment Hawk had grabbed Briksanna. She wanted to get away from him because he was handsome man and made her heart beat fast. She knew him to be one of Briksanna's adopted children and had chastised her internal reaction the moment her eyes had landed on him. Knowing he was a man and had been raised by her dearest friend did not sit well with how attracted she was to him.

Brushing her wayward thoughts aside she believe now would be a perfect time to steer the gathered into the safety of her keep. She cleared her throat and spoke out loud. "Please everyone, follow me to my keep and allow me to see to your comfort for a time. I have been eager for your arrival and have everything prepared anticipating this very moment."

Stepping quickly around Striker, who had nudged himself closer every time she moved, she instead reached out her arms making the come gesture with her hands towards the twins completely ignoring him. "Quick give your Aunt Kat a hug, girls, I have longed to hold you since you were infants."

That was all it took for the twins to turn to her giving a shrill squeal when they hit her arms in a fierce embrace. She glanced at Gabriella not wanting to leave the impression the girl did not have her affection as well, she made the gesture again directly at her. "Come Gabby, I have a hug waiting in my arms for you as well. Do not think Briksanna has kept you a secret? You are her daughter as much as I am your aunt. Come let me hold you as well and let us hope to be the best of friends."

Gabriella strode over not with resignation but with face of anticipation. She reached around the twins to grab the girl close to her. After holding all three girls for a minute she let them go, and kissed each one lightly on the check. "I love you all."

Stepping back she looked around, "Well lads you are all hale enough and fair on the eyes, I see Briksanna has done well with the lot of you in your realm. Now let us be away from this place as cook has made her famous pasties I for one am hungry. Please, if you all will follow me."

She kept her head held high when she walked towards the castle not once expecting further trouble from the people behind her. Except she could not shake the sensations she felt in the brief moments when the blonde man had grabbed and threw her behind him. He stood sentry in front of her until she had stepped around him. She did not think he realized how he had handled her not to mention the fact he never took his hand off of her wrist the entire time.

She could almost hit herself because when he did grab her wrist her traitorous body instantly recognized him for the potential mate he could be. Never in her two hundred years had her energy source flared to life so quickly and so fiercely as it did in those few moments with that man.

"God's, what am I to do now?" she mumbled as she lead everyone towards the castle.

"Go with the flow sounds good to me." Came from a voice too close for comfort.

Startled at the answer to her outspoken question she stumbled in her step and almost fell. She looked at the hands that held her waist steady and she chanced a glance at the face whom the hands had belonged to. She was in trouble because no man could look so beautiful and smile without reserve as the man before had. Internally groaning she knew she was in serious trouble by the way her thoughts were heading.

"You are safe with me Princess Katerina, always. Do not be frightened, I promise no harm will ever come to you while I am around."

She pulled out of his grasp quickly feeling him hesitate before he let her go nodding to him once for his genuine assurance. "Thank you."

As she continued to walk towards the castle the feeling grew within her this man was her other half and those thoughts scared her to death. Could this night hold any more surprises? She did not think her head or heart could take much more.

"Anything is possible even for a Princess," he replied.

He couldn't resist the temptation of responding to her. The more he thought about what he had just said the more right it felt in his heart. The craziest thing was he had felt that jolt of electricity when they had touched back there in the forest just like she had felt it and again when they touched a few seconds ago. The biggest crazy of them all was he could hear her thoughts and that about freaked the both of them out. So for now he would tell Briksanna later in privacy realizing she had spoken of each person's abilities possibly becoming more advanced or more, which no one knew what more was, but this soon? A guy could take what he could get and Katerina Kastekanos was everything he wanted in a woman and more.

Smiling his megawatt smile feeling lighter than he felt since his parents had locked him in that bunker years ago. He couldn't remember their faces and they didn't leave a big impression on him. At times he felt real guilty about knowing he loved his current family unconditionally unlike the way he felt about his real parents. If he loved his mother like he loved Briksanna wouldn't he still be able to remember her?

It didn't matter to him anymore. The people around him meant more to him than anyone else in the world and he, for one, didn't believe in wallowing in the past. He was all for moving forward in life. He watched the woman in front of him lead his family towards the castle and it felt right to him. He had that same unconditional feeling he held for Briksanna when his thoughts turned to the beautiful green eyed, blonde haired beauty in front of him. She had no clue how she was torturing him with being close to him right now. When he had first laid eyes on her stepping out of that portal all the pain of being shocked had been forgotten. He just stared at her hoping like hell he held it together long enough for his open mouth to close. He watched her while she waited anxiously for everyone to step through. Her eyes were the deepest color of green he had ever seen in his life like emeralds plucked straight from a mountain. He could tell they were that color despite the hindrance of full light. Her hair was more of a sandy blonde with highlights weaving in and out hanging in a similar fashionable thick braid Briksanna always wore with ribbons woven throughout the braid matching the color of her golden gown. Her face appeared light in color small in size resembling a woman who was used to commanding yet she managed to hold herself according to her station despite her excitement from everyone's arrival.

He knew by the way he was having trouble keeping his heart regulated he was in deep trouble when it came to her. Never had he been captivated by a single woman. He wasn't blind, he'd seen beautiful women but no one grabbed his focus as this Princess had. None of his brothers or sisters had dated and they didn't mind being single on bit. They skirted the issue of intimacy only on missions and solely with intended targets. They were all well versed with the art of seduction, arousal and sex however; no one in their group with the exception of Nate and Briksanna, had paired with a member of the opposite sex. Oh, he knew Gabby had a crush on him, he'd known that for years. Neither one of them ever acted inappropriately towards one another, nor did he feel for her in that way. He knew in time her childhood infatuation would go away so he left the topic alone. Kenneth knew. How could he not, he was her brother. Her feelings for him were not obvious with the family at least he didn't think so which suited him fine, but he was very happy with the woman walking in front of him like a grinning fool happy and that caused him some alarm. Where did his feelings come from? He was literally held captivated by her presence from the moment he stepped onto her soil and knew instantly she was the one he'd been waiting for all his life.

Running his hands through his blonde hair he did his best to erect mental shields from her mind thinking she might be able to read him as easily as he had read her. He needed to talk to Briksanna right away. He didn't know if he was going to be able to last long in her presence before he acted on his instinct to claim her. He wanted her like he wanted his next breath and that worried the hell out of him.

Reaching a side entrance to the outer baily, Katerina glanced over her shoulder eyes going wide to his close presence. He was stood beside her ready to hold the door open once she had opened it.

"After you, My Lady." He smiled hoping his mental shields held so they could have some peace from the mutual bombardment of desire affecting the both of them. He looked at her mouth noticing she had licked her lips not taking her own eyes off his mouth.

He grinned knowing she was just as affected as he was.

"I did not realize you were so close"—turning back pulling the door open she quickly spoke over her shoulder—"this door is the quickest route from the outside into the keep. It is usually barred only accessible from the inside. I will lead you through the inner bailey to the kitchens entrance. My guards above have been briefed and are anticipating my guests. Please follow me."

Kicking the rock away that had held the door ajar, Katerina walked through. He made sure everyone understood where they were heading by a two chirp whistle. Catching Stark's gaze he gave a nod and followed Katerina into the castle grounds mentally sending word to his family to follow him.

Whatever happened now didn't matter. His fate had been sealed the moment he touched her. He also knew without a doubt, just like she did, the signs that lead to their connection where deep within him. His soul recognized her for the woman she was. His other half and one true mate.

Grinning that megawatt smile when she looked over her shoulder she responded with a smile of her own making his heart stutter before he pushed the door leading to the keep open. What an adventure his life was going to be standing beside his woman.

His woman? Oh, man was he screwed. Briksanna was going to kill him for falling for her best friend. Mentally shrugging his shoulders he thought back to his earlier words, *deGoing with the flow sounds good to me.*

They passed through the gates with their cloaks drawn wanting to keep their identity a secret. He quickly walked through the kitchen which led to a large room. It was hard to see what type of room they had entered and wanted to avoid unnecessary interruptions if anyone was in them. The time to look around would be for later. They had much to say to one another and little time to say it in. So much had transpired in both realms over the past couple of days how could she be here feeling the excitement of coming home when at the same time she knew there was so much turmoil she had to sort through with her kingdom?

Whenever she came in the past it took so much time to unload her energy back into the realm before she was rushing back to the twins. Later she began to feel cheated by not allowing her family or herself the opportunity to be a part of her homeland. Not in the sense she had dreamed too often to do. Before her adopted family she spent more time visiting Katerina sometimes arranging High Council meetings in effort to continue an active role as High Queen while she hid from Lord Drakkoon in effort to prevent war. Later in her life there had been her family to come back to so staying no longer held appeal when she looked forward to going back to the Earth Realm. When she saw Hawk and Katerina stand, in the clearing earlier, it was as if she had finally come home.

Many were there times Hawk would travel with her to visit Katerina before Lysinous showed any sign of interest in her as a woman. They would ride for miles together often camping under the moon, while she listened to tales told by the great General. Stories of his home, the family he missed and the children he was waiting to be born; twins if memory served correct. What had happened to everyone? Why after all these centuries, with no word of survivors, would he return now? Why would Katerina keep such a secret from her knowing she mourned the loss of her family thinking he had been lost along with them?

She carefully brought her thoughts back to the present and swallowed her burning questions. They were led to the servant's stairwell which traveled to the second floor then proceeded through a large hallway towards, what Briksanna already knew to be, Katerina's solar. Everyone entered the room while Stark to it upon himself to close the door behind them and folded his arms across his chest not taking another step further electing himself as their guard.

The room was the same as she remembered. A large fireplace had already been lit with the promise of, bookcases filled with books surrounded the room on all walls with the exception of the fireplace. The entire room was large enough to seat twenty people comfortably with settees and wing back chairs placed strategically in the room along with several more chairs placed in the corners of the room allowing whomever the promise of comfort. Four windows were in the room each with heavy drapes drawn purposefully to keep the cold out along with cutting off any visible access of the occupants currently residing within the room.

"Please sit down, all of you, and rest easy. You may hang your cloaks on the rack to the right of the fireplace if you wish. You have all travelled far and are my most honored guests within the Second Realm. There is plenty of food and wine to share amongst ourselves while we discuss what has occurred within our realm as well as in yours. I understand time is different in your realm; however here it is much slower, according to Lady Briksanna, therefore what has us in a state of worry has only occurred hours earlier. Do I have the right of it Briksanna?"

Being the first to pour two goblets of wine, one for Nate and the other for herself she motioned for everyone to take a seat and mentally announced the food and wine were safe for them to eat. At once there was a lot of shuffling while they got comfortable. The girls sat on the settees and grabbed pastries along with wine for themselves; while the boys dragged over a couple of chairs so they too could be included within the group, but not before they made sure the windows were in fact sealed and drapes covered the windows completely. The meat pies looked to be their pick for the night as Kenneth grabbed some for Stark but he waved off the wine preferring to have one hand on his sword and the other filled with food.

"You are correct, Kat, however while here there is no notice of time passing except when in the Earth Realm. That is why I was always was in a rush to head back after releasing my energy."

Looking over her shoulder she noticed Hawk did not move from where he stood sentry behind her and Kat. His stance was tall and stiff mirroring the exact same pose as Stark. His face used to show emotion once they were in closed quarters, but now he stood silent, no doubt aware of everything and everyone within the room. The only thing that seemed odd was the way he continued to glance at the twins. He would look at them and riot of emotions would flash across his face before they disappeared replaced by his stoic expression concealing any hope of learning what he had been thinking of moments ago What had occurred that made the person who looked so familiar seem like a complete stranger?

Brushing her thoughts aside she looked at Kat and smiled hoping to assure her the hospitality had not gone unnoticed. She quickly realized Kat had said something about safety while her mind had wandered. "You are correct Kat. I believe in what you say in regards to our safety. The food looks delicious judging by the appetite of my family; however I do believe we have much more important matters to discuss other than our immediate hunger pains. Kenneth please seal the room from possible outside interference." Kenneth nodded closing his eyes for a few seconds gaining curious glances from Kat and Hawk while everyone else continued to eat. He opened his eyes and nodded to indicate he was done at the same time he shoved food in his mouth. She smiled at him in response.

"Kenneth has the ability to seal anyone from seeing or hearing within a perimeter he establishes so when we want to speak privately we can truly do so without the fear of interference or magic." Nathanial supplied for Kat and Hawk gaining a nod from both.

"Let me start by addressing everyone in this room. Allow me to introduce to you my family first and foremost. There are the boys Striker and Kenneth followed by Gabriella; Kenneth's sister and the twins Harmony and Trinity. Stark over by the door and my mate, Stark's brother, Nathaniel. Last we have two companions whom I must insist you are to keep their identities under the strictest of confidences. Their identities are not to leave this room. Actually, anything that we share in this room is to be kept within this room. If we decide to speak of anything it will be only in a need to know basis and only between the members within this room unless otherwise agreed upon. Do I have your agreement?" She held her breath hoping her statement would be met with no arguments.

"Yes of course, I have the utmost respect of you and that of your station. With that being said, you have my vow not to betray any confidences we may speak amongst one another." Looking each person directly in the eye seeking acknowledgment she continued, "I can vouch for Hawk as he has his own story to share that will require you to reciprocate the same you have just requested from us."

She knew Nathanial sat quiet this whole time content to let her lead the conversations knowing she was the familiar one, out of their family, when it came customs and practices within Skaldanna not to mention the fact she knew these people and would be best to judge how to respond given their responses. But something about what Kat said caught his attention enough so that she felt a ripple of anger flow through their mental link.

"I think Mr. Hawk needs to speak for himself on this. Not to call you a lair Lady Katerina, but I believe in this place, right here between us, I insist we must remain equals in all manner of discussion."

"You insist, what is this Lady Briksanna, which you would allow this boy to speak with insult to you?"—taking a hostile stance arms at his side he fisted his hands—"How dare you speak to the Princesses in this manner? You don't deserve her and until you prove otherwise to me you will remain silent!" Thundering the last statement so that no one in the room dared to speak let alone move. All were waiting to see how Nathanial was going to respond.

"I will not ruin this trust me Bri, I got this." Assuring her with what would be an equivalent of a caress across her cheek.

"I trust you my love always have and always will."

Taking a deep breath he never took his eyes off of the man that towered over him. Nathanial took his time to respond. Everything in his posture screamed to get ready for a fight this she recognized. What she knew was he needed to exert his authority not only as her mate but as the High King; however Nate believed this was where she needed him to be more than the man he had always been for himself and their family. She needed him to be more; he needed to be the mate of a queen defending the honor of the both their persons and their title.

Rising slowly from where he sat, he kept his eyes trained on Hawk. "I will allow you this one time to speak to me this way but that's it. Remember whom you are talking to. I'm not just some foreigner dating the Princess. I am the mate to the High Queen blessed by your Gods and you will show me the due respect to our station. Am I making myself perfectly clear?" Eyes glittering Nate had gone very still with his last demand.

Tension coiled all around him playing the game of wills. He never backed down from a stare down and Stark had taught him well how to master the look.

Then the most unexpected thing happened. One minute Nathanial and Hawk were standing inches from one another's face when they were thrown apart by an unknown force to be replaced by the Merridian. She never saw her move, she was that fast.

Eye color changing like a jewel glittering in the light reflected her unsettling mood. She knew she needed to do whatever she had to in order to reduce the distrust that had built between them just she knew help was needed within this realm possibly within the surrounding realms as well.

Listening to their posturing made her really angry.

"There will be no more challenging one another, nor is there time for distrust amongst yourselves. In this I will be understood. What Princess Briksanna was insinuating is that my companion and I require your confidence Princess Katerina and that of you Prince Hawk second son of the First Realm. Yes, I know exactly who you are and where you come from, but like Princess Briksanna here, I am curious as to your whereabouts even from a person such as I had no idea you had remained alive let alone whom else might have survived. I, like the Princesses, believed everyone had perished within the castle walls with the exception of Briksanna and Katerina. Come now and rise, let us all—what is that term you spoke of Stark—oh yes, lay the cards on the table...hmmm? No one wants to truly piss me off this early in the game."

"Who is this person, Princess, that you would allow to have such control over you let alone speak or act disrespectfully to me?"

Stunned from being thrown far against the other side of the room she noticed he still did not listen to what she had explained.

"I am done with these games. I am here on faith alone that the people I know in this room are the ones I would lay my life down for so they may live to see another day and here you all look at me in judgment because I am cautious not willing to give my allegiance to all of you so readily. I do not know anyone in this room but for both Princesses of which I have not seen either one in two centuries save for Lady Katerina only by a few hours prior to everyone else, and for that I am to give you my allegiance?"

Glaring at everyone in the room clearly for having to relent in the argument first with regards to his whereabouts he continued to explain. "I came looking for survivors once I woke from a century sleep, which no one will know any details until I bow down and give you everything within me when I have struggled with the most basic of motions for the past twenty years post my awakening, something no one in this room can comprehend. I battled the failure and loss to the marrow of by bones, for my family and the little girls I swore with my life to protect all destroyed by a lunatic in a mask. Seems I will be the one to speak first, but before I divest you of any more of that particular history mayhap you will tell me who these two people are as I believe I have much in value to protect besides the honor within this room." Chest heaving he visibly clamped his mouth closed to keep from saying anything else while he stood glaring at her.

The silence in the room was deafening. She did not want to lose this opportunity so she chose to be the first person to break it. "Prince Hawk I am the Goddess Merridian and this is my companion Lady Ellena. We are here to help rectify what has been broken amongst the realms by Lord Drakkoon. I, along with Lady Ellena, will remain with everyone to help with the task of reclaiming Skaldanna from the oppression of Lord Drakkoon as foretold by the seer Vakgdona long ago. There are many details surrounding the quest given to Lady Briksanna and Nathanial that we must share with one another and not all in one evening. We have much to learn about what has happened to all the realms not to mention most importantly what has happened to you. You alone, aside from both Lady Briksanna and Katerina, are the sole survivors of that fateful night in the High Royal House."

Keeping her eyes trained on him she tried her hardest not to exert her will upon him while she pressed him to extend his loyalty to everyone within the room. "I trust you will keep my true identity a secret. We had decided, prior to travelling here, each one of us will be needed to complete the quest thus make things right not only for Skaldanna but for the Earth Realm as well. There is much to lose if we do not unite as one team from the beginning."

She reached for his hand and clasped it tightly allowing Hawk to read her thoughts knowing he had the ability to read anyone through touch, just like Stark. He would know what she said to be true just by his touch alone.

She feared none of them could afford the time to discuss much by the anxiety she had felt grasping for her attention since she stepped foot on solid ground. She needed to open herself to him and he needed to do the same for their information exchange to work. She had to take the risk everyone else had been willing to take and so would she.

He closed his eyes and was able to see what was considered truth and what was to be a lie. He could delve into the depths of a person's memories just by a single touch. There had not been a person who knew his secret other than the High King and Queen beside his family and that secret had been buried when he grew to manhood within the High Kings court. How could this stranger know he was the prince of the First Realm without him saying so? He grabbed tighter attempting to delve deeper into her memories to seek any mistruth she may be hiding. He was met with an impenetrable block and it mystified him because he had never been denied access to a person's thoughts especially when his intent was determined as it was now. Suddenly, without preamble, the tables were reversed; she was tumbling through his memories and there was nothing he could do to stop it. The pain of her mental onslaught was horrific at the same time consuming. She ripped through each memory impatiently like pages of a book fluttering in the wind. Even the ones he kept buried deep within his soul not wanting to look or share with anyone the pain caused when his wife and unborn daughters were lost to Skaldanna and the sole reasons that had kept him from walking the first twenty years after he had woken up from his century of sleep.

The pain of that memory brought him to his knees ripping an agonizing scream from his throat in the process.

Stark was the first to move within the room coming up behind the Goddess, "Let him go Merridian, there is nothing more to see. You are hurting him."

Tuning her glowing eyes deeper into him she did not hear the man next to her speak. She did not acknowledge his plea focusing her attention on the man kneeling before her. The man behind her continued to speak bringing her back from whatever trance she had gone into for her to inflict such pain as he was in now. He hoped the man was successful because he did not know how much longer he would be able to hang on. The darkness threatened to take over and it took everything in him to remain awake.

The man rubbed his hands along her arms leaned in close to her ear. Despite his agonizing pain he was able to hear what he said to her. "Merridian, you're tired, let's go to our chamber and talk more in the morning. If you keep this up you will kill him. Let go Merridian. Let go for me."

Turning her head towards the man who spoke he saw the moment Merridian had heard his words. Suddenly she realized what she had done and immediately let go of his wrist. She looked down at him while he gripped his head knowing he had gone from a standing position to a kneeling one in a room full of people. All he could do was groan piti-fully while the pain continued to subside. He glanced up and saw her look at the man she called Stark with a face filled with utter humiliation. He knew that face, recognized it as a face he had worn himself when he failed to protect the High Royal Family. He knew what it was like to allow frustration to flow through his veins clouding his judgment. Her being a Goddess meant she more than anyone had to bear the responsibility to not allow emotion to influence her powers. He lived that statement every damn day of his miserable existence.

Tears filled her eyes when she stared at Stark clearly begging for his forgiveness in the unexpected display of her powers. Tears fell down her cheeks, "I did not mean to hurt him. I did not mean to cause pain. What have I done?"

Grabbing her in a hug Stark held her while he whispered soft words in her ears in effort to calm her anxiety. She pulled from Stark and turned back to his equally stunned expression and kneeled before him never taking her eyes off him while she spoke with true emotion and regret filled the tears that ran down her face.

"It is my turn to ask for forgiveness from a man worthy of honor. I have seen the truth in your heart and will not betray your secrets. When you are ready, sir warrior, they are yours to tell, this I vow to you. Likewise you have seen mine and I ask that you keep them to yourself until the time is right. You will know when and I will trust you will keep theirs as well. Time is important, sir warrior. Very important for everyone in this room. Do you agree?"

Looking at the Goddess stunned from what his pain free head had revealed through their shared memories all he could do was nod his head when she asked him the question then he did something he never would have thought possible since learning about the death of his family. He reached over and hugged her. His shoulders shook in what was unmistakably crying. He hoped there could be peace for them both for he knew her pain ran deep. Deeper than his ever could.

19

"Katerina, I believe Stark is correct and we should continue discussions in the morning. For now we have need of rooms and rest. We can adjourn in the morning." Looking at her longtime friend she knew it was not the course of action she had planned on, but it might be what was best for everyone involved.

"I disagree with both of you. We have some matters that need to be discussed," came a voice of authority halting everyone who had started to move when she had spoken.

"Stark, are you sure this is what is best for everyone?"

"Briksanna, you more than anyone know what this family can and cannot handle. We have had more distressing situations and will probably encounter a whole lot more while on this quest, so let's hop to it everyone now that introductions have been made."

She could always count on Stark to bring everyone back to task, including herself. "I suppose you are right. Let us try this again. Please have a seat Sir Hawk. Nathanial, is there anything you need to say before we get started?"

"Are you hinting at something my lady love?

"Only what you know you should do as the mate of the High Queen, my love." Sending feelings of encouragement she wanted to reassure him the way he had

spoken on both their behalf earlier had been handled appropriately in her eyes. He had displayed himself as the High King she needed him.

Extending his hand towards Hawk as an offering, "I'd say I'm willing to start over if you are?"

Grabbing the offered hand Hawk looked directly at Nate, "I agree with you. A new start is in order. Forgive me for my earlier outburst." He stood with his hand clasped with Nathanial's and she could tell whatever the Goddess had revealed to be true. His posture emanated honor and truth a warrior worthy of respect from the High King. This was the man she remembered him to be. The person she wanted to make proud while growing up more so than own her father. She loved him as family not as guard to the High King, but as another father figure in her life.

Letting go of Nathanial's hand she watched the man who had protected and nurtured her long ago engage in conversation with her mate. She was relieved he appeared more the man she had once known and loved than the stranger who had escorted her family earlier.

He stepped back and looked each person in the eye. "You have my vow not to betray the confidences shared tonight nor any other time. I will do everything within my power to assist you in your quest. I only ask that you allow me to speak to Sir Nathanial and Lady Briksanna, alone, with regards to what had happened to me since I had last been seen, when the High Castle had been attacked, before sharing it with all of you."

She studied him intently not needing to consult with anyone regarding his request. The question had been directed to the group, but it was she who was expected to respond. "You have our word, we will hear what it is you have to say tomorrow, alone. Fair enough?"

Nodding slowly hesitantly testing the foreign words on his tongue, "Fair enough," he smiled.

Stark had already led Merridian back to her seat beside Ellena and resumed his post at the door. Kenneth had gotten up during the commotion, but now checked the westward windows while Striker oversaw the ones on the opposite wall. "We're still clear." Kenneth called out making sure they were again in a state of solitude so they could talk without the hindrance of interruption.

"Please allow me to seal the room again, if I may? I would feel more comfortable doing so as Lord Drakkoon has many ways to find out the smallest of details. I for one would like to have our discussions continue to remain private."

She knew for Merridian to ask permission to do something as simple as sealing a room had to of meant a lot. She was more than likely used to giving orders or at the very least executing action before asking for permission.

"Yes, of course," she replied quickly.

Closing her eyes she watched her serene face void of expression with the task Merridian undertook. They waited in silence to see what would happen. A moment later her ears popped she adjusted the pressure by yawning; however before she could open her mouth the pressure was gone.

Eyes trained on Merridian she almost jumped when she snapped her eyes open and blinked at her. "It is done."

"Thank you," feeling genuine gratitude for her contribution of gifts. Since declared her commitment to her family with their quest, she has proven with action she would support her in fulfilling The Prophesy easing the doubt she held against the Goddess. That did not mean she was going to call her a sister in arms, but her actions made the thought of her betraying them seem harder to believe. What Merridian had done was exactly what she had asked for when she told Nathanial what the Goddess would have to do in order to gain her trust.

Looking at her family she knew what she was about to divulge would be a moment in time were Skaldanna's history would change. The time of old had come to an end. A new era had begun and she was going to be the first to embrace it.

She took a deep breath and began the conversation starting with her longtime friend. "I have explained to my family what it was you had shared with me earlier concerning your realm. I would like to know, if since we last spoke, if there have been any new incidents?"

Nodding her head Katerina put her cup of tea on the table and replied, "After we spoke my captain took a small regiment out to survey the extent of damage. At the same time I wanted him to extend to all of our tenants if they should need shelter they have but to come within the castle walls and they shall receive it. Captain Drake returned with news that as far as the eye could see my lands have been lain to waste. Where there was life growing now exists death. The forest trees are dying. Leaves have fallen when it is not time for them to fall. The grass and fields are barren. The flowers in the garden have died. It is as if all things which have kept my land most beautiful died within seconds leaving the rest to follow in time. There are areas where the land is struggling to keep a hold on life, but from the looks before sunset, it remained to be a losing battle. There is nothing natural about what has happened. In the morning you will see what I have spoken to be true."

Taking a deep breath she continued, "It does not appear to have affected animals other than their homes are now destroyed along with their food supply, both ours and for the livestock. We were but a month away from harvest and all the crops are laid to waste as if a giant hand of destruction sucked the life directly from the land. I do not know how else to describe it. Within an hour of this occurrence Sir Hawk had arrived and there was not much time to investigate further before night fell. You were expected to arrive shortly thereafter so we spoke briefly on what could have caused the desecration of my lands, then switched our attention for the rest of the evening preparation for possible refugees as I feel we will have more people arriving due to my lands lack of resources come the morning."

Hawk picked up where Katerina had left off. "It is as Lady Katerina has spoken. When I entered the lands not but an hour past crossing her boarders there was a great pull on my energy. I stopped my horse and saw with my eyes the land turn from its lush prime existence to desolation. It was horrific appearing as a giant wave laying waste to everything in its path. When it passed over me both my horse and I were disorientated for a time but quickly regained our senses seeking the measure of Castle Kastekanos. I had feared the worst for the people if the land could be destroyed in such a manner. Everyone I passed was terrified but unharmed; some were sick to their stomachs but nothing more than that."

Eyes wide Katerina looked as if she had relived the moment with Hawk's description, "I saw the same here, Sir Hawk. Some people were sick to their stomachs but nothing more; passing a few hours post the initial event." Looking around the room everyone appeared captivated with their stories she continued. "This is all we know so far. I have readied the castle to the best of my abilities for I know the people will need our support, courage and understanding in order to survive this atrocity."

"Did you notice anything else occurring that might have seen off but had caught your attention once the initial destruction had ended? And were there any other reports of this type of occurrence from any other realms?" Striker looked at Katerina with intensity that surprised her at the same time she detected concern in his voice. She had not heard him speak that tone before.

"No Sir Striker, I did not send out any scouts to the neighboring realms. I believed it would be best to await your arrival and decide after we had the opportunity to speak what the best course of action should be. It has only been four hours since the initial occurrence."

He looked surprised with her declaration regarding the time difference, but she knew she had included all of her children in the countless explanations regarding the difference of time between Earth and Skaldanna.

"I apologize for my lack of memory regarding the difference in time. Why don't Kenneth and I take a look around the kingdom tomorrow along with Stark and assess the damage to your lands and report back say mid-morning?"

"I would like to be a part of the team that surveys the lands. There is this deep pull I feel from the land ever since we arrived here. You all know how much I become connected to the surrounding especially when there is damage. The longer I am near the site of destruction the longer it eats at my soul." Harmony rubbed her arms and looked towards one of the windows while she spoke increasing the speed of her rubbing enough to leave red marks on her skin. "I think I can fix what has been taken, but I have to see the extent of the damage in order to do that. Feel the soil run through my fingers before I can tell you exactly what needs to be done."

She turned her head so fast her long blonde hair whipped around her face when she focused her attention back on the group. "What do you think, Momma? Should I wait for them to report or ride out with them? The decision is yours."

Happy to hear her open reverence in the final decision that belonged to her made her feel better that they, her family, was behaving exactly as she had once behaved with her parents. She had raised them to behave in this manner from the beginning and should have trusted her children not doubting what they may or may not do according to the station they were now thrown into because of The Prophesy. Stark and Nathanial both behaved this way with regards to their family naturally from the beginning. She owed them an apology for her concerns. Maybe she had been the one who harbored doubts allowing them to fester unnecessarily when she should have focused on their quest. She needed to let go of her fears or she would forever find herself trapped in the past.

In that moment she decided to let go of her doubts regarding what she perceived Skaldanna needed from High Royalty instead choosing to believe in what she already knew in her heart. Her family was more than capable of being exactly what Skaldanna needed from High Royalty.

"I believe you should wait here until their return mid-morning. We are still strangers in this land and should remain cautious. Lady Katerina will send out the captain of her guards along with a small regiment in their reconnaissance to include the men in this room. This will help validate their story of being high ranking guests of Castle Kastekanos without giving too many unnecessary details. I still want to keep our presence here as quiet as possible. You, Harmony, will be overwhelmed with the need to heal the land if you go and you know this. We still do not fully comprehend what it is that has been done to make this happen but if what Lady Merridian has said is to be true then it will take more than your inherit healing energy to fix this problem. I believe it will take the both of us; an infusion of my energy combined with Skaldanna's energy core along with your healing power to reverse it."

"Briksanna, do you know what could be the cause of this?" Kat asked sounding more worried than before.

"We think it may be caused indirectly by Lord Drakkoon. Lady Merridian is twin sister to him and before you begin to draw your sword Sir Hawk you will remember what it is you felt and saw when the Goddess touched you." She waited for the room to calm down searching for any indication of hostility form Kat or Hawk. Surprisingly she found none. Not a single sword had left its sheath.

"Let me explain something to you before we speculate further. Living on the Earth Realm, for many centuries, I have had several occasions where I did not rest properly nor was there an opportunity to feed myself properly. The result was an indirect autonomic energetic reaction, a force of self-preservation so to speak by my personal energy source. Our bodies within that realm runs at a higher metabolism, meaning Skaldannian's burn through personal energetic stores much quicker than in the Realm of Skaldanna; therefore I needed to be vigilant about my personal care. Eating and resting regularly or my body would go into self-preservation."

"What is self-preservation?" Katerina asked with a frown clearly trying to understand the difference between both realms. "In all the years we have kept in touch you never mentioned this being a problem for you."

"Remember the time difference Kat? For every one year here on Skaldanna ten years had passed within the Earth Realm. Honestly I couldn't remember everything that occurred over time nor did I have adequate time when I did visit. To me I came to see you twice per Earth calendar year. That was my time frame living on Earth in relation to time here on Skaldanna. For you it was once every six weeks that I saw you. I did not keep it from you; there was just so much time passing between visits I honestly shared what seemed most important to me at the time. I hope you understand."

"I think I do, but I believe you had the harder part to endure. Truly so much time passed between seeing me or Skaldanna must have been horrible for you not to mention the length of time you have lived in the Earth Realm. Truly I am so sorry if I sounded childish earlier; it has been so long for the both of us to spend time simply sitting beside each. You should have told me the depth of your sacrifice, Briksanna. No one should have to live as long as you have endured alone." Reaching out her hand, Katerina looked to reassure her that she understood.

She squeezed Kat's hand and smiled already forgiven her for her earlier comment and continued with her explanation. "Self-preservation is when our body's personal energy source becomes threatened with death and draws energy from the living surrounding it to survive. First from the land and secondly from any living creature, man or animal. When Lord Drakkoon performed his spell he had to have pulled energy surrounding him in order to complete it. This is why we are determined to keep our arrival a secret and need to determine the extent of the damage."

This time it was Hawk who looked confused. Shaking his head speaking out loud but to no one in particular. "I do not understand this drawing of energy to feed our personal energetic stores. How can this be? If it were so, then no one would die of starvation or illness, our personal energy stores would provide for us; however we know this not to be true as there is illness and death abundant throughout our history. How can this be now?"

She needed to explain herself more. Maybe what she said was not in a manner which they could understand. "I hear what you are saying and I understand what I am saying can come across as confusing. In the Earth Realm, whenever I had not paid attention to what level my personal energy store was in I would accidently draw upon the land, literally dropping on the ground and passing out as my body subconsciously pulled energy from the surrounding area to feed me so I could awaken enough to get myself to a place where I could recuperate as I should have done from the beginning. When this occurred I would awaken to the surrounding land, no more than fifty feet in diameter, dead of life. While I had slept my subconscious self-had drained the life of the surrounding vegetation restoring my own personal energy."

She thought over what she had detailed for Hawk and was quiet while he absorbed what she had explained. When he looked up at her his eyes where wide with astonishment understanding. "You think this is what he has done, inadvertently drained the energy of the land feeding his spell? Even I know whatever Lord Drakkoon does he does with intent. There is no accident here. What you will see was done with purpose and malice. This was an act of intent to do harm to everyone in contact."

Merridian immediately jumped in, "Yes, we believe this is what he has done. Being his sister I chose to believe he did not know the extent of the damage he had caused to the Upper Realm. We were there when it occurred, both Ellena and I. We would have been able to detect any malicious intent on the people of Skaldanna if he had intended to harm them. What I want to know is why has he not harmed a single person in all the two hundred years since the fall of the High King? I tell you why, because that was not him who caused it." Sounding sure of herself as she spoke judging by the tone in her voice she could tell Merridian was relieved to have given voice to her thoughts.

"Yes he sent the masked man to retrieve Lady Briksanna, but never did he intend for all for which had happened to her or the High Royal Castle. When he found out what had happened he was enraged for years after, searching the lands not only for her, distraught with regards to her safety, he was filled with a vicious anger when he was unable to secure the culprit who committed the heinous act in his name. He sought out the masked man to murder him, the person who had tortured the woman he loved. He sent scouts to, Gods knows where, for decades in hopes to present to you the truth. He did not have anything to do with what happened to you or your family or all of the people in Skaldanna two hundred years ago."

Shaking her head vigorously not wanting to give anyone a chance to stop her train of thought. "No I tell you there is someone who feeds this dark obsession he has had for princess and therein lies the true evil source. I do not excuse my brother's actions since that day you were cap-tured, not for a moment." Merridian made eye contact with everyone in the room before she continued.

When she glanced around the room she noticed everyone had been held captive with her story and when she turned back to Merridian she no longer appeared lost in thought. Her eyes appeared sharp and clear. Her lips were full and flushed as if she had spent the evening biting it in worry. She held herself still with hands at her side. "I can vouch his sole desire is that of Lady Briksanna not the destruction or harm of Skaldanna or any one person. That is not the brother I love who has sac-rificed everything for the continuance of the Under Realm."

The room was quiet while everyone absorbed what Merridian had just shared. Could it be true that there was someone other than Lord Drakkoon at work here this entire time? If so, then it would only mean a bigger player to the bad guy theory. He and his brother knew what it was like to live with the people who were sucked into working for the Mob, like their father had been when they were younger. He felt like the whole scene with Lord Drakkoon was the same scenario except he wasn't the mob. Chancing a look at Stark wanting to get his brothers opinion out of habit, he held of saying anything because he could see the wheels in his head visibly spinning already just by a glance in his direction. He already felt trapped on a merry-go-round within his head with learning about The Prophesy then the Quest. This shit keeps getting crazier by the hour.

Glancing at his brother he thought, *"Do you think what the Goddess said is true? That there could be another person who is the mastermind behind everything? That would defiantly explain the extent of damage Katerina claims to be throughout the land and the harm done to Bri and Merridian recently."*

"I don't know little brother but I am defiantly starting to think there might be some truth to what Merridian has been saying all along. We might have two to tango with instead of one badass. Whatever, we've had worse to deal with so don't go worrying your pretty little head."

"Hey, I'm game. Let 'em bring it. I so am ready for this to be over with before anything else is destroyed or anyone else become affected. Yesterday was enough. We both almost lost them."

Briksanna was very quit throughout their mental exchange so was the Goddess, but what bothered Briksanna out of the entire conversation was what they had said about the people not being affected. He could hear her thoughts while he and Stark talked. It was weird how he could multi task telepathically with conversations now. Maybe it was one of his enhanced abilities Merridian had talked about yesterday.

"Kat, did you or Sir Hawk find anyone incapacitated, harmed in any way other than an upset stomach?"

Shaking her head looking to Hawk for confirmation. "No Briksanna I did not. Did you Sir Hawk?"

"No My Lady, I did not. As a matter of fact only one family I came across had an illness and that person had already taken ill prior to the event occurring."

He looked around at everyone it all began to make more sense to him. Rising from where she sat, Bri walked around the room pacing back and forth. He could tell she was thinking because she would do the same thing back home in preparation for missions, running scenarios through her head before shared her thought with anyone. Merridian was right; the only people who lives had been threatened were hers and Bri's. Ellena was with the Goddess that was why she was affected too or maybe she just knew too much and it was better off to get rid. That had to be why they were drained energetically to the point of death. They may have long life spans but energetically if they are drained there would be nothing here or on Earth that could repair that kind of damage leaving death the only alternative.

He needed to be the first to agree so the tension could be taken off Bri's shoulders. She had enough on her plate as it was to admit the possibility the person she had placed all of her hatred towards may not have been the true villain. "You are right Merridian, it was a strike to destroy what Lord Drakkoon covets most. This was an attack on him not towards anyone else. I believe everything past and present has been a strike at Lord Drakkoon not the inhabitants of Skaldanna. Think about it, you and Bri are the only things he values most. He would not try to kill you. I don't believe a man who chases a woman for two centuries would harm a hair on her head or allow anyone to touch her in the wrong way. No Bri, I believe Merridian has the right of it. The who or what of it is not as important as to knowing that there is something out there that wants to destroy everything associated with Lord Drakkoon including the Upper Realm if need be. This makes everything appear different, yet makes complete sense to me."

She stopped pacing around the room and looked immediately to Stark, "I need to know, at first light, the extent of the damage to the land. I have a feeling Lord Drakkoon maybe closer than we think if only to cause damage within the lands of the Second Realm because of my connection to Katerina. Think about it; historically, when I would pass out, the damage to the surrounding land was thirty feet surrounding me. For the damage to only be here within the Second Realm then he would not only have to be here, but so would be our mystery villain."

"Or it could be just this mystery villain finally making a strike out on their own?" Throwing his two cents in just to keep everyone focused on this mystery person. If what his gut was telling him to be true then it would be this mystery villain behind everything and not Lord Drakkoon. The death of her parents, the destruction of multiple realms not to mention the torture and exile Bri had to endure. That didn't sound like it was the behavior of a love obsessed individual.

Rubbing her arms hiding the goose bumps he could see crawling up her arms at the mention of encountering her enemy whomever they were made him want to reach out and comfort her. He wanted to walk right over there and pull her in close while he rubbed the chill of fear away. After all this time she had waited to come home she had to come back to this mess. It broke his heart to see moments of despair leak out of her like this. She wasn't one to nervously twitter about rubbing her arms when in thought. She was the bull of the team always clear headed, determined, and methodical, but the single thought of their family being caught in this quest nauseated him. He knew she was upset more than anything else to think she might have sacrificed two thousand years of hiding so some unknown villain could torture her some more? A nights rest and some Intel in the morning should bring more light to the situation and a lot to settle her nerves. At least he hoped it would.

Feeling her distress spike he decided to steer the conversation from its intensity into more strategic planning. "Sir Hawk, take the boys, Kenneth and Striker in the morning when you go to survey the realm. I want them to accompany you with your assigned regiment. Scout the area but do not engage with anyone nor with the tenants of the land. I want to formally introduce my family later, with the Princess, at a more appropriate time and place dictated by our station. Our immediate interests are only that of the destruction done to the land and its repair."

Picking up his lead with their current mission Bri shook off her worries dropped her nervous rubbing and put her concerns out of her mind. He was proud of her and that was all that mattered. He saw her straighten her back and put her game face. He was hot for his woman and couldn't wait until they were alone so he could show her.

"Trinity, you and Gabriella are to deal with any people within the castle who may still be ill. Lady Katerina will escort you with the explanation that you are guests in the house who have the skill to help those who are ill. I changed my mind and I believe, Stark, it will be best served if you were to protect Merridian and Ellena until the men return from recon."

"Harmony you will stay with me; Nate will be our guard. I want to get a feel for the immediate grounds and release some of this energy while I am at it. You will be the best person to see how that is done as you are the only person in the family who is close to me in my powers energetically. Now if you all do not mind, I am very tired as I know you are as well."

She stepped in the center of the room and looked carefully assessing them for any disagreements to her declarations. He half expected there to be arguments considering it was the first time their family had come through the portal and here she was pretty much telling them; 'Hey time to go to bed' like they were little kids needing to be tucked in at night. He chuckled out loud at his thoughts gaining her sharp look of promised retribution for the outburst. He did catch the twinkle in her eye before she turned back to everyone noting the grin she tried not to show. She must have read his thoughts. Damn woman and her mind reading.

Shaking his head he listened to her when she addressed them again, but this time with a genuine smile. "I promise we can play tomorrow in a real old fashion sporting ring Lightning Strike style, until then, remember who you are and most importantly where you are and that there is a very real threat out there waiting to strike out at any us at any time. You all matter to me and I would hate to have to come searching for anyone. We will meet late morning after our initial assessments."

The family headed to the table holding food, a one last ditch effort to grab something before they headed in for the night. She spoke out loud to Katerina instructing her in what she thought would be the next step with communication to the other realms and he agreed.

He walked over to them and stopped beside Bri sliding his hand into hers linking their fingers together as she continued her conversation with Katerina not breaking stride in thought. "Kat, I want you to send messengers, tonight, to each of the royal houses. I want a meeting in one day's time here in Castle Kastekanos. Explain they are to come themselves with the exception to bring their heir. No regents are to come meet the High Queen's invitation. Let them know in the meantime the royal families are to travel immediately to Castle Kastekanos for a royal ball with promise of announcement to all realms of the High Royal Family's return. Only the royal families and their regents plus their companions are to attend the ball. The celebration will take place here at Castle Kastekanos in three days' time. It will have a masked ball. Can you do this tonight Katerina?"

Hoping not to put too much strain on her friend he mentally shrugged off any worries and offered his assistance anyway. "I can help you with writing the messages."

Running her hand over her waist straitening her gown she replied, "Not at all Briksanna, I can have those messages out before you lay your head on your pillow."

Sounding very confident Kat tilted her head towards the door and walked regally towards the hall passing around Stark who had moved aside during her approach. She raised her voice to address everyone in the room. "Allow me to show everyone to your rooms. I have prepared rooms for you in the west wing with each of you having your own quarters. No one will share this wing with you it is a space solely for your purposes. I and Sir Hawk will be the only persons with permission to enter your floor, but not into your personal quarters. That is for you and each of you alone."

"Sir Hawk has seen to the posting of guards at the entrance of your wing. No one will be allowed into your wing without your expressed permission. These guards are loyal to me and have my complete trust. You are to feel safe while staying in my home."

Katerina walked to the right leading them up a giant staircase. Everything looked brand new from the carpet to the staircase banister surrounding the area. The wall held brightly lit sconces bathing them in light along its steep corridor yet not bright enough to lighten the entire area. He leaned over the railing nothing seemed unusual from what he could. There were a couple of portraits which hung along the walls lining the staircase and along the hallway of the second floor landing they arrived on. The only people around were the two guards posted at the top of the stairs.

20

The two warriors at the top of the stairs stood at least six foot six, long hair one dark while the other had blonde, both similar in looks; blue eyes crooked noses screamed too many fights. Dressed in typical warrior fashion found on Skaldanna they both wore leggings with knee high boots loose peasant shirts covered with leather vests which visibly hung various knives affixed to several belts hung along their bodies. They seemed to take after the children caring more than what the eye could see. The twins would be excited to have competition with someone wielding knives. They had been itching for a good knife fight and those two looked like they could give them a run for their money.

Long swords strapped sheathed within scabbards on their backs. Appearing not as royal guards indicative to the secretiveness of their situation the men leaned more towards the mercenary side of things. Something she was familiar with back on Earth.

Stopping everyone at the top landing; Katerina pointed to each guard. "Allow me to introduce you to your appointed guards"—pointing to her right—"this is Khrysaor"—pointing to her left—"this is Pegasos. They are your personal guards watching the only entrance leading to the west wing. Tonight they will guard your floor but as of tomorrow they will be personal guards to whomever you feel will serve best, Lady Briksanna."

Kat turned moving forward down the hallway with everyone following behind her. She and Nate were the last of their party to stand on the landing. She hung back purposefully to look -each guard in the eye more to assure herself of their worthiness in protecting those who were most important to her. Khrysaor and Pegasos held her stare with a look of curiosity. With high cheekbones, large noses resting above full lips, both men closely resembled each other with the exception of a scar that ran from Khrysaor's brow to his lips.

"Do you know who I am?" she asked.

Squinting his eyes as if the direct light from the torch beside him was too dim for a response. "An important guest of Lady Katerina, whoever you are, she has asked that my brother and I guard you with our lives, which is how important you must be for the lady to require our assistance. It matters not to me who you are only that Lady Katerina has asked it of us and we will honor her with this task. Do not worry, you and the rest of your family will be protected," Khrysaor responded.

Already dismissing her with a glance at his brother they presumed their stares off into the distance beyond her. It was insulting the way they both had dismissed her. Not even the people in her own family treated her in this manner when they were angry with her.

Stepping closer to the guard earning a growl from Nate who had been behind her, she stopped herself from moving.

"That is close enough Bri; I don't know them and neither do you no matter who they say they are committed to protect or why."

Khrysaor turned his blue eyes to her mate. She noticed how careful he tried to be when choose his next words before he spoke next by the way he swallowed before responding to Nathanial's statement. For a man as tough as he looked it must have been something he struggled with in order to behave with respect to their stations as high ranking guest in Kat's home. What she really saw was the look in his eyes right before a mask fell over his face. He wanted to wipe the floor with her mate.

"I would listen to what your mate has to say Princess, my brother and I are not anyone's lapdogs; however I will tell you this, Lady Katerina has saved one of ours and for that my brother and I are eternally grateful for her assistance. With this debt of gratitude we honor serving Lady Katerina and any of her wishes to the death. I don't know you nor your mate over there, but my brother and I will guard you with our lives if need be in honor of the debt owe to Lady Katerina. Will that do Sir Nathanial?"

She held her breath allowing her mate to be the person he needed to be here. This was his second test of authority and she knew it would not be last one

He stepped around her placing his body in front of her effectively cutting off any immediate threat while he moved his body closer to the guard who had spoken. "What are your names?"

She did not want to give too much away but he knew her fears for the rest of the family and to ensure their safety she knew he would have to do whatever was needed to gain their immediate respect. Loyalty would come later. As long as he held their respect he could lead them to loyalty in no time. She knew he would not ask more from anyone that he was not willing to give of himself. Revealing all that he knew was not what he had in mind, she could tell from their mental link those were not his intentions, but that was not going to stop him from saying enough to gain their trust. Would it be enough to protect everyone? She hoped it would, they seemed like the type of men who would not give up even when the situation proved bad enough to run.

This time it was the second guard with that spoke, "My name is Pegasos and this is my twin Khrysaor. We are grateful to have this opportunity to protect you, Princess. Assisting Lady Katerina in this adventure is the least we can do," he said winking at Nathanial. His easy attitude in the way he spoke to both of them did nothing to quell the thought of this tough giant of a man who seemed to know too much yet continued to reveal very little.

It was her turn to speak placing her hand on her mate's arm assuring him she was not worried telepathically. She tried to sound as regally as possible playing the role of High Royal Queen, she spoke carefully.

Nathanial moved slightly to the right allowing her a better advantage to address the warriors.

She looked at the both of them while drawing her inner energy which made her eyes cast a light violet glow in front of her when addressed the two of them. "Khrysaor and Pegasos I see your dedication to Lady Katerina in the words you have so carefully spoken; however do not mistake my mate's worthiness with your innuendos. There is nothing needed from him to prove to you his worthiness. My word is satisfactory enough and that of Lady Katerina. You will be wise not to test this further; however I will settle this curiosity of yours."

Stepping back so she and Nate stood side by side she announced, "Consider yourselves our personal guards tomorrow morning. You will both be given ample opportunity between now and then to change our minds of this decision if you feel this is not the path you wish to walk upon. If you do choose to move forward with the assigned position you will be given more information than which you have already gleamed from our auras. Yes, I know from which realm you hail from, the true question should be from which house do I hail from?"

Pausing to look each warrior in the eye squinting as Khrysaor had done to Nate earlier, "I not only know from which realm you hail from but from which house you once were seated upon so choose wisely warriors as all realms of Skaldanna need for us to complete our mission and our safety will require men such as yourselves to complete the tasks along with my family whom you have just met."

Grabbing her elbow Nathanial not so politely excused them from the men and proceeded down the hall dragging her in his wake. She was walking fast trying not to trip as they still had half a hallway to go in order to catch up with the rest of the group.

Whispering loudly to Nate, "Why are you dragging me? Why did you pull me away from them? I did not hear their response. I was not finished talking to them." She couldn't help the sneer in her voice when he ignored her questions and continued to grip her elbow roughly. He had never manhandled her before. Was that a ringing sound she heard?

Sounding aggravated running his free hand through his hair he stopped dragging her to looking over anger written on his face. She had never seen him so irate in her entire life. He was livid with her.

"Why did you interfere back there? Those two needed to be put in their place. I haven't been challenged in such a polite way since Kenneth and Striker thought they could best me four years ago. They learned their place and so will those two jackasses. God, Bri, do you know how frustrating it is for you to stick up for me when I don't need you to? I am your mate, the High King. Let me be the man you believe me to be without you running to defend me every time someone says or does something you don't like or is it that you don't think I am man enough for the task?"

Pulling back from him as if the words had physically slapped her across the face causing her head to physically kick back from the impact his words had caused. His words held a great deal of venom when he spoke to her. What happened to the man who just hours before had held her in his arms while he whispered his undying love before they had left the Earth Realm? Within hours of his declaration he would question her commitment to him.

"Bri, I'm sorry, I should never spoke to you like that. I don't know why I did, I just got so angry and for a minute that is all I could see and hear was your disappointment at how I handled them back there. Do you hear a ringing sound?"

Closing her heart to the words he had spoken she recognized his half attempt to apologize. Insufficient words for the amount of pain she felt while her heart cracked from the force of his words. A blooming ache starting from the depth of her soul spread like wildfire throughout her entire body ripping a cry cut from her throat. She pulled out of his grasp flashing her pain filled damp eyes at him before looking back at the guards who in turn were looked at the them with their heads cocked to the side. She looked to the other end of the hallway where her family was and noticed Merridian had stopped and was watching before holding her hand up for what she did not know or care.

How embarrassing it was for him to question their relationship publicly. Did he forget so soon where he was and who he was talking to? Who they both were and what it meant for them to appear at all times unless behind closed doors? They were to always maintain a presence of royalty wherever they were despite how they may feel about anything. That was what it meant to be King and Queen. That was what they needed to be in order to succeed with the quest. He said he would be the only person she would need for the rest of her life. He promised he would never do anything to harm her and here he had spoken a few words that had cut her heart wide open.

What was with that ringing sound? Her head was starting to hurt from that constant ringing sound in her ears.

Who does he think he is to talk to her that way? She felt her anger mount higher and higher with every thought. She looked back towards Merridian once again knowing she was a Goddess and she had to of heard how Nathanial had talked to her completely humiliating her not to mention the guards had seen the entire confrontation. Did she not say they would have to be united with everything they said and did?

Bending over slightly, she grabbed her abdomen, a result of sharp pains that stabbed her in the stomach in tune with the pain now in her head splitting it in two.

What was that blasted ringing sound?

Finally settling her eyes on Nathanial who cradled his head while leaning against the wall He scowled at her when yelled, "This is all your fault! If you had listened to me when I told you I could handle them we wouldn't be having this argument in the first place. You would do best to just listen to me in the first place and this relationship wouldn't be in question. This isn't going to work if you don't listen to what I say."

Gritting his teeth he spoke to her as if she were someone he hated not someone he loved deeply. How dare he look upon her with disgust in his eyes. She was the High Queen and this was her realm. He had no right to harbor an ounce of contempt towards her, not one damn ounce.

"How can you look at me like that and speak to me in such a manner when you are just hours from our bed declaring your undying love? 'I go where you go Briksanna. Nothing can come between us Briksanna' was that just a pile of shit you declared!"

She screamed at him while she gripped her increasing cramping stomach and looked at him with hatred. Her stupidity led her to believe in his words of love feeling a fresh wave of grief when she repeated his declaration of love for her. She had opened her heart to trust him and look what had happened. He betrayed that trust at the first possible moment shredding her heart in the process. She closed her eyes as a wave of pain in her head caused a wetness to run down her nose. She ignored it not bothering with anything except letting her anger replace her grief.

"What is that ringing sound?" he yelled.

Opening her eyes a crack she fell to her knees at the same time she heard yelling from far away. "You want this do you not? Me on my knees begging for the pain in my heart to end so you can feel justified by your actions? That would make you happy to see me in such a subservient position would it not?"

Reaching for her inner energy to heal herself she was startled to find nothing there. What was wrong with her? Why was she unable to pull her energy forth? It must be his fault. What a worthless human.

Squinting her eyes at the man she once thought she loved she allowed hatred to flood her reminding her of the time she had been betrayed by her betrothed long ago. Her body filled with the energy reminding herself with self-loathing the acts she committed in moments of passion granting him free reign in her bed and in her heart. "You are nothing but a worthless human and as such you will die as one!"

Lifting her hands above her head she began the thought to pull the energy from the surrounding area to aid her in destroying the object of her hatred as she had done so long ago. She needed more energy and she would be damned if anyone tried to stop her. He was going to pay for his betrayal just like her Tormentor had. Her heart felt as if there was nothing left to beat for just like she did when she escaped her torment years ago, except this time the pain was a thousand times worse. She had loved him.

Nathanial gripped his head blood running down his nose and out his ears. "Stop the ringing!" He looked at Merridian and screamed, "Stop the ringing! It's in the ringing, stop..."

A loud scream rent the air, "*Noooo!*"

Everything around her went dark hearing a scream she felt herself falling to the side from where she knelt succumbing to the agonizing pain in her head and stomach. Before she lost consciousness the last thought she had before losing consciousness was the scream had come from her own mouth.

She could see the spell weave itself between Nathanial and Briksanna. She feared she would be too late to stop what she could already see happening. Dark magic was threading itself between them, through them faster and faster grabbing a hold of their words feeding them negative energy in return. For every word spoken, before it could leave their mouths, the dark magic would twist the light energy into dark turning concern and anxiety to fear and distrust; breeding hatred as a result.

They were not aware of what was happening to them. She chanted a counter spell to release the threads woven, but was afraid it would take minutes to break the hold on them possibly leaving damage she could not repair. In the state they were in they could inflict harm on one another and it would be instantaneous and permanent.

Choice made she began to chant loudly holding her hands out towards them literally pulling the threads down with her hands quickly countering the spell with her thoughts. She silently prayed Briksanna and Nathanial had enough love between themselves not to act on their evil fed emotions no matter what their mind, ears and eyes showed them. Their soul would know the truth in their love. It had to be enough because she couldn't spend any more time thinking on it.

She closed her eyes and put on a burst of speed cleansing the remnants of dark magic around them all. Just as the last threads snapped apart dissipating in the air she opened her eyes and saw Stark in front of her shouting, but she could not hear what he was saying. She could see that the two guards were leaning over Briksanna and Nathanial trying to ascertain the state of their welfare, but for the life of her she could not clear the confusion in her mind. She was drained from working so much light magic after being drained to the point of near death the day before.

"Stark, are they alright? I cannot hear you. Are Briksanna and Nathanial alright?" Worried she could not hear what was going on around her like someone had blotted the sound from her ears with pieces of cotton. She could see him talking and people around her shouting when they ran back to Nathanial and Briksanna, but she could not hear any a single sound.

Suddenly the sound came rushing back to her sounding like a great wind blowing her and Stark back against the wall. He had been able to grab a hold of her so when they hit the wall he had turned to take the brunt of the impact hitting the wall first then sliding to the ground.

"Oh Gods, Merridian, are you alright? Stark wake up!" Ellena shook them wanting them to wake up noticing they were coming around. "You have to get up in case there is more coming. We must get the Goddess out from here. Stark wake up, we have to get everyone out of here."

Shaking her head she could hear Ellena yelling at her about Stark. That was when she remembered they had been thrown against the wall. She got to her knees and looked for Stark and found Ellena hovering over the both of them trying to wake him up.

She scrambled over him to look for any injuries that might be fatal relieved she did not see anything that could have caused major injury. His eyes fluttered and she was relieved he was trying to wake. She knew her heart was only for this man confirmed by the way his heart was beating a panic rhythm under her palm.

She nudged him with her hands, "Stark, you have to get up now. I need to help us get to safety." No response as he closed his eyes again. She waited for him to open them again knowing she did not have the energy to continue feeling the blackness of sleep try to claim her once again. She was so drained. It was the sheer will of strength as a Goddess that had kept her going so far. She had to get him to wake up or they would all be in danger.

Shouting at him more out of fear than for safety, "Stark wake up now we have got to move!"

His eyes snapped open glowing bright. He did not look hurt he looked pissed. He got up quickly looked at her briefly before he nodded jogging off towards his brother and Briksanna. Oh God, Nate and Briksanna. She had forgotten about them shaking her head she held of the blackness of exhaustion putting on one more burst of speed back the way they had come noticing everyone had surrounded the two people lying on the floor.

"Don't touch them Trinity!" She let a small blast of magic shoving everyone away from the two people lying on the floor. Some fell flat on their butts others hit either sides of the hallway. She didn't mean to throw them so hard, but she did not want any remaining dark magic threads to latch onto them.

"Let me see to them first. I need to see how far the taint has infected them if any at all." She quickly knelt between them and put each hand on either head closing her eyes. No one made a sound there was utter silence. Everyone held their breaths waiting for Nathanial and Briksanna to wake up. Her hands began to glow emanating a white light onto the tops of their heads. A light passed through their bodies from their heads all the way to their feet before dissipating cleansing them from a few residual threads of evil she had found. As her healing magic faded so did the last bit of energy she had left keeping her upright.

Opening her eyes she looked at Stark and said, "They are clean you can move them now." That was the last thing she said before her eyes rolled into the back of her head letting the darkness take her away. The last thing she heard was the frightened voice of the man she was coming to love yell her name before strong arms wrapped around her in safety allowing herself to let go completely knowing he would protect her with his life.

— ⁓

Glowing eyes looked watched the scene of scrambling people above him and smiled. Sitting cross legged he ignored the pain in his legs from sitting several hours waiting for them to arrive. He had obeyed his Mistress's instructions to, at the appropriate time, send tendrils of hatred directly at the royal couple. He palmed the amulet that hung from his neck and welcomed the dark caress that slithered across his face congratulating him for a job well done further feeding his hatred for Lord Drakkoon giving it freedom to fill him then directing that hatred up to Briksanna and her lover above him.

How he wanted to lash out at the twins more but was reassured by his Mistress they would be his to deal with when the time came. He rubbed his scar and thought of the ways Harmony would pay for the mark she had left on him. She was good with blades, that one was, and beautiful to boot. He would have her naked strung up for his pleasure before he slit her throat to watch the blood drip dry. Attacking Briksanna and Nathanial took care of two birds with one stone. It appeased his Mistress because it would devastate Lord Drakkoon and it would make him happy to hurt the one obsession his overlord held over him for centuries. She was the reason he had been brought to the Under Realm and the reason he had been denied a second chance at life.

Feeling the dark magic link break he directed his attention back to the scuffle above him seeing the Goddess had broken the spell and everyone had surrounded the two people lying in the hallway. He held his breath afraid to get too excited before their deaths had been confirmed knowing simply breaking the spell did not rid the intended recipient of dark magic once infected. He felt his grin start to spread believing he had accomplished what he set out to do for the first time in his new body and what an accomplishment it would be to take down Briksanna and Nathanial in one fell swoop. Lord Drakkoon told him only to monitor the Second Realm not to interfere and definitely not to harm Briksanna or his sister for that matter.

Hell, if she fell he would fucking celebrate all night long, because that bitch needed to die for all her words of hope and faith she spewed every time she set foot in Deepsong. The bitch did not know when to keep her mouth shut? She had freedom when everyone else had been trapped in that depressing pit with no chance for redemption serving an obsessive bastard who cared for no one but his own hide pining for a woman who did not want to speak to him. No, he had no pity for her or her companion. Well, maybe a little for her companion because like him she was servant to Merridian. No, he didn't want anything to happen to Ellena, she was just as trapped in this mess as he was. Maybe he could convince her to serve his Mistress instead?

Training his thoughts on the people above him he focused on Briksanna and Merridian while she attempted to heal them from his dark magic threads of hate. He did not know what he was going to do if this did not work. The Mistress said she used the same spell two hundred years ago with great results so he knew she would not give him a spell that would not work. She would never betray him that way not like Lord

Drakkoon had. He believed in his Mistress and trust was something he would only give to her. He would never again trust anyone else again. Too much pain. Too much betrayal to let his heart believe in words spoken again.

He closed the mental door on his emotions and let his past float away just in time to see Merridian announce they were healed before she passed out in Stark's arms. Cursing his failure in killing Briksanna and Nathanial he decided right then and there he would do better next time thinking this trial run as the leader of the Shadow Riders did not turn out too bad. He hurt them badly and who knows for how long they would be out not to mention the Goddess was incapacitated. Not too bad for a couple hours of sitting in a room with his presence cloaked. Not too bad at all.

He unfolded his legs and left the room while masking his presence using the power of his amulet slipping out through the secret passageway below the castle that had not been used in many centuries knowledge gifted to him by his Mistress. He wondered if he could speed up the damage his Mistress had caused the surrounding land in the Second Realm by releasing the same dark magic spell directing it to kill everything that grew upon it with instructions to continue laying waste beyond its borders until nothing living remained on Skaldanna. That would keep the people in the castle busy while he planned his next attack.

Smiling he thought he could still celebrate the evening by destroying the one thing Briksanna had always talked about missing most when he would spy on her in the Earth Realm.

He would do his damndest to destroy what she found beautiful just as she had destroyed his hope for a new life.

21

Stark caught her cradling her in his arms. "Lady Katerina show me the nearest room that has connecting doors now! Hawk grab Briksanna, Kenneth and Striker get Nate. Everyone follow me. Khrysaor and Pagasos follow us and guard the doors to both rooms. No one gets by you two. Do you understand me?"

Both giants nodded bending to assisting the girls to their feet as Ellena's worried face came into view. "Will she be alright, Sir Stark?" Lifting her gaze to meet his eyes, "I have never seen her in all the time I have known her to be this depleted of energy. Whatever she battled here she won by sheer force of will. I am worried how much more she can withstand without rest. She needs to restore that which she has expelled or she may never wake up."

Eyes glistened while she searched his face for reassurance. All he knew was that the woman he was coming to have deep feelings for felt broken inside while he held her like a rag doll tossed aside. This was what he felt while he held her knowing her companion expressed the same things he had thought himself.

Softening his expression he tightened his hold on the woman in his arms, "I intend on doing just that Ellena, making sure she has the opportunity to recharge if I have to carve it into existence with my bare hands. She will get what she needs to heal you have my word."

Feeling a hand brush his cheek just as he was about to turn on his heels following Lady Katerina he looked down to see Merridian stare back up at him. He pulled her close and leaned his forehead against hers inhaling her sweet scent of rain forest allowing his senses to register what his mind had battled a few minutes ago. She was alive and breathing.

"Woman you just took years of my life pulling a stunt like that." Trying to slow down his beating heart he felt her relief knowing he held her in his arms. He thought she would push him away or say something about him encroaching in her personal space. He was surprised when she said nothing. She just snuggled closer burrowing deeper into his personal space. His heart constricted with her gesture.

She whispered with a slight smile on her mouth, "It had to be done and I am the only person who could see what was happening. There is more going on here than we suspected. I am tired Stark please protect me while I sleep. I am afraid I am not at full strength to lift a finger."

Lifting his head he scowled when he saw the dark circles surrounding her eyes, the worry she held etched in the furrow of her brows when she spoke. She was a dichotomy of emotion one half fighting the pull of exhaustion trying to figure out who was attacking them and the other half was too tired demanding her to let go and sleep.

"Nothing will harm you while I am here. You are safe Merridian. I will lay you in a room and stay with you until you wake. You have my word as a warrior who cares deeply for your life."

At his words the Goddess smiled and closed her eyes, "Thank you my warrior."

He looked up to see Ellena was still standing beside him with Kenneth next to her looking pissed off. They had to of heard their verbal exchange but he didn't care if they heard what was said or not. His priority was to their safety and that included Merridian and Ellena. By the look on Kenneth's face he was thinking along the same lines. They needed to get into the rooms now.

"Will the Goddess be alright?" Running her hands along Merridian's brow, "I fear this is all too much to endure not only for her power but for her heart." When she looked at him he saw the desperation in her request. "Promise not to hurt her heart, warrior."

Meaning it more than he believed he meant anything in the world he nodded. "I promise Ellena, I will protect her with my life."

Knowing there wasn't time to go into details he quickly turned following the direction he had seen Katerina lead earlier he strode into a room two doors down and laid her on the bed briefly looking for any injury to her body. Seeing nothing other than what he and Ellena had confirmed was only exhaustion he allowed room for Ellena to attend her.

Turning around he saw there was an adjourning door that lead to the next room. He could see Hawk lay Briksanna on the bed next to Nate. Kenneth must have helped Striker lay Nate down before coming back out to escort Ellena. He really needed to remember to talk to Kenneth about what was going on between him and Ellena.

Walking further into the room he looked down at his brother and his wife he felt a pang of fear recognizing how close everyone had come to losing the both of them. The sharp pain stabbed his heart knowing losing his brother would bring him to his knees. If it wasn't for the sharp look from the warrior named Hawk reminding him that this was not the place nor the time to succumb to such childish behavior he took a deep breath and forced his eyes to see what was really in front of him. They both appeared to be sleeping nothing else, yet he couldn't shake the desperate feeling from his heart with thoughts of life continuing on without Nate. Trinity hovered over Briksanna with her hands on her trying to get a read on her current state.

"Trinity, what do you see?" His voice cracked when he spoke realizing his emotions were still raw and up close. He rushed to tamp down his treacherous thoughts pulling on his strength as a leader to hold him upright.

"Static," she replied with a faint voice.

"What do you mean static?" He asked with words that sounded sure and strong.

Opening her tear filled eyes she spoke as emotionally torn as he had felt moments ago. "Static like their energy is jumping all around the place. I can't get it to settle in a normal rhythm. Each of us has a rhythm where our energies flow through and around us. It is what makes each of us who we are and keeps us functioning as the individual people operate as."—waving her hands over the two people lying on the bed—"Their energy is sizzling within like drops of water in a hot pan. I am trying to stabilize each of them by grounding their erratic energy. Mentally it's like driving a post in the ground tying their individual energy strands directly to the post to hold it. After their energy has settled I can remove the energetic grounding post and hope their inherent energy will have found its natural grounding post. I think it's starting to work. They are going to need time to heal and a lot of rest." She turned back to the task at hand and closed her eyes.

"Kenneth, go back to Ellena in the other room and see if she needs any help with Merridian. Stay with them not leaving the room until you are relieved by family and by my direct order only. Understood?"

Nodding he turned to head into the other room when he felt he needed to further explain himself to Kenneth giving himself a burst of speed to intercept his leaving. A dread of desperation poured out of his voice exposing his vulnerability for Merridian. "Don't let them out of your sight and don't let anyone other than your family near them. I don't know what is going on here but we are on red alert."

He looked back in the room that held the love of his heart knowing his actions had gained all eyes on him he added mentally to the rest of the family. *"That goes for all of you, we are on red alert and anything from this moment forward goes through me until otherwise noted."* He nodded for Kenneth to head back to the room believing Kenneth would alert him if anything were to happen.

Gabriella was checking out the room simultaneously lighting a couple of lanterns. Striker was helping Katerina light the fireplace while he spoke to her in hushed tones. Khrysaor and Pegasos were inside the door with the door cracked peering out. The must have spoken telepathically because they looked at each other when Pegasos started to head into the other room.

Stark lunged grabbing his arm in a tight grip. "Where do you think you are going?" he growled.

Looking at his arm caught in the vice of his grip. "You would be wise to let me go so I may guard the other door. From this point my brother and I can only see so much of the outside hall. There is an area where we cannot see."

"I don't know you and I don't trust anyone I don't know. Everything was fine until we came across you two." he growled.

"You would be wise to let my brother go." Khrysaor spoke quietly to Stark. "We are here to help and had nothing to do with what happened out there. Do not mistake the dark arts for my brother and I."—spitting on the floor—"We have nothing to do with that dark sorcery. It has killed many of my kinsmen, left orphans and spread deceit throughout our lands. Now I tell you again let my brother go so we may do what we do best and defend your family."

Stark struggled to reign in his temper desperately trying to hold his strength close to him not wanting to break the man's arm. Starring at Khrysaor, "I have your word that you and your brother will protect, defend and assist my family in this quest?"

Both speaking as one eyes casting a faint yellow glow briefly before disappearing. "You have the word from the House of Wolves that no harm shall occur by our hands while there is breath in our bodies. We will protect yours as if they were our own, this we vow to you."

Nodding once Stark let his arm go. Having read his honesty through his touch as well as the sincerity in his promise he believed they were one of the good guys, but he still felt on edge having only been here a couple hours and they were down three people.

"No one is to get into these rooms, alert me of anything you don't see as being normal." Already dismissing them he stepped deeper into the room to reassure himself she was resting. He saw Merridian was lying on the bed with Ellena sitting next to her holding her hand while Kenneth stood sentry over them both. His anxiety eased knowing everyone was as secure as he thought they could make it for the time being.

"Stark, you'll want to hear this." Striker said walking over to him with Katerina in tow close behind.

He noticed Striker seemed a bit possessive of the lady but there wasn't any time to deal with more couple drama now. It seemed as if everyone was suddenly paring up with the opposite sex when their entire lives no one had displayed a hint of interest. He filed that information for a later conversation with both boys. This wasn't the time to chase tail himself included.

Clearly agitated with his own thoughts he couldn't help the bark in his tone. "What is it?"

"Katerina has information more a possibility of what happened." Striker encouraged the lady beside him, "Go on love, Stark won't harm a bug; there isn't a reason to be afraid. He doesn't blame you for what's happened." He noticed Striker place his hand on her elbow gently guiding her forward.

Not saying a word Stark took the measure of the quiet mouse of a woman before him. This was Brkisanna's closest friend. It was hard to see this slip of a woman as anything especially a warrior compared to Briksanna. She was shorter than Bri, maybe by two, three inches tops, slight in figure. It was hard to see what she looked like with her modest gown. To think she was royalty was a stretch. Her face was not what he had expected either. Waist length blonde hair, green eyes, straight nose held up by full lips framed in dimples that peeked out every time she spoke made her a pretty woman even to his eyes.

Now only if he believed there were fairies then he could rest at ease with all of this magic portal, mysterious villain, magic wielding world. He was already stretched to the limit with his own family's abilities to think not only were their abilities going to become more but that there were more people with abilities in this world. Times like this he felt out of depth wanting desperately to be the man who sat in the background barking orders while he watched everyone else do the dirty work. At this point he didn't know what to believe all he knew was that his family had arrived and has been attacked hours after stepping into her home.

Steeling herself, before the giant of a man before her, she knew she needed to reassure them she had nothing to do with the attack within her own home. Maybe sharing what she suspected was a way to achieve their trust; however, she knew she was not going to let anyone intimidate her not even the mountain of a man standing in front of her. She was Briksanna's dearest friend and if anyone knew the sacrifices she had to endure over the centuries it was Briksanna. She was just as angry as the warrior before her regarding the attack. Looking at his hardened expression all thought of reassurance him went out the window. She felt her temper spike when his scowl deepened.

"Briksanna is my sister in heart, warrior, I do not care what you think or believe. I do know that what you just witnessed was a trap set for Briksanna specifically that is why no one else felt the negative energy. Nathanial's love for her provided a closed circuit for the negative energy threads to weave themselves around grabbing them both. The Goddess felt it before I did and she was the only one here with the ability to counter it. I have my healers in the castle but none would have been able to release them as quickly as she had. They both would have killed each other becoming the very monsters we fear."

Glancing to the fireplace, "May I sit while we speak? The chairs are close enough to the bed that everyone will be able to hear what I have to say and what it is I believe we have witnessed." Not waiting for his approval she moved to sit in the chair glad she decided to go with instinct and speak her mind. She was not going to allow anyone intimidate her ever again.

"Tell us what you know." Sounding matter of fact no hint of emotion could be detected in his voice.

Entranced by the light of the fire she wrapped her hands into the folds of her gown closing her eyes bracing herself for the onslaught of memories threatening to fill her with fear. With resolve to see the nightmare come to its end she vowed not see history repeat itself.

"We have not seen this type of magic since the attack on the High Royal Palace. I was with Lady Briksanna when the High King and Queen fell to their deaths from the same insidious dark magic. It happened several days prior to the great ball that was to announce the wedding of my brother to Briksanna. The High King argued with the High Queen within their private chambers so loud Briksanna and I heard it in our shared chambers. We were shocked when we recognized the voices belonged to her parents. We had never heard them speak to one another with such malice and hate. Her father left her mother storming through the castle. Briksanna was worried that it was something that she and I had done that might have displeased her parents."

Taking a deep breath she continued, "Sir Hawk had taken over our training once we entered our teenage years schooling us in the art of self-defense; but Briksanna and I took it to another level becoming so good we had decided to add our inherit abilities to our tactics with fighting. As a result we become extremely skilled in the art of combat. Not all of the Royal Guards within her parents' palace were as skilled as the princess and I. Knowing our level of skill, Sir Hawk agreed to share with the High King his praise. When we heard the argument we believed his talk with the High King did may not have gone as well as we had hoped."

"They were arguing because you both became good at fighting? That doesn't make sense." Startled by Striker's proximity she was grateful regardless for his presence.

Flames within the fire held her captive to her memories. "They argued because we beat the Royal Guards in a display of our new founded fighting techniques. The men we beat were responsible for the safety and protection of the High King and Queen and we had just laid them on the ground as if they were children on their first day of training."

"And there stood two princesses who had beat them." This time Stark did not sound as stern as he had before. He sounded guarded holding his arms across his chest, but no longer angry.

Nodding her head she acknowledged him, "Yes, not only did we defeat them we used tactics no one had used or seen in hundreds of years. We used our abilities to aid and direct our assault. We succeed not by strength or skill with a blade but in a combined effort to gain the upper hand. We beat them because we strategized within the mist of battle allowing our energy to flow through us as if our arms were extensions of our energy not the other way around. We trounced the Royal Guards within minutes, without breaking a sweat on our brow nor did we become heavy in breath. Even Sir Hawk had claimed he could not have had better pupils as he had found in the two of us. Briksanna worked her magic with her two swords and I with my knives."

Coming from striker with a bit more pride in his voice than Stark would have liked. "How many were you up against?"

This time Hawk spoke up moving opposite Striker, he laid a hand on her shoulder squeezing gently. She did not look up but smiled at the gesture keeping her eyes trained on the fire. "There were sixteen guards in total and the princesses defeated them within minutes. Not one of them got up from where they laid when all was done, yet not one person bleed. The princesses proved that with tactics used properly combined with energy victory could be achieved without bloodshed."

Glancing to where Briksanna laid, he continued, "Something not even I could do. That day they proved what they had argued to be right since they had been allowed a blade in their hands yet repetitively they had been told they could not do it simply because no one had mastered the art. Bloodshed could be avoided if energy combined with controlled abilities were allowed in combat training. Until then, abilities were not nurtured or used publicly. Those who had energetic skills were sent to the temple so they could be trained in honing their talents in feeding the energy used by the High King to give back to Skaldanna. It was frowned upon and considered punishable by the High Council if caught practicing such tactics."

Hawk searched Stark's face for understanding. She had glanced up when he had spoken wanting to hear his view of what happened that day. "We did not have wars, there were no battles only small skirmishes and posturing between boarder clans. All realms knew of peace for many centuries and we had become complacent in our teachings especially those concerning the training of our warriors. The knowledge to use energy had not been passed through the generations stifling the use of abilities combined with fighting tactics. Not even I thought it to be possible when they brought their thoughts to my attention; however I knew them since they were little and could refuse them nothing. I allowed them to show me what they believed they could do as a father would allow a child to play with a toy. Choosing to help them grow and learn how to properly wield a weapon while I guided in lessons of energy so no harm would come to them or others only practicing in secret. What they accomplished had merit worthy of the High Kings view and praise. The

Princesses were magnificent that day; however the praise was not shared by the High King and Queen. They were appalled with their skill in the art of combat and embarrassed they had defeated a contingent of High Royal Guards believed able to protect the High King and Queen."

"Why would they be upset and what does this story have to do with what just happened?"

She quickly turned her head toward the speaker not knowing what she would see as the tone of his voice was again filled with frustration. Stark's anger was starting to show and he no longer seemed as if he wanted to listen to a story. It was obvious the stress was eating at his nerves.

Not minding the exasperation written on his face Katerina looked back at the man clearly in charge and let him know with the same amount of exasperation in her voice over his impatience. "We were punished for not only displaying our abilities publicly but defeating an entire contingent of Royal Guards in front of the Ruling Council. The same council that was descendant form the original ruling council who banned the practice instituting energy was to be used only to feed peace and prosperity throughout Skaldanna. We were not just sent to our rooms but to the dungeon directly from the council chambers. If not for Sir Hawk and the High King's interference, the Ruling Council would have left us there for as long as they deemed necessary until we were purified from our scandalous behavior."

Voice shaking, "We not only embarrassed ourselves seeking praise and recognition for our acts as silly girls but dishonored our families in the process."—tears now spilling down her cheeks as she turned to looked at each one of them—"I felt more at guilt than Briksanna as it was my idea that we show them their laws were archaic and our tactics were deserving High Council consideration to change such stupid laws. She was the High Princess and I was the sister of her intended mate. No one was allowed to do what we had done and to do so publicly was a slap in the face of the all that our realms had believed should be the way of life for every person in the land. We had defied everyone believing the High King and Queen would be proud of our ingenuity. Instead we knew, by the looks of shock on their faces, we had shamed them instead."

Returning her tear streaked gaze towards the flames heating the room, "They wanted to send us to the High Temple for conditioning; a proper punishment for our crime as decreed by the High Ruling Council. We knew we had taken a chance by doing what we did; but we had hoped for praise and recognition as warriors worthy of status within the Royal ranks only to receive scorn and condemnation for our efforts punishable as decreed by law. We did not believe we would be treated as traitors to our government. Lead to the dungeons hands bound we were thrown in cells separated and frightened to be released hours later escorted to the Princess's room under armed guard. We were told nothing of our fate and saw no one. We cleaned up from having been in the dungeon and waited solemnly not knowing what was to happen. That was when we both felt a dark disturbance in the air around us. It felt like threads of hate seeking a target. Thinking back on it, many years ago Briksanna talked on the matter and believe it was a spell specifically made for individual persons targeting in on their particular energy pattern. That was the only way to describe what we saw and why not one thread that passed by affected had affected us."

Wiping the tears from her eyes shivering she rubbed her hands together trying to rid herself of the past and fear tonight's events had filled her with. Forcing herself to settle her nervous hands she noticed her fidgeting was apparent. She did not want them to know how shook up she really was so she decided to resume the story before she scrubbed her hands raw.

"We believe it is the spell that belonged to a dark witch. One that was told by the seer Vakgdona, before she left the castle, warning us of a taint to the land that used threads of magic to capture light energy turning it to hate. Because Briksanna and I had recently accepted our high energy in our earlier display, before the High King, it takes a while for the effects of that much energy to dissipate from our systems. Because of this we think that is why we could visibly see the dark threads floating throughout the room seeking its intended target."

"You mean you could actually see the energy in the air?" Trinity asked.

"Yes"

"Sometimes I can see energy plain as day while other times it's just a knowing like tonight. I could feel something floating past me as we were heading down the hall, but I couldn't place what it was I was sensing because I had nothing in my experiences to compare it to. It just felt wrong enough for me to stop and think about it until I heard the commotion behind us."

Nodding at her she continued, "For us it was like seeing many small black snakes floating in the air passing through the walls and doors. We were locked in our rooms and couldn't follow the snake threads, but almost immediately after the threads left we heard the yelling from Briksanna's parents and knew something had happened."

"What were they saying?" Hawk demanded visibly shocked in the direct the conversation had led to.

Feeling uncomfortable with Hawk's request she did not want to share the words that had forever seared themselves in her mind and heart. "What they said is irrelevant other than the fact the High King and Queen never argued. They never spoke ill of anyone even the subjects when they brought their issues before them during weekly court sessions to settle disputes. To do so would encourage dissention that could lead to anarchy within the land. They believed this with all their heart, practiced it, taught it to both of us since we were little children so for us to hear them yelling Briksanna and I believed we were to blame for their discord. We were so distraught we were willing to do anything to reverse the damage our actions had caused to shame Briksanna's parents."

Bending down on one knee in front of her, Striker placed his hand over hers stilling her fidgeting fingers. Looking right at her he did not blink when he spoke in a tone of voice that demanded her attention. "It wasn't your fault or Briksanna's for what happened that day. What you both did was brave and we, here, know what it's like to go against a group of dangerous people and come out the winner. You feel exhilarated and that is nothing to be ashamed of. You did nothing wrong and probably taught everyone a lesson in warfare that they had never experienced. I want you to hear me right now. No one in this room places blame on you for what happened on that day. It was not your fault. Please finish the story without worry of us judging you or Briksanna. I give you my word no one blames you. I don't ever want to hear you say that of yourself again."

She stared into the bluest eyes she had ever seen and felt the caress of his words wrap around her warming what the fire failed to touch. How long had she felt the guilt over her choices she had made that day always wondering if they had chosen to do things differently would it have prevented the events that had changed their lives forever? Hindsight was not clear and there were no longer seers in the land to confirm the course which had already been set in motion. Could it be as simple as he said? Could she let go of the self-inflicted guilt she had nurtured over the years following the hardships the people of Skaldanna had to suffer under the fear of Lord Drakkoon's oppression to arrive? When was the last time she had not looked over her shoulder making sure there was nothing to cause harm lurking in the air behind her?

"I will stand behind you to guard your back so no one will ever cause you harm, Princess. This I promise you. You are safe now. I mean what I say. Nothing will get past me without a fight. Ask anyone of them. I am pretty ruthless when it comes to winning when I set my mind to it." He smiled showing dimples deeper than hers and in that moment she wished everyone would disappear so she could reassure this man who had stolen her heart, with a look and heartfelt words, she truly believed him.

She squeezed his hand choosing to let him know she had accepted his protection acknowledging his words of reassurance with a smile. "You are most worthy, Sir Striker, to make such a vow to me publicly. I appreciate your concern; however I know what happened to everyone that night had nothing to do with what Briksanna and I did and everything to do with Dark Magic. At times when I remember it takes me a while to let go of the guilt in my heart when in my mind I know the attack on her parents had nothing to do with the two of us."

Letting go of his hand she shrugged off her melancholy allowing her own words to empower her effectively chasing the sordid memories away. She placed her hand within his outstretched palm and allowed him to help her stand before everyone in the room. No longer did she feel guilt or shame but fortified in releasing the hold her memories had held simply because she did not believe she should let them go fearing she had let her best friend down and as a result there were catastrophic events that had propelled their whole world into fear of the unknown. She saw Ellena standing in the connecting doorway listening with Pegasos a distance behind no doubt receiving a telepathic communication from his brother so he too could be a part of the conversation. Striker rose resuming his post at the left of her chair.

"I know now what I knew then, this magic is nothing but a targeted act specifically for the High King and High Queen. There Nathanial and Briksanna lie as quickly as did her parents; when they too had fallen under the spell. The only difference is Merridian was able to do what we could not do many years ago."

"What you are saying is wrong. I was there that night, Lady Katerina. I did not witness sorcery as I did this eve." Sir Hawk shook his head not believing her explanation.

"You were not near the High King and Queen as Briksanna and I had been nor were you full of energy from Skaldanna's energy core as we had been. We were witnesses to the heinous act in person, Sir Hawk. When the arguing began we were stunned with the venom they spoke to one another. We left our rooms escorted by the guards under the pretense something must have been terribly wrong with the High King and Queen. The guards did not need much prodding allowing us escape from our rooms for they too had never heard their liege speak in that manner."

Turning around the room she wanted to make sure every person understood what happened next. "We immediately searched out the pair finding it easy when their shouting led us right to them standing outside their chamber doors with electricity crackling all around them. Both of their guards had been struck down with the force of their negative energy there was no one to help intervene with argument, it was too far gone. We ran towards them and screamed for them to stop but all we could see where the threaded snakes clinging to their bodies covering them while they fed on their hate. The sight of those threads covering the High King and Queen will forever haunt me until the day I die. A most gruesome sight and I know Lady Briksanna was devastated by what she saw because it took her years before she would even speak of what happened because she was afraid the nightmares we had both been plagued with reliving the night would return."

For a moment she closed her eyes to let the ugly memory fade practicing what she had taught herself years ago to rid herself of the haunting memories. She took a cleansing breathe wanting to finish her story for she was tired, heart and soul. In a clear voice without horror and pain she did not want to scare them with her childhood fears. "Her parents did not hear our shouts of warning because before we could get within thirty feet of them they both struck each other down with the force of their angry energies, killing each other instantaneously in the process."

She watched the stricken expression on Hawk's face appear once she had finished her story and it was nearly her undoing, but she knew she had to go on for there was more for her to tell. She could no longer keep this information only between herself and Briksanna. Standing taller she steeled herself for what she had to say next because if she did not get the words out she did not think she would ever be able to say them again. She felt Striker's hand at her back steading filling her with the determination she needed to finish what she had dreaded to remember what happened all those years ago.

"Briksanna was so overcome with grief she screamed and would have kept on screaming if it was not for the quick thinking of the guards assigned to us. They pulled us away from the bodies of her parents and told us to return to her rooms for safety while they sought help. We were on our way back comforting one another when we heard the first sounds of swords clashing within the inner baily. It was then we knew we had been set upon by some unknown enemy. Briksanna convinced me we needed to get to her sister but her sister's rooms were on the opposite side of the wing near the children's nursery as she was much younger than the both of us. We changed our direction but were caught off guard by the sounds of fighting within the castle walls headed up the stairs directly where we had been standing. We ran into the nearest room and waited listening for any clue to what was going on. Briksanna knew a secret passageway through the walls that lead throughout the castle."

Feeling the vivid memories fill her with anxiety she hurried with her story worried they would overwhelm her. "We both refused to separate but knew we were defenseless without our weapons standing there. She was determined to get to her sister regardless and I felt as she had for her sister was all she had left of her family. We headed slowly towards her sisters room through the walls but when we arrived it had been too late. The moment we entered the chamber we saw her room had been torn apart with several Royal Guards dead in the middle of the room. We never found her sister and nothing has been known of her whereabouts since then and not for a lack of trying on both our parts. Briksanna was so distraught I was barely able to keep her silent we returned to the hidden passageways. I knew her screaming for her sister was going to give us away. I promised to continue our search as long as Briksanna kept silent and moving. I did grab the swords from the men lying on the ground before sealing us back into the darkness of the passageway."

Pausing as if she was again trapped in the dark with her heart beating sporadically she closed her eyes momentarily and remembered the smell of spilt blood as the walls closed in front of her. She would never forget witnessing the deaths of Briksanna's parents and then to find her sister missing with her guards lifeless eyes staring back at her all the while she heard the sounds of people screaming throughout the castle. Her mind tried to tell her body to run and hide so she could survive, but her body had frozen where it stood.

Opening her eyes she trained them on Stark while she continued, "I needed to get Briksanna out of the castle. For all I knew we were the only survivors. We had become separated when she charged through the tunnel while I was securing us in. I feared speaking too loud and being caught so I kept going forward in the dark as quickly as possible running my hands along the walls for a guide to find the correct direction I was trying desperately to remember led us out of the castle. That was when I heard voices next to me, but I did not know where it came from because I was in the tunnel alone, yet the voices sounded right beside me. There was only enough room for one person to walk in single file and no one was around me at the time."

"What did the voices say?" Sensing Stark wanted answers for the horrors she had just described. Hearing stories and the senseless deaths of the people within the story infuriated her. From the look on his face he appeared like she felt. He would rather destroy something right and she could relate to his feelings one hundred percent. She could feel his aggression mount kinetically while she struggled to take deep breaths to calm himself never taking his now glowing eyes off of her showing anyone who dared to see his temper had indeed returned.

She wasn't intimidated by his demeanor one bit. She felt she had found common ground for them to walk upon as she shared a part of her life with them.

"Come out, come out wherever you are or the little royal brat will get it just like the King and Queen did." Came a softer whisper from the back corner of the room, yet loud enough for everyone to hear.

All heads snapped to the bed afraid to say anything to the lady sitting up in bed with vacant eyes starring as if she still slept. She looked pale with her hair thrown all around her but she still held herself upright, regal and imposing trying to rid herself of her of the nightmare she was caught in.

"Momma!"

"Briksanna!"

Everyone took a step towards Briksanna but it was the soft glow of white light that held the couple on the bed once again surrounding them. At everyone's gasp, it was Trinity who smiled.

Needing to explain Trinity responded, "Merridian, is protecting them with her own healing energy allowing them to recover faster than I could ever hope to accomplish."

"I would not expect you to understand other than the shield is necessary for their energies to settle within their own inherit rhythm rather than a forced rhythm in hopes to steady their pattern. No offence young Trinity but this is the best solution for an immediate and safe recovery."

"Goddess!"

"Merridian!"

Both Ellena and Stark ran to her when she spoke, but it was Ellena who reached her first hugging the Goddess with relief. "I am so glad to see you up and about."

Before she could respond Stark pulled Merridian into his arms and held her tightly. "I swear woman, I can't handle seeing you hurt anymore. It about made want to tear this castle down just to blow off steam and I've never torn down a castle."

Wrapping her arms around the tall warrior's waist she appeared as if she reciprocated his feelings for mimicked his tight embrace. "I seem to keep finding myself in your arms warrior. I do not know what to think about that."

Sounding as relieved as Ellena had sounded moments ago, "Don't think just feel."

She pulled away and glanced up at him to smile, "I feel good right here with you, but now is not the time for us. We will have our moment, mark my words warrior, I shall not forget what awaits us when we do have the opportunity to explore each other more. I look forward to it."

"And that would be?" Sounding more relaxed than he had been a few minutes ago.

Smiling up at him looking mischievous, an emotion she had never seen played upon the face of the Goddess. "Possibilities, sir warrior, possibilities."

22

*A*fter all had been shared they were happy to have the peace to simply rest. It was agreed everyone should rest in the rooms they currently occupied. No one was in the least bit concerned with propriety a reflection of their exhaustion.

After Briksanna's brief outburst she simply closed her eyes and laid back down instinctively curling her body towards Nate falling into a deep sleep. Both of them appeared to be sleeping peacefully so no worries there. He could feel the connection between him and his brother growing stronger as each moment passed and felt at peace knowing they were on the mend. He believed Merridian was right telling everyone both of them would be better off once the effects of the dark magic had time to dissipate. His head was ready to blow thinking about all the magic that had attacked them so far. It was like story straight from a child's fairy tale book. He didn't know if he wanted to be a part of it anymore and that worried him. It was the first time he wanted to cut his losses grab his brother and run, but he knew they both were in too deep not to feel the connection building between everyone in the room with the exception of tweedle dum and tweetle dee guarding the doors.

Pegasos explained what Nate and Briksanna had said to them right before they fought and collapsed in the hall but none of it made sense. He guessed they would have to wait until they woke to see what they remembered. He looked around the room while everyone was settling down for the night thinking it might not be a bad idea, God knows his ass was tired.

Sprawled on the settee with her sister, Harmony, she leaned heavily on her shoulder when she spoke. "I think I have an idea how this dark magic thread spell works and I have an idea how to counter it. I've been thinking on everything we've learned both first hand and historically. I think this is all tied to the High Royal Family Throne and I'm thinking this doesn't have anything directly to do with either Nathanial or Briksanna, but more to do with this mysterious villain. I keep thinking about what everyone said earlier about striking out against those that Lord Drakkoon covets most. He would never hurt Momma and this thing we said earlier would not only hurt her, but kill her quickly judging by the rate of their tempers it wouldn't have been long before they would have attacked each other. If Merridian hadn't intervened I don't think any of us could have broken the hold that spell had on them. I don't know about all of you but that would have broken my heart in two."

Harmony grabbed her hand and squeezed, "She's all right twin. I feel your anxiety and mark my words we will take out the threat that would harm our mother that I promise you right now." Patting her hand already closing her eyes again settling her body in for much needed sleep she yawned real loud then smirked closing her mouth, "Besides Sir Hawk here needs a demonstration of our skills, isn't that right twin."

Looking at the man in question lying on the floor between Aunt Kat and Momma with one hand on his sword, he looked relaxed then a slow grin threatened the corner of his mouth. He mirrored their grin to a tee. It was like looking in a mirror and she didn't know what to do with that information.

"Yo Kenneth, I think the twins here want to show their skills publicly. You think us men should lend a hand and help them along? We wouldn't want the poor people of the Second Realm to have to see such a poor sighted show, now would you?"

Chuckling trying to keep the air playful everyone could always count on Striker to flash his quick comedic comments settling any anxiety she or her sister held.

"I'm thinking you may have something there, Striker, my man. We could hold a couple of skirmishes after we go on our scout tomorrow with Sir Hawk. A little swordsmanship with the twins may be just what the doctor ordered after a day in the saddle. Maybe you and I against the girls, but if Gabby wants to play then we'll have to ask another man to join the mix. How about it Sir Hawk? You up for a battle of skill, men against the women with a couple of swords? Striker and I won the last round against the twins although they are the champs in the family with a pair of blades; however my man Striker here is wicked with his Sai swords against Harmony. Those two make it look like their dancing, it's pretty incredible."

Turning on his side so that he could look at Kenneth he remained silent while he studied all of them. From Kenneth to Striker then to Gabby he settled his gaze upon her and Harmony who had fallen asleep now resting her head in her lap. He stared at the both of them for a couple minutes not saying a word. She almost thought he wasn't going to answer Kenneth but at the last moment he said quietly, "My Helen used to be very wicked with the blades. I will watch and participate if you still want me. Let us see how tomorrow fairs."

Looking from Hawk then down at Harmony she could tell something was up between them. Whatever it was she couldn't put her hand on it but it was bothering both her and Harmony a lot. He closed his eyes and appeared to be asleep. Whatever was with the guy she would not let him harm her family. Stark was right *keep your friends and family close, but your enemies closer.* She knew if she had any chance in finding out she would have to ask the Goddesses.

She decided everything could wait until later. She settled into the settee with her head back and closed her eyes. Right before drifting off she heard Kenneth say, "This shit is just enough to make a grown man run the other way"

Her last thought was he wasn't' the only one who felt that way. She had thought that the moment the Goddess had appeared two nights ago.

She was worried from the look Kenneth held on his face his words did not match his feelings inside. She knew there was a deeper reason he had said what he said but she could not get a clear reading from him. He was good at closing himself off from everyone. Would he ever understand she did what she had to do in order for him to survive all those years ago? She knew that by intervening she was doing exactly what Merridian had warned her intervening would do, break the laws of balance, but how could she leave the boy and his sister to the ravage streets of the realm he had been born to when she had dreamt of the man he would become with her.

It was a never ending plague of dreams that tormented her with a promise of hope she kept hidden deep within her soul. Always the same, she was with a man holding her, declaring his love for her while she wrapped herself in his arms begging him to come back to her and their child, but always with the same ending. His whispers to go back in time to save him and his sister from the nightmare they were all trapped in promising then could they all be saved.

None of it made any sense to her always passing it off as a nightmare that felt, smelled and tasted real leaving a hole in her heart the size of a fist every time she woke. Who was she kidding? It was an honor to be the personal guardian for the First Princess. A better fate than that of spirit awaiting rebirth which was what she would have been if not for the First God's request of her centuries ago unlike her love lying across the room. She prayed with all her heart she would have the chance to meet him in another life swearing never to make the same mistakes again. She accepted her position with Merridian never and had never regretted the choice she had made especially when she had lost her brother to the task set before him. Merridian had been grief stricken with the loss of her twin.

Watching Kenneth sleep brought back the moment of her dream when his arms were around her while he cherished her as a man desired a woman holding her as if his life depended on every moment spent. She wondered if he knew she had dreamt of him daily. She wondered if he felt the same desire she had carried in her heart since finding him again. She tried desperately to go to sleep and closed her eyes hoping her mind would follow. It did not.

He could not know how much those moments in her dream had helped her put one foot in front of the other while the years passed sometimes leaving her drowning in want of the man she could not hold. She longed for his touch and felt desperate to reach over and grab him. It took centuries of restraint not to display herself in that room.

"You'd be surprised what it is I dream about Lady Ellena. I have seen you many times in my dreams. I have never forgotten how it felt to hold you in my arms or how you taste with my lips upon you. I am that man and one day soon I will show my gratitude for your intervention for the rest of my life. You Are Mine."

Snapping her eyes open she stared at him in silence afraid to breathe lest she think it was her mind playing tricks on her. He was lying across the room eyes closed and had not changed position since the last time she looked at him with the exception of the words he had whispered in her head.

She would not be surprised if her own desires for him manifested his declaration falsely. Her feelings for him went beyond anything she had ever imagined possible. She had learned long ago to bury her thoughts deep, paying penance for the mistakes she had made that ruined their lives the first time. She watched him intently shredding the last bit of hope searching for a sign he had said those words to her in truth. Believing it a figment of her passionate mind she let the fantasy go closing her eyes once again.

"Let it be known, Lady Ellena, I Kenneth spoke those words to you and meant them. I have never wanted anyone or felt this way about any woman before. I have waited for you since you last appeared to me as a young boy. Give us a chance before you write this off as nothing more than a silly girl's fantasy. I am real and desire you above all else and make no mistake, Lady Ellena, You Are Mine."

This time when saw him he stared back at her mentally sending her the equivalent of a gentle caress across her brow while arms telepathically held her. She did not move instead felt every brush of his hands as they trailed her brow sending shivers down her spine.

She was embarrassed he had heard her thoughts and did not want him to know she battled her desire for him. She wanted him to be proud of her in the warrior woman she had become, capable of defending what she failed to do during her first life. Truth, honor and justice were equally important as was the man or woman fighting for freedom. She wanted him to know she had become woman of their dreams not the failure from their past. She was a woman who would send her love off to do what was right despite the grief and fear because it was the honorable thing to do. She had become woman she should have been to him before and it took losing him to understand.

"You are that woman to me. It doesn't matter if we've know it only in our dreams. I know it in my heart. Don't worry love I'm going nowhere. We will have our time. Go to sleep. We have a lot to do in a few hours."

She watched him wink while his mouth turned into a grin before he closed his eyes settling in for the night. She smiled at his flirtatious gesture finally able to close her eyes with peace in her heart for the first time in centuries.

— ~

She could hear voices around her but she felt weighted down like she was trapped under water desperate for the surface. She did not remember being in water. What was the last thing she remembered? Something about her and Nathanial talking to some men in Katerina's hallway while they headed to their rooms.

She reached up to rub her head surprised it hurt not to remember what she did to make it hurt so much. Shaking her head sitting up she opened her eyes to find herself on a bed with Nate lying beside her still asleep. *When did we go to bed? I do not remember entering the room.*

Something was wrong about them being in that room. Still rubbing her head she looked around and noticed the room was filled with her family.

"What happened?" she asked grimacing from the pain in her head.

"Momma!"

"Briksanna!"

Immediately people jumped up from they were lying and walked to the bed. "What happened? Why are Nathanial and I in bed? What are you all doing in our quarters?" Worried something had terribly gone wrong coupled with her loss of memory.

"One question at a time Momma." Trinity reached for her hand holding it securely to read her energy pattern. "You and Nate were caught in a dark magic spell. One that Aunt Kat said you two are familiar with. She said it looked like the same one that affected your parents. Merridian was able to stop the spell from wrapping you both in a match of hate and reverse the damage. You and Nate have been resting here for the past six hours. We have been waiting for you to wake up so we can talk about what happened." Trinity backed away from her so she could absorb what she had been told.

With a nod she gave mental command for them to leave her and Nathanial alone. They followed her request only when she promised she would be with them shortly.

Feeling stunned at what Trinity had told her was nothing compared to what she felt at being reminded the cause of their current situation was due to the same dark magic that had killed her parents. News such as that was enough to keep her silent for a long time not moving from bed. She did not want to remember what had happened that night or the horrible words her parents had said to one another. The sight of them killing each other in a fit of rage had seared itself in her memories forever. It took her centuries to burry that memory from her conscious thought. Now what was she supposed to do? The mere mention of the same dark magic brought those buried memories rushing back at her.

She squeezed her eyes closed from the onslaught of memories caught on a wave of old pain. She did what she had done for thousands of years when reminiscing of past hurts proved too dangerous to the function of her daily life. She breathed in and out while fisting the blanket with her free hand until the waves of painful memories were once again buried deep within her where they belonged.

It was several minutes before she realized a hand rubbed her shoulder with an attempt to soothe her. She turned to see Nathanial still held his eyes closed, yet his hand reassured her of his presence while she fought for composure.

"I'll always be here for you lady. You and I are not finished yet. Bri, those things I said…"

Swinging herself around she leaned over him flinging herself upon where he laid wrapping her arms around him. *"I love you Nathanial, more than you will ever know. There is nothing in this universe that can keep us apart. Not even death. I will always love you."*

He wrapped her in his arms fully awake while he rose up to hold her closer to him. He took a deep breath from the woman that held his heart. She heard his thoughts, knew his heart when he held her this close. He thought her hair reminded of fresh pine directly following a rain shower. It amazed her he felt so much love for her with regards to the simplest things like the smell of her hair. He tightened his hold on her while images flashed through their minds of his raging hatred for her back in the hallway. How he felt contempt towards her very existence. The memory of wanting to commit harm to the one woman who was his other half left a huge hole in both their hearts. She wanted to take those images of remorse away for she had felt the same way moments ago when the memories of her parents fight brought back the words she had said to him. He held her as if there was not a moment left in the world and if he let go their love would disappear.

"I don't ever want to feel that about you again. My hatred for you was more intense than I've ever felt for my worst enemy." His voice shook while he pleaded with her to understand.

"That is because those feelings is not natural. It is hard for me to explain what I know because doing so reminds me of witnessing my parent's death all over again. Katerina was with me when that happened and she is the only person in this universe who knows the struggles I had to overcome for me to bury that horrible moment from my mind. I will share it with you in time; however, I believe the best way will be able to show you is through our personal mental link. Can you give me time to reconcile myself to what happened in the past and not compare it to what happened between the two of us?"

Pulling back adjusting himself on the bed so they could see each other better. His green eyes stared back at her opening his soul to everything he had shown her. He loved her and would do anything to protect her from further pain. Her doubts fluttered away and gave chance to something more than she had ever believed possible.

Absolute and complete trust for the man before her.

"Even after all the things I said and the contempt I felt for you, you would continue to love me? I hurt you back there"—bringing her hand to rest on his chest for emphasis—"I saw your pain at my words as if they were a living being while I continued to spout my venom. Please forgive me for words spoken for they were not from my heart?"

She held her breathe hoping the sincerity of her words had been rec-ognized while she poured her love for this man one energy wave after another begging for his absolution. She heard someone clear their throat reminding her they were not alone and her pleading might have been viewed by everyone.

She felt like she could fall in hole and let it swallow her up. Would they ever have privacy again?

Nate put both hands on her face cupping her cheeks with one hand he brushed away strands of hair that had fallen from her thick braid. "Don't you worry about what everyone hears or thinks about what we just said, that's between the both of us. The important part is the words have been said and we both needed to hear them. We're a family, Bri, and there isn't anything said that we all doesn't already know about one another. You and I are one in the same. What happened between you and I was because some asshat out there tried to destroy what we have. Who knows what the real reason was and frankly I could care less. What I do know is that you are the most important thing in the universe to me. My love for you consumes me. I wake up thinking about you, walk around my day think-ing of you and can't wait til the next moment when I can hold you in my arms again. You are on my mind, in my heart and in my soul every damn minute of the day. What you don't realize is that there isn't a thing in this world that can make that go away. Never ask me for forgiveness when you were forgiven the moment I woke knowing you were still alive right beside me where you belong."

She felt tears spill down her check and leaned her head against his forehead while she released the breath she had been holding waiting for his acceptance. "I did not realize I needed to hear the words until you said them. My mind needed to hear the words my heart already knew existed. I could not bear to be the one to cause so much pain yet I was the one saying and thinking those horrible thoughts. I would never betray you and what our future holds. You are my reason I have begun to believe in myself again. You are the reason I have found the courage take the steps necessary in fulfilling The Prophesy. You are my hope for a new life."

She no longer searched his eyes for absolution. "For the longest time I did not believe I could succeed at defeating what had been spoken about

Lord Drakkoon, yet, he has continued to plague my existence so much so I did not think there was any other way to live until I met you. You are the one person I have been waiting for. You are the other half of me. The sole reason I know we can not only win but have a child born as a result of our unconditional love. I am honored to be that person for you and for our child. You are my life, Nathanial, and I cherish every moment the Gods have given me to spend with you now and forever."

His mouth took possession of hers mixed with tears catching her soft breathy sigh when he deepened the kiss, parting her lips while his tongue touched hers sealing their promises with a lovers kiss. His hands wound their way into her hair held tightly while he continued to ravage her mouth shattering any lingering guilt shared between them from the night before. She kissed him back pouring her love into each swipe of her tongue savoring the taste of his mouth set her blood on fire. Fingers finding their way to his chest she brushed them across his taught nipples.

Pulling away abruptly panting as heavily as she was he leaned his forehead against her, "I want to make love to you all day long, I love you, but right now we have too many people in this room and plenty to do today before I let myself indulge in you." His voice was choked with a harsh sound of desire.

Watching his emerald eyes deepen she knew there was nothing left to say regarding forgiveness, he loved her unconditionally and so did she. Sighing she responded, "We will have all night to devote to what you and your mouth want to do, that I promise you."

Reluctantly pulling away from him she briefly closed her eyes for composure more than anything only to open them to see his green eyes merrily twinkling in front of her.

"I'll hold you to that Mrs. Angelo." Winking at her turning his grin into a full smile no longer holding any regret from the night before.

They had renewed their love for one another verbally sealing it with a kiss. She decided she liked this type of play with him and wanted to do more of it.

She smiled herself while before she turned away from him and decided two could play at that game. "It is a date then?" Winking back at him in the casual manner he had just displayed hoping it had the same effect on him as it had on her.

Laughing at the groan he let out, she hopped out of the bed looking cheerful and beautiful in the sunlight knowing she left a man fully aroused with no recourse to appease that hunger. Nothing was going to ruin her mood. She loved him and he loved her. They could accomplish anything set before them standing side by side and for the first time in several millennia she believed that with her whole heart.

He ran his hands through his dark hair, "You kill me lady, seriously kill me. Let's get this day over with. The faster we do the closer I'll be to making you keep your word." He winked back at her bounding off the bed like the children had when they were teenagers.

Snapping into his familiar commanding mode, looking at his brothers cocky swagger grin still in place and just like that he was business as usual. "Report!"

Laughing out right clearly glad to have his brother back Stark grabbed his arm and pulled Nathanial into a full hug pounding on his back as men do. "Now that's how I taught you to represent the Angelo name little brother."

"Yeah well I missed you too brother."

Squeezing his older sibling tight she watched Stark and Nathanial hold each other longer than she had ever witnessed them do knowing they were not the type of people to display such types of emotion publicly. Stark had of seen the way they acted last night for him to have endured the possibility of his brothers loss The thought of them leaving their family with the same kind of pain she had endured was enough to entice those horrible memories to reappear.

Nathanial was very intent on reassuring his brother they were fine, but even to her Stark appeared as if there were more to the problem than their attempt to kill each other. What else could there be?

"Anything you want to share with me brother?" Nathanial asked hesitantly.

"Nothing that can't be explained once when you and Briksanna have some time getting changed. While you were sleeping we checked the castle out with tweedle dum and tweedle dee over there and I have to say I am glad they're playing on our team. They seem to take their task of guarding our family very, seriously wherever they go, so they have my vote to stay with our group."

"Everyone is well? No one else had been hurt?" She was worried the children might have been affected by the dark magic that had attacked them.

Stark turned a serious face in her direction reluctantly letting go of his brother. "Home base is clear. No more disturbances or any weird signatures of energy that Merridian can detect has been found. She placed a spell of some sort, a protective barrier, outside the perimeter of the castle extending a full two hundred meters out. Katerina was able to send out her messengers last night to the other realms assuring me they would be delivered by this morning. How that is possible considering they had to have covered some distance to get the messages where they were supposed to go is beyond me, but she assured me the horses were familiar with the tasks and the distances and that it was not unusual for royal houses in each realm to have several of them in their stables for occasions such as this."

He rubbed his head in the nervous habit Stark was accustomed to when he was feeling awkward speaking about something. "We should have the Ruling Council meeting by tonight." Stark looked between the both of them finally giving up on his nervousness. "There aren't flying horses living here are there?"

She was afraid Nathanial was going to laugh out loud over his brother's nervousness. She kept her face devoid of any additional emotion not wanting to bruise his pride for having the courage to ask what he was having a hard time accepting. It must have taken a lot of courage for him to ask the question considering the two of them came from a time and place where magic was not common place.

Her expression reassured him of his fears. "No they most certainly do not fly, but they do travel very far very fast. They are breed by Fenrir himself at the High Royal Stables. They are known to travel the distance of what you would consider a continent in a single night. Only the Royal Houses within the realms utilize this mode of transportation and are allowed ownership. The riders are hand-picked and trained by Fenrir himself. Each Royal House has five horses within residence at a given time and the riders are housed near the stables with enough room for families if they acquire them within their lifetime. Katerina and I can introduce all of you to them when they return. To answer your question they do not fly but gallop very, very fast."

Satisfied with her answer he nodded to the both of them mumbling he needed to get everyone downstairs to eat so they could head out within the hour to survey the surrounding area as discussed last night. Walking closer to where both men were standing she went right up to Stark and held her arms open to the one person who remained steadfast during their time of need. He kept the family safely together protected them while he held his own fears at bay. Her head turned into his chest she radiated her love for him feeling his arms wrap around her in a brotherly hug. The type of trauma he had experienced she was familiar with and understood without a doubt how hard it was to bounce back after an experience like that. Nothing was hard to witness than to watch someone you love get hurt.

Stretched up on her toes she kissed him on his cheek earning a blush in return. Stepping back she put her arm around Nathanial's waist finding herself content to let her love continue to radiate through her mental link. Stark nodded his head again turned around and left telling Nathanial he would see him outside when the time came to go.

"You're going out with them today?"

She looked up to him and time slowed down to a standstill while she was held captive in his encompassing stare holding her in place while he devoured her with his smoldering green eyes.

Smiling at her, she realized he had heard her thoughts, mentally slamming the doors on her mind she pinched his side earning a chuckle from him when she spun out of his arms wagging her finger at him. "You will not get out of answering me that easy Mr. Angelo."

With the playfulness set aside, Nathanial looked serious. "I need to be there with them on this Bri. I am your partner, but I am also the High King. Waking up this morning I realized I need to not just play the part I need to be the part. That includes surveying the surrounding lands of the Second Realm. I don't like leaving you ladies here, but I know you are skilled in your own right as warriors. I have no doubt you will be able to take care of anything if it were to occur. I just ask that if you leave the castle walls you don't venture past the perimeter Merridian set up until we have a better understanding of what we are dealing with. I think she was right this thing is directed at you and her not any of us so on that note, please, do me this favor and stay close to the castle."

Concern etched on his worried face fearing for her safety warmed my heart. She wanted to spend time with Katerina and the girls. It was not difficult for her to give in to his request without causing a big discussion like they had when they strategized mercenary missions on Earth.

Glad to give him what he wanted she pouted her mouth feigning disappointment then broke in a grin when she knew she could not keep a straight face even if she had wanted to. "I promise."

He nodded sighing with relief then stretched his arms over his head while he took in their surroundings. It was a large room for a bedroom even she had noticed that. There were two settees pulled close to the fireplace which dominated the living area. There were two chairs opposite the settees. This must have been where her children had slept. Knowing them they would not have wanted to leave them unguarded knowing there had been danger earlier. No, they would have camped right and only the thought of food would break their concentration or if Stark ordered them leave which would explain his presence a moment ago.

She noted very few things inside the room indicated it had not been used prior to their arrival. No paintings hung on the walls, no knickknacks rested on the armoire, just simple pieces of furniture; an end table here and there along with closet from the looks of the clothes hung within it next to a partially opened door similar in looks of their bathroom back home.

Walking to the only window visible in the room she stared horrified by the ravaged land stretched out before her. Eyes watered when she looked at what should have been the royal gardens and found nothing but row after row of dead plants as far as the eye could see. She had expected to see damage but nothing as horrific as she was seeing at this moment. Peering at the edge of the glass she tried to get a better look at the devastating picture before her. As far as she could see she was astounded with how complete the damage to the land actually was. Nothing that grew from the ground remained alive. The sight was disturbing to view.

Putting back into the land what energy she had carried from Earth she prayed Skaldanna's core energy would help her create the new growth needed to bring life back on Skaldanna. Between her and Harmony she knew they could accomplish it.

"I need to get out there now. Nate where is Harmony? Did Stark tell you where she went? If I know that girl, she will be itching to lay her hands in the dirt singing right along, but she is unfamiliar with Skaldanna and its energy. This is why I need to be with her."

Walking stiffly towards the closet she grabbed the first gown she came across that wasn't too fancy ripping off her outfit knowing she had been wearing the same clothes for the past twenty four hours. She was glad to be putting on a gown familiar to her station yet casual in its wear. She deafly laced up the gown while she walked in circles looking around the closet floor.

Walking up to her he thought how beautiful she looked in that dress. He reached behind her and grabbed a change of pants along with a loose fitted shirt to put on. She tried to ignore his heated thoughts while she dressed but it would not last long. He was hot for her and that was not going to go away any time soon. She did not know if she had the will power to resist him if he kept that train of thought much longer.

Sounding curious he asked, "What are you looking for?"

"Some shoes to wear and my knives, I cannot leave weaponless," she replied exasperated, "I cannot find anything in here, there is no light. I have forgotten how modern conveniences like light in a closet can make life a lot easier."

Blowing her hair out of her face she knew the look he was gave her he thought she looked beautiful working herself into a snit. She folded her arms across her chest frustrated and knew all along her anger had to do more about him than not having a light in the closet. He pulled her close and held her tightly against her playful struggles all the while kissing her nose and cheeks before fully capturing her mouth in a heated kiss.

They broke apart panting. She tried to keep a serious look on her face stressing the importance of completing her task when all she wanted to do was succumb to his advances and make love to him right there on the dark closet floor. "We do not have time for this Nathanial. There is so much to do. How can anyone do this to the land knowing what kind of havoc it would reap on Skaldanna's inhabitants? How can anyone consent to such an atrocity? It breaks my heart to come home and see what has been inflicted upon my homeland." Resigning into his embrace she allowed him to comfort appreciative of his presence while her heart grieved.

"We can fix this, Bri. I know it in my heart our family can fix this. We can't afford for you to question the why of it; we just forge ahead and deal with the problem like we always have." He turned her so she could face him while she searched his eyes believing his words of hope would be enough to calm her heart.

Her thoughts were scattered enough as it was while she wondered how far the destruction had actually extended its reach. It was worse than she had imagined and that was what frightened her the most. She knew with the witnessing what happened to the both of them had already reminded her what it had been like to witness her parents behavior long ago. She was desperate to try and keep her fears tucked away doing a poor job that had been evident with her breakdown a moment ago. Being in tune with him, in this place of her upbringing, she knew there was nothing she could hide from him no matter how hard she tried to bury it.

"We will do what we always do; assess the situation, formulate a plan of attack and solve the problem. All of us can do this, Bri, you can't start doubting your family now. Let the memories go. They don't belong here in the present. Let the past lie where it's been all this time." He lifted his hand to brush his fingers along her cheek.

"What if we fail or worse what if one of us gets hurt. I do not think my heart could recover from that kind of pain. This is what I have feared for so long refusing to acknowledge The Prophesy for anything other than a story told to me a long time ago. There is so much pain I have had to overcome through the years surrounding my parent's death and not knowing what happened to everyone. No one knows what happened to the people of my father's castle or my sister for that matter. It's as if they all disappeared that horrible day. Only Katerina was spared because she was in the tunnels when I had been taken. I thought I could get to my sister faster only to put myself directly in my abductors arms. My heart wants to believe in what my head knows to be true one minute then in the very next I am afraid we will not walk away from this unscathed and that has me more worried than ever before."

With bereft feelings floating through her heart she knew he was right to let go of her past. If she was ever going to move forward she had to let her self-incriminating doubt die for good. It did nothing for her but left her miserable inside not able to fully function until she exercised her treacherous thoughts. Some days that took longer to get rid of than other days. She was no longer the same person who had once lived as Princess of the High Royal Court. She stood before her mate and knew she had become more.

"You and I, together, can do all that we set out to do. I believe that with all my heart. So get this crazy talk out of your head, lady. Those kids are damn fine soldier's even finer people. Do you doubt their capabilities?"

Appalled at the mere suggestion she quickly answered, "Never."

He leaned in and kissed her lightly on her forehead, "Then trust in us to do all that we can do to save the universe while keeping our family safe along the way."

Her mouth threatened to smile when she felt warmth tingle throughout her body from his gentle kiss. He sent his love to fill her up where her memories had left her cold inside. Overwhelmed by his tenderness she took his advice and choose to let go of memories that had held her in fear for centuries.

She tested her resolve the moment the decision had been made surprised to find the weight ease from her shoulders instantaneously. "Well said soldier, now let us not be late in what we need to do before those peacocks arrive tonight."

Laughing outright at her assessment of the High Ruling Council, he let her go handing her the knives she had seen him grab from the top dresser when he entered the closet made her groan in embarrassment. Strapping her knives around her body she chanced a glance at Nathanial grateful she had a man like him in her life. If she thought his looks distracted her before they certainly did more now that she knew what it felt like to have his arms wrapped around her. He belonged to her and she did not want to take her eyes off of him for a single second. He continued to dress attaching his own weapons along the way. Gods she needed to leave the room or she would not be able to step away from him. When she saw him strap his knives around his waist her mouth watered. She was considering the time needed for a quick tumble before leaving their rooms.

While her traitor of a mind was mentally calculating the time it would take to unlace his pants and hike up her skirt he interrupted her thoughts. "I beg your pardon. Could you please repeat that?"

The left side of his mouth quirked up in obvious approval to where her mind had been. She had to do something about these raging hormones. She wanted to jump his body every time they were in close proximity.

"I think I will walk with Kyrysaor and Pegasos catch up on the lay of the land while I head out to meet Stark and the boys. I'm curious to what they think might have happened to the land. I'll meet you at noon if not earlier in the dining room." Frowning at what he just said, "There is a dining room here isn't there?"

She outright laughed, "It's called a Dining Hall; we are civilized beings here Nathanial. We do sit and eat with utensils and all."

Picking a throw pillow off one of the settees he playfully tossed it at her. "Ok laugh it up, I deserved that one. Seriously, take care of yourself. We have a date tonight remember?" His brow scrunched in doubt if he should leave her alone. She felt his mind fill with worries and rushed to send him her reassurances through their mental link.

"I love you. I will see you at lunch time or as they call it here Noon Meal." With her parting words and warm thoughts she left, but not before she threw the pillow back at him before exiting the door hearing his laughter while she proceed down the hall.

She hardly believed she was back in her homeland walking the halls of her best friend's home for a period longer than a couple of hours. In the beginning of her self-appointed exile she had spent longer time in Skaldanna, but once the twins were in her custody she never left their side nor did she leave them unprotected. They had been guarded by either Fenrir or Katerina via telepathy while she tended the infusion of energy on Skaldanna.

Mentally groaning thinking of Fenrir she knew he would have to be told of her arrival in the realm and was probably chomping on the bit as to why she had not alerted him of her presence or intentions in person.

Mentally searching for his presence in her home realm she called for him. Her summons was met with silence. She worried because Fenrir had always answered immediately.

"Fenrir, answer me are you in need of aid? I am here in Kat's castle and plan to stay this time for good. I need you to come immediately. It is in regards to The Prophesy."

Already felt your presence love and am on my way to your location as we speak. Tell Kat, I'll see her this eve and will require my usual quarters in the South Wing, no guards. I have my own.

A bit sure of yourself are you? she replied

Laughing mentally at her remark, *"Not much gets by you does it?"*

Not saying anything for a couple of seconds she hesitated how much to fill him in on what had transpired. On one hand she looked forward to seeing her longtime friend and on the other she did not want to involve the people she loved in the quest fearing they may be harmed in the process. "Damn, damn and double damn."

"I can hear your thoughts, love. Do not worry about me, all will and can be discussed when you are ready and the appropriate parties are present."

"Arrggh, I hate it when you do that. You are better at telepathy than I am, nothing is private when I am around you."

"This surprises you?" Laughing a deep rich baritone he filled her mind with thoughts of confidence and assurance.

"I have missed you, Fenrir. It has been so long that I have hidden myself, there were times I wondered if I would ever be able to find myself again." She spoke softly afraid someone would over hear her thoughts. *"You are the only person besides Kat who knows how much I have endured and sacrificed in order for all the realms to survive without additional harm."*

Not addressing her specifically, *"I will be there this eve, love, in the meantime, try not to engage in anything too hazardous until I get there. Oh and Love, She Is Here. I felt her come with you. I just wanted you to know, no matter who it is I will do my best to not say or do anything until you and I have spoken. I know how you feel about this when we last spoke, but I cannot guarantee I can keep my distance. I promise to try my damndest to give her time to know me before I tell her the truth about who I am."*

"I trust you Fenrir, just be careful with my daughters. I trust you will not harm their hearts or we would not be having this conversation. Just promise you will not engage with her until you and I have spoken. They are my children and as a mother I want to know who she is first as will my mate."

Letting those last few words sync in she waited for his response. She knew Fenrir was like her he had waited centuries for his other half never committing to any one person all the years she had known him. When she asked him, long ago, he told her he would know her energy the moment she entered any realm for she would be his destined other half and he was the only person besides herself that was tuned into Skaldanna's energy core and because of his own heritage he was an exception to the rule here in the Four Realm Kingdom regarding High Royalty. He was High Royalty from his homeland.

Sounding tired Fenrir responded to her request. *"Agreed. Now let me conserve energy and break this link. I should be there by evening meal. I promise to wait to talk to you and your mate before engaging with her, whomever she may be. Now you promise not to do anything too hazardous until I get there."*

What does that mean, too hazardous? Eyes glaring at the empty hallway in front of her as if he could see her expression when she had stopped walking irritated by his remark.

He did not reply, nor did he reply to her unsuccessful additional attempts to gain a response. Worried over his continued silence, she knew he could take care of himself should the need arise and hoped he arrived sooner rather than later.

She continued in the direction towards Katerina's apartments opening the door without knocking. Katerina sat at her writing desk engrossed in whatever was in front of her dismissing her presence as if she had never heard the door open. She stood with her eyebrow raised in mock concern when she did not address her upon entering.

"I know your there and we have been friends long enough that you do not need formalities when entering my private chambers," she replied nonchalantly.

Katerina sat stiffly in her chair dressed in an everyday gown same as she had two thousand years ago. Blonde hair pulled back in a long braid similar to hers, small earrings hung from her ears, rings adorned each finger. She looked regal and fierce yet she still managed to maintain a look of ease coupled with grace when she first looked upon her entering the room. Anyone who took Kat's first impression saw only a pampered princess. They were seriously mistaken for she knew how ferocious Katerina Kastekanos could really be if and when the need arose.

"You look too pretty to be ready to fight in this battle before us." Baiting her into a conversation hoping to provoke her longtime friend to shake off the melancholy that surrounded her. Things from their past they both had spent many years trying to bury deep in their minds hoping never to witness again, yet for some Gods forsaken reason seem to have reappeared in their lives again.

She did not want her best friend to get hurt in the process nor did her friend look like she wanted to talk about any of it. Frankly, she did not blame her one bit. For thousands of years she did not want to even look at her past let alone become its active participant, yet they were faced with a threat from their past. The question plaguing her mind was, what were they going to do about it?

23

Scoffing at her friends words she looked up from where she was reading seeing her longtime friend stand in gown similar to hers with hair braided in the same fashion as hers except she had hers draped over her shoulder twirling the ends like she used to do when they were younger. The skirt of her gown was floor length, but like herself she knew Briksanna carried several weapons on her person just like she had. Swords in hidden sheaths within the skirt along with knives strapped to their legs and arms. To the naked eye you would not be able to tell from the way the gown hung around them, but they had been trained from the moment they could carry a sword to be prepared for anything no matter what attire they wore and they had never stopped practicing that habit. With last evenings spectacular events she would not be surprised if her friend carried no less than five knives on her possession at this very moment. She carried no less on her own body.

"Feeling better?" she inquired.

"Much"—flopping down into a large chair across from her—"from what I hear you had an eventful night. I understand you shared with everyone the dark magic snake threads we saw attack my parents."

"What happened last night was exactly like what happened to your parents with the exception of death. It was pretty hard to see that a second time, Briksanna. A person could go their entire life without having to witness that nightmare again." Shuddering at the memories and the too close encounter was enough to send her back to bed for the rest of the day.

"I can only imagine." Briksanna reached for her hand clasping it while she spoke. "Thank you for everything including protecting me all these years. I know how hard it has been to be alone; not knowing who you could trust with your words or your heart and without the means of communication. I realize the years have passed with the same fate of solitude for the both of us. I can only imagine how hard it has been for you to be responsible for both your realm and those within it."

She squeezed her hand briefly before letting it go while she rose from her chair striding towards the window that overlooked the same desolate scene she saw yesterday. Where the forests had not been completely ravaged yesterday except for the trees lining the fields were now completely barren and destroyed. It was if something came like a thief in the night and stole what life remained from her lands. It broke her heart this morning to wake and see the absolute destruction of the grounds that surrounded her castle. She prayed Briksanna had the means to restore the horror that had become of her home.

"Did you happen to see the gardens? They were our favorite place to play growing up. It was my mother's favorite place to be when she was alive. Over the years when you would leave I would walk through them, and as long as the flowers continued to bloom I knew peace from the curse of The Prophesy could be accomplished because the garden had remained untouched by the taint of evil. Nothing had been beautiful as those flowers had been when I looked upon them every morning and they were just as magnificent when I went to bed each night. They were what helped to ease the pain from my nightmares when I felt trapped in my past. That garden was what kept me believing there could be hope for our worlds to survive The Prophesy. I made up a mantra in that garden saying to myself, put one foot in front of the other and one day you will look back at all those steps you took and see time has passed then it would no longer look so bad to stand where I stood. I did that every damn day for decades when finally the day came when I no longer needed the words but only needed to smell the flowers or look out my window to see it was all still there to feel I could and if filled me with hope, but now it is gone and I am afraid I may truly lose my hope." Her voice cracked revealing the depth of her grief for what has happened to her realm. "Those flowers helped me all these years hold my head up high for my kingdom and now they are gone and I am very, very angry."

Half turned back towards Briksanna she knew her eyes had gone dark with rage. Gone was the regal expression she held at her desk. It had been replaced with hard cold eyes she was sure her best friend had never witnessed before. The thought of the destruction before her spreading the remaining realms left her raging with anger and her expression was a direct reflection of that anger.

"I want to murder the persons responsible for this destruction to my home, Briksanna that is how much anger I have festering within me. I thought I could be strong and maintain the balance you need in a ruler to help set an example for the High Ruling Council, but now I find myself so full of resentment towards the mastermind behind this not even I, fair Lady Katerina Kastekanos, can see straight. Then I hear you and Merridian speak of the possibility in there being another madman; the possible mastermind behind every wrong deed. How is this possible? More importantly what am I to do with all of this anger? This is not who I am, yet I have always held in my anger about what happened to our families that night, yours and mine, for we both lost them that day.

Taking a deep breath not wanting to dump all of her anxieties on her best friend she needed her to know she had a hard time reconciling what she had learned against the history the nightmare had left in her memories. She had to learn how to stand up on her own just as Briksanna had all this time. "The crazy part is I do not know where to begin fixing the problem with my lands. My mind is a complete blank with regards to this subject, never mind how to begin finding a solution for it. In all the years as a ruler I have never come across a task that I could not manage nor have I come across a situation I could not find someone who could provide the solution until now."

Rising up to comfort her longtime friend Briksanna knew the feelings she had shared were experiences she had come to terms with as well. The topic was nothing new to either one of them. She could feel her thoughts from the sisterly bond they had shared since they were children. She knew Briksanna had felt those same feelings time and time again residing in the Earth Realm when she would visit. She could see it in the longing expressions her friend carried with her when she arrived and the solemn expression each time she left. She had told her more so in the beginning of her self-imposed exile than she had in recent years. In fact she had not spoken about it since Briksanna found the twins a few years ago...well decades in the Earth Realm. Their way of life had evolved over the years with them both living around people yet they had remained alone the entire time. Both of their families were gone and there was nothing in the universe that could change that fact.

In that moment of realization she felt her two hundred years of age more than she had ever felt it before. She was so tired of being alone. Tired of having to strategize everything pertaining to the management of her realm by herself. She craved a mate of her own more than anything. A man she could share her heart and world with along with all its problems like the one facing her in the window below watching her before he rode off with a smile on his lips.

"We have more important things to accomplish than to feed the anger within our hearts, Kat. You above all people know what can happen when anger is let into the equation; it breeds nothing but misery. I too find myself struggling with that one simple concept and you know what Nathanial reminded me just a bit ago? Let our memories lie where they belong...in the past. Do not give your memories the power to hold you prisoner in this time and place. We will find the problem and exact the proper solution to what has happened to your lands. Mark my words, we shall succeed in this today."

Taking her by the hand Briksanna steered her out the apartment door out into the hall while she continued to speak. "Besides you have two loving nieces whom you have never met in person who are greatly gifted to help rebuild along with three of my adoptees to complete a family for both of us. What better way to mend your traitorous heart than to spend time with my children? Hmmm..."

Green eyes lit up along with her chuckle, "Those two blonde beauties of yours sure know how to raise Sir Hawk's hackles."

"Oh no, what did they do now?" Enjoying Briksanna's company she was happy to redirect the conversation away from matters of her heart. Her warrior's instincts screamed to retaliate against the ones who dared hurt her best friend. She had a sinking feeling the culprit behind everything had lured Briksanna back to Skaldanna thinking they could send their black magic in to destroy her along with all the realms in the process.

Whoever they were, they were in for a world of hurt because she was not going down without a fight. Knowing the rest of her family they would not tolerate anything less than giving it their all to destroy the threat against her friend. Mentally cursing herself for allowing her angry thoughts to gain control of her waking mind she shoved them deep down for reflection later.

Almost laughing outright she pictured what had happened this morning. She tried to hold her giggles to a minimum or she would never be able to tell the story. "Nothing, the girls thought it would be great to trick the boys this morning while they were sleeping. They each held wet strips of cloth over their eyes and as one dropped them on their faces while they slept. At this all the men afflicted jumped up out of their slumber reaching for their weapons to find that the girls had done something to the scabbards locking their knives and swords in place."

Outright laughing at the memory, "You should have seen three grown men hopping around the room shouting struggling to relieve themselves of their weapons. I hadn't laughed like that since we used to play ticks on the lads in training when we were younger."

Smiling at Katerina's infectious laughter, "How did Sir Hawk take the girls humorous attentions?"

"Sir Hawk was the one who cussed the loudest once he realized there was not a threat to anyone in the room other than his pride." Laughing louder holding her sides, "You should have seen the expression on the girl's faces when they realized he was serious.

Laughing right along with her not holding back her own humor, "I bet they laughed the moment the men jumped up."

Let me tell you those three girls not only kept their silence until the men had tried several times to relieve their weapons, but they had told everyone who was awake of their intent before so as not to cause alarm with the commotion. It was Stark who laughed first followed by the Palapanos twins. Those two had a bet with Gabriella that the twins would not be able to pull off not wakening the famous Sir Hawk in the process. Gabriella not only took that bet but made sure the twins accepted it only if they could complete the trick without waking him and if he woke they would have to pay up, their words not mine, at a later date and it could be anything she wanted. If they won Gabriella would have to pay, at a later date, of course."

Wiping the tears from her eyes reliving the memory brought to life by Briksanna's family acting affectionately towards on another within her realm was a testament to their kinship.

Briksanna inquired with raised eyebrows, "What did they say when they realized they had won."

Slipping her arm through Briksanna's she steered her to the grand staircase leading down to the first floor. "Of course being the rough men they portray themselves to be; mind you I have seen them in full protective mode and have no doubts of their skills or their loyalty to our mutual cause, but seeing them enjoying themselves clearly remembering they are a family foremost was a blessing to witness. Oh Briksanna, it is good to finally have you home. I have missed you so much."

Stopping at the top of the stairs Briksanna asked, "Has everyone eaten already?"

"Your family has already left with Sir Hawk's regiment to investigate the land within my realm. Trinity is working with my healer to help with the few remaining sick. Merridian and Ellena opted to go along to see if any dark magic had been used to alter their health and to render their services settling in our flux of people flocking to my castle."

"Is Merlita still healer here? I have not seen her in long time. It would be a pleasure to speak with her again."

Patting her hand Katerina looked up with pain filled eyes. "Merlita passed five summers ago, Briksanna. Her daughter Sierra is healer now. She has many gifts in the art of healing that Trinity has taken an avid interest with herbs and potions for healing declaring it be her calling as long as she remains in this realm. She stated if anyone had need of her they could start looking where there they sick lay. Again her words not mine. Frankly that girl is amazing. I can see much of you in her when it comes to empathy for those who suffer."

Glowing at the comment she smiled. "Trinity is a powerful healer in her own right and great warrior to have by my side. I have not forgotten what you and I believed in so long ago and I raised those girls to fight in the old ways, the way you and I believed it should have been, not dependent solely on the practices of the realm, but in how we always dreamt it should be to raise our children." They walked towards the dining hall, "Where is Harmony and Gabriella?"

"Gabriella is with Pegasos touring the castle discussing ways to improve our home defenses with an influx of inhabitants within the castle walls. He will guard her. Khrysaor is guarding Trinity and Sierra in the sick ward. Besides the Goddess and Ellena are with them."

Feeling uneasy because she had not come outright asking after Harmony's whereabouts, "Where is Harmony Katerina? Tell me you did not let her outdoors until I had awoken."

Feeling dread at what might have happened to her baby girl she did not realize she had gripped Katerina's arm tightly while franticly searching the room for her daughter. Letting go of Katerina not hearing her friend cry out in alarm. "Where is Harmony, Katerina?"

Not waiting for her friend to answer she immediately called out for her mentally, *"Harmony, where are you? Report this instance."*

"I'm in the solar momma. I promised I would wait for you and I have, but don't doubt for a second I am happy about it. The land has been rapped of its glory. Striker had to put me in here with all of Aunt Kat's plants or I would have ventured off without you. Something about being here magnifies my need to heal the land."

"I am on my way. Stay put little one, I am coming."

Snapping to attention as Kat spun her around fury lighting her eyes. "You forget yourself Briksanna, what I have done for you all these years and how far I am willing to go to continue to help you and that of your family especially while here in my own home does not warrant you treat me like common waste. Do not for a second think I would place any of your family members in harm for the sake of petty anger or vengeance I may be holding." She glared at her while she continued to rub her arm.

She stared at the flashing sea green eyes of her best friend taking few moments to realize what it was Katerina was talking about. "I do not forget what you have done and continue to do for me and mine own. I am grateful for everything you have done to protect me. When it comes to my family I am very possessive of them especially knowing they are here for the first time and Lord Drakkoon along with this unknown enemy is out there looking to strike back at anything to get a hold of me scares me witless."

Hoping to reassure her best friend through explanation of her action before apologizing might help her cause, because from the look on Katerina's face she had some serious groveling to do. "You are as important to me as they are. Second to all the people in Skaldanna. You deserve the same amount of concern and worry from me that my family receives on a daily basis and that is saying a lot. I am truly sorry for grabbing you the way I did with no regard to the pain I might cause. That is not how I want to treat my best friend. I will work on not letting my worries get the best of me and especially on acting them out. Please forgive my behavior?"

The look of contempt relaxed form her face before she turned around. Not saying a word she stepped forward a few feet before turning back. "Well are you going to follow me to check on the girl or do you like standing in the entry way by yourself?"

"I swear one of these days…"

"Yeah you keep saying that and I am still waiting for you to finish that sentence."

Glad the tense mood had dissipated she approached her wanting to reassure her their friendship had been before her family came to be and would remain steadfast in the future. "You know I would never betray our friendship for that of my family Katerina. You are just as important to me as they are. I hope you know and understand this."

Once again looping her arm into hers she led her through the solarium doors to pause for emphasis. "And that, my dear, is why you make a great High Queen."

Entering the solar anyone venturing in would be enamored by the water fountain center stage of the room. Four large columns of flat rock stood half hazard facing outward within the middle of a large enclosed pond cascading water to a beautiful rhythm heard by anyone willing to listen. Within the pond's enclosure floated dozens of white lilies. Beyond and around the pond plants grew enormously; standing tall at least ten to twenty feet, in some places, reaching out with their long leafy arms begging admirers to come and touch them. Flowers littered below in various colors with varieties bathing the floor in a colorful array of height and texture. The entire room was a floral paradise, cool on her skin and flavorful to her nose. It was a wondrous garden inside a castle.

"How did this happen?" Kat whispered reverently beside her.

One word explained everything, grinning at her daughter; she knew she had waited for her to wake and it must have been torture for her to sit idly by. She did the only thing she knew she could do. She created life within the confines of the castle obeying what had been asked of her, to safely wait for her mother to wake creating a place of beauty in the interim.

"Harmony," she answered.

"What do you mean Harmony? How could one person do this in the matter of hours? It is impossible. No one I know or heard of has this kind of power, Briksanna." Bewildered her friend looked all throughout the entire room spinning herself in the process. It reminded her of the day they had been given permission to play in Kat's mother's garden for the first time.

"Harmony has the power, yet it has been magnified here while on Skaldanna, that is for sure. Come, let us find her." She took Katerina's hand and led her towards the pulse of her daughter's energy signature.

Harmony was seated facing away from the solar entrance in an overstuffed chair surrounded by what appeared to be hundreds of roses surrounding a smaller water fountain set in the corner of the large room. Ivy snaked up behind the wall behind the fountain reaching to the ceiling hanging like a giant fan over the pouring water. She had been able to cast the effect of a giant umbrella protecting the entire bed of flowers on the floor below from harm.

"I have always taught you when you are in a room you are never to sit with your back to the entrance or you leave yourself vulnerable to intruders no matter where you are."

Jumping up Harmony spun around and ran into her embrace gripping her tightly around the neck. "You scared me." Harmony looked up see her genuine smile.

"I love you too daughter mine." Kissing her on her forehead she pushed Harmony back to survey the room. "You have out done yourself this time. I think this is the best you have created yet."

Blushing, "I wanted to make a place for Aunt Kat to have for herself. What happened out there is horrible and I wanted to bring beauty back to her homeland. I decided I would start in here." She kept her eyes averted nervously fidgeting with the sleeve of her gown. Very unlikely behavior for Harmony and she wondered what concerned her daughter that she could not find it in her to look her in the eye while she spoke.

"You're not mad that I did this are you? I mean you told us all to wait before doing anything, not to reveal our abilities, but I couldn't help it, Momma, and I just wanted to give something back to Aunt Kat. I have wanted to come here my whole life and to finally be able I come to see purposeful destruction of something you both have always described as beautiful breaks my heart. Knowing how much it hurt Aunt Kat; well it was too much for me not to do anything. Please don't be mad at me. I don't want to disappoint you or Aunt Kat."

Did she think she would condemn her for creating such incredible beauty within this time of great sadness? Katerina was the one who reached for Harmony's hand pulling her in for a surprisingly strong hug.

"I am so honored you would grace me with this place. I am overwhelmed by the serenity and beauty of what you have done here." Tears glittering on her lashes, "You have given back to me something I was starting to fear I had lost for good."

She had to wipe away her own tears at Katerina's praise when Harmony asked quietly, "What is that Aunt Kat?"

She raised her hand to smooth back her daughter's hair in a loving fashion reminding her of what her own mother used to do when she felt lost.

"Hope. Hope that not all is lost nor can it be fully destroyed. You have reminded me to never forget there is always hope even when we cannot see it right in front of us. Hope resides within us not just around us.

Thank you little one from the bottom of my heart." Kat smiled revealing deep dimples framing her mouth happy to praise Harmony with heartfelt words. She saw for the first time what it would be like in the future when Katerina had children of her own. She would be a very loving and wise mother.

The desire to hold her daughter grew too much for her to keep still. She gently pulled her from Katerina arms and embraced her seeking the familiar scent that identified her from Trinity. She took a deep breath closed her eyes and burned the moment within her memories for safe keeping. She knew in her heart this would be one of those moments as a mother where she would associate beauty of a garden with the hope shown by her daughter's love. Things between all of them may get rougher than they had already experienced and she did not know what the future held, but she knew remembering this moment would be enough for her to believe there would always be hope for a future.

"I am so proud of you. You are beautiful sweetheart, absolutely beautiful. Everything you create is a deep reflection of your inner beauty."—pulling her back so she could look her in the eye—"I am glad you waited for me before going outside. It is safer that way. We have no idea what trap may be out there in the soil. Look how quickly Nathanial and I were attacked and that was with everyone around. No, you did right. Whatever may lie out there we will find out together, understood?"

Smiling at the praise she had been given Harmony looked deeply into her mother's eyes nodding with knowledge she could do anything to protect her and those she loved. Never doing anything in half measure, she knew the beliefs and values she had taught all of them was just as important as knowing when to remain silent. What was right and true had equal value with the consequences met by justice for what was wrong and what happened outside was done with malice and contempt.

Katerina would always tell the girls when she watched over them during one of her many visits that their mother was a great princess who all women of Skaldanna admired because of the great sacrifice she bore for all of their sakes. Hiding within the Earth Realm had been her sacrifice. Today she realized she no longer viewed her time away as a sacrifice but chose to view it as a necessity to grow up. She had a deep feeling her greatest sacrifice had yet to be met and she was afraid to feed her fear of what has yet to come.

Bringing her thoughts back to the present Harmony spoke up. "Thank you Momma, I appreciate your words and take your advice to heart regarding safety. I'm hungry and I can tell you are hungry too. Let's go get something to eat and head out to the royal gardens. That is the first place I want to restore, with your help of course."

"Of course, you are right. I am hungry." Her stomach chose at that moment to growl furiously making the women laugh out loud.

"Then by all means let us adjourn to the dining hall to break our fast before creating more miracles, hmm?" Waving her hand for them to follow, Katerina had already turned around and was out in the hallway before she or Harmony could follow.

Whispering in her ear leaning closely, "Aunt Kat looks more delicate than I had pictured my whole life. Kind of like what Gabby has always described a princess should look and behave like. I had this mental picture of a Zena warrior princess that wore leather skirts and ate with a sword on her back."

Laughing out right at the crazy picture Harmony painted of Katerina; she quickly covered her laugh hoping not to gain the attention of her longtime friend allowing the both of them to speak freely. "Do not be surprised to find yourself on the flat of your back in the lists when your wee delicate Aunt Kat brandishes her sword. Remember, I told you it was her and I who trained under the careful eye of Sir Hawk and she and I bested the High King Royal Guards in a matter of minutes using the same techniques I have taught your brothers and sisters. She and I were the first of our kind to use psychic powers in combination with fighting. Your Aunt Kat and I broke the mold." Grinning at her use of slang words the kids liked to throw at her. She chuckled and winked at Harmony.

Squeezing the hand she held Harmony chanced a glance at Kat and saw that she had a smile on her face. It was then that she knew Kat had heard what had been said about her and by the looks on her face was pleased with what she told Harmony. She laughed out loud again at the thought of Katerina wearing a leather skirt and a bra carrying two swords on her back while eating in the dining hall. That picture was worth a thousand words.

Grinning at her foolishness, Harmony pulled her hand out of her grip saying loud enough for the both of them to hear. "I love you both, you know that right? I am very glad you included us in your quest to fulfill The Prophesy. In a way I get to participate in a large clean-up of sorts. Yes, that's what I will call it, The Great Clean up."—holding her hand out accentuating each word for emphasis—"It's what we are doing, cleaning up the Realms of Skaldanna and the Earth Realm too, from the evil presence afflicting both realms."

With her daughter's word of wisdom ringing in her ears they entered the dining hall and proceeded to eat breakfast from the abundant food left on the main dining table chatting about what they thought would be the most important area to begin restoration in hopes for quick betterment to their situation offering all people a chance for hope.

Katerina believed the fields would be the best place to begin this way they could ensure crops regained their growth supplying with the biggest fear, food for the upcoming winter months. Harmony believed the surrounding forest would be a good place to start because the vegetation would ensure food for the animals thus supplying the people with meat for the winter months; whereas I believed the gardens would be a great place to begin with because the beauty of the castle grounds gave the people hope within a realm that had always reflected hope with its beauty and peace for all the realms.

This is what she wanted to give to the people of Skaldanna. Hope for a future without fear.

Katerina put her goblet down and looked at her two dining companions, "I believe you each have brought forth good arguments as to what needs to be done today; however I believe you have forgotten what power you have in restoring the faith of the people Briksanna. Your presence here in the land of Skaldanna will restore hope within the people far and wide not flowers. The longer your presence remains word will travel restoring their belief of victory over the ever presence of evil no manner who's hand wields it."

Harmony chimed in, "Aunt Kat is right Momma, just you being here is enough for everyone to believe good will triumph over evil. Let's try restoring the fields first then if time permits we can work on food for the animals. With the solar being a testament of my power here on Skaldanna between the both of us we should have the land completely restored in a matter of days. What do you say, shall we begin?"

From where she sat she could see the people outside no longer troubled with what was beyond the castle walls instead they bustled about caring for one another right down to the dogs who chased the little children. It painted a picture of what life looked like when it endured the demands often placed upon a person by someone else's will. Katerina had done well with her people for them to continue on this way. Seeing the servants do what needed to be done to accommodate the influx of people had been a testament to Katerina's leadership. Could they all make it out of this mess alive? She did not know the answer to the many questions that rattled in her head. She did know she had the courage to seek them out because everyone, right down to the dogs making the children laugh, were important to the cycle of life and she would do anything to preserve that for all people.

Tearing her eyes away from the scene outside, she answered her daughter, "I believe you are right Harmony, let us not waste another minute. Your plan sounds perfect. Let's do this thing you and," winking at her daughter while she stood.

They left the dining hall and quickly passed the inner bailey without interruption despite the activity. They continued through outer bailey hearing the men at arms training with a nearby arena. She smiled remembering her earlier conversation with Kat about the girl's bets. She wondered what else her children have agreed to compete in. It was a wonder she had not awakened to a crowd gathered below while they beat each other up. Snorting at her funny thought she glanced at Kat saw her friend look back at her with the same knowing smirk on her face.

"They all are good men and women. They just have a tad bit more enthusiasm when it comes to besting one another than may seem normal around here." She coughed on the laugh she tried to hide, "In all honesty they act just the way we were had at their age. All is well Briksanna, do not worry about your children for they are no longer children but strong warriors to be proud of. Besides, I can't wait for you and I to dance with our weapons in that ring. It would do them well to remind them who it is they learned their skills from.

Both women erupted in laughter no longer able to contain their amusement at the thought of all the open mouths from the children when they saw their beloved Aunt Kat pull out her sword to dance. She believed she would place a wager on who would be the winner of match herself.

They neared the outer gates where Katerina waved her hand at the tower guard alerting him of her intent to leave the castle grounds. Almost at once the gates groaned while they rose above not having to break stride. "Hello Sir Thomas, how is the Missus?" Katerina called to the guard above smiling warmly at the man who looked down.

"All right, My Lady, doing well with the extra blankets you sent over for the kinfolk. We thank you much for your generosity." Replied the stout older man who leaned over the portcullis responding to Katerina's question. "Be careful, My Lady, there is danger lurking about. I feel it in my bones. Take caution when strolling about this day," his concern for her well-being obvious.

"We have no plan to linger long Sir Thomas. Please tell your wife I will stop by soon to check in with her. I'd love a moment to chat if she has the time to spare."

"I will, My Lady, have a care." With those parting words he disappeared over the wall while they continued to walk under it.

Directing her attention to where they walked Katerina pointed to the left from where they stood. "The fields begin to the south of the castle. We can reach the edge of the fields by walking around the corner along this path."

Before they could exit the gates three men stepped from around the corner effectively blocking them from where they intended to go. Each man held a resemblance to the other clearly a relation of sort. They stood as tall as Stark's six foot eight inches, dressed similarly to Khrysaor and Pegasos knee length boots, leggings, long shirt under worn leather vests adorned with various knives filling their scabbards both at the waist and chest. Their swords were held on their backs while bracers adorned their wrists. Each set of bracers represented a different shade of color. Maybe to identify themselves, she did not know. They were attractive and shared the same color of blue eyes along with sandy blond hair, long noses and straight chins; ripped lean they stood before them effectively blocking the direction in which they had been heading. Were they friend or foe? Kat did not seem to appear to be worried as if she knew them so she would not overly concern herself unless they spoke rudely to her or her daughter.

The man on the left had a scar running from his left eye down to the corner of his lip, yet this did not take away from his beauty. She should know for she was covered with them. He appeared curious like he was trying to figure out what they were doing taking a walk outside the castle walls. The man in the middle had small silver hoop earrings in both ears; his hair was worn a bit longer than the man on the left and it curled at the ends. He smiled a bit as he checked out Harmony more than I cared to like. The last man had no scars or jewelry adorning his body that I could see but he did have the longest hair of them tied back in a queue and was the only man who wore gloves. He too stood separate from the group starring at us I could tell his focus of attention was on us as a whole, but her instincts said the intensity of his stare was solely on Harmony. He appeared startled upon first seeing her but quickly masked his wide eyed shocked expression before she could study it any further. She did not know if she liked his apparent interest in her daughter, but she would hear what they had to say before she made any assumptions. Harmony could take care of herself, this she believed without a doubt.

"Ahh, seems like the ladies are heading out for a wee walk, wouldn't you say brother?" came from the man with the earrings.

"Seems to me that Lady Katerina would have more sense than to leave the safety of the castle with nothing but beautiful women in tow. What if something horrible were to befall them, then what would these beautiful women do?" The man with a scar looked directly at Harmony while he spoke.

"I think it might be in their best interest if we tagged along, you know, for protection. What do you think brother?"

"I think you might find yourselves in a wee pickle if you did not take my brother here up on his suggestion, My Lady." Smiling more at his confident statement than what the man with the earrings out. "We are just the men for the task. If all goes well maybe later you can catch us showing a bit of skill, you know just to show you how real warriors protect women in this realm."

She had had enough of their insult and disrespect not just to her but at the way the two men kept looking at Harmony. She had a feeling judging by Harmony's heart rate it was the gloved man, who had yet to speak, affected her emotionally and that irritated her. If Katerina did not say something in the next ten seconds she was going to show them just whom they were dealing with.

Noticing Katerina was about to open her mouth to speak, she decided against her earlier thoughts mentally sending Katerina a message to keep quiet while she handled these louts herself.

Painting a smile on her face erasing all signs of irritation she decided to bait the trap. "Might I ask, Sir Warriors, what are your names that way I know whom to thank for the kind gesture of guarding us women in search of a walk?" She purred out the words effectively batting her eyes capturing their attention with a single question.

The man with the earrings, the most talkative of the trio, spoke first bowing slightly in a show of respect. "My name is Alkimos, I am the spokesperson for this merry group and master swordsman." Pointing to his left, "This is my brother Kainam the youngest of us but not to worry he is just as strong as I and deft with a sword to boot."

Pointing to his right, "The silent one on the right here is Alexio, our oldest brother, but do not mistake his silence for anything less than deadly. He is the most skilled among us with a set of blades than all of my brothers put together. Fine women, such as yourselves, would count themselves lucky to have the Palaponos brothers to guard them."

Feigning her interest raising both her eyebrows at the name association to the twin guards currently out with Stark and Hawk after Kat received word they left Gabriella and Trinity in the safe hands of Kat's personal guards prior to their leaving for the gardens. She was curious to their association with the twins. Were they brothers or cousins? Clearly there was a relation of some sort.

"There are more than the three of you? Oh, my, Lady Katerina, how exciting." Grabbing Kat's hand to calm her snickering hoping her friend could keep her silence her for a bit longer. She wanted to string them along for few more minutes before revealing who she was. It was becoming difficult to stifle her laughter at their expression, especially the two talkative ones on the right.

"My Lady, should we employ their services and be about our business or continue as we were? I fear our time outside the castle will soon run out. I was looking forward to the time spent at the fields." Harmony spoke out loud hoping she would catch her meaning to get on with what they came were to do. She never took her eyes off the silent gloved warrior. The stare had been met at first sight and neither one had yet to change their visual position. She could tell the effect he had on her daughter was a mixture of worry and excitement. She wanted her daughter to be happy. She always chose to remain aloof when it came to matters of the opposite sex, until now.

Mentally shaking her head trying to rid herself of thoughts about romance she knew she had to get her royal head back on track with what they intended to accomplish that day.

Speaking up for the first time in response to Harmony's statement never once breaking eye contact from her daughter inclining his head politely indicating his respect to her station. "It is very dangerous outside the castle grounds, My Lady. There is evil out in the land and it is not safe for anyone to venture out. I must insist you choose to take your walk upon the battlements where it is much safer to see the lay of the realm. You can see the lands well from within the safety of the walls." He pointed behind them towards the battlement walkway they had just passed.

Both his brothers whipped their heads towards him in surprise with their mouths open when he spoke. Their expression made her want to roar in laughter again. That and the absurdity of Harmony needing protection from harm in a hand to hand combat was just plain stupid. She was as deadly in combat as the men before her likewise her and Katerina have handled men more intent on killing than all three men combined.

Katerina turned with a raised eyebrow in question strain evident from withholding her laughter. *Shall we show them what we can do Briksanna? It has been a while since you and I danced with our swords.*

Laughing out loud no longer able to hold back how humorous the entire conversation had been. Harmony was right they needed to keep their minds on the task at hand and all else could be dealt with later. They were running out of time and needed to be about their business restoring the Second Realm.

Shaking her head at Katerina she knew she could not let loose on these men. They genuinely believed they were doing them a service trying to warn them of the dangers beyond the castle walls. If she and Kat were to engage with them to prove a point she would lose all respect she had hoped to build with the High Ruling Council later that evening. She could see it now tales of Royalty fighting outside the castle walls. Her intended political gain would become a mockery especially when she had hoped to establish Nathanial as the High King. They both would lose respect from the populace believing their ruling monarchs did not take their positions seriously. No, she would show them who she was in another way.

"Let us be on our way master swordsman lest us mere women shall fall upon trouble and need a skilled warrior such as yourselves in which to defend us." Raising her finger halting anyone from taking a step further, "I think it would be in *Your* best interest to know whom it is you are guarding. In case anything should go wrong while on our walk. I was always taught it was wise to know who it was you were protecting whether it be lady or man who be the protector."

"Well spoken, My Lady, I could not agree with you more." The man with the scar said grinning like he was the cat who had caught the canary.

Katerina spoke wiping the tears from her eyes trying to stem her laughter. "You crazy louts! Wipe those grins off your faces for you have really stepped in the muck this time. Let us be on our way; we have wasted time dealing with you thick headed lackwits." Sending a mental note to Briksanna, *"I would encourage you to hold your tongue on who you are for the time being. Let these simple brained lackwits learn a lesson here. Besides it will be fun to see how they act once they figure it out. Stupid fools."* Sending laughter through their mental connection.

Grabbing his heart Kainam looked at Kat and grinned acting as if struck by an imaginary blow to the chest, "You wound me Lady Katerina with your words. We are merely here to provide you with our most skilled services."

Finally fed up with the conversation, Harmony stepped around all of them speaking from over her shoulder, "Well if you've decided to guard us then hop to it lazy bones. We have things to see to that urgently need to be done." Mumbling a few choice words clearly meant to insult the men Harmony stomped off in the direction Katerina had indicated earlier.

Following her daughter still grasping Kat's hand she laughed enjoying herself fully for the first time in a long time. "Keep up gentlemen; eyes wide open, you may learn a thing or two while on this walk."

Kainam hand still holding his chest when she passed him, "You wound me with your words, My Lady. Just plain wound me."

— ~

Alkimos looked between his two brothers and tapped him, the ever silent older brother by one year, on the shoulder. "What was with spouting all that safety shit?"

He looked where Alkimos had just hit him and brought his gaze up to meet his brother trying to decide if he should tell him what he knew about the mysterious women they were now to guard. Thinking it wise to let his brothers stand in their own dung a while longer he held silent leaving both his brothers gapping at him.

"You say hardly anything longer than four words to any of us and all of a sudden you're speaking sentences to the pretty lady. Is that it, you like the lady. Ok well you can have that one only if you can win her affection big brother. She wants me, I can tell." Not realizing how his words were affecting him as they trailed the women at a safe distance, but still within range of protection. Kainam missed his brothers' fists closing and opening evidence of his agitation in the direction the conversation had gone.

"Close your mouth about the lady, boy. Do your job lest you boys plan on failing the women ahead." Speaking very quietly he made sure his words were short and to the point. He did not like to talk much. He never needed to. His words were absolute and had carried a lot of weight whenever he spoke over the years. They always had and they always will. His brothers closed their mouths and began to seriously observe the surrounding area.

He knew how to carry on a conversation if said conversation were warranted. With the blonde haired beauty; the conversation was defiantly warranted. Gods, seeing her for the first time hit him straight in the gut. He was so surprised he was not sure he could speak coherently if any questions were to have been directed at him. He prayed no one asked him anything right now because Gods help him he was too caught up observing the way she walked.

Sparkling pale green eyes with many flecks of brown thrown around them had starred back at him. She had pale skin with row of freckles thrown over her pert nose set above the most delicious mouth he had ever laid eyes upon. She was tall for most women of the Second Realm, but he liked that for he was a tall man himself. She filled out her gown letting him know she would be one to keep him happy for hours locked in room. What he would not do to lose everyone save her and spend time worshiping that body currently tempting him.

Where did that thought come from? He had not been with a woman for years almost to the point where his brothers stopped giving him grief with regards to his celibate life. An occasional conversation with the cook or cleaning person was all he ever did. Upon occasion he would talk to a female merchant or a store owner, but never would he court them or take them to bed. He could not do that knowing there was the one person out there that his inner core would recognize belonged only to him. The other half of his soul. This was what he had been waiting for. The relationship he saw, a long time ago, while visiting the High Royal Castle, between the High King and Queen, was a shared love that had endured centuries. What happened to them belonged to dark magic and everyone believed the dark arts where responsible for the travesty that had occurred. If dark magic had not been present that day life as they knew it would have been completely different.

Shaking his head he tried to keep his thoughts on task, he had not seen her within the castle or the surrounding villages in the time he and his brothers had been residing within Castle Kastekanos. Where did she come from? What about the lady she was with, who was she? Both their auras had shone brightly almost beckoning him to taste the wealth of energy they contained within their bodies. Looking at them was tempting for a person with abilities such as himself.

Which house do they claim and from which realm? There were so many questions he had rolling around his head be began to think he would never have the answers at least not as quickly as he would without pissing off the golden haired beauty. He had never seen anything like it although their energy did look familiar. He could not place where he had seen auras like that before, yet they remained familiar to him like an old memory he could not place. It was very frustrating tempting his irritation to boarder on anger.

Risking a glance at the blonde woman in front of him his thoughts went right back to what he might say if he had the opportunity to speak with her again. What things did she like? Was family important to her like it was to him? How many siblings did she have? What dances does she like? Does she dance at all? He wondered what she would look wrapped in his fire...he meant the fireplace or candlelight. That would be even better. Arrgghh, what was he saying?

God's could he keep his head out of the trenches? "I have got to get away from these two lackwits."

"Did you say something big brother? Are we free to talk now without offending you?" Kainam replied sarcastically.

Sighing knowing his brother would not let it go until he answered him. He looked over and saw Kainam still searching the perimeter for any possible threats despite the words that had recently exited his mouth.

"You are both free to talk," he barked.

Looking at the women gaging their proximity to him and his brothers, Alkimos waved his hands urging his brothers to walk closer so they would be able to speak privately.

"Did you see their auras?" He spoke softly not wanting to alert the women of their conversation.

"Lit up like the sun," murmured Kainam

Looking from one brother to the other Alkimos asked the one question they all had hanging on their minds. "The new comers' auras were bright; yet Lady Katerina's aura seemed stronger. Does that make sense to any of you?"

Brows furrowed he scanned the path they walked on irritated with every step. He did not like surprises. He hated not knowing what was around the corner that was why he persisted to stalk his enemy gathering all the information he could about his opponent before announcing his presence. With what evil had occurred in the Second Realm followed closely by the bright new comer's meant something did not add up. He was determined to find out what that something was. Never again would he allow any threat to fall upon his family or those of the people in all of Skaldanna as long as he held breath in his body. Family came first, that was their motto, no matter how much the hazel eyed beauty ahead captivated him.

"We protect them but never let them out of our sight until we know more about them, understood." Not waiting for an answer expecting his brothers to obey his command without question. He felt edgy and did not like how his thoughts kept sliding back to the tall drink of water currently in front of him.

Growling he kicked the dirt in front of him. Blasted woman. Taking in the scenery around them he knew they were headed towards the fields. Why would they want to tour the land the way it was now? It made no sense. Lady Katerina should not be touring the grounds with the new comers putting her guests at risk. Anything could happen out there knowing they were lucky nothing had happened yet. Shaking his head at his pessimistic attitude he noticed the women had stopped once they had rounded the side of the hill that bordered the southern fields. What were they standing there looking at? Something was not right. They had stopped abruptly holding his attention. He and his brothers held their breath waiting for their next move. Before them laid the vast devastation brought upon the Second Realm by evil no one had seen the likes of in all of Skaldanna's history.

"Lady Katerina, is everything well? Do you need our assistance?" Kainam spoke loud enough for them to hear.

Katerina turned and spoke to them directly, "All is well Sir Kainam, and keep watch for our attention is currently diverted and will continue to be so while we are about our business here. I trust you and your brothers are up to the task?"

This time Alkimos spoke bowing to her one hand over his heart grinning. Always the flirtatious one, "With our very lives, My Lady."

"We shall see Sir Alkimos. Let us hope it never comes to that. This land has seen too much death as it is."

Eyes locked on the blonde beauty he chose to speak up, "That it has My Lady. That it has. Go about your business you will be guarded well."

24

Silence filled her ears. Not a sound could be heard for miles out. The stillness in the air enhanced the barren desolation before them reminding her there was no life left to behold. She hadn't seen such destruction in her two thousand years of life as was witness to this day. Trees had shriveled pulling their long branches close within themselves to keep the pain from radiating out towards the next branch. No leaves could be seen on any of the trees even though the leaves were not set to fall from off the arms of its mother tree for several months to come. Shriveling down to the base, each tree had curled in on itself as if trying to escape the horror it had been forced to endure.

The grass was gone. The crops were gone. The flowers and shrubs all were gone.

Not a single stalk stood in the fields for as far as the eye could see. There were only rows of dirt where just days ago they must have stood tall and bountiful pending the upcoming harvest. There was no life left in the land anywhere her eyes travelled. It was all gone in a matter of minutes ripped from its home kicking and screaming. She could feel the agony from the land through the soles of her feet begging for her aid. It was crying out to her resonating its grief alongside her mournful soul. It took everything within her not to wail out in miserable companionship.

She clamped her mouth closed biting her tongue to keep from screaming at the injustice of it all.

She could not close her mind from the lonesome sound around her. It wasn't only the land that had been grieving; everything around her grieved because they were all connected. The sound of silence she heard in her ears wrenched a cry from her mind. She felt her heart mourn deeply resonating the wrongness done upon the land around her. If the sky could cry with the wind and rain it would, yet a solemn silence remained. The only thing that fell were the tears her eyes no longer could hold dripped from chin to the dry dirt below. A loud gasp brought her out of her thoughts. She spun around to see what her mother had seen that would cause a reaction from her.

Tears matched her own as her mother reached out for her hand holding it tightly within her grasp. "This is not of Lord Drakkoon's taint. I know him. I know his energy as if he were standing beside me just as you are, but this"—waving her hand in the direction of the fields before her anguish became visible—"this is not from that man. He has never destroyed something so completely in all the thousands of years that I have known him as my enemy. Oh Gods, Merridian had been right, this evil is something separate from Lord Drakkoon, yet much more sinister than he could ever have been."

She saw both her mother and Aunt Kat with tears falling freely down both their faces. She had never created life from something destroyed as she was witness to in that moment. Could she do this? She still had no answer to her own question.

"We can heal this land restoring it to its splendor, Harmony, I am sure of it. Are you up for the task child?"

Squeezing her mother's hands feeling empowered with the knowledge that her mother stood beside her while she attempted something great. She nodded feeling her own tears spill over not caring how she looked. "Feed me your energy mother and I will sing birth into the land."

"You are sure about this? There is much here to heal. I do not want you to over tax yourself. Let us concentrate on the field first then see what happens, hmm?" she spoke confidently.

Her mother squeezed her hand once more before releasing her grip walking several feet ahead of her before coming to a stop. Facing the direction where the fields would have extended she pulled her sword from the hidden folds within her gown stretching her sword arm in the air she immediately commanded lightning to strike the sword in one long continuous arc. The lightning went on longer than was natural striking her sword at its tip lighting the entire area with a bright violet light. The sky was blue not a cloud in sight could be seen that would encourage such an act from the heavens. Momma had created magic in the air.

The moment the lightning struck the sword all hell broke loose behind her. The men screamed for them to come out of the fields in fear for their safety. Something kept them rooted where they stood staring at the point where the lightning met the sword as if it wasn't a surprise to them after all. Several minutes passed before she turned back to saw Alexio staring at her and her mother as if he could see the energy she felt building up within her. She knew there had been a shift in energy because the kinetic energy on Skaldanna was a living presence reaching for her soul. She felt it the moment she stepped foot on Skaldanna as if she were part of its life force and it had welcomed her home surprising her with its resonance. It had creeped her out and was part of the reason she had reacted when Sir Hawk threatened her mother. Drawn to her mother she notice her aura had become brilliant, more so than she had ever seen before. Startled she looked down at her hands putting them slightly out in front of her to view. She saw they were just as bright as her mothers were, almost too painful to look at.

She felt she could become one with her surroundings and this overwhelmed her so much her rational thought no longer wanted to be heard. Her mind was becoming one with the realm. She could feel the powerful change threatening to take her over and she welcomed it. Chancing one last glace at the man behind her she let all thoughts of him fly away while focused on relinquishing herself to Skaldanna letting go of her will believing it was the right thing to do. She let herself go willing her magic to blend with the energy her mother had begun to build around her, for her and for the whole land.

It dawned on her, in the moment she turned herself over to Skaldanna, she was exactly where she should be in this precise moment in time. Momma had screamed at that point startling everyone but her. She was too absorbed in becoming one with her surroundings the words of the mother land crept closer towards her heart begging for a voice. Her voice. She whispered, her mouth moving, weaving magic she had never heard or felt before. Her chant was not loud enough for any one person to hear yet loud enough for the realm to obey her command.

The flashes of lightning stopped leaving Momma's sword glowing a brilliant white. She thought for a second it might be too hot to handle, but like her they could handle all types of energy whereas others would die from the force of it. There was too much raw energy in both the sword and in its master she was in awe to watch her move. Pointing her sword at the field Briksanna shouted loud enough for everyone to hear within a half a mile radius. In a commanding sonic boom her voice had carried by her command to repeat the same words over and over again eyes never wavering from her task fully expecting what she had said to be obeyed.

Puste nytt liv. Puste nytt liv.—Breathe new life. Breathe new life.

"Lady Katerina, what is going on? What is she saying? Shall we aid her?" Alkimos sounded confused by what he was seeing.

Stepping closer to Alkimos, Katerina leaned over to translate what the woman was saying speaking loud enough for all of them to hear. "Breathe new life. It is she who commands Skaldanna's energy."

Jerking his head to the side studying Lady Katerina like she was a dolt Alkimos replied, "Only High Royalty can command Skaldanna's energy in such a manner, and everyone knows all High Royalty had been killed except..." stopping mid-sentence he looked at Katerina's patient expression waiting for him to figure out at his own in his slow witted pace never needing to say another word.

He searched his own memories when he remembered a flash of violet eyes when they had spoken by the portcullis back when he and his brothers thought to charm the women to do their bidding which would be the safer place for the women to be. He did not put two and two together then, not completely. The way she carried herself about and how Lady Katerina looked completely at ease in her presence. Why they would want to walk out in the middle of all this destruction looking as if they had a picnic planned. His thoughts were flashed in his mind faster than he could grab them. This new comer was High Royalty, but who he knew had yet to be seen; the older or younger sister, neither body had ever found.

Mentally sharing the news with his brothers telepathically he did not wait for a response. The energy surrounding the Lady who commanded the lightning grew brighter encompassing an entire section of field they stood in front of. An arc of energy shot from her sword into the center of the field blasting the destined area for several minutes yet no one noticed the younger woman who walked, in a trance, further into the field but him.

He did not care what happened around him only that of the safety of one woman who seemed intent to put herself in danger. What was she doing? He shouted to her several times pleading with her to step back. She was too entranced in what she was doing by the time he slowed his racing thoughts he was able to study what she was doing and prayed his instincts about who the lady wielding the lightning was correct then the woman he was enamored with had to be just as important and just as powerful. Women of High Royalty were perfectly capable of handling the levels of energy being wielded at the moment this he knew without a doubt.

He heard his brother talking about the woman with the sword who drew the energy from Skaldanna, no matter which sister she was, her being High Royalty seemed to fit her just by watching the way the energy flowed from the sword settling itself on the land like a soft blanket would warm a body. She laid the energy all around her simultaneously commanding the land to breathe in new life.

The woman who caught his eye and held his heart walked until she was about thirty feet from where she had stood originally. He still could not shake off the deep rooted fear for her safety. Something about her aura and how strong both newcomers energy fields glowed told him they were not in immediate danger. In his mind he could see that, process that, but his gut was clenched tight with worry. He did not want anything to happen to the woman in front of him. He wanted more than anything to pull her into his embrace knowing his strong arms were wrapped around her to protect her from the world around them. This was where he needed her to be safe within his arms and that desire is what had him tied in knots.

He closed his eyes, keeping his feet rooted to the ground by shear will and reached out with his senses. He checked around them to make sure they would remain uninterrupted; accessing the perimeter for any hidden dangers finding nothing and he still felt riled up emotionally for her safety. Letting go of his thoughts he noticed he had been so intent on his personal feelings he had forgotten to be the man he swore he would be for all the women there. A warrior to protect them all.

Shoving his personal thoughts aside, for the one he believed was made for him, he once again wore the mask of the man he had become since his older brother had been taken by the evil that had permeated their realm. He would not allow any distractions to befall his family again because if it should then all hope for the universe would fail for The Prophesy could not be complete without The Blacksmith.

Focusing on his other half he let go of his worry and forced himself to watch her be the woman he believed her to be.

High Royalty.

Something started to happen with the dirt around where she stood. Something he thought he would never see in his lifetime. Hearing strained he listened for the words she said in hope to learn what she was doing.

She knelt in the dirt drenched in the pain the land had experienced when its life had been robbed. With Momma commanding the combined Realms Energy directing, changing it to a healing energy with her words of command she knew she held the power to channel her own ability to instigate new growth.

Digging her hands into the soil she felt the energy deep within the center of all realms responding to Momma's request crying out for retribution against the one who had caused the travesty. Many voices chanted in a language she did not recognize, yet the song they sung resonated within her soul reaching a crescendo of music made solely for her ears to hear. Instinct compelled her to recognize what it meant to hear the music in the voices, but somewhere inside her she held back not fully connecting with the words of the unknown voices because she did not know what would happen to her if she did. Instead she let the song drift through her, around her giving it the freedom to share her life and her mind taking a chance on something foreign never once believing her mother would put her in harm's way. Fortified with that thought she knew the time had come to release her magic into the world she had come to connect with. Taking one last look at the surrounding area, she committed to memory the absolute horror that had been forced upon the land beneath her by a monster invisible to them all.

There were no doubts her family would defeat this creature of evil this she resonated without words to the voices letting their cry for life fill her until she could hardly contain the magic of their song. She etched her own vow to that knowledge; whoever was responsible would pay for what they had done to this world. Bending over she closed her eyes plunging her hands deeper into the brittle soil and gripped a handful while releasing a thread of her energy blending her will for new life with the voices she heard in her head. Deep within her conscious thought she faintly felt the grains of dirt flow through her fingers when she pulled her hands out of the ground, but her instincts were driven by a force larger than her conscious thought. Her actions were woven within the notes of the most beautiful healing chant she had ever heard filling her with the necessary actions needed to complete the task before her. She took a deep breathe releasing the last grains of soil from her fingers while she stood lifting her arms expanding her lungs to its fullest preparing herself for what was the next step all the while knowing she was the one that would breathe new life to all of the Realms of Skaldanna.

Mentally she saw her own energy blend with the new energy that made up the molecules of every living thing around her. Concentrating on the swirling band of combined energy she instinctively began to spin around in a circle no fear of tripping of falling. How she knew it was the right thing to do did not matter to her, it simply was what her instincts drove her to do so she could spread her magic out far and wide. Weaving her arms in a sword swiping motion she released bright streams of light full of fire and color along with the voices chanting magically within her. They leaped with ease obeying the song of life her arms commanded.

Some strands of energy leapt from her hands targeting Momma's bright energy. For a second she almost fell over distracted with worry for her mother's safety, but she let go of that thought when soothing words floated through her mind reassuring her of the realms welcome to the daughters of Skaldanna whispering happiness in their rapid response to a cry for help.

She recognized what her mother had done now that she was fully connected to the living molecules around her. They had become a kaleidoscope of healing colors filled with a promise of renewed birth that left the land breathtakingly beautiful. They were the only ones who could heal the land recognized by the greatest living source of energy she had witnessed reaching into the soil. Skaldanna's Energy Core was a true living source of life. A blending of what once was, what is and what will come to be. She was humbled to have been recognized as a daughter, by the voices in her head, the next in line as successor in the House of Akmond, Princess of High Royalty, a position she acknowledge with the help of the information passing through her mind at a rapid rate. She would bear great power coupled with the responsibility of owning such power, yet she had been named the one to succeed, by this living source of energy, to be capable to wield it, hone it and shape it for the sole purpose to fuel all inhabitants with a continued gift of life.

She held the biggest well of energy deep within her while her mind whispered a song of new growth filled with her love and a promise of love and attention in return from the inhabitants who shared its realm. She continued to spin in a circle spreading her magic not increasing her speed but maintaining the same pace she had begun with earlier. She felt her energy dive within the soil race to the trees excited to touch the dying with the song of life it carried. She imagined sprinkling the foliage and flower beds with her energy willing them to obey her thoughts visualizing what must have been the outlying walkways full in bloom. Flying swiftly the energy continued to obey her command not stopping for one moment in its flight from any one particular area but swiftly moving to the next sight in need of her magic by the will she sent to create it promising new growth sealed in hope forming sustenance for the inhabitants of the realm.

Energy rushed all around her obeying her commands as if it knew exactly how she wanted the realm rebuilt. She could feel the sprouts of growth bustling below the soles of her feet readying itself to burst from the soil simply because it was the next phase of life. The creaking of the trees as they struggled to upright themselves grew loud in sound while buds of leaves unraveled themselves sprouting cries of birth upon the branches.

Foliage burst from the ground spreading throughout the nearby forest floor like dominos falling creating beautiful rows of different shapes and sizes. Flowers shot from the walkway growing in height until buds bursting with color opened to reveal the living nectar for all insects teasing with its sent to feed the living with its beauty and sustenance after days of starvation. Rows of vegetation burst from the ground spilling varieties of foods filling what was just moments ago a blank canvas of death.

Still spinning she caught sight of rows of what once was sorrow to her soul being replaced with a rich dark soil sprouting an abundance of various crops of grain quickly rising to the full of its maturity awaiting the upcoming harvest.

She closed her eyes from what she had started to see happening not wanting to be distracted by the wonder of what she was saw knowing she was witness to life instead wanting to cement the healing within the land around her. Her desire to heal what had been ripped away was the strongest feeling she had ever felt before. She recognized her strength to wield such majestic energy and found herself humbled. Sending thoughts of love and gratitude for the realms own life force she saw the ball of energy she had held in her heart along with the deep breathe she had yet to release since she started spinning. She followed the source of energy mentally trailing its voice through the soles of her feet accepting the gift of succession embracing her place within its circle of life.

Mentally stepping into the core of energy she was enveloped within its fortifying embrace. No longer did she have doubt in what was happening around her. She was made for this moment in life and by embracing it she had consented to its power. The very moment she accepted her role she was given the knowledge of what she had to do next.

She released her breath sowing the seeds she had commanded to life firmly in place planting the picture of what the land held in potential for all inhabitants simultaneously smelling the fruits of growth around her. What came out of her mouth was more than she had physically or mentally expected and was not afraid. A huge gust of breathe flew from her mouth infused with the magic she had kept within fueled by her mother's blend of energies. A combination of life and hope for everything it touched sealed in the promise made by her and her mother.

She kept up with her whispers and spinning until she felt confident her seeds of life had been firmly planted envisioning the potential of beauty she smelled growing around her. This was what she was made for; bringing life to the land. It made her happy. She couldn't help the smile on her mouth when she slowed her twirling knowing the strands of energy she felt drifting around her would continue on its course until the stench of evil had been rooted out. She didn't dare open her eyes to see the wonder she knew sat before her, but knew she needed to thank the energy for the life it had given and close the flow connected between herself and Skaldanna. Drawing her energy back she sang the stream of light to return from its beautiful work all the while sending thanks for its gift of healing it brought to the land. Her energy once more settled within her filling her with its joy for having a part in a beautiful creation. She felt connected to the living surrounding her now more than ever.

Tilting her head up to the sky she knew what was needed next, "Momma we need rain!"

A simple request knowing her mother could make it happen regardless of who was around her. They had already revealed too much to the surrounding people who may lay witness to what they had done. Knowing her mother would not question her, she kept her eyes closed head tilted to the sky waiting for the change in the air signaling coming rain.

Feeling Harmony's joy reminded her what it felt like when she had first commanded Skaldanna's core energy; majestic and powerful, yet filled with life. How complete she felt when the rush of energy flew through her veins; temptation at its finest if left in the wrong hands. Energy was meant for all Realms on Skaldanna and it is the legacy of the

High King or Queen to command. Always one from the blood lines of the Akmond family like her father and his father before him.

Can you see me now Father? Can you see your granddaughter Mother? We are still feeding the Realms as you have taught us; as the Gods dictated long ago for all people to survive. I am proud to be your daughter as I believe you are proud of me. I miss you.

Clearing her mind of the past she concentrated on calling the water from Lake Timnon along the northern border of the Second Realm. The elements had always been easy for her to command no different than putting one foot in front of the other. All she needed was a conscious visualization of what it was she wanted to do and she could bring it to life. She built the picture of rain in her mind step by step solidifying thought into action.

Knowing her request would be answered immediately she felt the air cool around her face, wind blowing through the loose strands of hair that had come undone in the time she and Harmony had blended their energies together. It felt good to be deeply connected to her home. Pulling the energy from Skaldanna's core channeling it to Harmony, aiding her in bringing the land to life, was awe inspiring. She had never done anything of that magnitude before.

Keeping with the command she had sent to the sky above, clouds gathered from the north rolling in a rush dark ominous force powerful in strength as it raced to heed her call arriving in time to deliver the much needed sustenance needed to nurture new the growth to thrive.

One drop.

Two drops fell.

Three drops lead to a steady pitter patter over the new vegetation.

She laughed out loud opening her arms up as a personal offering thanking the powers that be for the gift of rain.

Turning around to meet her daughter, Harmony looked around her for the first time taking in what she had done. Bright colors adorned the walkway where the warriors stood along with Katerina. She was a few feet away from Harmony knowing her eyes glowed violet in the rain. She felt her smile widen reflecting the joy she felt inside catching the first glimpses of what they had done together.

"Look what you have done, daughter. What you have brought back to life is truly magnificent. As far as the eye can see life begins again."—pointing to the nearby forest—"even the forest thickens under your command." Sounding excited and proud, "You have outdone yourself Harmony. I am very proud of you."

Looking around at what she had done, from the tall fields stretching to their full height to the trees in the forest down to the lush soil beneath their feet, Harmony took it all in. Pride filled her heart in what they had accomplished together, but mostly for what her daughter was willing to create without regards for the evil that had destroyed it. She knew Harmony created life only destroying in self-defense despite the reputation she had created shielding herself from people. She knew her daughter was selfless at heart. She was a creator not a destroyer.

"I did it. I pictured it in my head and felt it in my heart and willed it so feeding my energy into yours." Running towards her she jumped into her mother's waiting arms, "Momma I did it! I healed the land." Pulling back arm's length joy written all over her face, "I can't wait to tell Trinity. This is soooo cool!"

Just like she ran to her father many years ago when he first showed her how to command the core's energy to sustain the realms of Skaldanna, she closed her eyes knowing her soul had recognized the next in line for succession to the throne. Skaldanna had accepted her desire to make her family High Royalty and had chosen the heir of its Realms well.

This is the one who will be charged to maintain all that is in my place should I fail. Such a burden yet a wonderful joy when facilitated with the love of all gains through proper use of this knowledge. Oh Harmony, can you survive where I may not? My love for you goes beyond what my heart holds. It is shared by the unborn son I now carry. Life grows within me at an accelerated rate. I must tell Nathanial.

Pulling back from her daughter's tight embrace, she pushed her hair away from her face in a motherly manner she had always done with a children. "I love you."

"I love you too momma." Leaning in to kiss her on the cheek she pulled back laughing, "I love what I can do!" Running away from her mother she watched her grab Katerina by the hands and pull her around in a circle dancing in the rain laughing at the miracle of it all. Harmony was a sight to see.

Thoughts of what the both of them accomplished filled her mind and heart with hope conveyed the depth of her courage to put one foot in front of the other. She knew deep down she would have to pay The Prophesy with her greatest sacrifice. Her life with Nathanial would be the price she would have to pay. While bathed in the warm wisdom of Skaldanna's energy she had seen clearly what it was she would need to do despite her free will, in order for the quest to be fulfilled. Someday soon she would have to sacrifice the love of her life for the next step of the quest to be taken. It was the way it was to be. Like bleeding a wound to clean it, in order for the bleeding to stop you had to stich the wound closed. She would have to close her heart to the pain of loss for her to see The Prophesy to the end surrounding her broken heart with the promise of hope.

She would hold the dream of a place and time where she would be reunited with her other half and that would be the hope that would sustain her while she fulfilled her role in The Prophesy. Her dance had already begun between her and Lord Drakkoon and she had finally found the will to see everything to the end. She now had the courage to put one foot in front of the other without Nathanial by her side knowing Merridian promised he would not die, but be held in safe keeping until the day they would be reunited once again.

She believed what the Merridian said, but did not understand what it meant when she said he wouldn't die. Her head spun thinking of possible scenarios, but the nagging feeling bothering her the most was what if her heart could not last the outcome of his absence physically left an aching hole in her heart. She could not help but bring her hand to the place above her breast in effort to stop the imaginary pain flowing through her heart.

Did she have the courage to do what she believed was the greatest sacrifice possible? Could she give up her family for the sake of thousands of lives? The end result was bigger than all of their hopes and dreams put together and without her sacrifice there would be no path for them to walk upon during their quest. Only faith that good would triumph over evil.

Not wanting to depress herself with her thoughts she tamped down her greatest fear rubbing her heart. Turning around she felt a grin poke her mouth as warmth seeped from the soil through her feet tickling them in the process. Looking down she could have sworn she recognized Skaldanna's energy reached towards her trying to gain access. Closing her eyes she ignored the tickling sensation and gave way to the warm energy while it moved throughout her body. A burning sensation began to sizzle on the inner sides of both her wrists to the point of pain. Ready to rip whatever was hurting her off she was about to open her eyes when a voice filled her mind.

Do not fear child for we are always apart of you and will be for your family as well. You have done well daughter. Stay strong and true to your path and all will be right in the end for everyone. You can do this for we believe in you, always. Our love for you has never strayed. You are our heart as you are theirs. You can do this for you are Queen of Skaldanna and as such you will always have sacrifices to contend with. We believe in your wisdom to do what you must. Follow the daughter with the black hair, she will lead you to the Emerald stones. From there let the voice of the prisoner guide you on your next steps. Do not stray from the path before you no matter what the heart feels for to do so would destroy everything you hope to gain leaving heartache and misery for everyone in both worlds. We have faith in your courage. All you have to do is believe you have the strength within yourself to endure. Allow the quest its pace and all those involved will have their moments as you shall have yours, but know this, you will succeed for your unconditional love will be the greatest sacrifice of all. Stay well daughter for this will be the last time we shall speak. Your mother and I love you forever.

As quickly as the energy had filled her with warmth it left leaving her cold and desperate for his voice again. She wanted to bend over and dig in the soil after her father's voice like a little girl begging for him to say one more word. How many times had she dreamed of him speaking to her wondering what her parents would have thought of her if they could see the woman she had become? It took everything she had learned over her two thousand years not to fall to the ground like a little girl caught in the middle of a tantrum and beg for his return. She let the tears fall unchecked for she had her wish come true and the words spoken gave her hope by her actions she could save both worlds. Her father had spoken to her from wherever it was he had gone to. She had always believed her parents were with her because they were a part of her heart and mind, but to feel and hear his voice solidified her beliefs.

Remembering the pain she felt on her wrists before he spoke to her she looked down to see them for the first time gasping at what she saw. Rubbing her fingers over it no longer feeling pain she was shocked it could have happened to her searching her mind of any story she had been told similar to what happened to her. Coming up with no memory she marveled at the intricate lines of the mark that had been seared into her skin. Two oval circles woven together in a sideways figure eight repetitively starting small then growing larger no bigger than an inch and a half in length with three lines flowing from the center both above and below. Looking at her other wrist remembering she had felt pain there she saw she had been marked there as well with the same symbol. Not familiar with the mark she closed her eyes knowing this was new territory with known relationships concerning Skaldanna's energy. She accepted her fate believed it was a sign given to her by her father and would wear it with pride as a daughter of Skaldanna.

Distracting her from her solemn thoughts she heard Harmony's infectious laughter and it was not long before Katerina laughed right along with her stomping in rain puddles like a couple of children reminding her life went on just like the new life had grown all around her.

Shoulders back she dropped her hand from her heart allowing the women's laughter to fill her with joy instead of sorrow choosing to tuck it away in the past where it belonged. She walked over to them finding each step closer brought her one step closer in solidifying her courage to accept her role within The Prophesy. She would do what was expected of her for the sake of the greater good. That was what she believed a good queen of the people should do. She hoped she had the courage she believed it would take to keep on living after all the dust settled.

25

Ever since he heard the first sound of lightning from the direction of the castle, he couldn't keep the dread out of his heart something was wrong right along with the bitter taste of fear for Bri's safety. Yelling for his brother not waiting for a response he turned his mount around feeding his horse and the horses of their party speed from his own energy resources, enabling them to fly with the wind, while he raced back to the castle in hopes to interrupt any problems he feared could have provoked the onslaught of her lightning.

Shouting for his mount to hurry, he almost choked on the thoughts feeding his fear desperately trying not to let all the horrible things enter his mind. Had he told her how beautiful she looked this morning with the sun shining behind her hair disheveled lips wet from his kisses? Did he tell her his worries of being the High King were starting to go away? How he now believed he was able to step into the roll she had always professed he could fulfill never to embarrass her simply because traditions of her homeland demanded etiquette. Did he say those things to her? God there were so many things he wanted to tell her. There were so many things he wanted to show her, do with her, laugh with her. Please, please God, let nothing happen to her.

"Stop thinking that way little brother. You keep on that train of thought and you'll be writing her off in the next minute," Stark spoke reassuringly through their mental link. *"I believe they are fine. I would have detected evil from what Merridian has shared with me regarding our master villain. She tuned my energetic frequency to the protection barrier she set around the perimeter of the castle so if anything had happened from our mystery person I would have picked up traces of their static trail. From what we've seen so far all the destruction to the surrounding lands are from that single source and I don't detect any other energy trail right now."*

"What are you saying?" Not sure where his brother's conversation was supposed to lead to he was still struggling to not choke on his panicked thoughts. He knew Stark tried to distract him from worrying over nothing by talking about the mission at hand. It was the best way to get his mind back on track.

"I don't think this has anything to do with Lord Drakkoon."

He processed all the information they had gathered while scouting the Second Realm in the matter of seconds. Listening to the accounts leading up to, including the event itself, everyone said the same thing. They were about their day no major strife in the land nor in the homes that could have led to the widespread death currently in view, there was no other way to put it. Seeing the destroyed vegetation everywhere made no sense to him. It was absolute destruction like nothing anyone in their traveling group had ever seen.

Knowing he wanted to share what they had seen with the rest of the family, he leaned closer to his horse spurred it faster at the same time he kept rhythm of the horse's heart so he did not hurt his animal with his energetic impatience.

"I would be curious to get Kenneth and Striker's opinion, hell even Sir Hawk. That man can track like I've never seen before. It's almost as if he can smell the scent of his targets next step before they make their move. I think our discussions will be productive and fruitful now that we have a better sense of the how far this destruction extends."

"You're right, hey what the hell?" Reigning in his horse a mile from the castle walls he could tell something was happening to the ground in front of them. Something stirred in the soil causing it to swirl not only in one spot it was happening everywhere around them. The ground was swirled around like a great hand had rubbed the soil loosening it prior to planting.

"Whoa!" Holding his hand up signaling everyone to stop reigning in the energetic thread of speed linked to all riders. "Do you all feel that in the ground?"

Sir Hawk circled his horse around searching the ground for some invisible force. "I do not sense anything."

"Look in front of us!" Striker yelled pointing in the direction of the castle.

Heart in throat Nate whipped his head up from the ground expecting to see some great battle before him, instead what he say left him speechless. In the distance he could see new growth evident everywhere, in the trees, in the grass, in the crops, filling the forests like a sonic wave heading straight for them leaving the ground in birth with new life in its wake.

"What do we do?" yelled a panicked Pegasos.

Nathanial connected with Briksanna mentally but was met with too much static he physically cringed from the force of her energy. "I can't connect with Bri. Whatever she and Harmony are doing is too intense for me to connect with her telepathically. Stark try Harmony."

"Already tried, brother, same thing here; I get too much static."

"Brace yourselves. Steady your mounts telepathically; they will know your fears and anxieties. You must reassure them less you will be thrown." Holding onto his prancing horse Sir Hawk commanded obedience from the riders in the group. "It is up to us, lads, to be brave despite the unknown. Remain steadfast."

"Briksanna knows we are out here and that of the people inhabiting the realm. She would not allow harm to fall on anyone. I trust her with my life." He spoke with authority enunciating the last sentence making his point clear.

"Here it comes!" yelled Pegasos.

"Steady lads!" bellowed Sir Hawk.

I trust you Bri, I trust you Bri. You are my light in darkness. I love you." Sending the message with everything he had projecting the words to the heart of his mate hoping she received it with knowledge his affection and loyalty were absolute in all decisions she would make. He let her know he trusted her with his life.

With that realization he felt at peace with the litany of doubting questions that had plagued him for the past several days. It didn't matter how he was perceived by the people of Skaldanna; as long as he supported the principles he and Briksanna had always shared leading their family nothing else mattered.

Mentally laughing out loud, nothing mattered except what mattered to the both of them. It really was as simple as that. Beside her, he was High King to his High Queen.

With that thought lingering in the forefront of his brain the giant wave of energy hit them rolling with incredible speed, yet upon contact, it felt as gentle as tub of water with the cold bite of the Pacific Ocean. It wasn't painful, but crazy as it sounded, it felt good.

Like a caress bathing him with promises of renewed strength, encouragement and hope. All thoughts of doubt were completely erased while wrapped in the magnificence of their combined light.

He felt great power around him which begged to be let in, reassuring him that he was part of the promise made long ago. The call commanded his attention and he couldn't deny its voice even if he wanted to. Lowering his mental walls he welcomed the energy into his being filling him with recognition of what he did not know.

Closing his eyes he allowed the warmth of acceptance to spread throughout his body giving him sight to threads of magic weaving ropes of strength and surety around his once unsure heart. He could see light threads of magic floating around in his body recognizing the violet energetic signature belonging to Bri. He noticed a separate bright thread of magic wrapped around each thread of Bri's energy strand knowing it belonged to Skaldanna. How he knew didn't matter, he just did and that didn't bother him in the least.

The threads of magic blended together with an equally bright honeyed band of energy riding on top like a surfer who caught the next wave. Bri's magic was the wave and the surfer belonged to Harmony. Flowing nutrients were being fed energetically to everything the wave came in contact with creating new life. At the exact moment he saw this he felt the energetic threads within his own body build in excitement burning him from inside out raising the energetic vibration to where he could barely tolerate the strength of it. A searing pain hit the inside of both wrists at the same time energy exploded out of his body ripping a scream from his throat leaving him with a force of renewed strength.

Glancing around he noticed two things; one he wasn't the only one who had shouted, looking stunned, they all had. The second was each and every pair of eyes staring back at him glowed.

All around life was growing at an exceptional rate, faster and broader than he had ever seen Harmony command. The fading pain in his wrists he recognized the infinity symbols etched onto his skin. Two oval circles, repetitively marked on his skin, starting small then growing larger no bigger than an inch and a half in length with three lines flowing from the center both the top and the bottom.

"We won't know until we get there little brother." Spurring his horse in the direction of the women Stark took off followed by the rest them, with him snapping out of his thoughts not bothering to worry about the marks on his wrists. Not wanting to be the last to see what had happened he spurred his horse to the front of the riders taking lead alongside his brother.

The closer they got to the women he noticed there were three men standing near them armed to the teeth. They stood apart from them but close enough to determine they were not a threat. He did see they weren't wearing the coat of arms as Lady Katerina's knights and that left an uneasy feeling in his gut.

"Do you know them?" Nate asked roughly clenching his teeth while he tried to reign his sudden anger at the unknown men standing too close to his wife.

Glancing quickly to his brother surprised in the tone of his anger. "Haven't seen them before, but they look harmless. Harmony could have them all on the ground bleeding before anyone drew a sword, so could your woman. I bet Lady Katerina has some serious skills with a blade as well. We won't know until we ask."

"I don't know them and already don't like them. They'll have to prove their loyalty to me before I'm ok with them hanging around my wife." he snapped.

"Reign it in bro, we're almost there and you are going to lose brownie points with the wife if you keep it up with this caveman shit."

Shaking his head before losing control, he remembered about last night, how quickly frustration turned to anger and just as quickly that anger had turned into hatred which led to actions he would never have committed if he was in control of his own mind.

"Breathe, I am safe and will be in your arms momentarily. We are fine and looking forward to your return with joy." She sent reassurances via their mental shared link. *"I heard what you said when you were approaching. I love you more than my own life. You are my other half, Nathanial."*

Relieved to hear her voice, he finally let the last bit of anxiety go. *"You scared a few years off my life again woman."*

"Silly man, only a few this time. Must be an improvement."

"Impertinent wench"

"Whom you love and adore." she laughed.

"To turn you over my knee!" he countered chuckling at their banter.

Giggling mentally all the while sending warmth and soothing thoughts, she continued to reassure him of her welfare knowing his anxiety was due to the unknown evil waiting to destroy her at any moment. He was glad she understood him and promised himself, not caring if she heard his thoughts, he was going to be thankful every day for the rest of his life she was his.

"I am no longer afraid, Nathanial. I am connected to all the Realms once again. All will know I have returned now including Lord Drakkoon. I am finally ready to fulfill my part in The Prophesy."

"Is that any different than how you felt this morning?"

"I know it sounds weird, but I did not fully believe in everyone's hope we would succeed. I always allowed my fears to rise up in front of me clouding my judgment and faith in both myself and in our family. Not only that, but in the worries of the people who would be affected by this quest for the great sword when we would split up to search for the missing pieces."

"You thought we would fail." It wasn't a question but a statement that he himself had felt ever since Merridian first spoke of their need to fulfill

The Prophesy. He always hoped they would win but didn't count on it because sometimes things didn't always go as planned and people could get hurt.

He didn't feel that way anymore. *"There are a lot of changes Bri. You aren't the only one who had the light bulb turn on. Back there I was able to let go my fear of not measuring up to being your partner throughout all of this. The other half is you need me to be your High King, the warrior you need to fight alongside you when you battle this evil villain as well as be the lover who would share in the vulnerability as you've shown me this past week. I knew I loved the woman just like I love the warrior and the High Queen. It was realizing you are three in one that made it so I didn't have to pretend to be mate to any one in particular but husband to Briksanna; the only woman I love with all my heart and soul. Because of this I can be The Sacrifice for the sake of our unborn son. I am the man you need me to be. I am confident now in my feelings surrounding this. I knew you were worried. I even had a feeling you were trying to come up with a way around that, but it doesn't matter anymore to me. Our love will never die therefore neither will I. I believe that with all my heart and with the Goddesses promise to me, we will never really be apart only separated for a time. Don't ask me how I know this, I just do."* Taking a deep cleansing breath after releasing so many emotions during his speech he knew he needed to wait for her to speak before he said or did anything.

He felt her emotions crack under the force of the truth in his words. Her heart overflowed with love for him, but not revealing an ounce of it visually. Their bond had become impenetrable. Only through their mental link did he know Bri was ready to launch herself at him seeking the comfort of his arms. Riding up to her he knew pulling her into his arms was going to be the first thing he did before another moment got away from the both of them. He needed to hold his woman now.

"Riders approach from the North!" Kainam shouted.

Instantly Briksanna was in battle mode protecting those that she loved nearby. She lifted her sword just as their makeshift guards were attempting to pull them to safety.

"Stand down, sir knight. That is my mate approaching with your twin brothers in tow. Do not approach any closer than you have already so nothing untoward is interpreted prior to an explanation."

She with the violet glowing eyes held her sword half way up in an attempt to deflect any blows made by whom would be a good question; the men or the riders? She did not care as long as she was prepared for anything. Then there was Katerina who held her own sword standing with her legs apart in a ready battle stance mimicking her position opposite from where she stood. Where the hell did that come from? She didn't remember seeing her move.

Harmony had her two sai swords out and ready, one in each hand feet apart as well, all traces of laughter gone replaced with determination should anything threaten the two women beside her. Her protection was clearly for her and Katerina. She looked just as fierce as Katerina did.

"What the hell woman! We are your guards not the other way around. Where the hell did you pull out your blades from?" murmured Alkimos. "It is not supposed to be the other way around. It is not done," sounding like a child who had been scolded one too many times.

Glancing quickly at their surroundings, she took in everything from the new vegetation to where everyone stood to the riders quickly approaching. She could feel Nathanial's anxiety regarding the three men. He was upset they were outside the castle walls with nothing but three young men for protection. She could imagine him scowling in front of her upset at another one of her many choices that could have gone south a million different ways according to his one to many rants regarding her going about with both feet in on most missions.

"That's right my love, you come first and that of our family. You risk too much at times but I trust your judgment regardless how it makes me feel."

His absolute honesty floored her. That he would bare his insecurities to her alone in the mist of his fear was one more notch higher on her trust ladder.

Laughing mentally, *"You will see for yourself what gallant knights we have guarding our well-being. Katerina trusts them implicitly as do I. I believe there is a story behind them all, which I will gain much pleasure in sharing this information with you privately."* What would equate as a mental kiss was sent to reassure him of her well-being.

"When I get there, and I will get there, you will let me decide for myself if they're worthy. Preferably in the lists with these two knuckleheads you shackled me with."

Rolling her eyes mentally, *"Blah, Blah, Blah. Were you saying something?"*

"You have seconds to retract that last statement before I haul you draped over my horse back to the castle butt in the air."

Losing her composure Briksanna laughed out loud as the riders trotted to them. Nathanial vaulted off his horse and stalked her never taking his sights from her, lust flowing from his emerald glowing eyes she felt his desire punch right through her making her insides clench with the anticipation of his touch.

"You can certainly try, but I warn you, I will happily demonstrate my skills in the lists first before anyone of these children can step foot in the arena that is if you are determined to follow through with that absurd thought." Still laughing she hugged her mate closing her eyes to breathe him in. He smelled of soil, wind and a hint of rain. With the rains gone she could still smell the cleanliness brought on by the drizzle floating through the air. "I missed you."

Squeezing her tight, "I missed you more than I thought possible. I love you Briksanna with everything in me. There is no me without you. I am your King, my Queen."

Pulling back from their embrace not letting go of her hand but taking in the state of Lady Katerina and Harmony as they were busy re-sheathing their blades. It was the three guards who held his attention.

"Who are you three? My Mate claims you are her guards, is that so?" Nate demanded authority dripping from his voice.

Alkimos started to speak but with a raised hand Alexio effectively halted all speech from his brothers. "I am Alexio head of the Palaponos family line. This is my brother Alkimos and Kainam, you have already met my twin brothers Khrysaor and Pegasos." Indicating to the grinning fools astride mounts nearby. We meant no disrespect to the women when you approached, we did not know if you were friend or foe with all that has happened recently. We thought it would be better to be prepared and ready than not.

Starring at the man who had spoken to Nathanial, she judged him to be a few years older than Striker and Kenneth. He held himself responsible for any offense he or his brothers may have caused by their actions, asserting himself as leader of the family clearly by how his brothers submitted to his authority in his response to what had been asked. His expression was granite, there was no fidgeting, no nervousness about him only patience awaiting a response.

Nathanial did not appear as if he liked Alexio, but the way he shielded Harmony raised her hackles not to mention she let him shield her as well.. Their actions made it obvious to her they felt there was reason to worry so she chose to pick her battles and allow her mate be.

"Do you know whom it is you protect, Sir Knight?" Nate asked tilting his head trying to get a read on his loyalty to the High Royal Family.

"Yes"

"No"

Harmony and Alexio spoke at the same time.

"Now is not the time Harmony." Stark spoke for the first time since coming upon the scene, "I think everyone should return to the castle and we can make proper introductions out of the cold air."

"Harmony ride with Stark and I will ride with Nate..." She spoke but was interrupted halfway through her instructions.

Maneuvering his horse closer to Katerina, Striker gave his own demand. "I will take Lady Katerina back." Reaching his hand out not brokering for any arguments he simply pulled her in front of him settling the horse from stomping due to the additional weigh.

Sighing at the undercurrent of attraction between the two, she rolled her eyes grasping her mate's hand settling in front of his stallion. "You three can ride with your brothers; Kenneth will offer his horse to you Kainam."

The dark skinned man approached offering his hand, "I am Kenneth."

Stepping away from his brothers, "I am Kainam, let us venture off. I'm starved, wet and in need of a warm fire. What say you Master Kenneth?"

Laughing at the warrior's audacity to break the tense mood within the group, Kenneth liked him already. "I agree, let's bounce." Turning his stead away back to the castle not waiting for anyone's censorship for his choice of words he cantered back towards the castle following behind Striker.

Alkimos and Alexio mounted behind their younger brothers and everyone turned their mounts towards the castle as a group.

Ridding ahead of the group, Nate clearly wanted to get out of the cold drizzle left over from the recent downpour. She held onto his arm secured around her waist and smiled at Kenneth and Kainam's antics. "Those two are going to be a handful, you know that right?"

Leaning onto her mate's chest she rested her head relishing the moment of closeness and grinned, "But what fun we will have while dodging the bogeyman."

Laughing out loud, "So says the woman who taught all of her children to fight. Nothing frightens them, the scarier the better.

"I have to talk to you before we all speak this afternoon, privately. It is very important." The latter was spoken in hesitation.

26

He whipped his head down surprised by her tone of voice. "What is it? Are you all right?"

She leaned up to him and kissed him on the check, "I am fine, my heart, really. I simply need to talk to you privately before we speak about all we have seen and done with everyone else. There are things I prefer to speak to you first, mate to mate, King to Queen without an audience." She was positive she was making the right decision to share with him privately what she had learned this afternoon.

With an edge in his voice internal alarm bells ringing loud enough for her to hear. "The castle is only a short ways ahead. We will be there in minutes."

Trying not to gallop Nathanial set to steadying both his horse and its group of riders to a pace not to cause concern with the men guarding portcullis or the outer baily. They have had enough to deal with in the past two days with the land first being destroyed and then with her and Harmony renewing its growth. Awaiting groomsmen flurried about eager to attend the riders as they halted to dismount.

"Please head up to the castle and attend to yourselves. We will convene in one hour in the dining hall. That will be my only command for the day." Smiling at her statement, Katerina headed into the castle doing exactly as she wished.

Stopping a maid hustling about Nathanial asked, "Could you please see that there is a bath set in each chamber for Lady Katerina's guests within the West Wing."

The maid curtseyed, "My Lord, it has already been seen to. They are being drawn as you speak. We all figured when the rains came and you were not back from you trip you would be caught in the downpour, so we began preparations at once to heat the water."

Keeping her eyes downcast when she spoke she noticed the maid did not look or sound intimidated when she spoke, but neither was she disrespectful for being pulled aside and questioned. She liked her instantly. Her energy read truth and loyalty to her castle and its occupants.

"What is your name good servant?" Gently patting her arm reassuring her all was well. "I'd like to call the person by their first name who thought with genuine concern for me and my family before we were even able to take care of those needs ourselves."

"Isabeau, My Lady." Curtseying again with gratitude in the praise she had been given.

"My daughters and I will be in need of the services of personal maids. Would you be up to the task? Of course, I will check with Lady Katerina before a firm decision can be made, but I wanted to make the offer to you so you have time to think upon it. You can return to me an hour before the evening meal and I will let you know of Lady Katerina's decision and you can give me yours. How is that, Isabeau?"

Face lightning up, "Would you consider my daughters as attending maids to your daughters? They have been trained by my hand and are as loyal as I. You can inquire for yourself from the Lady of the castle or meet them at the appointed time later this eve."

"Bring them with you and I will speak to Lady Katerina prior to our meeting."

Bobbing another curtsey, "As you wish My Lady." She hurried off in the direction of the kitchens with a whole new purpose than she had when they had first walked in.

Kissing her on the top of her head, "You made her day you know that don't you?"

Squeezing his hand turning around, "Yes I did, but I am freezing in these clothes and am already dreaming of a bath. Let's go to our room."

Abruptly scooping her up off her feet and throwing her over his shoulder she shrieked appalled by his behavior. "What are you doing, you brute. You cannot pick me up and carry me off like a sack of potatoes." Pounding on his back, "Put me down!"

Slapping her bottom, then rubbing it, "Keep it up and I will have to spank you again. Now while we are headed to our rooms, you will explain why you decided to scare the living daylights out of me by not communicating you had planned on doing something of that magnitude."

Feeling the blood rush to her head, she suddenly felt sick to her stomach, "Nathanial put me down. I am going to be sick."

"I'm not going to fall for that. I'll have you know…"

"Nathanial, I am going to throw up!" Barely keeping the bile from rising up her throat.

Abruptly swinging her upright holding her steady she franticly searched for something to throw up in. Recognizing her panicked distress, he spotted a potted plant and reached for it, thrusting it under her nose. She immediately bent over the pot losing all the contents in her stomach.

Rubbing her back holding her hair out of the way she noticed he had been very quiet while she was threw up her guts in the hallway. She was thankful he had been and even more grateful no one had passed them in the corridor. It was a humiliating sight to hold a pot with her vomit in it and she was completely embarrassed.

A few minutes passed before she was sure her stomach would stop revolting before she put the pot down and stood and wiping her mouth with her sleeve.

"At least it's wet," indicating the state of her gown sleeves, looking up at her mate concerned etched in his face, tears immediately sprang to her eyes.

Wiping the tears that had spilled over with his thumb, he asked her gently genuinely sorry to have caused her pain. "What is it love, what's wrong? Are you sick?"

"I am with child." There she said it searching his face for any hint to what he felt about her revelation.

Stupid, Stupid, I should have waited to tell him romantically like a wife would to her husband not in a corridor standing next to a pot of vomit.

He had gone very still, not trusting his mouth to say a thing, waiting a few seconds for his brain to process what she had just said before opening it again.

"A child are you sure?" He choked out while he held her face still searching for any trace of doubt while he continued to wipe her tears away with his own hands.

Nodding she waited for his rebuke, but found his mouth turning into a huge grin lighting his entire face. "We're going to have a baby? Our child?" Pulling her into a tight embrace he gave off a loud whoop. "How can this be? I mean it's only been two nights since we were together last and it should be several weeks before you would even know, right? I mean look at us, we'd be wonderful parents. The kids are going to freak. I can't wait to let Stark know. He's always razzing me about how I need to dispense more of the famous Angelo charm…what is it Briksanna? Are you not excited about this?" He slowed his vocal enthusiasm when he noticed her calm demeanor.

"Let us go to our chamber before I share more with you." She pulled his hand heading towards the room they had shared the night before.

Trying to mask the worry from his voice, "Is everything ok Bri? Nothing is more important than your well-being."

"I am fine Nathanial, the child is fine. There is more I need to share with you about what I have discovered about this pregnancy while connected to Skaldanna."

Keeping his questions to himself he knew she was right to keep anymore conversation about the matter to themselves instead choosing to talk about it in the hallway.

Following behind her they entered their room while he shut the door allowing her time to strip out of her clothes. He strode over to the fireplace adding a piece of wood to the existing fire bathing the room in additional heat. He wanted his wife, his mate, the mother of his child to believe her well-being was the most important thing to him. Not

Drakkoon, not the mysterious villain, not the well-being of the universe, just her. She the other half of his soul.

"Everything about you matters to me. I do not want to see you upset. It eats me up inside. I want to strip that anxiety away from you and replace it with my love. There isn't a thing I wouldn't do to ensure your life and the lives of our children are kept safe. Do you understand what I am saying here?"

Looking over her shoulder pulling the wet gown she could saw his devotion burning within his eyes. He couldn't hide his desire from her in this place. This was their private sanctuary. Here he could be the man he wanted to be for her. More importantly this was a place he could show her.

"I believe you and that is why I need to share with you what I have learned today before we do anything further. No planning, no Intel sharing, no lovemaking. This is important to me. This thing is what I fear the most."

He walked over to her purposefully taking his time allowing her the needed seconds to gather her thoughts. He knew what she was going to share was what scared her most. He didn't want to read her thoughts to gleam the information, like his instincts were screaming for him to do; instead he gave her time to share in her own way allowing her voice of reason be the outcome of whatever it was she wanted to vocalize.

"Before you say anything, know this; whatever you are about to tell me, we can handle together. I consider us one being two people who have become one in mind and spirit. There is nothing that can separate us. Nothing you or anyone can suggest to me will ever change my mind about that. My devotion to you is absolute. We will endure and survive anything thrown our way. I am yours completely, reverently wrapping my love and faith in us even when you have doubts I will remain your rock. There is nothing shameful in your questions about our life. I want you to come to me first with all concerns. I will not tolerate less than that from you nor can you expect any less from me. I am your mate first before I am King, before I am father, before I am brother, do you understand me? I love you." He poured his belief and trust in his words searching her face for any sign of doubt.

Tears spilled over when she looked at him, the man who was her chosen mate, the High King, father of her unborn child, a warrior completely devoted to their family. She had to share what she knew or he would rip the information from her mind earning her wrath just to keep her safe.

Closing the gap between them she kissed him pouring all her love into that one kiss, wrapping her arms around his neck holding onto him for dear life. After a few minutes they broke apart, starring at one another when Bri spoke first, "I believe in us, my trust and commitment to you and you alone is absolute before anything else in the universe. You are my chosen mate."

Pulling his hand towards her flat stomach, "The prophesy says 'Her first son born too shall bear the same color eyes as his mother marking him as the Instrument of Peace. He will be born of this world and of the one called Earth who only by his hand will be the instrument of death for Lord Drakkoon thus freeing all the worlds from imminent destruction'. If this child is a son he is a key player in The Prophesy."

She continued, "I am pregnant Nathanial, now, not like when we talked about waiting for later."

Choosing his words carefully seeing the panicked look in her eyes at what she just shared he pulled her to his chest. "Does the idea of a child, our child, scare you so much? I know this is the first time you are pregnant, but it isn't your first child, Bri."

"That is not the reason I am upset. I am upset because while I was connected to the energy core all things were made clear to me"—rubbing her temples trying to ease the headache brewing—"this child will grow at an exponential rate, not like the pregnancies of your culture but that of mine. In a matter three months I shall be ready to deliver this child. I cannot be on the front lines with this quest while pregnant. Almost all women of Skaldanna are confined to bed by the ninth week simply because they are exhausted from the rapid growth that happens. To my culture it is a celebrated event and that of royalty even more celebrated. Women are cherished, revered and protected. Above all else, never in the history of Skaldanna have I known an enemy to harm or allow harm to a woman who is with child. I have no idea if this pregnancy will even follow those rules."

Moving her hands out of the way turning her around so her back rested on his chest, he began to gently massage her temple sliding his hands down her neck making sure to ease the tension within her. "What does your instinct say to you? The first thing that pops into your head."

"This pregnancy will not follow those rules mostly because of the combined genealogy and a sprinkling of fate." Sighing she thanked him for the attention by squeezing his hands turning her head giving him the best smile she could muster given her state of anxiety. "I think I will have even less time carrying him than the women of my kind usually do. I believe this child conceived by the two of us will be extremely gifted and his rate of growth will not decrease until he reaches maturity, with the quickest of his growth being in my womb. Nate, I would be lying to you if I said I was not worried. I am deeply concerned because there is so much to be done and I am the center of it all."

Pulling her back to him, facing front, he held her not saying anything because her fears mirrored his own while she had been explaining her thoughts. The one thing he knew there wasn't anything he would allow to happen to her or their unborn child as long as there was breathe left in his body. If it was the kingdom she was worried about, no sweat, he was ready to step up and be the High King. If it was the quest the seer put in front of them, no problem, the rest of the family could team up and take up that mantle. His confidence in their abilities to act independently was solid.

Feeling her shift in his arms he held on tightly bringing back to where he held her whispering, "Not yet, just a few more minutes. I want to fill you up with my strength because that is what we are going to do from this moment forward. You and I are a team and being a good team player means we are going to share all the responsibilities with one another right down from your health and well-being to the kingdom and quest. We have family and friends who will partake in that responsibility while you can't. That is what ruling a kingdom requires, sweetheart not for us to be team leaders but a ruling monarch where we delegate."

Lifting up his hands he turned hers over so her wrists were visible. He knew he'd seen the inked marks on her arms when she was throwing up in the hallway but was distracted with her news. Feeling her head shift down knowing she could see the matching markings on his wrists he heard her gasp. "We are the other half of one another. I can't be without you and you can't be without me."

"Oh, Nathanial, you make it sound so simple." Running her fingers over his new markings she sighed.

Rubbing his chin on her head he continued with his train of thought. "It really is, baby. Trust me to handle this with you. It goes against everything within me to steer you wrong, so you don't have to worry in that department. We will still remain partners in all decisions and concerns."

"I trust you completely, you do believe that, right? We are connected, I hear your thoughts, I know your feelings as if they are my own. We are one in every sense, which is where my love lies, within you."—pulling his hand up to cover where their child grew—"This child is a child born of our love and with it I cherish not condemn. Do not ever think that of me; I am very happy to find myself pregnant, proud even. I only tell you my fears because everything has been happening so fast. I can hardly get my mind wrapped around a topic when we are being thrown into something else"

Pulling her back into the warmth of his embrace not letting go of his hand on her stomach he kissed the top of her head, relieved to hear her reassurances over her love for their child. "That is why you will let me help you. I love you Bri and will do everything in my power not to let any harm come to you and that includes your worrying."

Abruptly pushing her away from him turning them towards the tub resigned to let him lead her to the tub she sighed allowing him to finish undressing while assisting her into the warm scented water. Closing her eyes she slide into the tub allowing the water to do its magic, chasing away her chilled worry filled bones.

Slipping into her thoughts he could sense her letting his words sink into her own thoughts pushing her doubts out of her consciousness. He could also hear her concerns. *Can this truly work out for the best? Is it as simple as delegating responsibilities?* Feeling him rubbing her arms with a soft cloth, he sensed her allowing her mind to be at ease replacing her worries for the quest with the excitement of healing the Second Realm.

She sloshed up from her sitting position in the tub, "Nathanial, I almost forgot to tell you, while Harmony and I were healing the lands

I was connected to Skaldanna's energy core deeper than I have ever been before."

"Jeeze Louise, you just made me jump, lady!" Bending to the ground using a towel he mopped some of the water she had spilled over the side of the tub when she jumped up.

Leaning over the tub still talking, "Do you remember when I told you I had adopted our family as the royal family in my heart and soul, declaring before the Gods in our return you all will be as such, High Royalty, my family belonging to the House of Akmond, my family name and seat in our government."

Seeing him nod she continued, "Well while we were connected I declared such in spirit to The Energy, willing it to accept my family in the event I am unable. Now do not get upset that I would think that, I just realized I was pregnant and may not be able to attend to the releasing of energy throughout the lands like I have been."

Seeing his brow furrow she must have thought it would be best to hurry up with the telling because she quickly added, "That was when The Energy connected with me deeply and also with Harmony. She is my successor in the event that I cannot disperse the energy to the lands."

"Nothing is going to happen to you Bri, I wish you would stop saying that." Brows drawn deeper he pushed her gently back into the tub warming the cloth in the water and returned to bathing her.

"Nathanial you are not hearing what I am saying; when I am confined to non-active responsibilities I will need a successor to continue aiding the realm of Skaldanna with the energy disbursement. Harmony is that person. The Energy Core has accepted her as High Royalty of my bloodline."

Smiling in triumph because she could finally cross something off her giant list of things to see done before the next round of hell and brimstone, he stilled bathing her to look her in the eye. "You're sure it accepted Harmony? She isn't from your world Bri and I don't want anything to happen to her because she isn't from your bloodline."

Shaking her head sending water wiping around her in a halo, batting his hand away to rise out of the tub. "You are not hearing me. You and our family are now considered my High Royal bloodline. Skaldanna has accepted all of you and there is nothing that can deny what The Energy has decreed." Flashing air quotes.

She said this so matter of fact; he was having a hard time wrapping his brain around it. Whenever she would talk about them being accepted here on Skaldanna as being her family, he had associated this concept to that of adoption. What she was saying was in reference to all the energies of the various realms that were gathered and channeled back into the realms after she had infused it with her own integral energy, effectively making herself the stir stick to a giant mixed drink of energy.

"I get it Bri, it just sounds so crazy. I thought you said only High Royal bloodlines, specifically your fathers bloodline could oversee the blending of energy feeding all the realms. How can Harmony be included in that bloodline?" He said while he watched her dry off by the fireplace.

She caught his lingering gaze she smiled. "Simple that wave of energy everyone in the Second Realm felt altered the bloodlines of my adopted High Royal Family; all of you are truly my family from the House of Akmond. From that it was a matter of deciding who would be the best person suited for the job and I chose Harmony. She already has an affinity for healing the lands as her sister heals its inhabitants. I guess Skaldanna recognized my thoughts and accepted my decision, because as you can see by the events of today, her powers are powerful enough to support my decision."

Walking over to her he thought how happy she looked talking about Harmony and what she had discovered in their outing. It was such a difference compared to the panicked woman he held in his arms earlier that morning. She was right, it didn't matter how they delegated the vast responsibilities he knew was going to be shoved at them as long as they all stepped up to help shoulder it with her.

Reaching her side he gently pulled the drying cloth away from her and lifted her chin up to meet his eyes. "You're absolutely right, I am officially checking that one off the royal list; however you forgot something Mrs. Angelo."

She licked her lips watching his eyes glitter in the firelight, "Which is?"

He didn't stop to answer; he just took what he had been waiting to take since he set her naked body into the tub of water. He claimed her mouth with everything he was worth, not giving an inch pouring all his love, confidence and trust into that one kiss. Gripping her waist tight, he didn't hear her moan over his growl as she pummeled his scalp with her nails.

He was swamped in their rising hunger for one another. Her desire consumed him and he knew there wasn't anything in any world that could damage the love they had for one another. He loved her more than he loved life itself. He would do everything in his power to keep her and their unborn child safe.

He claimed the last piece of doubt she had sucking it out of her mouth replacing it with a kiss filled with love straight from his heart. He felt it flood her system starting with her mouth shooting throughout her body effectively shredding any thoughts she had hidden away deep inside. He was right in everything he had said to her. She acknowledged his affirmations deepening the kiss with every swipe of her tongue. No matter what they faced, they would triumph in the end together. They had proven this over and over again with every assignment they had been assigned in the past, always family first team second. Nothing was going to be any different living here with their new mission than it had been on Earth. She would gladly feel the same way if the tables were reversed and it was another family member who had a great quest to attend to. He knew this about her by the way he had studied her all these years without her knowing. She was a woman of her word and he was a man of his.

It took everything in him to pull away from the kiss knowing somewhere in his brain that now was not the time for intimacies. They had several more things to do and share this evening with everyone. Her love for her family was unconditional and she fully trusted every person within including several members whom were friends as being a part of her inner circle. Because of this trust, he too had no doubt of their loyalty.

For the first time in days he finally believed they could be the persons everyone needed them to be; a mate, a friend, a mother, a father, a king and a queen. Their love would endure the sacrifice.

27

The leader of the Shadow Riders sat deep in the forest watching the castle from afar wondering what he was going to do now. He had thought the Mistress would be proud of the work he had helped her do, completely destroying the lands of the Second Realm, but looking around feeling his own eyes begin to glow by the yellow haze he cast on the new blades of grass still growing beside him he spit on the ground to rid the disgust knowing she might not be happy because he had failed.

She had told him that it was her that had drawn the energy from the Second Realm transferring the necessary stolen energy to fuel Lord Drakkoon during his creation. He was grateful for her intervention because of how strong he had become. If it was left entirely up to Lord Drakkoon, he would not be the feared warrior he was now.

Looking up he could barely make out the riders heading towards the castle. They had already picked up the party he had been watching. "Your time will come my pet. That I vow." Absently rubbing the scar on his neck he made a promise he would have his revenge on Harmony as soon as he did his Mistresses bidding with Briksanna and Lord Drakkoon.

He watched them enter the keep while he kept vigil an hour longer to see if any further visitors approached before heading back to camp.

Rising he went back to his horse leading the magical stallion deeper into the forest. Several miles in the forest his men lay in wait for his orders. He needed to speak to the Mistress one more time before he did anything next. Then he would have to speak to Lord Drakkoon to reassure him Briksanna and her family had arrived.

He spit on the ground to rid the sour taste of defeat, spittle flying from his mouth as he spewed his words out laced with venom. "Those bitches will pay for their interference."

Acknowledgements

To Rayna, my editor, thank you for your help. I would not have made it past the first draft it if were not for your time and dedication to work with my POV and Verb Tenses. To my Dad for his insight on story line and character development. Our weekly Friday morning phone calls kept me plugging along with the integrity of the novel. To my Mom for the encouragement and excitement every time I completed a scene. Your enthusiasm continues to fill me up.

To all the Beta Readers who took the time to read early drafts pushing me to the edge of my literary boundaries—LauraLee Hairgrove, Sam Taylor Mullens, Michelle Escamilla, Jessica Hammon, Kelly Sachko. Sloan Johnson you brought the idea of what it meant to be an Indie Author home. Thanks for keeping me going during those late night conversations, you are one of the best. Victoria Alday, you showed me not only how to brand my product, but that it was ok to give myself a title. I am a Professional Dreamer and I thank you from the bottom of my heart for your hours of literary influence and ingenious designs. I believe, my dear, I got this!

To my wonderful family and friends, for the long hours they suffered while I sat at my computer effectively tuning them out. I love you more than you can possibly understand. To my children, thank you for listening to my countless thoughts and ideas you are my guiding light. Guess what? Mom is ready to listen! And to my husband, my champion, thank you for pushing me to write one more line, edit one more page and when I wanted to pull my hair out you were there to brush it back in place. And when my cancer got in the way of writing you helped hold me up so I could dream a little more.

I love you forever.

There is no passion to be found playing small - in settling for a life that is less than the one you are capable of living.
Nelson Mandela

About the Author

Although Sabrina began physically writing two years ago the ideas that conceived her first novel have been percolating in her mind for many years. She lives in Sonoma County heart of the wine country of California enjoying her rural life happily married to a wonderful supportive husband. You can always find her reading a book, cooking a meal for her multitude of children or playing with her dog, Taylor.

You can reach her at:
Like: http://facebook.com/authorsabrinarawson
Follow for photos, history and book tour information: www.sabrinarawson.com
Email me at: sabrina.rawson@outlook.com
Follow: Twitter@SabrinaRawson